The

by

Diane E. Lindmark

To
Carole
Family, Love, Loyalty and
Honor the things worth
fighting for.

Diane E. Lindmark

I

Bloodstone found herself chained to a chair looking up at Bloody Fang. A moment later, he hit her again and again. "You know you can stop this anytime you want, all you have to do is tell me what I want to know," he said in a persuasive tone. In response, Bloodstone spit at him; he backhanded her.

"You are pathetic and weak, Breton; you and your army will never defeat me and my men," said a woman from the shadows. Bloodstone twisted and turned trying to see her, but the woman was always just out of sight. A moment later she added, "After all, you're so pathetic you got your own father killed."

"Who are you? How did you know about that?" demanded Bloodstone.

Bloodstone was walking through the encampment when the Duke fell backwards into her. She caught him and laid him down on his back. Seeing he had been shot by two arrows, she tried desperately to stop the bleeding. "Stay with me, don't leave me!" she said frantically.

The Duke reached up and grabbed the back of her neck, pulling her down to him, "Had you been a better soldier, I wouldn't have had to save you. You're pathetic. My sons are worth a hundred of you," he gurgled out, blood splattering on her face and tunic as he spoke. Then blood was running out of the sides of his mouth. A moment later, his body convulsed. Bloodstone tried frantically to stop the bleeding, but there was so much blood, her hands were soaked with it. Blood gurgling out of his mouth, he struggled to speak. More blood splattered on her face and his bloody hand touched her cheek. "You failed your brothers." Then he died.

Bloodstone screamed and pulled him to her. "No! Father, Father, you can't leave me!" She held him another moment, then gently laid him down. Bloodstone stood up and took several steps back, standing there seething with rage as she looked down on the corpse of her father. A moment later, her head snapped back to where the archer was still shooting at her. She drew her sword and pointed it at her and as their eyes met, flames leapt into hers. She screamed out, "I'm coming for you, Bloodstone! You killed my father!"

Bloodstone sat up with a start. She was soaked in sweat and breathing hard, her heart racing. "It was just a dream. It was just a terrible dream," she told herself. Hearing Blackwolf crying, she got out of bed and went over to soothe him. After a few minutes he settled down and went back to sleep. She could hear her four guards arguing softly outside. She ignored them. The two Barbarian guards were new. Eden's last act before leaving the encampment was to assign a young Wolf Tribesman named Dex as the head of her personal guard, a Barbarian guard - which conveniently for Eden and not so conveniently for her - she had no authority over, and unlike her Athenian personal guard, these men followed her wherever she went. He also had given orders that Katya and Blackwolf were to always be under guard as well. She ran her hands through her hair in frustration and looked at the hour candle; it was shortly before four. As she looked at the candle she asked herself, *Why does something always happen at four? Why not at five? Or nine?* She stood rubbing her face. It was the second morning after the death of the Duke of Stone Reach. Eden, her brothers, and their wives had left yesterday to escort the Duke's body back to the Duchess - well, Dowager Duchess now. Knowing that she'd never be able to get back to sleep, she decided she might as well get started with all of her extra work; because in addition to her normal duties, she was now doing Black Stone's and overseeing the repairs to the walls that she had set on fire somehow, which she still didn't understand how and was afraid to even contemplate.

Two hours later, Dex and Sergeant Simon arrived at Eden's tent. They did so at nearly the same time each morning. Each man drew a little aside to receive their men's report from the night before. Dex found himself to be a little nervous; he never before commanded a group of men like this. He'd led men in battle, but he didn't feel it was the same thing at all. His King had entrusted the life of his woman and child and the life of another woman to him. It was his responsibility to make sure nothing happened to any of them. "Is there anything you wish to report to me?" he asked the night guards.

Both men seemed reluctant to speak. Finally, the older of the two said somewhat warily, "Very early this morning we started hearing noises coming from inside the tent. At first they were just noises and then they became more audible. According to the two Breton guards, this has happened before. The ..." the man hesitated. Finally making up his mind, "General apparently suffers from horrible nightmares. We were unsure as to what to do about it. Finally we decided she could not be permitted to go on in this manner and we went to enter. The Breton guards argued with us and there was a little bit of ..." the older man cleared his throat and looked uncomfortable, "unpleasantness between us and the Breton guards, but then things got quiet and we've heard nothing since."

Dex considered for a moment then he said, "I would like you two to remain on guard for a few minutes longer while I speak with the Sergeant." He did not wait for a response, but turned and headed for Sergeant Simon.

Sergeant Simon, observing Dex heading his direction, drew apart from his men and awaited

Dex. "Is there something I can do for you?" asked Sergeant Simon.

"This morning your men informed my men that this nightmare was not an unusual occurrence. Given the fact that I too am charged with the defense of your General, I would prefer it if we could come to some kind of agreement that would allow us to work well together, rather than at odds with each other. After all, she is my Queen," replied Dex, trying not to sound too annoyed.

"To the best of my knowledge it has been nearly a year since she has had any trouble sleeping ..." Sergeant Simon hesitated a long moment. "Not since Eden and her began to reside under the same roof, for lack of a better word. I would presume that it was the brutal method in which her father was killed, coupled with the ..." again Sergeant Simon hesitated, "necessary departure of her husband that has brought them back."

"Your men prevented my men from entering and checking on her. Are you informing me that is the custom of your men? To just permit her to suffer through it?" demanded Dex, his irritation evident.

"My men and I are charged with her protection, and if we know that she is in no physical danger, it would be inappropriate for us to enter her quarters without being summoned or without permission.

After all, she is our commanding officer, it is not for us to presume upon the relationship," Simon stated carefully.

Dex found himself unsure as to the meaning of what the Breton had just said. Something about it felt wrong. He felt as though there was something he was supposed understand, but since he wasn't feeling sure of his footing, he merely nodded to Sergeant Simon and excused himself.

He returned to his men; his other daytime guard had arrived. He turned to address the older of the night guards. "Tonight I will take your watch, enjoy your night off." Turning to face the younger he said, "I need you to go and inform Reef that I will need him to take my watch tomorrow." The men nodded.

It was a little past three the following morning when Dex would swear he'd heard a little whimper. A few moments later he heard a little cry. He was just in the process of trying to decide whether it was Eden's woman or Eden's child when he heard a scream. That settled it. He didn't even hesitate. He turned and entered the tent. As he did so she cried out again, but he had only taken two steps into the tent when she came flying out of the bed reaching for her sword. Their eyes locked for just a moment; then Dex quickly looked her over. Her thin cotton nightie was soaked with sweat and clinging to her body, and her hair was all hanging loose. He blushed as he realized he was staring at his Queen in her nightie. He quickly turned his back on her. What irritated him most was the uncomfortable knowledge of how he reacted to her as a man. *By the gods!* He mentally kicked himself. *That woman I was just admiring in her nightie was the woman of my King.* He kicked himself mentally again. The baby started crying. Bloodstone sighed and dropped her sword on the bed. With where Dex was standing, she was forced to walk around him. As she walked past him, he inadvertently permitted his eyes to trail down the back of her body. He mentally kicked himself again and turned to look away. He knew he should leave, but having come in, he felt stupid just leaving.

Picking up Blackwolf, Bloodstone turned to face Dex. He had turned to face the right wall of the tent, so that his back was again fully to her. "Dex, is there a particular reason you felt the need to come into Eden's tent in the middle of the night?"

"I came in to investigate some noises I was hearing," he replied quickly.

"I'm not going to pretend I don't know what you're talking about; I'm just going to say I'm used to it. Don't worry about it, and there's no need for you to enter my tent again. Do I make myself clear?"

"Your Breton guards may be content to stand out there and listen to you suffer. I am not," he stated firmly.

"Well, Dex, since there's nothing you can do about it, you're just going to have to learn to accept it and deal with it. Now good night, or good morning, or whatever it is, I am going back to bed and you are leaving."

Dex didn't argue; he left the tent. He spent the rest of his watch deciding what he was going to do about it. He was not merely content to allow the status quo to continue. And so, as Reef arrived to relieve him, Dex went to seek counsel from the Elder. Dex felt strongly that he could not permit the situation to continue and since there were none of her brothers here to consult and since he knew she and Eden's brother Viktor were not getting on, he felt that the only logical choice was to consult Eden's grandfather, Hafgrim.

Arriving outside the tent of the Elder, he cleared his throat and asked, "I know it is early, but are you awake, Elder?" A moment later, the old man opened the tent flap.

"Do I know you?" questioned the Elder.

"No, Elder, you do not know me. Your grandson left me in charge of protecting our Queen. My name is Dex and something has arisen and I wish to seek counsel and there is none of her family of which to consult, so I felt that I should consult you as Eden's grandfather," Dex said hesitantly.

Hafgrim nodded and stepped aside, gesturing for him to enter. He indicated a chair at the table. Seating himself in another chair he said, "Is my granddaughter making your life particularly difficult, or is it something else?"

Dex quickly recounted the events of the past two mornings to the Elder, being careful to conceal his own inappropriate thoughts. Hafgrim sat considering for several minutes. "I do have to say, I like that man Simon. He is very aware of the fact that in this particular matter his hands are quite definitely tied, but yours are not. I feel it is obvious that Simon wishes you to do something about it," the Elder replied.

"But I do not know what I'm supposed to do about it," Dex said, feeling as though his King had not even been gone two days and he was already failing him.

"Well, I would suggest that you speak to her father on the matter," replied the Elder.

Dex stared at the Elder, wondering if perhaps the man's memory was starting to go. Then to his surprise, Hafgrim started laughing. "You are aware of the fact that the Duke is her father, but the woman that he was married to is not her mother.

Her mother is married to a man in this encampment. I believe I heard my grandson refer to him as Sergeant Major Fletcher. I would suggest he might have some thoughts on the matter."

Dex nodded slowly, then stood up. "Thank you, Elder, for your advice. I will go in search of him. I, myself, am not familiar with him; hopefully he will not be too difficult to find."

To Dex's surprise, finding Sergeant Major Fletcher was actually quite simple. He stood back and watched as the Sergeant Major was exercising his troops. He waited for some time for an opportunity to speak with him; finally his moment came. "Excuse me, Sergeant Major Fletcher. We do not know each other, but I was wondering if we might be able to speak about your daughter."

Fletcher turned quickly to see a young Barbarian. He looked him up and down in an appraising manner, twenty-three or twenty-four he guessed, carried himself well for his age. "I have several daughters. Of which of them would you like to speak?" Fletcher, of course, knew the answer, but he wanted to see how the lad would react.

"I wish to speak to you privately about General Bloodstone, my Queen," Dex replied quickly.

"Very well, why don't you come with me to my quarters?" Once inside Fletcher's quarters, he indicated a chair on one side of his desk. He walked around and sat down on the other side. Crossing his arms over his chest, Fletcher leaned back in his chair and asked, "What about my oldest daughter do you wish to discuss, young man?"

Dex did not hesitate. He quickly introduced himself, then relayed the whole story to the older man and awaited his judgment. As Fletcher sat listening, he knew he was treading on dangerous ground. After all, he was merely a sergeant major and she was a general. Nevertheless, he'd grown quite fond of the girl and viewed her very much as he did his own daughters. He hoped to continue to develop this relationship and that one day she might actually think of him as a father. He knew Eden would not appreciate them allowing her to continue to suffer like this, but he also knew her own stubbornness was going to make this very difficult.

"I believe I may have a solution to the problem. Mind you, I do use the word 'may'. But I think you may trust my judgment on this matter. I will endeavor to deal with the situation."

Dex stood up quickly. "You are her father. I am more than willing to hand the situation over to you and to trust your judgment on the matter. If there's anything I can do to assist you, please do not hesitate to ask." He bowed and excused himself.

Bloodstone found that as she walked back to Eden's tent, she was dragging her feet. She was exhausted. As she approached the tent, Sergeant Simon opened the flap, saying as he did so, "You have a visitor, General. I permitted him to wait inside. I hope you don't mind."

"No, of course not, thank you, Sergeant Simon." When she entered, she observed Sergeant Major Fletcher stirring something over the cooking fire. He turned at her entrance.

"I hope you're hungry, I've prepared you dinner," he said. Not waiting for a reply, he was spooning up stew and placing it on the table.

"Is there something I can do for you, Sergeant Major? You do know I'm quite capable of preparing my own dinner," she said, looking at him suspiciously as she seated herself at the table.

"I am well aware of that, but you've had a lot on your plate the last few days and you look like shit. I figured you didn't need to prepare your own dinner. So why don't you just sit down and eat," he said, cutting some bread and cheese and placing the food in front of her.

"Who's in charge here?" she asked, looking annoyed.

"In charge of this encampment? You are, Sir. In charge of this family? I am." Bloodstone rolled her eyes and began eating her dinner. They ate in silence. As soon as she was finished with her dinner, he got up and poured her a cup of coffee. "I apologize now for the taste, never been a good hand at making coffee. I make better tea if you'd prefer that instead of the coffee," he said somewhat apologetically.

"Actually, I don't remember the last time I had a cup of tea. I think that would be nice." He took her cup of coffee and made her some tea.

"Well, thank you for dinner, Fletcher, but I think I'm going to go give Blackwolf some hugs and kisses and then I think we'll both turn in for the night. So, good evening."

"You can give him hugs and kisses, but I wouldn't recommend picking him up. I wouldn't want you to drop him," he said, casually drinking his coffee.

She glared at him. "I find it insulting, Sergeant Major, that you think I would drop my son."

"Under normal circumstances, Sir, I would never believe that you would drop your son. However, I took the liberty of drugging your tea. I was a little nervous about it, but Viktor said that you'd never be able to taste it in that particular brew of tea. He also said that try as you may, a half an hour is the most consciousness you're going to have this evening; so I suggest you go and give my grandson kisses good night, get changed, and get into bed before you pass out. I'm going to go outside and have a nice conversation with your guards, and I'll be back in about a quarter of an hour. Then I'm going to go and sleep next to my grandson and hopefully my daughter will find my presence comforting, whether she likes it or not." With that, he rose to his feet and exited the tent.

Bloodstone quickly picked up her mug and looked at the dregs. She did feel unusually tired, but she thought that was just because of how hard she been working and not sleeping the past two days. She slowly got to her feet and staggered a little. She said under her breath, "I may just kill you tomorrow, Fletcher." When Fletcher re-entered her tent a quarter of an hour later, she was already in bed asleep. He was carrying with him a bed roll. Pulling off his boots, he made himself comfortable and went to sleep.

Bloodstone awoke with a start as she looked around to see what had awakened her. Her eyes alighted on Fletcher walking back and forth softly cooing to Blackwolf. "What time is it?" she asked groggily. She rubbed her face with her hands trying to make sense of her muddled mind. It slowly came back to her. "You ass, you drugged me! I can't believe you drugged me! What in Hades were you thinking, Sergeant Major Fletcher?"

"I think it's a little past five in the morning and yes, I drugged my daughter."

Bloodstone glared at him and cut him off. "Why do you call me that?" She bit back an angry retort, hesitated a moment, and then went on. "I would think that you would want me to disappear, never hear from or see me again. I'm an ever present reminder, yet in spite of everything, you go out of your way to befriend me. Why?"

"Because had I been able to return home to you and Rosie, I would've raised you as my own and killed any man who said any different. You know, I have had longer to think about this than you have. I've suspected it for some time. But as much as I wish that would've been the case; I'm not sure it would've been the best thing for you. Despite how hard your life has been, you're a soldier through and through. I don't think you ever would've been happy as an innkeeper's daughter. Though if your passion for the forge is as great as General Black Stone says, that might've placated you somewhat; but I think one way or another, you would've ended up right where you are. I may be coming to your life a little late, but you still need family and I think you're not too old yet for a little fatherly advice every now and then. Whether you like it or not, I'm going to continue to call you my daughter; but of course, only in private, General," he added with a smirk.

"Don't ever drug me again. If you have problems or concerns, talk to me about it, please."

"Very well. How did you sleep? Your new guard, Dex, is very worried about you. I think Sergeant Simon is too, but he tries very hard to respect the differences in your station. Dex doesn't care; all he cares about is taking care of you. He's a good lad. I like him."

She hesitated a long moment considering. "Last night was the best I've slept in three years without Eden." She regretted it the moment she had said it. It made her uncomfortable admitting such a thing. She added quickly, "I appreciate what you did for me last night; however, your presence will not be required again."

He looked at her sternly a long moment. "I have a late duty tonight; however, if I learn that you have a nightmare tonight, nothing will prevent me from sleeping by my grandson's cradle until my son-in-law returns. And if you do not like that, daughter, you may take it up with my son-in-law when he returns, because I am certain he will approve of my actions."

II

It had now been five days since the Duke's death. Bloodstone found that no matter how hard she tried, she counted the days. It was the first thing she thought of every morning and the last thing she thought of every night. It was no wonder her dreams were haunted by his death. She looked over her shoulder at her new shadow, though over the past few days she had grown used to Dex being there. She now found herself wondering if he knew about her near screaming nightmare last night and whether if he had as of yet informed Sergeant Major Fletcher. As she approached Eden's quarters, Sergeant Simon opened the tent flap. "Katya brought the baby and put him to bed a little while ago. He's been sleeping soundly. I told her to go and get something to eat and I'd keep an ear out for him. He hasn't made a sound." She nodded to him.

As she entered the tent, blinking for a moment as her eyes adjusted, she slowly became aware that she was not alone. Looking quickly, she saw a man standing over Blackwolf's cradle. He had his back turned to her. All she could see of him was shoulder length, black, curly hair, a brown studded leather shirt, brown spiked leather bracers, brown homespun britches, brown leather grieves, and brown leather boots. As she slowly gripped her sword, her heart began to race. As her fingers flexed around the handle of her sword, the man spoke. "I don't think you want to cross blades with me."

Bloodstone stared for a long moment. That voice, it was so familiar. Bloodstone shook her head to herself. It couldn't be; it just couldn't be. The man bent down and scooped Blackwolf up in his arms, turning around to face her. Bloodstone had simultaneously drawn her sword, though as soon as their eyes met, her sword slid from her hand and clattered to the ground. Her jaw dropped open and she stared in disbelief. She knew she should say something, do something, not just stand there gaping like a fool. *There has to be a reasonable explanation. I am not looking at the Duke of Stone Reach. This merely has to be another of his illegitimate children who chose to be a Soldier of Ares,* she told herself. That made a lot more sense than the twenty-five-year-old man she was staring at, who looked and sounded exactly like His Grace, the Duke of Stone Reach, actually being the Duke.

"Do you know, throughout the centuries, I have quite literally sired hundreds of sons; but before you, I had not sired a daughter? And out of all those hundreds of sons of mine, most of my sons did not even live to be men. They all ended up getting themselves killed stupidly and rashly, so consequently, before you and your brothers, I have only had seven sons live long enough to produce grandchildren. And only two of them lived long enough to raise their children; the others got themselves killed before their children were even born. And before Daniel, only one of my sons had produced multiple offspring." He looked down at the boy in his arms. He smiled fondly at him. "That makes this little guy something very special, something rare. In fact, if you include your two oldest and Murtaugh's, which of course I do - after all, Rebecca is exceedingly fond of Murtaugh and Helena as am I - you and your brothers have damn near doubled the number of grandchildren I've had." As he had been speaking, he crossed to the table and pulled out the chair Eden always used. Turning the chair to face her, he dropped down in to it. He made a face as he shifted. "Does Eden actually find this chair to be comfortable? I can't imagine him doing so." He wiggled his backside into the chair more, and to Bloodstone's amazement, the chair grew and shifted. A moment later it was something very nearly resembling a throne; it also changed from a light oak to black lacquer with a crimson velvet cushion padded back and arms. He then shifted in it sideways so that half of his back was leaning against the back of the chair and the other on the left arm, then throwing his right leg over the right arm, he sat Blackwolf in his lap, positioned so that he could look down on the boy.

"You're Lord Ares?" she said in disbelief.

"There are those who call me Lord Ares. There are those who call me Ares, God of War, Battle, and Bloodshed. I'm not exactly into titles," he replied nonchalantly.

All right, so it was Lord Ares messing with me the other day when Father was killed. Why all of a sudden is Lord Ares getting involved in this? What is the game he's playing at and why is he deciding to masquerade as a younger version of Father? Bloodstone asked herself as she watched him with Blackwolf. She wasn't concerned. Lord Ares may have a reputation for being a womanizer and a bloodthirsty killer, but he did not make war on the innocent. He believed in fair combat and he and his soldiers felt that those who would prey on those weaker than themselves were not soldiers, but cowards.

Ares started laughing. "Well, I've been moved from the Duke to Father. Pity it took me dying for you to make that leap, but no, I am not masquerading as the Duke of Stone Reach. Where do you think I've been the past sixty years? I know people say eighty, but people do like to exaggerate. I've only been missing for fifty-nine years."

Bloodstone interrupted. "You're telling me that Lord Ares decided to be born a mortal and has spent the last sixty years living as the Duke of Stone Reach?"

"Yes."

Bloodstone ran her hands through her hair trying to make sense out of her reeling mind when she observed a Corinthian helmet sitting on one of the chairs at the table. She crossed over to it and picked it up. It was the same style worn by all the Soldiers of Ares, however, Soldiers of Ares wore a much simpler version, and theirs were also shiny brass and did not have a tail. This one, however, was shiny steel with crimson horsehair. Turning it over in her hands, she examined it. It was incredible craftsmanship. She'd never seen its equal. The red horse hair began at the forehead and went straight down the back. It stood about eight inches high until it got all the way down the back, then it had a long tail which must've hung at least eighteen inches. The design on each of the cheek protectors was identical; it was a fearsome looking dog charging, and racing behind him was a pack of wild looking dogs. She set it down on the table.

She turned to face him and demanded in an irritated voice, "Why? What possible motive would you have to do that?"

"Why, to win a bet with my sisters, of course. They're always nagging me about my morals and my behavior ..."

Bloodstone interrupted again. "Whoring," she supplied.

He shrugged his shoulders unconcerned. "Yeah, that too."

A bet? I and my brothers were mere side effects of a bet? The unmitigated gall of the man! Bloodstone growled and ran her fingers angrily through her hair. She turned around, so she didn't have to look at him a minute longer. If she did, she might just throttle him. As her eyes alighted on Eden's bed, her fury found new heights as she saw a shield tossed casually on it. A round leather shield with the 'A' for Ares going from edge to edge sitting on top of the sword of battle; the hilt of which was at the bottom right, but it laid at an angle with the blade pointing to the top left, so it too went from edge to edge. This, of course, was the symbol for the Soldiers of Ares. She turned on him. "How dare you! Get your damn shield off of Eden's bed!"

Ares shrugged his shoulders and held out his hand. The shield flew past her. He caught it and set it next to him. "My apologies."

"You should be sorry. This is Eden's home and you should not just walk into it and start changing things. And while we're on the subject of changing things, why did you have to become a mortal in order to win a bet with your sisters?" she demanded.

"I was always going on about how much I loved mortals. Freya being Freya said that it wasn't mortals I loved. It was just mortal women I loved. And Athena said that I only loved mortality because I could go back and forth at will; that I wouldn't love it if I had to stick with it. I told them that I would greatly enjoy being a mortal. One thing led to another and they bet me that I was incapable of living a normal mortal life span, that it would only be a matter of time before I would give it up and use my abilities. And as you can see; I was right. I won." He rose and crossed over to Blackwolf's crib. Kissing him gently on the forehead, he placed him in his bed. Blackwolf started to cry and Ares put a finger to his lips and said, "Not now, Mommy and I are talking, back to sleep." And to her great annoyance, he did.

"Oh, yes, must been a great hardship for you being born into the family of Stone Reach," she replied sarcastically.

"I know, daughter, that it must be hard for you to believe this; but I would've much preferred to have been born a peasant. However, I had no say in the matter; that was Freya's decision. She knew I'd find it much harder to be a nobleman then a peasant. Man, sisters can be a pain sometimes." He threw himself back in the chair and again cast his leg over the arm, leaning back, stroking his chin, studying his daughter. He considered. "Although, in the interest of complete honesty, I will say I did somewhat enjoy the pompous arrogance of Grey Stone; but I also greatly enjoyed having the time to raise my sons. And get that thought out of your head, your brothers and you are not mere side effects of my bet."

Bloodstone glared at him. "You have informed me of the terms of this bet; however, you have not yet informed me what exactly was the wager."

"Well, of course, any time one makes a wager with a god, of course it is never anything as trifling as money. The terms are always much more … shall we say … creative, or interesting," he grinned broadly.

"So in other words, you have no intention of informing me of the wager."

"Not the slightest intention."

"Why are you here, Lord Ares?" she asked, crossing her arms over her chest.

"You know, Daughter, when I informed you earlier that I wasn't exactly into titles, I believe I may have misspoken, because in your case," he pointed his finger at her as he spoke, "I shall make an exception. Do not refer to me again as Lord Ares, you will call me Father."

Bloodstone tapped down her irritation and bit back an angry retort. "Very well, Father, what do you want?" she demanded.

"You know, I might just have to torture that man Ellsworth. You and I were having such a lovely Father/Daughter conversation, and you even looked happy to see me. Now, because you know I'm Ares, you distrust me and in fact, I fear you might even hate me. What will it take for us to go back to that moment?" He rose and crossed to her, all arrogance gone. He reached out and touched her cheek with his hand. "I may be a god, but I am merely a god of war. This, of course, causes me to make many mistakes in relationships, especially where women are concerned. But you are my daughter. I don't want to make mistakes with you - anymore than I've already made. Please give me a chance to be your father."

"I don't know what opportunity there would be for you to be a father to me. I am fully grown, married, and well able to take care of myself."

"Speaking of your husband, I have to say I was pleased to find Eden the man he is."

She looked at him suspiciously and then asked, "Why?"

"Because even as Grey Stone, I could not have suffered my daughter belonging to a lesser man. Had he not been a man truly worthy of you; I promise you, even as Grey Stone I would've found a way to arrange an untimely accident. Fortunately for Eden, he is quite worthy of you." He reached out and gripped her face with both hands and bent down and kissed her on the forehead. "Regretfully my daughter, I must take my leave of you now; but

I promise you, we will continue this conversation at a later time. However, I suddenly find there is someone else I must speak to urgently." He turned back and glanced at the chair, cocking his head to the side. "You know, something tells me that chair is not exactly Eden's style." He stroked his chin, then bent down and picked up his shield, sliding it on his arm. He crossed to the table and pulled his helmet on. As he walked towards the tent flap, he glanced back at the chair, flicked his right hand in the direction of it, turned and walked out. Bloodstone looked back quickly to see that the chair was now a dark oak, stained nearly as dark as fresh churned earth, and the once crimson cushions were now a beautiful emerald green.

Sergeant Simon stuck his head in. "You opened the flap, General, but you didn't come out. Is something the matter?"

"You mean when the flap opened, nobody walked out?"

"No, Sir, I saw no one." He hesitated a moment, looking confused and then asked, "Is everything all right, General?" Bloodstone could see Dex looking over Simon's shoulder. They both looked concerned.

"You heard nothing of what transpired in here?" she asked, still looking confused herself. Both men slowly shook their heads.

Ares – God of War, Battle and Bloodshed. Known for his skill in swordsmanship as well as his ability to manufacture weapons and armor. He is not only known for his escapades on the battlefield, but in the bedroom as well. He is the older brother of Athena and Freya and gets along well with his sisters. When he is not making war, Ares prefers to take his ease around the campfire, tavern, or forge, anyplace he can socialize with soldiers. Unlike his sister who believes that wars are won by the officers through cold, calculating strategy, he believes that wars are won on the battlefield at the hands of the common foot soldier. He is a striking man of six feet six inches tall, and extremely well built. He has long, raven black, curly hair and very blue eyes. His animal is the war dog. His preferred weapon is the Longsword. Both countries follow Ares.

III

As Ares walked out of his daughter's quarters, he said in a grim voice, "Hades, I think we need to have a conversation."

"Where this time?" asked Hades.

"Appleshire, just outside of the magistrate's office." As Ares continued to walk, flames coiled and wrapped around him. He did not even break stride as he walked from one place to the other. To those in Appleshire, they saw a ball of fire appear about seven feet off the ground, and then it slowly coiled around something. A moment later, a Soldier of Ares appeared walking towards the magistrate's office. He came to a halt directly in front of the building. A moment later, the earth shook as a hole in the ground opened up and a murky gray fog seeped out of it. The fog did not scatter about the ground, but went straight up. A moment later, the fog disappeared and a man stood there. The man stood about five foot eight, average height for a Breton; his gray-blond hair pulled back in a tight queue. He wore a rich, black velvet coat, a fine linen white tunic, and expensive black velvet breeches. His feet were sheathed in fine black leather boots; every article clearly fashioned by expert hands. His costly raiment was a stark contrast to the common foot soldier towering over him.

"Is there something you require, Nephew?" Hades asked in a bored tone.

"I would like to begin by making sure we understand each other, Uncle. I am not here to ask a favor of you, I am merely here to inform you of a situation you may or may not be aware of; but make no mistake, I am definitely not asking a favor of you," Ares said in a voice so cold, it chilled the blood of those who heard it.

The magistrate had come out of his office at the commotion. He now stared at the two men. He had not seen the arrival of the first. He had, however, seen the arrival of the second and though one part of his mind refused to believe his eyes, the other acknowledged with no doubt that the man he was staring at was indeed Hades, God of the Underworld, and to the last detail the other appeared to be Lord Ares, God of War. Indeed, he had even just heard him refer to Hades as Uncle. The magistrate continued to stare fixedly on the sight before his eyes, unable to turn away, despite his desire to flee before two of the most dangerous gods in all of Olympus.

Hades raised his right hand and made a circling motion, as to indicate Ares was to get on with it. "Yes, yes, I acknowledge that you are not asking me a favor, Nephew. So what is it you feel I need to be made aware of?"

Ares made a gesture with his hand. Though he and his uncle never ever discussed business in private, it was safer for everyone that way; he did not wish these villagers to overhear the rest of his conversation. "There is now a man in your domain. This man has caused untold grief and pain to a member of your blood. I merely wanted to make sure that you are aware that amongst his many victims, one of the girls that he has raped, tortured, and beaten, is my only daughter." Ares' voice had shook with barely contained rage, and now flames erupted in his eyes. As he took a steadying breath and observed his uncle, he saw his Uncle's usually calm gray eyes cloud over with a dense fog, an unusual sign that his emotions were getting the better of him. Something he did not usually permit to happen.

"What is his name?" The voice that spoke was as cold as the grave.

"He called himself Bloody Fang," Ares replied with equal coldness.

"Does my great-niece still live?" demanded Hades.

Ares removed his helmet and ruffled his hair. Looking down at his uncle he said, "She is my daughter. Do you think a pathetic weak man like him could end her life? Torture her and make her suffer, yes, but he's not strong enough to kill her. I look forward to watching my daughter and my sons kill his mistress and slaughter his father. Before my children are done, you will have many more inhabitants. The River Styx will positively swell from the number of boats that they will cast upon the water," Ares boasted.

Hades knew his nephew well enough to know it was not an idle boast. If Ares said his sons were good enough to do it, they would do it. As of yet, he had not found himself interested in this war; perhaps he needed to take a closer look at the main players. He might find it an enlightening experience. "You have my assurances, Nephew, I will attend to his comfort personally." Ares nodded, donned his helmet, and again flames coiled around him, and then he and they disappeared. Another hole opened in the ground and again dense gloomy fog covered Hades. When the fog lifted, their quiet street was returned to normal and it was as though nothing had happened, though the magistrate could not remove his eyes from where he had seen Lord Ares stand. Ares's face had been turned three quarters of the way towards the magistrate. Well enough that the magistrate could see him and what he had seen had staggered him.

Hades entered his throne room. Crossing to his chair, he sat down. As he leaned back in his chair, his hand began petting his dog. The dog had glowing red eyes and a thick black hide, with a lean, quick body, and razor-sharp teeth - though of course, its most dangerous feature was its ability to launch poison spikes out of its tail. He looked up at the rafters where his birds all perched. He liked crows; their calling soothed him. He didn't understand why other people found it annoying. He shrugged his shoulders as he considered the best way to deal with the foul creature. He turned to two of his guards. "Bring me the one called Bloody Fang." They scurried away to do his bidding.

Hades spent the next three quarters of an hour staring into the gazing pool. He began with Bloody Fang's death. As he watched the scene unfold that led to his demise, he observed two sons of Ares. Then he waved his hand over the pool, going back to when Bloody Fang was about ten and worked his way forward over the man's life and past transgressions. It disgusted him to his very depths to observe the cruel, abusive nature of the man. As he watched the man's life fly by - he had no need to watch it in slow motion - his evil deeds were so prevalent, one bled into the next, but a quick glimpse of raven black hair halted him. He flicked his wrist for the image to go back. Finding the beginning of his encounter with the daughter of Ares, he watched as the scene went from bad to worse. Gritting his teeth, he had to remind himself this was nothing he had not seen a million times before when weighing a man's punishment. His guts twisted as though to remind him that this was different. This was his own flesh and blood, Ares' only daughter, his grand-niece. He forced himself to observe a little longer before he became so

32

sickened by the sight he smashed his fist into the gazing pool, shattering the image.

A moment later, commotion outside caught his attention. He looked just in time to see Bloody Fang was being dragged in. Hades' face was a stony mask, and when he spoke, his voice revealed nothing of his emotion. "Release him. Let him walk to me of his own accord." He concealed his amusement as he watched the man walk forward. He could see his gait was uneven. "Did you receive that injury at your death, or at some prior time?"

Bloody Fang stared, trying to decide what he had done to warrant a visit to the Lord of the Underworld. "That ruddy bastard who killed me brought his sword up into my bollocks."

"You should be grateful that he waited until after you were deceased to decapitate you and sever your arm, otherwise you would now be missing those as well. However, I might consider dismemberment as part of your punishment," Hades said with a smile.

"Dismemberment?" Bloody Fang ejaculated.

Hades slowly grinned. "Oh yes, I have given my word that I will see to your comfort personally. It is fortunate for you that you were completely unaware of whom you were mistreating, because had you had an inkling of an idea, I would feel myself compelled to permit my nephew into my realm to deal with you personally. However, since you were ignorant of her lineage, I will deal with you personally."

Bloody Fang swallowed hard. "Her lineage? Is this about some girl I rolled? You know how women are, willing enough until their father finds out and then they say he raped me." He hesitated a moment trying to swallow, the heat in here was unbearable. "You have a nephew?"

Hades laughed, though there was no amusement. "You are clearly a fool if you are not aware of the fact that Ares, God of War, Battle, and Bloodshed, is the eldest child of my long dead brother, Zeus."

Bloody Fang's eyes bugged out of their sockets. "But I thought none of the gods got on well with each other!"

Again Hades laughed without amusement. "I may dislike my nephew and I might look for an opportunity to stick a knife in his ribs, but that doesn't mean I appreciate some pathetic mortal daring to rape, beat, and disfigure the daughter of Ares. After all, she is my flesh and blood as well, and what amuses me most about this entire circumstance is you are still so foolishly clueless." As Hades spoke, fog clouded his eyes, his skin turned ashen, and then the room slowly started to fill with a murky gray fog so dense Bloody Fang

34

could no longer see the floor. Then Bloody Fang felt a cold hand grip his heart. As Hades grinned, there was something so evil about the grin it made Bloody Fang gasp for air. Hot air from the room filled his lungs, despite the cool fog nipping at his feet. "You know, a thought just struck me. It is within my power to give you back your life."

"What would you ask of me to give me back my life?" Bloody Fang asked nervously.

"If I were to give you back your life, I would place you right outside my grand-nephew by marriage's tent. He has many times bemoaned the fact that he killed you too quickly." Hades rather enjoyed watching the man go from pale to ghostlike. He was quite certain had the man had anything in his stomach, he would've either retched, or wet his pants. Apparently, he was quite afraid of this Eden - which made Hades like Eden all the more.

"What would be the purpose of that? I would just end up back here."

"Yes, but I would get to watch Eden kill you again, and who knows - my nephew might get there in time to kill you himself. And I promise you, if Ares learns that I gave you back your life, he will know why I did it and he will be quick to pounce on you." Hades made a gesture of annoyance and then said, "Guards, take him to the River Acheron and cast him into it to await my pleasure." Bloody Fang cried out in protest, but the guards quickly removed him from the throne room. Hades crossed to his chair and dropped into it. A few decades in the River Acheron will be a good start to his punishment"

*****

Hades – God of the Underworld. Weighs the souls of the dead to decide their final resting place – Elysian Fields or Tartarus. He has graying blonde hair and grey eyes; five feet eight inches tall, athletic build. Brother to Poseidon and Zeus. Uncle to Ares, Athena, and Freya. His animal is the crow. His preferred weapon is a scythe. Both countries follow Hades.

IV

Five days earlier, Grey Stone stared up at his daughter's face. She was fighting to hold back tears. She also foolishly was trying to stop the bleeding. He knew he was dead. He was dead the minute the arrows hit him. *Dumb ass! What was I thinking stepping in front of her? I should've knocked us both clear, then the two of us could have taken on the archer together. But I had to react foolishly, to ignore years of training and die because I acted stupidly. Now I am leaving my daughter to face that man alone.* Blood gurgled out of his mouth as he tried to speak. A moment later, a fire of pain shot through him, and then Ares was standing over his daughter, looking down on the corpse of Grey Stone. He gave a little shudder. There was something so disconcerting about looking down on your own dead body. He took several steps to the side, watching his daughter's face.

A voice from near his elbow said, "You mustn't interfere now, Ares." Ares did not even turn to look at his sister, Athena. He continued to watch his daughter as her face contorted with grief and then rage. As she turned towards him, looking past him where the archer now stood, he caught his breath at the unmasked rage in her eyes. She drew her sword and pointed it at the archer, and as their eyes met, flames leapt into hers, and a moment later, the flames in her eyes grew and spread, as her entire body became flame. She screamed with fury. As Ares watched his daughter stalk past him, having eyes only for her prey, he turned slowly to see an astonished look on Athena's face.

"Did you have any idea she was that near?" he questioned, his voice full of awe.

Athena slowly shook her head. "I knew she was exceedingly powerful. I had no idea she was that powerful. I knew that she and Eric are more powerful than any child you ever sired before them, and more powerful than any child Freya or I have ever given birth to."

"Eric is that powerful?"

"Had Eric been in a temple where he had received divine training, I shudder to think what the two of them could accomplish together. They have already accomplished more than any two mortals should have been capable of accomplishing. And Brother, I should warn you that several of the gods have become concerned by all your offspring. They feel that they are growing too powerful under your tutelage, and they have begun to whisper that we should destroy them before they are too powerful."

Ares grinned broadly as he watched his daughter bring her sword down in a fiery arc, cutting off the assassins escape. "Has she always learned this quickly, or is it just rage driving her?"

"She has always learned this quickly. Everything she turns her hand to, she learns with the greatest of ease. Even when she was merely a priestess of mine, her power was great. I knew she was going to be powerful. Even at the small age of three I knew that." Ares frowned as he thought of his daughter a priestess of Athena. Athena laughed. "Would you prefer I left her in the woods to die, Brother? I sat up with her all night, keeping her warm until Father Thomas arrived. I even went so far as to draw his ear to her cries."

"No, Sister, I would not have wished you to do that. But you must confess, you would no more like a son of yours becoming a servant of mine, than I do my daughter serving you." She nodded her head in grudging assent. The two watched as the battle died down. "I understand the gods having it in for Bloodstone and Eric. Why the others?" he asked suddenly.

"Perhaps you are too close to it. You have not observed that Andrew is perhaps as fine a swordsman as you have ever been, and Daniel is nearly as good. Patrick has the potential to be as great a weapons craftsman as you or Bloodstone, and Bloodstone is nearly your equal - if not your equal. And the others are young, and under your tutelage their ability would continue to grow; but now they have their elder siblings, demigods

39

trained by Ares himself. And I may have made sure that my niece had the finest weapons training available from mortals." She blushed and looked a little sheepish. "And with Eden the werewolf to train them, and of course, one cannot forget Murtaugh. Murtaugh has no truly extraordinary ability, though he himself is quite extraordinary as far as mortals go. And I would not want to go up against him or Big Bear." She gave a little shudder. "The unpredictability of that man's mind is a little scary. The group of allies that has formed here is really extraordinary. If they were to set their minds on conquering the world, they would do it. And I doubt that there's any army that would withstand them."

Ares couldn't help it. He knew he should be taking the situation a little more seriously. He grinned broadly as he said, "What do you expect? They're my family." He sighed and took one last look at his children. His heart ached for the pain Black Stone was feeling, and he winced as Bloodstone became hysterical. He looked back to his sister. "Well, Sister, I believe my corpse lying over there dead at the hands of a mortal wins me the bet, does it not?"

Athena glared at him. "And which one of my temples are you going to claim?"

"Well, Sister, you know that my men and I aren't exactly into temples. We tend to be more into … fortresses." He almost managed to sound casual.

Athena turned one of her most hate filled glares on her brother. Her eyes flashed sky blue for just a moment, and she said through clenched teeth, "You wouldn't dare take that one, Ares!"

"Don't bet … what you cannot afford to lose, Sister, and you said any of your temples. I find it so convenient that my daughter has already vacated the premises for me." He continued to sound casual, being sure not to sound even the slightest bit gloating. He knew that that would irritate Athena even more.

"Ares, not that one!" she said angrily.

"But Sister, you and I both know that it is the only one of your temples that would suit the needs of the Soldiers of Ares. I think my banners will look very nice hanging from the spires. Granted, it does needs some repairs and my daughter did block that pass, but …" he shrugged his shoulders. "Nevertheless, I think we will make good use of it, don't you?"

"Ares, have I informed you recently what a complete and utter ass you are?" she said coldly.

"I've missed you too, Sister. Now may I suggest we go and have a talk with the other gods and remind them that my children are strictly off limits?"

41

*****

After his conversation with Hades, Ares retired to his chambers so as to make use of the gazing pool. A hand on his shoulder startled him. He looked up quickly to see his sister Freya standing there. "What do you watch so intensely, Brother?" She leaned over the pool. Wincing, she looked away quickly. "Why do you watch that, Brother?"

"I am merely attempting to get a better understanding of my child by viewing her life. I would've thought it would please you that I was taking an active interest in my offspring for a change."

"Your interest in your children does please me, Brother; however, you have no need to torture yourself over this."

He turned on her. "And who should be tortured by it? Her, for being a child and unable to protect herself, or her father Ares, God of War/General Grey Stone and neither one of us protected her! Neither one of us looked after her! We have both failed her!"

Freya rolled her eyes. *Men could be so silly, even when they're gods.* "I'm assuming your prickly disposition means you're still irritated with me?"

"Why wouldn't I be still irritated with you? You did it deliberately, giving me a daughter at the worst possible time to do so. That malicious act of yours, Freya, caused her to be harmed."

She grabbed him by the arm and jerked him around to face her. "My intentions were not malicious. Mischievous, yes, but not malicious. There were circumstances beyond my control. I gave her to Rose, a good woman who would have taken care of her. I could not have seen what was going to happen. You know as well as I do, the Fates do not share information."

Ares sighed and hugged his sister tightly. "I know. I'm just angry."

Freya embraced her brother and kissed him on the cheek. "Without directly interfering in her life, Athena and I have gone out of our way to keep an eye on her. I know that that did not prevent her from suffering much harm; but we made sure that even when she was suffering, she was not alone. I'm sorry we could not do more for you and for her. Please forgive us our failing."

*****

Athena – Goddess of War, Wisdom, Truth, and Knowledge. She has a passion for the plight of the common people. She is a fierce defender of truth and justice. She has always felt it was her duty to protect and guard her baby sister, Freya, so consequently her followers also defend the followers of Freya. Of all the gods, she is the most powerful. Athena is elegantly featured, with long blonde hair and crisp blue eyes. She is nearly six feet tall with a shapely muscular build. Her animal is the owl. Her preferred weapon is the Longsword. Goddess of Bretony.

Freya – Goddess of Fertility and Nature. She is a gentle and peace loving goddess, who prefers to expend her energy with more fruitful tasks such as farming and healing. Freya loves her brother, but disapproves of his complete disregard for the feelings of the opposite sex. Freya is delicately built. She is five feet eleven inches tall with long, curly, auburn hair and green eyes. Her animal is the rabbit. Her preferred weapon is the bow. She has a large following in both countries.

V

Dex and Simon exchanged concerned looks and stepped into her tent. "General, you've been alone in here. Nothing has transpired. What's going on?" questioned Sergeant Simon. He started to look around the tent, but his eyes got no further than the new chair. "Where did that come from? It was not here when Katya brought the baby."

Bloodstone began shaking her head and running her hands through her hair. "Out! Both of you, I have work to do!" Simon grudgingly took his leave.

"General, you'll forgive me for questioning you; but something is clearly disturbing you. Perhaps it would be best if you confided in one of us, or I could go and get the Elder," Dex added somewhat hesitantly.

Bloodstone narrowed her eyes and fixed Dex with a cold stare. "I said I am fine and that I have work to do tonight and at this time I do not require either one of your assistance. Sergeant Simon may return to his duties, and as far as I am concerned, you and your men may go away. And while we're on the subject of you and your men, do not get used to lurking outside my tent or following me around. As soon as Eden returns, it is my intention to make sure you and your men go away and never bother me again. I am not a child who needs a bodyguard. Is that clear?"

Dex moved to stand directly in front of her as he glowered down at her. "You may not feel that my presence is necessary, Your Majesty, but my King and the Council do. And whether you like it or not, you are my Queen and it is my duty and the duty of my men to give our lives to protect you. We all made a mistake. We did not make sure you had a guard to begin with. You may blame yourself for the death of your father; but there is not a man in Wolf Tribe who does not also blame himself, because we should've been there to protect you. He should not of been called upon to give up his life for yours. I may have come too late to this task to have prevented his death, but I'm not too late to protect you and those around you, whether you like it or not. So it is you, Your Majesty, who had better get used to our presence." To Dex's surprise, she gave a curt nod.

"If your men are going to be my guards, we need to come to an understanding." She hesitated and looked up at him. Dex nodded for her to continue. "As a General of this army, sometimes things that are said in my quarters must remain in my quarters. Conversations that you will overhear while we're here or moving throughout this encampment are private, which means you and your men are not to repeat anything you overhear to anyone. This includes the Council, or Eden. If this is something you and your men are not willing to do, then I will be forced to put you and all your men in the stockades until Eden returns."

"I do see the necessity for such a statement; however, my men are to report to me anything that concerns them. Once it is repeated to me, I will decide whether it is something I need to pass on to someone else. I am not Sergeant Simon. I am not under your command. My sole responsibility is the protection of you, your son, and Katya. If my men report something to me, or if I overhear something that I feel jeopardizes any of your safety in any way, even if the danger is yourself; then I am forced to act upon it. You cannot throw all of Wolf Tribe in the stockades," he added with a grin.

She sighed and gave a curt nod. "Then for the moment, we have a tentative understanding. Now I have dinner to prepare and much work to do, so be gone." She gave a gesture with her hands to the door. Dex bowed and excused himself. Once he was gone, Bloodstone growled and ran her hands through her hair in increased agitation. She growled again and began preparing dinner. Normally in Eden's absence, she wouldn't bother to prepare dinner, she'd just go to the mess tent and get something to eat. But something told her that she was going to have at least one, if not two, guests for dinner.

That having been done, she crossed to her desk and picked up her box. Opening it, she pulled out the bloodstained documents the Duke had been carrying with him at the time of his death. Her hands shook as she broke the seal. She as of yet had not been able to bring herself to read them. The reports were written in the Duke's bold hand. The papers on Hawthorne were on the top. She read through them carefully and then at the end he had written, "I know you may have concerns about this man, Hawthorne, but I see nothing in any of his records that would give me pause. He appears to be a good, honest, loyal soldier. He's had his bouts of trouble, but what soldier hasn't?"

Flipping on to see who the Duke had chosen to tackle next, she saw Ellsworth's name. She gritted her teeth as she read the report, again at the end the Duke had added something. "I can't say as I like this man Ellsworth. I've spoken to several of his former commanding officers and fellow officers. They all say the same thing. They never saw him do anything wrong, but there was always something just not quite right about him. And I also found one Athenian soldier, purely by accident - I should say he overheard me asking questions about Ellsworth - who swears to me, Ellsworth is not to be trusted. He has always suspected that Ellsworth had something to do with the death of the Captain who he conveniently replaced. I will endeavor to find out more about this Captain's death, but in the meanwhile, all I can say is he just doesn't seem real."

About Captain Cutter he wrote, "He appears to be the standard upstanding soldier. He has a few complaints lodged against him, nothing major. I could find nothing in his records that gave me any concern, though I should add that he has been directly under Ellsworth's command for five years." Bloodstone growled in frustration and threw the papers in her box, slamming the lid.

As she sat there considering, she realized how impotent she felt. She needed to find some way to feel useful. There had been just too much tragedy, death, and destruction. She needed to do something constructive. Then she slowly smiled as she thought to herself, *I wonder if it's possible for a mortal to save a god? Well, I can at least try, not dead yet.* She picked up the paper and began writing orders. When she was done, she had letters going to all the large villages in the area, as well as all the villages between here and Capital City. "Sergeant Simon, could you come in here, please?"

Sergeant Simon entered and crossed to her desk. "Yes, General?"

She handed him the first stack of letters. "Would you have a church messenger take these letters and see that they're delivered immediately?" She picked up the second stack of letters and handed them to him. "When the regular messenger leaves tomorrow for Capital City, make sure that he is aware to deliver these along the route."

"Of course, General, I'll see to it immediately." He bowed and excused himself.

Bloodstone got up and went over to the fire, stirring dinner. She determined that dinner was ready and pushed it a little further away from the fire, so that it would just stay warm. As she looked down at the fire, a thought struck her. She slowly slipped to her knees in front of the hearth, rolled up her sleeve on her right arm past her elbow, and thrust her arm into the flames. She stared as she felt the warmth, but was not injured. She felt no pain, no discomfort. She wiggled her fingers in the flames. She reached down and scooped up a handful of burning embers, again she felt no discomfort. Turning her hand, palm down towards the fire, she concentrated, willing the flames to burn out. To her surprise, the fire did not die down, but actually absorbed into her hand. A moment later, the light in the room dimmed, the only light coming from the hour candle and the lantern hanging over her desk. She lifted her hand and stared at her palm, then waving the back of her hand over the fire, almost as though she was caressing Eden's chest, she willed the flames to return. This time, the flames did begin to spark and kindle from amongst the logs. A few seconds later, the fire was burning bright and hot.

She had no idea how long she'd been kneeling there by the fire staring into it when a voice from beside her startled her. "General, is there something the matter?" questioned Fletcher.

"I've been sitting here pondering on that same question myself. I hardly know what to think of it.

I hardly know what I am to do." She swallowed hard. *Great, just what I need, more things in my life that I am forced to conceal for fear of what people will think of me,* she thought to herself.

Fletcher dropped to one knee and squeezed her shoulder. "Bloodstone, you're scaring me. What's the matter? The dark look on your face is …" He broke off, unsure of how to continue.

"Is what?" she demanded in a distant tone.

"It concerns me."

"Do you think I'm mad, Fletcher? Do you believe I am dangerous? Do you think I'm losing it? Do you think I'm at my wits end?" She turned to look at him. "Do you think I am unfit to command my men?"

"Why would you ask such questions?" he said in a gentle voice.

"Because you, Dex, and Sergeant Simon all think I need coddling and protecting like I am an ordinary woman who isn't perfectly capable of taking care of herself, like I'm not perfectly capable of protecting all of you," she said angrily.

"I cannot speak for Dex or Sergeant Simon. I can only speak for myself, and though I know you are perfectly capable of protecting yourself, me, and every man in this encampment, you are still my daughter and I feel obligated to try to protect you. And as of late, you have seemed a bit fragile, and though I see the strong, determined warrior, I also see the eighteen year old girl. Sometimes I wonder at what point is the eighteen year old girl going to break? There's only so much a mind can take and deal with before it does break. And it does not matter whether that mind is the mind of an eighteen year old girl, or a forty-five year old man. We each have our breaking point, and I fear greatly that watching your father die is going to be yours. So I hoped if I was here, I could keep the break from being irreparable." He squeezed her shoulder tightly, then looked at her sharply. "I understand the other questions, but why did you ask if you're dangerous?"

She hesitated only a moment. "If I tell you, you must never repeat it to anyone. Is that clear, Sergeant Major?"

"You have my word on it, General." Bloodstone could see the lines of concern creasing his face, then she thrust her arm into the fire. He cried out, "What do you think you're doing?" As he grabbed her around the waist and jerked her back from the fire; they both fell back, him landing on top of her, his nose to hers. He stared down at her, but before he could speak; they heard a cough from the doorway. Fletcher looked quickly to see a Barbarian he did not recognize, standing just inside the doorway looking stunned. Dex was standing to his left looking furious, and Sergeant Simon to his right looking surprised. Fletcher looked down. Finally, fully grasping how the situation must look, he started and jumped to his feet. Clearing his throat and looking very uncomfortable, he stammered out, "My apologies General, I ... I tripped." Fletcher mentally kicked himself, that had to be the most feeble obvious lie he'd ever told in his life. He felt his cheeks grow hot. As he knew himself to be blushing, and try as he may, he couldn't seem to stop, nor could he meet the eyes of any of the four people in the room. He just stared at the ground. *By the gods you damned fool, you're a forty-five year old man. You're old enough to be her father, surely they can't think anything inappropriate was happening, could they?* he asked himself.

Then Bloodstone cleared her throat. "Father, permit me to introduce Hafgrim, the Elder of Wolf Tribe, and Eden's grandfather. Grandfather, permit me to introduce Sergeant Major Fletcher, my mother's husband. And of course, both of you are familiar with the other two lurking in the doorway." She hesitated a moment and then decided to go on the offensive. "Speaking of which, I do not recall summoning either one of you." Both men shook their heads and excused themselves.

Once they were gone, Hafgrim openly glared at Fletcher. "I may be unfamiliar with Breton culture, but I cannot imagine that kissing one's daughter is considered an appropriate thing for a man to do," Hafgrim said in a frigid voice.

Fletcher looked insulted and glared back. "I am insulted that you would even imply that I would cheat on my wife - and with her daughter no less."

"Then I'm sure you have a logical reason why we walked in on you on top of your woman's daughter, kissing her?" Hafgrim questioned coldly.

Fletcher tightened his jaw as he realized nothing he was going to say was going to convince the man otherwise. In his mind he knew what he had seen and that was that. "You will believe what you are going to believe no matter what I say so I will merely state for the last time. I was not kissing her." Fletcher crossed his arms over his chest and continued to glare at the older man.

"If you have done nothing wrong, then explain to me how you ended up on top of my granddaughter," Hafgrim said calmly. Fletcher remained silent. After all, he had given his word to say nothing. Remembering about Bloodstone's arm, he looked back at her quickly, his eyes alighting on her unblemished right arm. The skin was not even the faintest bit pink. He knew he had moved quickly, but not that quickly. The arm should be red and burnt. She had thrust it directly into the hottest part of the fire. He looked up to meet her eyes; she merely shrugged her shoulders.

"Sergeant Major Fletcher is under orders not to repeat what had transpired. He gave his word of honor." She crossed her arms over her chest and looked at Hafgrim. "What I desire to know, Hafgrim, is what do you think of me in this situation?"

"I think that you are a very upset, traumatized young girl, who can easily be taken advantage of by men out for their own pleasure." He glared at Fletcher, who continued to glare back.

Bloodstone moved to stand in front of Hafgrim. When there was only two feet separating them, she glared up at him. "If that is what you think, Hafgrim, you will leave my tent and not return until your grandson does. Neither I nor Fletcher are required to explain ourselves to you." As Hafgrim watched her face, he saw fire burning in her eyes, and her skin took on a red tinge. Bloodstone felt herself become warm, she could feel sweat running down her back and her blood begin to boil. As her heart pounded in her chest, she stepped back quickly from both men holding her hands out, bidding them to stay where they were. Remembering that last time fire shot from her sword, she hugged herself, pressing her palms tightly into her sides. Closing her eyes, she took several long, slow, deep breaths, trying to calm herself, but her heart would not be calm. She was so angry that Hafgrim would think that she would ever betray Eden.

As Fletcher watched, he literally saw steam begin to rise from her soaked clothing. Her skin was turning an even darker shade of red. She was shaking with barely contained rage. He didn't think, he didn't even hesitate, he crossed quickly to her and grabbed her face in both of his hands. She was so hot to the touch, it was nearly painful to hold her; nevertheless, he forced her to look at him. When she opened her eyes, he saw fire burning in them. "Fletcher, you have to get back quickly, I don't know if I can control it," she said, her voice frantic with fear.

"Yes, you can. Just breathe. Look into my eyes and breathe. That's it, one breath at a time, slowly, breathe with me." As he continued to hold her face, the heat began to burn his hands, but he forced himself to conceal it. He took a slow, deep breath, and then let it out. He repeated this process several times, continuing to ignore the pain. He held her face, forcing her to look at him. After five of the longest minutes of his life, the flames left her eyes, and her skin returned to its normal bronze. Bloodstone sank to her knees exhausted. Fletcher fell with her, pulling her tightly against him. Putting her head on his shoulder, he stroked her hair murmuring softly in her ear, "It's going to be all right. We'll figure this out together."

Hafgrim watched the whole scene unfold, feeling worse than useless. He said just loud enough to be heard outside, "Send someone to fetch Viktor and send for my great-grandson's nurse."

Katya arrived only a few moments later. Hafgrim looked at her. "Would it be possible for you to keep my great-grandson overnight?"

"But of course, if the General requires it," she replied, a little hesitantly.

"It is necessary. Please take him and remove him quickly." Katya glanced at the General, still in Fletcher's arms.

"Is the General unwell? Is there something I can do for her?" Katya asked, looking concerned.

"Yes, you can remove my great-grandson, so she need have no fear for him," Hafgrim replied quickly. Waiting until the girl was gone, he then peeked his head outside and looked from Dex to Sergeant Simon and said, "When Viktor arrives, you and your men are to retreat over there to where you cannot hear what is going on." Dex opened his mouth to protest, but was silenced by a glare from Hafgrim. "Do not presume to question me." Both men nodded, their irritation was evident.

Viktor arrived a quarter of an hour later. He looked from the grim face of the Elder to the concerned face of Fletcher, finally to Bloodstone, whose eyes were shut. She was leaning heavily against Fletcher, both still kneeling on the ground. "What is going on?" he asked softly.

Hafgrim shook his head in confusion. "I do not know. I have never seen anything the like of it, not in all my eighty years. Viktor, flames literally burned in her eyes, her skin became red."

Viktor nodded his head. He crossed over to Bloodstone and dropped down on one knee. He put his hand on his little sister's shoulder and squeezed it tightly. She opened her eyes and looked up at him. To his sheer astonishment, she burst into tears and threw her arms around his neck and hugged him tightly. "Viktor, I'm terrified! I don't think I can control this!" Viktor and Fletcher exchanged worried looks.

"Bloodstone, do you know what is causing this to happen?" He felt her nod her head against his chest. "I think you'd better tell us what is going on."

Again, he felt her nod, and then she slowly pulled away. "You must all give me your word not to repeat what I'm going to show you or tell you." Viktor and Hafgrim both agreed quickly.

"I was trying to show Fletcher when he jerked me away, and that's when Hafgrim came in and everything went very badly after that - but I do not think telling you will convince you. I think I need to show you." With that being said, she stood up and walked to the fire, then dropped down to her knees and again, she stuck her bare right arm into the fire. Viktor moved to pull her away from the fire, but Fletcher grabbed his shoulder, wincing as he did so. Viktor turned to glare at him, but

58

Fletcher merely shook his head. All three men turned to watch her and the fire. For a long moment, she just left her arm in the fire, then she swirled her arm in the fire as though she was testing the water. Holding out her palm, she began to absorb the fire. When she was done, the hearth appeared cold. Viktor crossed over and tentatively extended his hand to the logs, he felt no warmth. He picked one of them up. It was cool to the touch. Bloodstone calmly took the log from his hand and placed it back in the fire; then holding out her hand, the flames slowly sprang back to life. When she was done, she turned to look at all of them. She was relieved to see none of them looked afraid. Viktor looked puzzled. Hafgrim looked worried, as did Fletcher.

Viktor was shaking his head in confusion. "I don't understand. You're a worshiper of Athena and, yes, you were a priestess of Athena, so you would have other abilities. But Athena does not have anything to do with fire. I think you'd better explain what you believe is causing this."

"Well, that's where things get interesting. You see, apparently," she hesitated and added in a soft voice barely audible, "I am the daughter of Ares." Viktor blinked, believing he could not have heard her right.

"So the Duke of Stone Reach was not your father?" questioned Hafgrim.

Fletcher, who was staring wide-eyed said slowly, "No, I think what she's telling us is the Duke and Lord Ares are one and the same … which means … that on a regular basis, there are seven half gods in this encampment." Bloodstone nodded slowly.

"Well, that explains where the fire came from. I've been wondering how you managed to turn into a burning …" Viktor hesitated, "… person."

"Viktor, I think I inadvertently did something that now I cannot control," Bloodstone said nervously.

"If you are the daughter of Ares, and if you have learned either inadvertently, or deliberately, to manipulate fire, you will learn to control it. When is your first recollection of you manipulating fire, before that day or only since then?" questioned Viktor.

Bloodstone considered a long time. "I've been thinking about that ever since I played with the fire here this afternoon. I don't ever recall being burned, never. The only time I was ever burned, and I don't think it counts, was when I was in the Dream World. And that's about your mind, not your actual body. And my mind would tell me that a ball of fire would burn me, because I did not know yet. I've grown up in the forge. I've worked with fire all my life and I never thought about it. But now that I have thought about it, I have never had trouble with the fires. Eric, sometimes the fires will not behave for him; sometimes they burn too hot, sometimes they won't burn hot enough. I never have that problem. I've never had that problem in all my years of metal forging, never burned myself, not once." She thrust out both her forearms, rolling up her left sleeve, she turned them over. "My arms and hands have no scars, not like most blacksmiths, and I've been trying to remember whether Patrick does either. Eric does, as do all of his apprentices, but not me, and I don't think Patrick."

"Then you've inadvertently been controlling fire all your life. I think the only reason you're having trouble with it now is because your mind is having trouble reconciling it. You've done it naturally all your life. I think you need to stop worrying about it and just go back to doing it naturally. I think you're worried because you're afraid of what it means. Stop worrying and embrace it as a part of you. It's always been a part of you," Viktor said confidently. She looked to see both Hafgrim and Fletcher nodding as well.

"But if you and Patrick are immune to fire, would not General Black Stone be as well?" questioned Fletcher.

"Not Eric 'Black' Stone, Eric 'the Blacksmith' Rosario, a Colonel in the Church Knights," she replied quickly.

"My apologies, General, I've never heard him referred to as anything other than Blacksmith." She waved her hand dismissively.

Hafgrim, who had been silent up till now, spoke. "I agree with Viktor. I think you're over thinking it, and that's why you're having problems now. However, I also agree with Bloodstone - we need to make sure that no one hears of this. It could be very dangerous for our allies if it gets out that we have seven demigods here. I also think that Viktor and Bloodstone need to find a secluded, secure place for her to work on mastering the skill, which means Dex is going to have to be informed." He hesitated a moment considering, then added, "And if we're going to inform Dex, I feel it would be inappropriate not to inform Sergeant Simon as well." His audience all nodded in assent.

Hafgrim returned to the tent flap and opened it, calling for Sergeant Simon and Dex.

When the two men entered, Sergeant Major Fletcher turned to face them. "There's something we would like to make you gentlemen aware of, however, before we can do this, we must first swear you to absolute secrecy. None of what we're about to tell you can be repeated under any circumstances. Do you so swear?"

Sergeant Simon glanced at his General, who gave a nod in assent. "On my honor, I swear to silence," he said quickly.

Dex shifted uncomfortably. "I cannot give such a vow unless I am first assured that Eden is either already aware of what you are going to tell me, or will be made aware of immediately upon his return."

Bloodstone glanced up at him quickly. "Now he's just Eden," she said, her irritation evident.

"He prefers me to call him Eden, but when I feel it is necessary to remind you of who you are, I will use more formal titles."

"What I'm going to tell you, I would never attempt to conceal from my husband. You have my assurance that I will tell him immediately upon his return," she said wearily.

"Then you have my word of honor - provided that you inform Eden within two days of his return - and I will check with him to make sure you do tell him. I will repeat it to no one else, under any other circumstances."

"What's the matter, Dex, don't trust me?" she demanded angrily.

"With all due respect, General, I think where secrets are concerned, you will keep them as long as you can." He hesitated a moment and then closed his mouth. Bloodstone glared at him in open hostility. Dex remained unperturbed by this.

Fletcher cleared his throat. All eyes turned to face him. "Now that you both have given your word, I think we should get down to business." Then he informed Dex and Sergeant Simon of the situation and enlisted their aid with plans and strategies on how to find a safe, secluded, quiet place for Viktor and Bloodstone to work on this together.

As soon as their plans were made, Hafgrim arose and said, "Sergeant Major Fletcher, I feel I need a private word with you. Would you mind escorting me back to my quarters?"

Though Fletcher did not look pleased about the matter, he nodded his consent and followed Hafgrim from the tent. Viktor quickly made his excuses and followed the other two. Simon also bowed and excused himself. As soon as they were gone, Bloodstone rolled her eyes knowing good and damn well they wanted to talk about her behind her back. She arose from the table and stretched her back. Heading for the washbasin, she pulled off her tunic, saying as she did so, "Clearly you want to say something, Dex, so go on with it."

Dex stared at her corseted back a moment longer than he should have. Turning around quickly, he kicked himself. He should've turned around as soon as he saw she was going to remove her tunic. A moment later he heard water pour from the pitcher, then splashing. She was clearly washing. "Is your custom to always remove your garments in front of men who are not your mate?" he snapped out angrily.

"Dex, I'm a soldier. Modesty is not exactly my strong point, but you're supposed to be explaining to me why you're still in my tent," she said as she began washing her face.

"I know that you think I insulted you a little while ago. It was not my intention to insult you; but from what I have learned about you, secrets have been your means of survival for a long time. And for whatever reason, you still find it necessary to make your own way and to survive on your secrets. To hold them tightly to you, but that is all you are doing. You're surviving. There is a big difference between surviving and living. You have survived long enough. Isn't it time you learn how to live?"

"You do not know me. Do not presume to act as though you do," she replied angrily.

"Unfortunately for you, I probably know you a lot better than you would wish me to. I've probably already learned more of your secrets than you would wish of me; but if I am to protect you, I must know everything. I cannot protect you if I do not know," he stated firmly.

She rounded on him angrily. Seeing that he had his back turned to her with his arms crossed over his chest, she stormed over to stand in front of him, glaring up at him. Dex looked down at her and swallowed hard. Whatever thin cotton garment she was wearing fit snugly, barely concealing the full curves of her very nicely shaped breasts and a waist so tiny he thought for sure he could wrap both of his hands around it. Gritting his teeth and reminding himself whose woman he was ogling, he looked up at the ceiling. "I do not need a guard. I will not be a prisoner with guards all around me telling me where I can go, telling me what I can do. I need no one! I am perfectly capable of taking care of myself!" As she continued to glare at him, it annoyed her that he was refusing to look at her. "Do not continue to look at the ceiling when I speak to you!" she added angrily.

Dex looked down to meet her eyes, forcing himself to maintain eye contact as he said, "I am not your guard. You are not my prisoner. I am here to protect you. I am not your enemy. Please let me and my men protect you and let us do our duty by you and our King. I know that you are a skilled warrior and I know that you are better than probably all of my men. Maybe even better than me, though by the gods, I hope not. But even the most skilled warrior cannot take on a dozen warriors by themselves. You know, had you been in that court yard alone, you probably would've perished, but fortunately, there was a large contingent of soldiers on your side. Please don't fight me every step of the way." Bloodstone gritted her teeth as she knew she had to acknowledge the justice of that statement. Finally she nodded. Dex gave a respectful bow and excused himself.

*****

Hafgrim waited until he was sure they were far enough away from his granddaughter's tent before he said, "Please forgive me for insulting you back there. I was mistaken and I'm sorry. Your love for your daughter is apparent."

"Apology accepted. I understand how walking in on that absurd situation, one could get the wrong idea." Fletcher hesitated a moment and then added, "If there is nothing else, I would like to return to my daughter. I really don't feel she should be left alone."

Viktor interrupted. "Not until I have a chance to look at those hands." Both men turned to see him following them.

"They're not that bad," Fletcher added quickly.

Viktor held out both his hands. "Then let me see them."

Fletcher sighed and placed his hands palms up in Viktor's. "It is not her fault. She didn't mean to do it," he said quickly.

"I know and I apologize for letting you suffer with it as long as I did, but I didn't want to upset her further by letting her know she had injured you." Viktor leaned forward and examined both hands. They were not bad, they would just merely be uncomfortable for a few days. "Are you a worshiper of Athena?"

Fletcher considered for a moment then shrugged his shoulders. "Truth be told, I wouldn't say I really worship any god, though if pressed I would say I'm more of an Ares man. Athena's a bit too formal for my taste."

"Good," replied Viktor quickly. A moment later, Viktor's hands began to glow a rich orange. The glow slowly seeped into Fletcher's hands, and after a few moments the glowing stopped.

Fletcher wiggled his fingers and looked down at his hands. "That's incredible. I've never seen anything like it before."

Viktor shrugged his shoulders. "Anytime." The three men parted ways.

VI

In the drawing room at Stone Reach Castle,
eight days after the death of the Eighth Duke of
Stone Reach, Lord Candleford cleared his throat.
The room fell silent. He picked up a large stack of
documents and surveyed the room. A quick count
told him at least a couple of people were missing.
"I know that at least some of you are curious as to
why I have requested this meeting. I would not
normally do this the day after the funeral, but since
His Grace ..." he indicated Black Stone with a
wave of his hand, "the Ninth Duke of Stone Reach
has informed me that all of you understandably
have pressing business elsewhere; I've decided to,
on this occasion, under these extraordinary
circumstances, make an exception to my usual
routine. However, before I can go on, I must
determine who is absent and whether we must wait
for their presence." He glanced down at the stack
of paper and began marking people off,
occasionally glancing up as he spoke. "There are
the seven sons plus Lord Greyhawk, all of the
wives are present plus one who is not listed ..." he
added, pointing at Tabitha. Then he looked
around. "Oh yes, I forgot the daughter is absent
due to call of duty. She is, however, represented
by her ..." he hesitated a moment and then said,
"mate, Eden Silvermane, and only the eldest
grandson is present ..." he pointed at Innish.
"Lord Danoher, though I should also mention that

His Grace makes note of three expected grandchildren, and then there is a Murtaugh Wolf and his ..." he raised an eyebrow, "woman, Helena Wolf." He glanced in the direction of Murtaugh who nodded, endeavoring to conceal his amusement. "Oh, good, I'm glad that makes sense to everybody but me, and of course, also present, is Her Grace, the Dowager Duchess of Stone Reach."

Lord Candleford picked up his glass and took a drink, then placed it back on the table. He surveyed the room. "Before I read the will, I'm going to inform all of you that His Grace made it quite clear to me that none of you were going to be happy with this will. He did not bother to inform me why, and I really don't care. Michael was one of my oldest and dearest friends, and he asked me to be the executor of his will, and that is what I'm here to do. And I am to here to make sure that no matter how any of you feel about this will, it is carried out in accordance with his wishes. So any arguments, any complaints you have, save your breath. They are pointless. This will is signed and witnessed by the King himself. And though unfortunately pressing business required our King to depart yesterday, it is nevertheless, unbreakable." He was pleased to observe that though they all shifted uncomfortably and looked mutinous, none of them dared to utter a word.

"'I, Michael "Grey" Stone, General of the Army of the King, and Eighth Duke of Stone Reach, being of sound mind and body, do hereby bequeath my worldly goods to my family as follows. And just so there is no confusion, if you're in this room, I consider you my family. To all of my grandchildren, both current and future, I leave the sum of one thousand gold each. To all of my daughters-in-law, I leave to each of you the sum of five hundred gold; this way you don't always have to be holding out your hand to those tightfisted sons of mine.'" To Candleford's surprise, all of the men laughed. "I would like to point out that he mentions Helena specifically as one of his daughters-in-law and he has also made provisions for all of your wives even though you're not all yet married. 'To Grayhawk, the first son of my heart, I leave you ten thousand gold to assist you in running and maintaining your estate. I hope you will find it useful. To Murtaugh, since I do not know where you and Helena will wish to settle down, I do not leave you an estate. I do, however, leave you the sum of ten thousand gold. That should permit you to buy an estate wherever you choose. To my six younger sons, I leave you each an estate. Candleford has the deeds and will present them to you presently. To go along with these estates, I leave you each five thousand gold. Since you are my sons, I expect you to keep, maintain, and grow your properties. To Eden Silvermane, I return to you the sum of twenty thousand gold, plus seventy-five.'" At that, Eden and Eric both burst out laughing. "'And I bequeath to you a sum of ten thousand gold to rebuild your country again. I hope you will find this useful. To my daughter, I give you this box and its contents. I

71

hope that Eden will make sure that you use them. To Rebecca, the love of my life, I leave you the Dower House for your life and the sum of five hundred gold a year to maintain your property. At last, I come to you Eric. Of everything else not yet accounted for, I leave to you. Of all of my children, it is you for whom I settle the heaviest of burdens. Some of these burdens will become apparent immediately, others will take time for you to truly understand how great they are; but first and foremost, I leave you the responsibility of your younger siblings. As the head of the family, the yoke of leadership falls to you. Though many would think that the Dukedom is a privilege, I know you will see it for what it truly is, a heavy burden. But I have no doubt you are up to the task. And if you should die before producing a son and this burden passes to Andrew, I have confidence that Andrew will step up to the mark and be as great a leader as you.'" As Candleford watched, he was surprised to see the looks of irritation and outrage on every face. This confused him. He did not understand, this will was more than generous for all parties.

To everyone's surprise, it was Patrick who could no longer contain his irritation. "Black Stone, I am so sorry. It was not right that Father should cut up your inheritance." The other six brothers quickly agreed.

Murtaugh added, "I am truly touched that the Duke would think of me, but it is not right. I am not one of his sons. It should go to all of you. It should be divided up amongst all of you." Eden nodded quickly in agreement.

"All of you stop being ridiculous. I think Father treated you shabbily. The estate could have easily born a much larger settlement on all of you. An injustice I intend to remedy immediately," Black Stone said firmly. The room quickly erupted into a dozen arguments.

Candleford blinked as it slowly dawned on him why they were all angry. He looked at the Dowager Duchess. To his further surprise, she looked pleased. Finally, he let out a loud whistle. The room again fell silent. "As I previously stated, this will is signed and witnessed by the King. So whether you all like what you were given or not; you're going to have to keep it. I would like to point out that in the dozens of wills I have read over the years, this is the first time people have ever been angry because they received too much. You have to be undoubtedly the oddest family I've ever had the privilege to deal with, and believe it or not, I mean that as a compliment." They all looked around at each other and then started laughing.

Amber asked, "May I ask a question, Lord Candleford?"

"But of course, Your Grace," he replied quickly.

"What is a Dower House?"

"A Dower House is a residence that most titled families keep nearby on their estate for the mother-in-law."

Amber sat quietly considering this for a few minutes, then she rose and walked over to the Dowager Duchess. "Mother, might I have a word?"

"Of course, Amber. What can I do for you?" the Dowager Duchess replied quickly.

"I know I'm still very ignorant on so many customs of Breton culture, but it does not seem right to me that you be exiled to something called the Dower House if that is not what you wish. This is your home. You have lived here since Eric was a babe. I do not wish you to feel that you need to vacate the premises." Amber blushed slightly.

"Amber, you are now the Duchess of Stone Reach. This is your home and though you are correct, the Dower House is not my preferential residence; I cannot help but feel that you and Eric would prefer to reside here in private and not to have your mother-in-law always peeking over your shoulder. I know that when I came to this residence, had my mother-in-law still been alive, I would've felt she was always judging me, thinking I was doing things wrong. And though, of course, I would not interfere in the running of your residence, would you not prefer to have me at some distance?"

Amber hugged the older woman tightly. "I'm certain that Eric will agree with me and wish you to remain here. Though I will admit, I'm sure there are things that I will change, I'm also certain that at least for the first year I will need your guidance desperately. So please stay with us. And I also must confess that my motives are somewhat selfish, because I intend to return with my husband to the encampment whether he likes it or not, which will mean that …"

As Amber hesitated, the Dowager Duchess quickly stepped into the gap. "You wish me to continue to run the household. I would be honored and privileged to do so for you. And I can't blame you; I would have wanted to stay with Michael too, though he never gave me the option." The two women embraced again.

Eden interrupted at this moment. "Forgive the intrusion ladies, but Xanhara, Patrick, Terrence, and I are going to take our leave of you now." Eden bent down and kissed both women on the cheek.

The Dowager Duchess quickly reached out and gripped his arm. "I wish you did not have to go so soon, but I know you're anxious to get back to your wife. And truth be told, I'm anxious for you to return to her. I do not like her being out there all alone. The gods speed you on your journey. Be safe. When do the others leave?"

"My understanding is Daniel and Innish will follow in a few days, but Brigid is going to remain with you until after the birth of her second child. Daniel does not like the idea of her being so isolated, even if it does put her closer to him. He prefers her to have you around her all the time, than him around once a month. Andrew, Tabitha, Murtaugh, and Helena will follow within the week. Fitzwilliam will leave in the morning to return Edward. I'm sure Eric and Amber will follow as soon as his business is concluded, though I expect it not to be for another couple of weeks. And Grayhawk is going to go over to his estate to check on things and then he'll follow." Both women embraced him again, kissing him on each cheek. He bowed and excused himself, anxious to return home.

VII

Six days later, Bloodstone rounded the corner and almost ran smack dab into Sergeant Simon. "My apologies Sergeant, I didn't expect to see you standing there." As she met his eyes, she saw he was pissed. "Sergeant, what's the matter?" She glanced past him to see ten of her personal guard and eight Wolf Tribesman all standing there, arms crossed, looking furious.

Dex, standing directly behind her, blurted out in Barbarian, "Who in Hades are those assholes?"

Bloodstone looked to follow his gaze and groaned. "I think you'd better report, Sergeant," she said, her irritation evident.

"My sincerest apologies, General, if I made the wrong decision, but I felt given the fact that you were not currently in residence, and Blackwolf was also not currently at home, you would prefer for me to yield the ground rather than start an all out fight. Again, General, if I made the wrong decision, I apologize and I will submit my resignation this instant for my grievous misjudgment."

"Sergeant Simon, don't be ridiculous. Tell me what happened and how in Hades they came to have control of Eden's tent?" she said, trying to sound calm, and failing.

"A little more than an hour ago, His Majesty, along with his full contingent of guards, approached and the Colonel in charge of his guard demanded to know if you were in residence. I informed him you were not currently in. The Colonel ordered myself and my men to go in search of you. There was a slight confrontation, where I may or may not have informed the Colonel that he had no authority and there might of been a little ..." Simon made a face trying to figure out the best way to say it. Finally he decided to just say it. "I may have been very disrespectful when I got in his face and told him to piss off. His men were reaching for their swords; my men were reaching for their swords. At this point, I decided we were outnumbered and backed down. I also decided that I wasn't leaving sight of your tent, so I ordered two of my men to go in search of you. Apparently, they haven't found you. I also sent for more of my men. Once they arrived, I sent one man to inform Katya that she and Blackwolf were to remain in her quarters out of sight until further notice, and I informed your Barbarian personal guard of the situation. They brought some of their men and here we all stand." Simon stood patiently, awaiting his General's judgment.

Bloodstone stood there, her mind racing as she contemplated the ramifications of any action. As she glanced past her men, it was obvious from the King's Guards' demeanor that they were watching the group. They had yet not spotted her, or did not recognize her for who she was. This was good; it give her a few more minutes to think. "Okay, Dex, you want to be my guard? You're going to get to be my guard. This is not going to be fun, and no matter what happens, we cannot start this fight. They attack you first, you have my permission to respond in kind. They hit you in the face, you hit them in the face. They draw swords, you draw swords. They hit you, don't draw swords." All the men quickly nodded in understanding. "Dex, you and your men take a position to my right. Sergeant Simon, you and your men take the left. Dex, you are going to take and hold the line that this is your King's tent, and they are trespassing. Also remember, and do not forget, you are standing on Barbarian land. They are the trespassers, and you are the defenders. Oh, and one more thing Dex. Remember right now, I'm a pissed off general. I'm not your queen, so whatever you do, don't get between me and my prey. Is that understood? Oh, yes and one more thing. No matter what happens, Dex and Sergeant Simon are to remain with me at all times." Both men nodded their heads in understanding.

"Just look over your shoulder, I will be standing right there, Your Majesty," said Dex with a grin.

As Bloodstone moved towards the front of her men, they began taking up position behind her. She saw one of the King's Guards poke his head inside. A moment later, the Colonel exited and moved to stand in front of his men. Bloodstone headed straight for him. She stopped barely a foot from him, and he was just as tall as she, though twice as wide. The two glared back at each other.

Dex interrupted them by clearing his throat and asked in a cold voice, "I would like you to explain, Colonel, on whose authority you have taken control of my King's tent?"

"I do not recognize your King, and I only grudgingly recognize that these are the quarters of the General of the Battle Knights of Athena, and unfortunately, the temporary commander of my King's army. Even if she is just General Grey Stone's pathetic bastard." He angled his head to the side and raked his eyes up and down her body in a familiar manner that made Dex's blood boil. "Though I must say, General Grey Stone did always have excellent taste in the whores he enjoyed rolling, and if your body is any testimony to your mother, she must've been a very enjoyable roll."

Bloodstone smiled prettily. She reminded herself of the punishment for attacking a guard of the King; then she shrugged her shoulders and bashed her fist into his face. A moment later, it was an all-out fistfight. Unfortunately, the Colonel was at a decided advantage over her, seeing as how he was fully armored, though fortunately in studded leather, and she was only in tunic and britches. The Colonel quickly retaliated with a hard right-left to her midsection, followed quickly by a hard right-left aimed at her face, which she was fortunately able to block. She even retaliated with a hard right to the face, sidestepping and bringing her knee up into his guts. She bumped into somebody and turned around quickly to see Dex standing there, fists at the ready. A King's Guard lay at his feet. Glancing back to her opponent just in time to catch a hard right to the jaw, a loud whistle split the air. All the King's men immediately dropped their fists. Bloodstone turned to see the King standing in the doorway. All of his men immediately bowed.

The Colonel bowed to the King. "Your Majesty."

As the King glanced around, he said in a bored tone, "I have to say, surprisingly enough, I think you might have lost, Colonel."

The Colonel quickly looked around him and bowed to the King. "My sincerest apologies, Sire, but I fear you are correct."

As the King walked forward, Bloodstone felt his eyes appraising every detail of her appearance, taking in everything, missing nothing. "General Bloodstone, I presume."

"You presume correctly," she said, looking irritated.

"Is there something the matter with your knee, General?" he asked casually.

"If you expect me to bend my knee to you, that is not going to happen," she said, crossing her arms over her chest.

The Colonel turned and glared at her. "If I were you, little girl, I'd find a way to bend my knee before I bend it for you."

Bloodstone turned to give the Colonel her full and undivided attention. "I'd like to see you try, Colonel," she said, wiping the blood from her mouth with her thumb. "Because so far, you haven't impressed me at all." She glared at him defiantly.

The Colonel stepped forward so that they were nose to nose. "If you think you're good enough to take me on, little girl, anytime, anyplace."

"If you don't want me to bash in your head, you'll back off, and you will remember when you speak to my Queen, you will speak to her with respect, or I might just cut out your tongue," Dex said coldly.

"Well, I guess that settles it in my mind. You can't be General Grey Stone's daughter, or you wouldn't have a lapdog fighting for you. General Grey Stone would never let someone else fight his battles for him, or is that the whole point? You're not as good as Daddy." To his complete and utter astonishment, General Bloodstone just laughed.

"You know, I find it very interesting, every time somebody wants to provoke me into a fight, they always choose the same things. First you insult me because I'm a woman, then you insult me because I'm a bastard, and then you insult me because my guard seem to think that it's their job to protect me. Oh, wait a minute, that's because it is their job, which you should fully understand, because you're a guard! And let me make one thing very clear to you, guard, you are a colonel and I am a general. I command an entire army. What do you command, two hundred men at most? You can insult me, you can question my ability with a blade all you want, it's not going to gall me, because I'm comfortable in my own skin. I know I got where I am because I fought for it and because I'm good enough to hold it. Let me make another thing very clear to you. Dex is my guard, and I can insult him and I can tease him, but you had better watch your mouth, because you insult him again, and you'll pick your ass up off the ground. Is that perfectly clear, Colonel?"

"Damn! Your Majesty! Grey Stone was not kidding when he said her balls were as big as Black Stone's!" the Colonel said, with a smile. He extended his hand. "Colonel Maxwell Carter, and it is an honor and a privilege to meet you, General. Before I became one of the King's Personal Guard, I served under your father."

Bloodstone tentatively took his hand and shook it. "General Bloodstone 'the Dragon' Silvermane, of the Battle Knights of Athena."

"I hope, General Silvermane, you will forgive the Colonel and his men for their outlandish behavior. They were, of course, acting on my orders. Grey Stone was my oldest and dearest friend and unfortunately I must state that he could sometimes be rather ..." the King hesitated a long moment.

Bloodstone rudely cut him off. "Besotted where women were concerned."

The King laughed. "It's good to see you have a good understanding of your father. If you will forgive our rudeness, perhaps the Colonel and I may enter your quarters and have a polite conversation. Of course, my men will relinquish the protection of your door back to your men; though of course, my men will have to remain as well. The disadvantage of having so many high heads in one building or tent." He shrugged his shoulders and entered the tent.

VIII

As Bloodstone entered Eden's tent, she glanced around. She saw that someone had been sitting behind her desk, and the chair Ares had given to Eden was pulled out and turned to face the room. She crossed to it and picked it up, turning it back to the table. She pushed it in. Grabbing two other chairs from her table, she yanked them free and placed them in front of her desk. As she did this, she gave a quick, almost imperceptible glance at Simon, indicating he was to go and stand behind her desk. He caught her meaning immediately and went to stand on the left side of her desk. Dex, following suit, took the right. She moved around to behind her desk, pulled out her chair and indicated the other two. The King narrowed his eyes at her, seated himself, then gestured for her and the Colonel to be seated. He waited until Bloodstone seated herself and leaned back in her chair waiting.

They sat there in awkward silence for perhaps a minute before the King spoke. "You would not offer your King the best chair in your house?"

"This is not my house. This is the home of Eden Silvermane, King of all the Barbarian lands. And that chair was a gift to him from my father, so no one sits in that chair but Eden," she replied coldly.

"You have an unusual way of showing your King respect. Then again, I would expect nothing less of an Athenian. That despite your status as General of the Knights of Athena, you have a lot to answer for," he replied just as coldly.

"What do you feel I need to answer for, Your Majesty?"

"To begin with, on whose authority did you destroy the mountain pass?" he questioned coolly.

"On my own. As far as I'm concerned, Your Majesty, you really have no complaint to make on the matter, given the fact that the portion of the pass that I destroyed is on Barbarian land. The only man who has any right to complain on the matter, is once again, Eden Silvermane," she replied quickly.

"You do not feel that you still need to explain yourself to your King for your willful destruction of a valuable pass that we could use to get into their country, and you also abandoned an important temple that has been protecting one of our northern most borders for hundreds of years?" he said casually.

"As previously stated, the section of the pass that I destroyed is on Barbarian land, and I made the best decision for your people. If you dispute this, then I feel all I can do is apologize for annoying you; but even had I had the opportunity to communicate with you, I would not have. I would have still made the decision that I did, because Generals do not as a habit wait to ask questions. We make decisions and we make the best decisions that we can make with the information and resources that we have at hand. And yes, I closed up and abandoned the Temple of the Mountain Pass because it was indefensible. It would've taken an entire team of engineers and stonemasons more than six months to restore it to its glory; six months we did not have. And at this time, we do not have the abundant resources required to focus on it. After the war is over, I will make it amongst my first actions, but until then it's going to sit and wait. Since the property in question is in fact the property of the Athenian Church, it is not your concern and since my goddess has no complaint with my actions . . . " she shrugged her shoulders dismissively. "Again, I can not help but feel you have no complaint to make on the matter. If you have problems with my actions, take them up with my superior. If Athena takes your side, I'm sure she will let me know." She hesitated a moment and then went on, quickly forestalling the King's complaints. "In fact, Your Majesty, it occurs to me that I am remiss in my duties. I should make arrangements to introduce you to your Allies." She picked up a piece of paper and a quill, quickly scribbling off a note. "Corporal, would you please come in here," she called loudly.

The Corporal entered and saluted. "General, Your Majesty." The King glared openly at the young Corporal.

"Yes, would you please see that this message is delivered to Viktor Silvermane, head of the Council of Wolf Tribe at once? Await his response and return it to me immediately." The Corporal took the note, saluted, and left the room.

"Are all of your soldiers so insolent to their King?" demanded Colonel Carter.

"As you should recall, Colonel, Church Soldiers swear no allegiance to the King. Their first and foremost allegiance is to Athena, followed quickly by their own chain of command. The little stunt you and the King played with Eden's tent is not going to endear you to them. So if you wish to mend some of the damage you did to the alliance with your behaviors, you will take my men's disrespectful attitudes with a grain of salt. You will remember that the Allies may need us; but we need them just as badly. Our Allies are important."

"The General's correct, Colonel, we do need these Allies. So before I meet them, what do I need to know about them? Are there any little cultural differences that I could inadvertently stumble into and unintentionally insult them?" asked the King quickly.

Bloodstone considered for a moment. "They've come to know and understand Bretons pretty well, as we have lived here with them. We have come to understand and know them pretty well. Most things they will not take as an insult because they do know that it is a difference between our two cultures. I would have to say the thing that immediately jumps to mind that would insult them is: do not refer to me as Eden's wife. It is not a word Wolf Tribesman use. They would consider it an insult. Refer to me as his queen, or refer to me as his woman."

Dex said softly, "Marriage."

Bloodstone nodded her head in quick understanding. "Yes, if any of your men are desirous of a bed warmer this evening, make sure that they understand that the women of Wolf Tribe are strictly off limits, unless of course, they desire to be married men. And if they are already a married man and they were to trifle with a woman of Wolf Tribe, her male relatives will kill them. In accordance with the treaty, we must respect their desire to do so. If they seek a mere fleeting night's entertainment, they might do better with the Amazons. They are perfectly willing to use men as breeding stock," Bloodstone said with a grin.

Sergeant Simon and Dex both let out chuckles that they quickly turned into coughs. "Do you care to explain what the two of them find so amusing about that statement?" asked the King.

Bloodstone made a face as she considered. "I'm not exactly sure. I can only take a guess, but I would guess that both of them are well aware of the fact that any of your men trying to get an Amazon will most likely get laughed at. Amazons are somewhat particular in their breeding stock. They do prefer men who have proven themselves in battle, though your rank, Colonel, might permit you to enter an Amazon's bed. But just remember, in their mind, you're the bed warmer and they're the master." Dex choked on his laughter.

"Are you trying to insult me, General?" the Colonel demanded angrily.

"Colonel, I am actually not trying to insult you. I'm merely informing you of how an Amazon mind works. Amazons view men as breeding stock and nothing more. They also view you as beneath them because you are a male. They also really only desire a girl child from you. They tend to dispense with their male offspring. These are not things I'm saying to insult you, but merely attempting to educate you on how Amazons work. Their villages are made up entirely of women." He stared at her in open mouthed astonishment.

The King chuckled softly. "When we return to the palace, Colonel, I will permit you to read the reports so you can better understand our new Allies."

"But I thought General Black Stone married an Amazon. Surely that woman who follows her around, who says she is her mother, is an Amazon," the Colonel said, still looking stunned.

Bloodstone laughed. "That Amazon, as you call her, is Xanhara, Queen of the Amazons and my brother's wife, Amber, is her only child. Though Amber is not an Amazon; she is a Wolf Tribesman. Her father, Henry Silvermane, was the oldest son of the last King."

"Your brother's wife is your husband's niece?" questioned the Colonel.

"Yes, which makes Xanhara my sister-in-law, and the head of the Council of Wolf Tribe is Eden's oldest living brother, Viktor. He is not eligible for the throne because he chose to be a shaman instead, and shamans are not warriors. Only warriors can be king. Does that clear everything up for you?" she asked smugly.

Both men nodded, but before they could speak, the Corporal reentered. "What message does Viktor send to me, Corporal?" Bloodstone asked.

"Viktor says that he and the Council would be honored to meet with your King in two hours time, if that is convenient. They would also be honored if he would meet with them in the Mead Hall."

Bloodstone glanced at the King, who nodded. "Also, Your Majesty, some of our Allies are not

Wolf Tribesman. I would be pleased if you would permit me to host an impromptu gathering in what we refer to as the War Room, which is half of Black Stone's tent, after the meeting with Wolf Tribe. This will permit you to get to know some of our other Allies." Again the King nodded. "Return to Viktor and tell him that we look forward to seeing him. Also, would you tell him for me that he and his lovely woman are invited to a little gathering afterwards, along with the Council and their women. I will send around notes presently with the details." The Corporal nodded and excused himself.

"You weren't kidding about that wife stuff, weren't you?" asked the Colonel.

Without glancing in his direction, Bloodstone said, "Dex, if I were to refer to Seva as Viktor's wife, what would that imply to you?"

"I would take it as one of two meanings. Either Viktor and his woman are not on good terms, or that you dislike your sister immensely," Dex replied coldly.

"Oh, that is the other thing I forgot to tell you. There is no Barbarian word for 'in-law'. Brothers are brothers, sisters are sisters, that's just the way it is. But I'm sure you would like to freshen up before you meet with your Allies. I will have one of my Corporals escort you to the VIP tents. Take over them however you see fit of course, Your

Majesty." Bloodstone arose and walked over to
the other side of the table. Extending her hand, she
offered it to the Colonel who took it and shook it.

"Corporal." The second young Corporal
entered. "Would you please escort His Majesty
and his entourage to the VIP tents?" The Corporal
nodded and held open the flap.

She then extended her hand to the King, who
gripped her fingers delicately and bent forward
over her hand, brushing his lips across her
knuckles in a most familiar manner, murmuring as
he did so, "Until this evening, when we can
continue this conversation more privately." Then
turning her hand over, he kissed her wrist.
Releasing her hand, he smiled at her knowingly.
Turning, he exited the tent.

Bloodstone stood there for a long minute.
Finally Sergeant Simon broke the silence. "What
in Hades are we going to do about that?"

Bloodstone rubbed her forehead as she crossed
to her desk. Sitting down, she began writing a note
to Black Stone's cook and to Sergeant Henderson,
informing them of the King's presence in the
encampment, and that there was going to be a little
impromptu social gathering in a few hours in the
War Room, asking them to prepare something light
and to make all ready. Then she quickly wrote off
notes to all of the Allies, inviting them. When they
were all done, she handed them to Sergeant Simon.

"Will you have some of the men deliver these at once?"

Sergeant Simon returned a moment later. "I've been thinking, Sergeant Major Fletcher will be no deterrent. He's a King's man and will easily be ordered away."

"If you're going to be helpful, Sergeant, make suggestions that have a possibility of working, not ones that we already know won't work," she said irritated. She crossed to the washbasin, pulled off her tunic, and began washing.

Dex quickly turned his back and looked at Simon. "Do all Breton females just undress in front of men who are not their mates?" To Dex's further annoyance, Sergeant Simon didn't seem at all bothered by her unclothed state.

"No, I think it's only the General," Sergeant Simon replied casually.

"It does not embarrass you to see her thus?" he demanded.

"I've served as her personal guard for more than a year. Between seeing her naked and walking in on her and Eden early in the morning …" Simon shook his head. "It would take a lot more than seeing her in her corset to embarrass me. Actually, I've seen her completely naked on many occasions. I've even assisted her in lacing her corset." Sergeant Simon laughed at the appalled look on Dex's face. Turning back to the problem at hand, he said quickly, "What about Colonel Blacksmith?"

Bloodstone turned, drying her face, to glare at Simon. "It can't be a Church or State Knight, or any Church Soldiers or State Soldiers, or be anybody under my command. It can't be a Wolf Tribesman because we don't want to inform our Allies of the lecherous nature of our King." It was Simon's turn to rub his face with frustration.

"What are you two on about?" demanded Dex, looking concerned.

"You heard the King say he wished to speak with her further later, right?"

Dex nodded. "What is bizarre about that? He wishes to speak to his general further."

Bloodstone rolled her eyes and sighed with exasperation. "He does not wish to speak to me further, Dex. It is his intention to bed me tonight."

Dex's eyes widened in horror. "But you are a married woman!"

"Yes, and our King only beds married women; women who are not his wife because he is not married and has no intention of marrying. He prefers the wives of his subjects. He thinks that they should be privileged and honored that he

95

favored them with his attention," Simon said with irritation.

Dex stood there considering as he tried to wrap his head around the situation. "And I'm assuming because he is a King, you can't just tell him no." Both of them shook their heads.

Bloodstone shook out her hair as she paced back and forth. As she quickly braided her five warriors braids that Eden had given her, then brushing the rest of her hair, she left it hanging loose. As she pulled out her finest blue linen tunic. "Not the blue one," Simon said quickly.

"Why? The blue one is my best tunic."

"Because the blue complements your eyes and makes you look far too pretty. Wear one of the plain linen ones," said Simon. Bloodstone shrugged her shoulders, but did as she was told.

"And re-braid the rest of your hair, don't leave it hanging loose," Dex added quickly. Bloodstone rolled her eyes, but again did as she was ordered.

She went back to pacing, discarding idea after idea. Finally, she froze as a thought occurred to her. She went over every detail in her mind. She tilted her head to the side. "I can find no fault with that plan beyond the obvious, which I'm not happy about either; but I can think of none better."

Both men exchanged a concerned look, but it was Dex who asked, "What's the plan, and why do I get the feeling I'm really going to hate it?"

"At this point in time, I'm afraid this is a question of the lesser of two evils. With that being said, the only way to deter the King that I can think of, is if he gets the idea that there's already somebody else in my bed."

Dex rubbed his hands up and down his face. Dropping into a seat, he looked skywards and rubbed his hands up and down his face again and into his hair. Groaning, he said, "I knew I really wasn't going to like this. Why can't I just tell the King if he touches you, I'll cut off his balls?"

"Because if you threaten the King, that would be an open act of war; which means he'll order all of you killed, which would turn this army into three definite camps. Which means we'd all be at each other, and by the time Eden and Black Stone returned, there would be only a shadow of the army that they left. So a flat refusal or a flat denial won't get us anywhere. This needs to be a subtle dodge, or maybe not so subtle, which means that there's only one man in this encampment suitable for the task I have in mind."

Both men turned to look at her and said simultaneously, "Who?"

"The Colonel of the Soldiers of Ares. He is the only man in this army I don't command."

"Why him?" demanded Dex.

"Well, several reasons. First, and most importantly, as the Colonel of the Soldiers of Ares, the agreement he struck with Black Stone was his men work in conjunction with us, not under us. So I have no authority over him, which means there would be no breach of military conduct. Also, he told me he owed me one. I told him he owed me nothing. I think I'm going to have to change my mind. Also, as a Soldier of Ares, his loyalty is to Ares and Ares alone; which as you both are aware, if I have to use this card I am reluctant, but willing to play. Due to the timing of his arrival in this encampment, Eden has never met him, so Eden will not feel betrayed by a friend. Also, Sidel trusts him, which means he's probably not a lecher."

"How do you intend to convince the King that you two are lovers?" asked Sergeant Simon.

"He's going to have to catch us together," Bloodstone said, looking directly at Dex.

"You do realize, General, this is a very dangerous game you're playing. Your mate is not going to appreciate you having any kind of involvement with another man, no matter how minor," Dex said, looking worried. *By the gods,*

Eden is going to kill me for being a complete and utter failure, Dex thought to himself. He rubbed his face in frustration again and groaned. He tried to think of an alternative. "Why don't I just stay here all night?"

"Because the King would merely order you, me, and any guards away," replied Sergeant Simon.

"I don't answer to him. I can refuse to leave," Dex replied quickly.

"Then he would shock and appall you by telling you that you could watch, or he just would order her to come to his tent," Sergeant Simon retorted with disgust.

Dex looked questioningly at Bloodstone, who merely nodded her head in reply. He groaned again. "What you want me to do?"

"First off, Sergeant Simon, send one of the men to find the Colonel and tell him I need to speak with him immediately. Then I want you to have a group of our men relocate Katya and Blackwolf to the Captain Stones' tent for the night. I don't want her anywhere near where she might run across the King. And Dex, I think for the night, you should double the Barbarian guard on them." She hesitated a moment and then added, "At the risk of shocking you, Sergeant, I suggest you might wish to spend the night there as well. There are three

cots after all." Simon nodded and went to carry
out his orders.

She then looked at Dex. "You and I need to
get ready to go to the Mead Hall. I'm assuming
you don't want to wear that. And you're going to
have to use your best judgment on how much you
are going to inform the night guards. My guards
will not interfere no matter what. Nor will they
repeat anything they hear. You will have to do
what you feel is best where your men are
concerned, and if you're going to be around you
have to be out of sight; the King is already well
aware of your distaste for him. He would not
expect you to swallow this blindly." Dex nodded,
but did not look happy about it.

Three hours later, Bloodstone considered as she
escorted the King to the War Room, that things
went very well in the Mead Hall. Both parties
made speeches about how they were honored to
have such wonderful Allies. Bloodstone tried hard
to ignore the political lies, though in truth, the King
had lied far more than Wolf Tribe had. As they
approached, Sergeant Henderson bowed formally
and opened the tent flap, then he announced them
in proper order. As she had expected, many of the
guests were already present, those who had not
been present at the Mead Hall. She immediately
began making introductions. Again, the King spun
elaborate tales about how honored he was to have
such great warriors as Allies. Bloodstone

concealed a smile as Autumn merely nodded her head curtly to the King.

"I, of course, Your Majesty, cannot thank you enough for the assistance that your army has given myself and my people," said Lawrence, bowing formally. The King continued through the room, making sure to speak to everyone, ignoring no one. Bloodstone had to admit she admired this about him.

As she was standing there idly observing the King, she felt a hand on the small of her back. She looked quickly to see the Colonel of the Soldiers of Ares standing there. "Colonel Foster, I hope you and your men are settling in?" she asked casually.

"Oh, please, call me Stephen," he said quickly.

"Very well, so Stephen, how are you and your men liking this encampment?" she asked with genuine interest.

"My men have found their few days here quite enjoyable, though of course my men aren't enjoying themselves as much as I enjoy socializing with our beautiful new ally," he replied flirtatiously.

They were interrupted by the King. "Well, ladies and gentlemen, I again must thank you for your delightful hospitality, but my men and I are weary and we have a long journey ahead of us

tomorrow; so I shall take my leave of you now.
He gave a casual nod to his audience and left.

Bloodstone couldn't help herself, she glanced
quickly at Colonel Foster who merely smiled at her
and winked outrageously. Then, giving a little
bow, "I, too, good lady, am exhausted, so I hope
you'll forgive me if I take my leave as well.
Perhaps I will see you again soon." Bloodstone
felt her cheeks flush with color at his
outrageousness. But as he turned and walked
away, she observed Colonel Carter watching them.
She glared openly at him. He smiled, bowed, and
excused himself. A half an hour later she was
heading for Eden's tent, her stomach twisted into
knots.

As she approached the tent her guard
announced, "The Colonel of the Soldiers of Ares
says he has important matters he wishes to discuss
with you. He's waiting inside."

She nodded and turned to Dex and Sergeant
Simon. "Well, you gentlemen have had a long day.
You may turn in for the night. I'll see you in the
morning. "Both men nodded and excused
themselves. Bloodstone wasn't fooled for a
minute. She knew neither one of them would be
going far. She turned and entered.

The Colonel was standing in her tent looking
incredibly casual, which somehow seemed to
irritate her. "I had one of my men watching, the

King apparently went to his tent. He will come and inform us if he leaves there." Bloodstone looked at him in surprise. She opened her mouth to speak, but he forestalled her. "Don't worry, he'll come around to the back and speak through the tent. No one will see him approach, though my men did a cursory scan of the area. They're pretty sure the King did not leave anybody observing your quarters, but he did leave a man outside watching the War Room. I expect to hear from my man momentarily that the King is hot on his heels."

To her further annoyance, a moment later she heard a whisper coming from the back of her tent. "The King can't be more than ten minutes behind me. I followed him for a moment to make sure he was headed in this direction, as soon as I was sure, I ran."

"Very well, you are dismissed, and remember what I said," the Colonel replied quickly. Not taking his eyes off of her, he said, "Take your boots and your tunic off quickly." Bloodstone swallowed hard, but did as she was ordered. The Colonel removed his tunic and his belt, but not his boots. Then, looking her up and down, he added, "Unbraid your hair." Bloodstone rolled her eyes. What was it about men and her hair, braid it, unbraid it; but again she did as she was ordered to do. A cough outside the tent caught both of their attention. She looked over her shoulder and didn't see Foster move forward.

He grabbed her around the waist and toppled her onto the bed. A moment later, his mouth was on hers, and he was kissing her with one hand on either side of her head. A moment later, he slid his hands down along the sides of her body. To her relief, he did not touch her breasts. He did slide his hands down her hips and grabbed her backside with both hands. She would have gasped, but he had his mouth immediately covering hers, and as she opened her mouth, he stuck his tongue in it. He pressed hard against her, and she closed her eyes and regained her composure, realizing that that reaction of hers would have spoiled everything. A moment later, he squeezed her thighs and pulled them up so that he was cradled between them. Still kissing her demandingly, he lifted himself up on one elbow. As he did, he slid his other hand between them and began unhooking her corset.

They could hear one of her men say softly, "Good evening, Your Majesty, the General is currently indisposed. Can I take a message for you?" A moment later, she heard the tent flap rustle; but she did not look.

She forced herself to focus on Colonel Foster as she ran her hands up and down his back and into his hair. A few moments later, she felt the last hook on her corset loosen, and he shifted to the other side. Only then, looking away as he pulled the corset out from beneath her; still holding her corset in one hand, he sat up and said in a very irritated tone, "What in Hades?" He growled out, "I'm a little busy here; you got something to say, come back in the morning." Bloodstone sat up and instinctively grabbed the Colonel around the waist and pressed her chest into his back to conceal her almost visible breasts. Knowing she was blushing, and feeling she could not meet the eye of the King, she pressed her face into the Colonel's neck. The Colonel discarded her corset onto the floor and reached back with his now free hand and caressed her hip.

The King and Colonel Foster continued to glare at each other. "Well, girl, I would've thought you had better taste than him. Soldier of Ares, how disgusting! What, you enjoy slumming it?"

To the King's further annoyance, Colonel Foster laughed and reached back and squeezed her thighs with both hands. Leaning back against her comfortably, he said in a smug tone, "Soldiers of Ares and Soldiers of Athena enjoy the confrontation between each other. It makes for some glorious battles, and what good girl doesn't enjoy a very, very bad boy every now and then?" Bloodstone dug her fingers into the Colonel's midsection. She heard the tent flap rustle again. The Colonel turned around to face her, grabbing her around the waist and jerking quickly, in one fluid motion, she somehow found herself astride him. Before she could utter a protest, he reached up and grabbed her by the nape of the neck and jerked her down forcing her to him, kissing her.

As he continued to kiss her, her hair fell all around them, concealing their faces. Holding her firmly there, he pulled his mouth away quickly and said, "Lass, you're torturing me. Stop teasing me like this and take off your clothes. I want to see you naked." Again, before she could protest, his mouth was roughly on hers She was just about to slug him when she heard the tent flap again.

This time it was Colonel Carter who spoke. "The King wishes me to inform you that he will be leaving at first light and he has no need of your company again."

The Colonel kissed her a moment or two longer and then pulled his mouth away and said with irritation, "Good. Glad to hear it. I intend to keep her occupied for some time, now get out." He immediately went back to kissing her. His hands slid down and gripped her backside with both hands pulling her down on him. As he rubbed against her, Bloodstone found it interesting that though she did not find him revolting, she also did not find his touch desirable.

After another minute or two, she heard her guard say in a low voice, "They're all gone, General."

The Colonel rolled her on her back and moved off the bed immediately. He walked slowly away from her. Bending down, he picked up her tunic and tossed it over his shoulder at her. She caught it and pulled it on. Looking around for her corset, she found it and began putting it back on underneath her tunic. He had walked up to her desk and was standing there with his back turned to her.

Bloodstone felt terrible. The Colonel hadn't been lying when he said kissing her was torture. He had agreed readily enough to help her. She didn't think he'd find the task that revolting, but apparently he did. "Thank you, Colonel, for helping me. I'm sorry it was such an unpleasant task for you."

He asked without turning around, "Why would you say the task was unpleasant?"

"I forgot to tell you in advance, I'm a Truth Seeker of Athena. I cannot lie, which means I also know when people are lying, or more importantly in your case, when they are telling the truth. You were not lying when you said that I was torturing you. I'm sorry. Had you told me that it would be that unpleasant for you, I would've found a different way."

He chuckled softly. "Apparently it is my destiny to always end up having to protect young, innocent girls. Though I would've thought you being a married woman would not be quite this naïve. However, given how honorable your husband is, it should not be that surprising you're so naïve."

"I'm not naïve."

Again he chuckled. This time however, he turned around to face her. "The task was torture because it's been a while since I've had such a beautiful woman kissing me; though fortunately, I still don't find young girls appealing, even if that young girl is of an appropriate age. I tend to like women more my own age, though unfortunately, most of them are married. I also have my own code of honor, I don't bed down with married women." He laughed harder as Bloodstone's face and neck, and then even her tiny little feet turned a rich crimson. "What are you going to tell your husband when he returns? I know you're too honest to not tell him."

"Don't worry. I won't involve you. You need have no fear; I will protect you," she said quickly.

"I'm not worried about myself. I'm worried whether he's going to take it badly," his concern evident.

"Eden might take it badly, but he'll accept it." *He might just never speak to me again,* she added silently to herself.

The Colonel picked up his tunic and pulled it on. Then tucking in his tunic, he found his belt and buckled it. "I am going to sit down and wait for my men to tell me the area's clear. You know, a lot of women wouldn't have gone to this much trouble to remain faithful to their husbands. I hope your husband knows how much he should appreciate you."

Three quarters of an hour later, Dex entered the tent. "My men, the Soldiers of Ares, and the Soldiers of Athena, have all searched the area multiple times. There's no one lurking around to watch and from the furious look on the King's face, I don't think you have to worry about him again."

"Well then," the Colonel stood up and bowed, "I shall take my leave of you."

IX

As Colonel Foster left the General's tent, he ran his hands through his hair and muttered to himself, "I need a drink." Deciding it wasn't a good idea to go to the bar in his part of camp, he decided to search out a different one. A few minutes later, having asked directions, he entered the bar. Looking around, he groaned. It wasn't exactly full; however, there were only State Soldiers present. He walked up to the bar, ordered a drink and threw a coin down. Picking up his drink, he turned around and surveyed the room. His eyes alighted on a woman sitting alone. He approached her table. "Mind if I join you? This isn't exactly a safe place to drink on your own."

She glared up at him and asked quickly, "You think I need your protection?"

Deciding she didn't say no, he pulled out the chair and sat down. "No, I didn't say you needed my protection. I need your protection. This is not a safe place for me to be drinking by myself."

The woman continued to glare at him. "If you think teasing me is going to attract me; it's not going to work, and I did not tell you that you could sit down."

Foster laughed. "I'm dead serious. Those are State Soldiers, I'm a Soldier of Ares. There's about forty of them, there's one of me. That is not a battle I want to get into. I'm good, but I'm not that good," he replied in all seriousness.

"Ares, he is the God of War is he not?" Foster nodded. "And the soldiers of your king and you do not get along?"

"Well, it would be a lot quicker to just say no one gets along with the Soldiers of Ares. They all kind of look down on us."

"Why? You are all of the same country. Why do you not all get along?" she asked with genuine curiosity.

"You're a Barbarian?" She nodded. "Do all Barbarian tribes get along?" he countered.

She leaned back in her chair and surveyed him. "All right, I'll grant you that point. You're right, we don't all get along." She hesitated a moment considering. "Actually, most of them do get along; it's only the Amazons that they don't get along with."

"And you are a …?"

"Amazon." She kind of gave a little start as something occurred to her, then she inadvertently muttered in a soft voice, "Oh shit, I didn't think of that!"

"What, you're going to become even more of a social outcast because you're talking to a Soldier of Ares, or something else you didn't think of?"

She leaned her head back, looked skywards, and groaned. She had just realized that when her niece married, she removed herself from the royal line, which means, *I am now Xanhara's heir.* She groaned again. *Damn it! I don't want to be Queen.* "It's nothing that concerns you, and why are you still sitting at my table?" she countered quickly.

"I'm Stephen and you are …?"

"Bloodrose, and are you going to continue to ignore the question?" Despite herself, she was smiling.

"If you wish me to leave, then tell me to leave; but I thought we could just talk as friends. This, as I said, is not a friendly place for me to be and I prefer not to drink alone; because if I drink alone, then I'll drink too much. Whereas, if I talk to someone, then I will not drink as much."

"So you didn't just choose to sit at the table because you heard Amazons are easy lays?" she said, picking up her cup and taking a drink.

"I've only been in this encampment a couple of weeks. Still really don't know how to identify any of the tribes, and I certainly don't know very much about them, though I am quickly learning. So apparently most people think Amazons are easy lays. Why is that?" he questioned quickly, as he took a drink.

She grinned at him. "Because we only use men for breeding purposes, otherwise we really have no need of you."

"Ouch! Okay that's a little harsh. But I can say with complete honesty, I didn't know you were an Amazon when I sat down. And I figured even had I made an attempt to get laid, I would have gotten rebuffed. Let me ask you another question, aren't you a little short by Barbarian standards? Was your father a Breton?"

She felt a little uncomfortable and changed the subject. "So you are not offended by an entire tribe full of women warriors who think they don't need men to protect them?"

"Why would I? My apprentice, until a couple of years ago, was a girl. Since she reached the age of maturity, I feel she is perfectly capable of taking care of herself and making her own decisions. Though I do look upon her as a daughter, and sometimes the father in me doesn't always agree with the decisions she makes. In fact, right now I think she's hiding something from me; but I figure this is one of those times if a father pushes, he's going to get rebuffed. And again, right now being rebuffed seems to be my lot in life. She's also a Captain serving under my command as a Soldier of Ares."

For the first time, Bloodrose took a good look at the man who sat down at her table. He was tall by Breton standards, about six foot two inches. He had wavy brown hair that hung a little past his shoulders, dark green eyes, a broad muscular body, and well-tanned skin. He was not at all bad to look at. She considered for a moment - not quite forty.

As she sat openly considering him, Foster was taking this opportunity to appraise her as well. There was something so tiny and delicate about her. Nothing like any of the other Barbarian women he'd seen. He thought she must not even weigh a hundred pounds. She had a sleek muscular body and clearly wasn't very tall. She had rich, chestnut brown hair, and amber eyes that almost seemed feline. Young, but not too young - thirtyish if he had to guess.

She interrupted his thoughts. "I guess I get my height from the man who fathered me. I'm only about five foot four inches, which as you correctly assumed, makes me incredibly short; but since I'm not a swordsman, I don't mind." Again, she looked uncomfortable and something in her tone bothered him.

"Archer?" he said quickly.

"Yes, I'm an archer and a hunter; I'm not a warrior. I'm also a priestess of the Goddess of the Wilderness." She watched to see if he looked disgusted, but to her surprise, he looked merely curious.

"Goddess of the Wilderness, am not familiar with that one. Is that a Barbarian goddess?"

"Yes, Seana, patron Goddess of the Amazons. She is the Goddess of the Wilderness and all things wild."

"Does that mean that Amazons are wild?" he asked with a mischievous grin.

She laughed. "But of course. But it's getting late, so I think I should turn in for the night, Stephen." She rose, and he rose with her.

"I'm not a great archer, but I do always enjoy friendly competition. Perhaps sometime soon we could meet at the practice field and you can embarrass me by showing my complete lack of skill?" he asked hopefully.

"I have watch in the infirmary tomorrow. The day after at noon?"

"Until then." He bowed and watched her go. *Wonder if I can manage to get myself injured tomorrow. A trip to the infirmary would be very nice, I think.*

*****

Bloodstone had passed a sleepless night. She felt so guilty for what she had done. She had become convinced in her own mind that Eden would never forgive her. Looking at the hour candle, she saw it was a little past four in the morning. She gave up any hope for sleep and arose and washed. Her mind not on the task, all she could think of was Eden. She grabbed a washcloth and a moment later, it burst into flames. She threw it in the basin. "Dammit!" She looked at her wet hands and face, taking a deep breath and trying to be calm, she gripped a towel and began drying herself. She managed to discard the towel a moment before it burst into flames, though it did have singed marks on it. She took another long, slow, deep breath and decided it was going to be a very long day.

*****

Eden and the others had gotten up before sunrise, all anxious to get back to camp. Eden estimated less than two hours and he would be in Bloodstone's arms. He allowed his mind to dwell on how pleasant that would be. He was startled from his imaginings by the sounds of many heavy horses moving at a slow pace in their direction. He waited a few moments, as was his habit, before saying, "I hear horses." A few moments later, the King and his entourage came into sight. Both groups reined in their horses and approached each other slowly.

It was the King who spoke first. "Eden, Xanhara, Lord Stone, Lord Patrick, I had no idea you were returning so soon."

"What brings you out to the encampment, Your Majesty?" asked Eden.

"Since I had no idea how long General Silvermane is going to continue to command my army, I felt I should at least know her. I found her to be a very forceful personality, very vivacious. Would you not agree, Colonel Carter?" The King spoke in a tone that implied he knew something they didn't and Eden didn't like it. He also did not like the strange emphasis he had put on the word 'know.' Eden found himself uneasy and more desperate to be back with his woman.

Colonel Carter hesitated and then said, "Yes, Your Majesty, the General is indeed a very passionate individual." This drew Eden's attention to him, and the first thing that caught his eye was that someone, probably yesterday, had given the Colonel a very painful looking black eye. Though the eye was not swollen, it did look rather ugly. Eden hoped it was his woman. "Your Majesty, if we're going to make it to the inn before nightfall, we need to be on our way." The King nodded dismissively, and they continued their journey.

"Terrence, what does that word vivacious mean?" demanded Xanhara.

As the two Barbarians turned to look at the Stone brothers, they were surprised to see both concern and fury on their faces. "It's unimportant. I think we should just continue with our journey," Terrence replied, his irritation evident.

Eden glared at both of them. "One of you had damn well better tell me what is going on right now."

"I'm sure everything is fine," Patrick said, sounding less confident and more hopeful.

"Be silent, Patrick, you know not of what you speak," Terrence replied quickly and angrily.

"I may not be as old as you are, Terrence, but I've heard the rumors too. You forget the Lord I was Squire to spent much of his time in Capital City. I know of our King's particular tastes."

Terrence turned on his younger brother with a murderous look. "Patrick, if you know what's good for you, you'll shut up."

"What does 'vivacious' mean?" Xanhara demanded again.

Terrence sighed and glared again at his younger brother. "I'm not sure I can explain it well, but it means energetic, vigorous, full of life, exciting, exotic, get the idea?"

Xanhara felt her stomach twist and heave. "Are you telling me that that pig tried to bed my sister?" she asked with disgust. Eden did not wait for a response, he turned his horse in the direction of the camp and took off at a gallop. Arriving back in camp little more than an hour later, he barely waited for the watch to open the gates before he headed for the stables. He dismounted and angrily tossed his reins at one of the handlers. He turned to storm off, but he was halted by his name.

"Eden?" Eden turned around to see who spoke. The man said again, "You are Eden, aren't you?"

"Whoever you are, I do not have time to deal with you now. If you need to speak to me, see me tomorrow in my quarters." He turned to walk off.

"My commanding officer says I am to bring you to him one way or another. He would prefer you to come willingly, but he must speak to you at once. He says it is of the utmost urgency."

Eden turned and growled, "It damn well better be, or I will make sure you personally pay for it." He gestured angrily with his hand for the man to lead on. Only as he was following the man did he realize he did not recognize the man, though he was sure he was a Soldier of Ares. The only senior ranking Soldier of Ares that he knew of was Sidel, and if she summoned him like this, he'd beat her backside, and then he'd smash in Brynjolf's head.

The soldier walked right up to a tent and pulled aside the flap. "He's here to see you, Colonel, as you expected." He turned back to Eden and gestured for him to enter. "The Colonel will see you now."

Eden entered the tent glaring at the soldier as he walked past him. "I hope you will forgive my rudeness for summoning you here so abruptly, and I hope you will forgive me for speaking to you before we are properly introduced, but given the gravity of the situation, I felt that it was better if we spoke first."

Eden glared openly at the man and said with some heat, "I'm very busy and I have pressing matters I wish to attend to, so this had better be good."

"I'll get to the point, but first permit me to introduce myself. I'm Colonel Stephen Foster of the Soldiers of Ares. I command the Fortress of Knee Deep and the matter I wish to speak to you about is your wife. I hope you realize what a remarkable woman you are married to, and I hope you are worthy of her. I was not long in this encampment before I observed that everybody speaks very kindly of you, Eden. You have the loyalty of not only your own people, but many of the Bretons as well. Which is why when the King arrived in the encampment yesterday, things kind of went from bad to worse. I as of yet do not have all of the details, but there was some kind of scrimmage over the control of your quarters, though I do have it on excellent authority that your wife won that battle most decisively. However, a battle she ran into some trouble with is the lecherous nature of our King, and that's where I come in to this. Our King has a particular taste, he likes women that don't belong to him. I also have heard he prefers women who are under his power, not under his spell."

Eden interrupted him. "I don't understand the difference. Do they not mean the same thing?"

"Perhaps I expressed myself badly. What I mean to say is, he prefers women who come to his bed because they have no choice, not women who are besotted by him." Eden felt his stomach tighten and his temper rise. "I do not know in what manner he made it clear to your wife he intended to bed her, but he did. Your wife, being intelligent and loyal, came up with a solution to avoid such an unpleasant task. She wisely assumed that had he found her in bed with another man, he would be disgusted by her and leave; which is, of course, what happened." Eden moved quickly. He punched the Colonel in the ribs just as hard as he could with his right and then delivered a hard left to his jaw. The Colonel staggered back, stumbled, and landed on his backside, coughing and sputtering.

"Dammit! Has anybody ever told you hit like a sledgehammer?" the Colonel said. Still coughing and then spitting blood, he slowly got to his feet. For a moment, he thought Eden was going to hit him again, but he didn't.

"You think telling me that you went to bed with my woman is going to make me feel better than hearing that the King took my woman to bed?" Eden towered over him and glared down at him. As Foster craned his neck to look up at the huge man, he felt somewhat intimidated. He wasn't used to being towered over by other men.

Foster took several steps back, groaning again, and holding his side. He said, "You didn't let me finish. Perhaps I should tell you from start to finish." Foster quickly and carefully related the story of last night's adventure to the big man. To his relief, Eden didn't hit him again.

Eden took several calming breaths, then allowing his common sense to take over, he smelled the air. He stepped in close to Foster and inhaled deeply. He could tell that the man had not bathed this morning and he caught only the barest hint of lavender and vanilla. After a long moment he said, "On your honor, all you did was kiss my woman?"

Foster cleared his throat and looked a little uncomfortable. "As I said, I did somewhat ..." he hesitated, considering. Shrugging his shoulders and condemning himself, "Allow my hands a limited free roam." Eden reached for him and he added quickly, "The King would not have been convinced otherwise. It had to look convincing."

Eden gripped his shoulder and gave it a friendly squeeze. "I know. I realize that as much as it pains me to admit it, it was probably what had to be done." Eden looked at him considering. "Why did you tell me? Why did you not to permit my woman to tell me?"

"As I said, everyone speaks of you kindly and says that you're a good and honorable man, but I didn't know you and I didn't know whether you were the kind of man who would beat his wife for what she had done. If you were going to beat anybody over the situation, I preferred it to be me."

Eden couldn't help it. He started laughing. He could not imagine Bloodstone allowing any man to beat her. "Do you think my woman is the kind of woman who would put up with such a man? She would have gutted me long ago."

"You would think that, but I have learned over the past few years that the strong, stubborn, proud ones are the ones more likely to suffer a man's abuse in silence; because they are too proud to admit that any man's beaten, abused, or mistreated them. And though I have not had many dealings with your wife, I think that she is the kind who would bury it down deep and allow the poison to fester until it destroyed her. I, unfortunately, have some experience with her kind." He coughed a

123

little and held his side. "Damn, I think you broke one of my ribs." As a thought struck him, he slowly grinned. "I guess I should thank you. I was trying to come up with a way to have to go to the infirmary."

Eden did not hear him at first. He was too busy meditating on what the man had just said. He had to admit there was more truth to it than he wanted to. Finally, the last thing the man had said seeped into his brain and he looked up in confusion. "You wanted to go to the infirmary? Why?"

"I find myself attracted to one of the priestesses."

Eden narrowed his eyes. "Which one?"

"Why does it matter? You're a married man?"

"Unfortunately, I'm related to several of them."

"Well, you can't be related to this one; she's an Amazon," Foster said with a little cough.

Eden groaned. "Bloodrose, she is my sister by marriage. It's complicated. You do realize she's an Amazon. You do realize how they feel about men, right? You realize if you mistreat her or hurt her, I'll break all your ribs?"

"Don't worry, I don't think I'm going to be seducing anybody until my ribs heal. Now if you'll excuse me, I think I'm going to go to the infirmary." Both men left the tent together. Eden turned and extended his hand.

"I know this might sound strange, but I think I would enjoy getting to know you better. Perhaps we could be friends."

Foster took his hand and shook it. "As long as you promise me in the future to pull your punches just a little."

X

Bloodstone was trying to prepare the midday meal, emphasis on the trying. She had so far turned two potatoes into meteorites and burned her hand print onto the knife. She also had to give up doing paperwork because she kept setting papers on fire. She was just on the verge of screaming when she heard the tent flap rustle. A moment later, she let out a slow, soft sigh as she barely breathed his name. "Eden." He moved up behind her and slid one arm around her waist, the other around her shoulders, and squeezed her tightly to him. He bent down and began kissing her neck gently, then he tentatively ran his teeth along her neck. Sliding his hand back across her belly, splaying his fingers, he gripped her hip. His other hand he slid across her breasts, making sure to caress each one, then sliding down, he gripped her other hip and rubbed her backside against him. Bloodstone felt her heart began to race and her face flush. Terror shot through her as she pulled away quickly. She started to turn to face him, to hold out her hand, but she quickly turned her back to him and hugged herself tightly, pressing her hands into her arms. As she stood there trembling, her breathing was rough and ragged and she was trying to get a handle on her emotions before she became hysterical. When she finally felt calm, she turned around and he was gone.

Eden had slipped quietly from his tent, kicking himself for his stupidity. He rubbed his hands up and down his face, thinking about what Foster had said. He decided to listen to the older man. He changed his direction and headed for the area allotted to the Queen's men. As Eden walked, he thought it was interesting that everyone still referred to them as the Queen's men. Eden found this ironic, since most of them were here in this encampment because of his woman, their true Queen. But then again, he also thought it was interesting how in so many ways they were separate units: Wolf Tribesman, Amazons, State Soldiers, Athenian Soldiers, Queen's men. Sometimes they all held very strictly to their own chain of command, other times they would respond to an order without question or hesitation, no matter where it came from. It was the strangest mix of enemy and friend, adversary and ally. It also always amazed him that despite these differences, they all held together with an iron grip and stood shoulder to shoulder, ready to brace the storms that would come. He smiled as he thought of what Murtaugh affectionately referred to as the Stone Wall. This was not the army as a whole, but a very specific section of the army. When Murtaugh had first given them the nickname, it was only the Stone brothers and Bloodstone - but over the past year, the Wall had grown and grown. He paused in his walk as he contemplated how many members there now were: Grey Stone, deceased - he felt a pang at the loss as he always would, Black Stone, Andrew, Grayhawk, Daniel,

Bloodstone, Fitzwilliam, Terrance, Murtaugh, himself, Big Bear, Xanhara, Fletcher, Amber - though no longer a warrior, still a force to be reckoned with, Tabitha - not a woman he'd want to cross, Innish - whose skill was quickly growing, the Dowager Duchess - another woman not to cross, Helena - quiet, but strong and stubborn, she could be fierce in defense of those she loved, Patrick - a decent warrior but an incredible armorer. He added them up in his mind, nineteen. There were others too, but he was not sure whether everyone would consider them part of the Stone Wall. He would have to speak to Black Stone and see what he had to say on the matter now that he was the head of the Stone Wall.

Arriving at his destination, he looked around, spotting a soldier. "Where's William's tent?" he demanded. The soldier gestured. Eden turned and walked into the tent without even announcing himself. To his surprise, William, Matthias, and two men he did not recognize, were all sitting around a table playing cards and having their midday meal. They all looked up at his entrance and got to their feet. "William, I would have a word with you." The two men he did not recognize excused themselves quickly.

Matthias turned and leaned in close to William, whispering in a voice he thought Eden could not hear, "I'm not sure I should leave you alone with him. He looks murderous."

William gestured for him to leave. "It'll be fine. Eden and I are old friends."

Matthias's eyes widened and he said louder than he had intended, "The last man who called him friend, he killed in a very ugly way. That's not reassuring, William."

William laughed and went over to the side table and poured a drink. "Out, Matthias, we'll be fine." Returning to the table, he set the drink on the other side and gestured for Eden to be seated. "So what do I owe this honor, the King in my tent."

Eden glared at him. "Don't call me that." He walked over to the table, picked up the drink, and downed it. Then looking at William he said, "I want you to tell me everything you know about what was done to her when she was in prison."

William swallowed hard and concealed his emotions behind a mask of calm impartiality. He then said calmly, "I know you don't like me, Eden, and I know we're not friends - but please believe me when I say you don't want to know."

Eden glared at him. "Do you honestly believe anything you can tell me is worse than what I've imagined?"

Williams sighed and said sadly, "I do not feel that it is my place to tell you. If you want to know these things, speak to your woman. Do not ask me."

Eden gritted his teeth and said in the calmest voice he could muster, "I am not asking you to tell me what happened between you and my woman. I ... I just want to know what he did to her."

William blinked as he tried to grasp the meaning of that statement. "What do you mean what happened between me and her?"

"I'm not stupid, William. I know what is required of a Queen's man to keep his life. You could not of had a woman in your quarters and not bedded her. Do not pretend otherwise. Don't insult my intelligence."

"Eden, I did not go to bed with your woman, I swear to you. I did see her naked, because I made her bathe, but trust me, at that moment in her life there was nothing appealing about her. Again, I did not even enjoy seeing her bathe. She was a bloody mess. The only reason I watched was because I did not trust her not to stick a knife in my back or break my neck. We talked a lot in my quarters, that is all." For a brief moment, William's mind went back over all their conversations. Something leapt out at him, and his mask slipped for a split second. He quickly re-affixed it, but he knew it'd been too late. Eden had not missed that one unguarded moment.

"What ... what did you remember? What don't you want to tell me?" Eden demanded coldly.

"I don't want to tell you any of it. You don't need to know. She loves you. She is in your bed, nothing else matters," William said firmly.

Eden snorted with irritation. "Oh yes, it doesn't matter so much that just now in my quarters I frightened her and reminded her of one the animals who raped and beat her. That's how much it doesn't matter."

William closed his eyes and looked skywards as he groaned. He picked up his drink and downed it. Groaning again, he said, "I don't know about other times in her life, but at the prison before I arrived the only man who had …" he closed his eyes and gritted his teeth, "raped her had been Bloody Fang. She was his exclusive toy. By the time I arrived, he had lost interest in her, but was still forbidding anyone else to touch her. Even after he lost interest in a woman, he did not allow other men to touch her until he was sure she wasn't carrying his child. Now please, for your own sanity, let that be enough. Just remind yourself she wants to be with you. Whatever else has happened, that should be enough."

Eden was looking at him in an appraising manner. "After you tell me what you realized earlier, something occurred to you, something you hadn't put together before. What was it?"

"Eden, it was nothing, we just talked about my wife."

Eden could tell he was holding something back. He glared at him, "You're not telling me everything."

"I asked her if she was married. She said that she had a lover once and she missed him ..." Eden glared at him. "His name was Eldrik. Eden, just because she missed him then doesn't mean she doesn't love and miss you now." William was staring at Eden, who looked ridiculously happy. "Why are you so happy about that?"

"When I knew her before this encampment, the name I was using was Eldrik." Eden couldn't seem to stop smiling. He knew he probably looked like a fool, but he just couldn't stop.

"Then you should stop worrying about everything else and just concentrate on how much she loves you. Now get out of my tent so my men and I can finish our meal before we have to go back on watch - and go tell your wife you love her." Eden turned and exited the tent quickly.

As Eden walked back to his tent, he contemplated the situation he was in with his woman. He had said it after his son was born, and now he felt it even more. He had had it. It was time to be done with secrets. It only continued to drive wedges between them and cause misunderstandings. He was going to have to put his foot down and demand that they dispense with them. But Bloodstone had said that he continued to keep things from her, and until he was ready to tell her everything, she would not tell him everything. Though in truth, he could not immediately think of anything he was still concealing from her. It slowly came to him. Sorrel, he'd forgotten all about Sorrel. He would have to tell her.

As he entered his tent, he felt his temper rise as he saw his woman's busted lip. He also saw what a state of extreme agitation she was in. "Where have you been? You come home and then you just leave. I need to talk to you. It's important." Eden knew he was being an idiot again, but he couldn't seem to think about anything else after she said home. She had referred to his tent as 'home', she had never done that before.

He crossed quickly to her and wrapped his arms around her, pulling her tightly against him. Bending down, he said just before he kissed her, "I'm glad to be home." For several minutes Bloodstone could think of nothing but Eden kissing her. It annoyed her that sometimes when he was kissing her, all she could think about was him. She was an intelligent soldier; she should not be so easily distracted by a man kissing her.

Finally, she remembered how dangerous it was for him to be this close to her and she pulled away quickly. "No, you can't do that. You can't touch me right now."

"I know we need to talk. You want to go first or do you want me to go first?" he asked grimly.

"I need to go first. I need to tell you about yesterday and what … what I did last night," she said as she stared at the ground, her embarrassment growing.

To her shock, Eden waved his hand dismissively and said, "As long as you don't ever, ever expect me to welcome your King into my home, you have nothing to tell me. Colonel Foster and I have already spoken at some length about this matter."

Bloodstone opened her mouth and then closed it. Though she was surprised, she also had to admit she wasn't that surprised. She liked Foster from the moment she had met him, but she also had to admit that might've had something to do with the fact that he was threatening to flatten Falcon, who try as she may, she always harbored a grudge against. "Are you terribly mad at us?"

He laughed and reached for her, but she backed away quickly. "Why in Hades will you not let me touch you?"

"I'm afraid I'll hurt you," she said shyly.

Eden blinked. "Why would you think that you will hurt me?"

"Because ... remember when I turned into a burning person?" Eden nodded, looking a little worried. "Well, I now know why I did that, and I will tell you - but you have to promise not to tell anybody else right now."

Eden crossed his arms over his chest and stared at her suspiciously. "I have no intention of being part of any more secrets that do not directly relate to military security."

"So you intend to inform my brother that you're a werewolf?"

"Okay, you got me there. I agree."

"You didn't notice the chair yet, did you?"

Eden quickly looked around. Seeing the chair, he raised an eyebrow. "Where in Hades did that come from?"

"Actually, interestingly enough, Hades had nothing to do with it. However, General Grey Stone and Ares, God of War, did." Eden raised an eyebrow, but waited patiently for her to get to the point. "The chair is a gift to you from my father."

"Bloodstone, love, you do know your father is dead," he said in such a gentle tone, so not to say that she was being crazy. Bloodstone almost started laughing.

"Now see, that apparently is where we were all mistaken, because as you will see, my father is not … well … General Grey Stone, however, is dead, but only his body because you see … as insane as this is going to sound, Lord Ares, General Grey Stone, and my father, are all the same person." She watched as he stared at her in disbelief. "I know you're probably thinking I'm crazy, but I'm definitely, unfortunately, not." As though to prove her point, she held out her hands, palms up, slightly to either side of her. A moment later, a ball of fire appeared in each hand. After a long moment, she turned her hands to face each other, and the fire spread from hand-to-hand until it was a bridge between the two. After a long moment, she closed her hands and the fire went out. She turned and casually waved her hand over the fire in the hearth. As her hand passed by, all the fire absorbed into her hand, and when she was done, not an ember was left. It was left cold. Eden dropped down to one knee and picked up a log that had been burning only a moment before. It was cold to the touch. He swallowed hard as he looked back up at her.

"When are you going to tell your brothers? Might they have such extraordinary abilities as well?"

"I have no intention of informing them. Lord Ares is going to have to do it for himself," she said, firmly and angrily. "And as to the other, yes I believe that they do. Theirs are still latent abilities,

136

whereas mine have come to the forefront. Though Viktor says I'm overthinking it, and that's why I can't control it."

"Viktor? You consulted my brother?" he said, clearly pleased.

"He's the most powerful shaman in the encampment, who else would I consult?"

Eden put the log down and went to the basin and washed his hands. Returning, he grabbed her around the waist and pulled her tightly against him. She began to panic in his arms, but he held her fast. "You won't hurt me, stop struggling, and just kiss me." He bent forward and kissed her. As always, she melted in his arms. When he thought he couldn't stand merely kissing her any longer, he pulled away and said panting, "We need to talk."

"Isn't that what we have been doing?"

"Yes, but I wish to pick up a subject we started on the day our son was born, and have not continued. I told you then, I wish to be done with secrets, and I meant it. You said then that you would not be done with secrets until I had told you everything. I could not then think of anything that I was still deliberately concealing from you. On the way back from William's tent ..."

Bloodstone interrupted him quickly. "What were you doing in William's tent? You hate William!"

"I may have done once, but no longer. I was there for him to tell me everything he knew about your imprisonment." She glared at him, then rolled her eyes. "But as I was saying before I was rudely interrupted, I did, however, think of something that I had concealed from you because I am ashamed of it."

Bloodstone interrupted him. Quickly, she touched her hand to his cheek and looked deeply into his eyes. "Eden, if you don't want to tell me, you don't have to."

He swallowed hard and shook his head. "No, that's where you're wrong. I do have to tell you. I should've told you long before this, but as I said, I was ashamed, and I mostly kept burying it to the back of my mind. In one of the villages we did business with, there was a beautiful widow." Eden smiled as he saw his woman bristle. He gripped her tightly around the waist and squeezed. "I promise you, not as beautiful as you. She was always pursuing me. Viktor thought I should marry her, but since I already had me a woman - even though Viktor did not know of her - I continually refused. But one night I got really drunk, really drunk, and when she kissed me, I allowed her to kiss me. And I allowed her to continue to kiss me and then she slid onto my lap and wrapped her arms around my neck. It was several more minutes before I came to my senses and put an end to what I should never have allowed to begin. Fortunately I came to my senses long before anything …" he blushed, "more than kissing and caressing happened."

"Eden, it was just a momentary lapse of judgment, and as you say, you did not go to bed with her. I'm not mad at you, promise. And anyways, after what I did last night, what room would I have to be mad?"

He looked down at her. "What you did was necessary. What I did was for my own pleasure. But I mean it, woman, we are done with secrets. No more between us. I will not be satisfied until you prove to me you will keep no more secrets from me."

She crossed her arms over her chest and glared at him. "Since clearly you do not intend to accept my word, how do you expect me to prove such a thing to you? And what if I do not agree?"

"I would accept your word, if it wasn't for the fact that you still conceal things from me. So until you come clean and tell me everything, you cannot give your word to keep no more. And if you do not agree, I will unhappily return to the floor. I will not share my bed with a woman who does not confide in me all of her pains and all of her heartbreak. I should also tell you that there are things I understand you do not wish to discuss normally; but going forward, if you have a nightmare, I expect you to tell me about it. If I do something to you that provokes a bad memory, I expect you to tell me about it. For now, I would be happy if you think of one thing you would never have told me, and tell me."

Bloodstone continued to glare at him. Every bone and every muscle of her body was in belligerent irritation. She made an exasperated sound as she tried to search her mind for something that would appease him. This was difficult, given the fact that she had very few secrets from him now. As she searched her mind, she alighted unexpectedly on something.

As Eden watched his woman's face, he knew the instant she had thought of something. All irritation left her quickly, as her entire demeanor changed, and she went from the agitated woman he had been observing to the soldier. Her face quickly converted to its unreadable mask. Her body straightened and stiffened into the stern unreadable soldier. Eden said quickly, "That, tell me that."

Bloodstone looked at him quickly, her mind racing, trying to find a way to avoid telling him. Her shoulders slumped. She was stuck and she knew it. "I'm not sure you want to know. This will probably truly shock and appall you."

"Tell me, Woman."

She blushed a vivid crimson. "The day you bought me, when you returned to the cottage that night, though a small part of me didn't want you - most of me did." Eden raised an eyebrow in surprise. "I know that that makes me a whore, but I knew I was never going to get married. No man would ever want to marry me, and you were a good man. I knew that, and I thought you would be nice to me. You wouldn't hurt me unnecessarily, so I wanted you. I wanted to know what it would feel like to share a bed with a man. I wanted to know what his hands would feel like on my body." She hesitated a moment as tears pricked at her eyes. Her hand went involuntarily to her belly - she splayed her fingers across it and pressed gently against it. Eden didn't catch the gesture at first, he was too busy remembering how shy she had been when she showed him her scars. He found it hard to believe that that shy girl wanted him. When her second hand moved down to her belly, and then she hugged her belly, and she looked away so ashamed, Eden realized she had not told him everything. He moved forward and cupped her cheek and turned her back to face him, but before he could say anything, she began nodding. "I know I have to tell you the rest." She hesitated a moment and then looked up at him pleadingly. "Would you believe me if I told you it was better you didn't know?" Eden felt a tightness in his stomach, but he slowly shook his head. "I know that it had to have been that night or the morning after that you gave me our first child." Eden felt his legs go weak and his stomach twist and turn into a hideous knot. He had expected her to tell him that she had found him revolting. "It was about three weeks later when I lost the baby." She burst into tears as her body became wracked with sobs. He pulled her tightly against him.

Eden felt a mixture of fury and sadness. Finally he asked, "Please tell me it was nothing I did."

"No, I believe it was just my body. It had sustained too much damage. You know the healers told me I'd never be able to have children. I consider the fact that we have Blackwolf a miracle. I know that Viktor feels another one would kill me, but I don't agree with that. And if you want to be done with secrets," she looked up at him and gripped his face with both hands, "When the war is over, can you please try to give me another one? By the time Blackwolf is up and really moving around, Innish will be full-grown and living on his own. I would like for Blackwolf not to be, for all intents and purposes, an only child. It wouldn't be good for him. It would make him into an arrogant person. He should have a younger sibling to thwart him on occasion."

"Why didn't you tell me? Did you not think I deserved to know?" To Bloodstone's surprise, he sounded very near tears. She didn't know why, but for some reason she thought a man wouldn't feel the loss as acutely as she did. That was unjust of her.

"I did not tell Eldrik because he had enough to worry about. He did not need to worry about me. He was too busy trying to keep us both alive, and my virtue intact. And when I met you again here, it seemed wrong to tell you two years after the fact. That was wrong of me, and I'm sorry. I should have told you."

"You're damn right you should of told me. A part of me died too." He choked on a sob and hugged her tightly. After several minutes, he looked down at her and gave a weak smile. "You know, if you expect me to give you another child, you're going to have to let me practice." He scooped her up in his arms and carried her to the bed.

Afterwards, as he lay there holding her against him, rubbing his hand up and down her back, he kissed her on top of the head. He reached out with his other hand and pulled her thigh across his middle. "All right, I've been laying here trying to puzzle it out, why were you so embarrassed to admit that you wanted me? A little surprising, I admit, but not so shocking."

"Because only a whore wants a man she does not know. My behavior and thoughts were scandalous."

"If you call yourself a whore one more time, woman, I'm going to blister your backside."

"You wouldn't dare!"

"I've done it before. What makes you think I won't do it again?" he said with a laugh.

"That was before I let you in, before I loved you."

Eden quickly rolled her on her back, pinning her beneath him. Pulling her thighs up around him he said, "You let me in long before that."

Bloodstone blushed and gave a little gasp. "Eden, what do you think you are doing?"

"What does it feel like I'm doing?"

"I said after the war, not during."

"And I told you I could not share your bed and not make love to you, and if I'm making love to you, there is always the possibility of another child. You can't have it both ways, Love."

XI

It took Foster three quarters of an hour to make it to the infirmary. He found it was extremely painful to walk quickly. Not just because of the movement, but also because of the increased breathing. That was the most painful part, breathing. It had been a very long time since anybody had broken any of his ribs. He was surprised to see that the infirmary was a solid wood structure. As he entered, a man sitting at a desk turned around to face him and slowly rose to his feet. "Is there something I can assist you with, soldier?" Foster looked up at the large Barbarian. Fifties he had to guess, and if clothes denoted tribe, he too was a Wolf Tribesman. He was just about to reply when Bloodrose came out of the back room.

Foster gave her a smile, then looked back at the man. "Yes, I'm sorry to bother the two of you, but I think I might have a couple of broken ribs," he said, clutching his side.

Bloodrose walked up and patted the big man on the arm, saying as she did so, "It's all right Viktor. Go back to your paperwork, I will attend to him." Viktor nodded and returned to his desk. She gestured to one of the cots. "Please sit down, and can you remove your tunic on your own, or do I need to help you?"

Foster refrained from making the obvious statement. Instead he replied, "I think I can manage it on my own." With careful maneuvering, he was able to remove his tunic without looking too much like a baby, though he sure felt like one with all of his complaining.

Once his tunic was off, she stepped between his legs and gently gripped his face and tilted it to the side. She then examined the bruising and cut to his mouth. After a moment, she tipped his chin back so that he was looking up at her, but only a little. "So who hit you in the face?" she asked. As she pulled on each one of his eyelids, she peered deeply into his eyes, her loose hair occasionally brushing against his bare skin.

It took him a moment before he realized he was supposed to answer the question. "Eden."

To his surprise, they both spoke simultaneously. Viktor said, "When did Eden get home?"

"Eden is back?" Bloodrose asked with obvious pleasure.

"Yes, he came in just a couple of hours ago."

Viktor rose and came to stand near him with his arms crossed over his chest. "Care to explain why my brother's been gone two weeks and the first thing he does is go and punch you?"

146

Great. Eden's brother is in charge of the infirmary. He didn't mention that fact. "We were just introducing ourselves to each other."

Bloodrose picked up each one of his hands and turned them over, examining them, then lifting his left arm, she examined the ribs. "It does not appear as though you put up a fight. So why did you just stand there and take it while Eden pounded on you? Do you enjoy being a punching bag?"

"No, not really. In fact, we agreed that if we're going to be friends, he has to learn to pull his punches."

"So my brother punched you twice really hard, and the two of you are good friends?" Viktor asked skeptically.

"As I said, we were just introducing ourselves, and we parted agreeing we would like to be friends," Foster replied with a grin.

Bloodrose and Viktor exchanged a look, then both shrugged. "Viktor, do you understand the mind of a warrior?" asked Bloodrose.

"Nope, never have. Eden and Murtaugh would beat the shit out of each other one day and then go and have a drink like nothing happened, and they've always been like that. I try not to think too much about it."

Bloodrose nodded and shrugged her shoulders. She stepped back in close and went back to examining his eyes. "I'm not sure you don't have a concussion. Did you see spots or anything? Did you lose consciousness for even a moment?"

Foster considered for a long moment. He remembered feeling his vision did blur, but he didn't think he lost consciousness. "I don't think so, but I know my vision was a little blurry."

"Then we are going to assume you have a concussion, which means I hope you got a good night's sleep last night, because you are not going to get one tonight."

"Well then, if I have to stay up all night, are you going to come and have a drink with me to keep me company?"

She smiled at him mischievously. "Sure, you can buy me drinks while you're drinking water, because you don't get to have alcohol until we're sure that brain of yours isn't leaking."

Stephen didn't think he liked the sound of that, brain leaking. "Sounds serious."

"Not if you can behave yourself and do exactly as you're told. You'll be fine, no sleeping and no alcohol."

He nodded and gave her a little salute. "As you command."

"Good, and glad to see at least somebody around here can follow orders. Now let's take a look at those ribs." She dropped down on her knees next to him and began carefully examining his ribs. He winced several times as she pushed, poked, and prodded him. Finally she stood up. "Two of them are cracked, one is broken, and two are badly bruised. Eden was really mad at you." He gave an indifferent shrug. She walked over to a cupboard and pulled out several rolls of bandages, and dropping down to her knees beside him again, she proceeded to carefully bandage his ribs. When she was done, she stood up and stretched her back. "Well, those will be very painful for a couple of weeks, and you have to take it easy for at least a week."

"So what time are you going to meet me for drinks tonight?" he asked with a smile.

She crossed her arms over her chest and looked at him suspiciously. "I told you, you can't drink."

"No, you said I had to drink water. That's still drinking."

"Colonel …"

He interrupted quickly, "Stephen."

She sighed. "Stephen, I don't know what you exactly have in mind, but … I don't think I'm the right person for you to have it in mind, with …" She mentally kicked herself for being inarticulate.

She was usually much more composed in her speaking. She sounded like an ignorant child.

Foster couldn't help it. He smiled as the faintest hint of pink crept into her cheeks. "It's just a drink. It's not a marriage proposal." To his delight, her blush increased. She looked lovely when she was blushing. And now that she wasn't standing close, brushing her hair against him, rubbing her hands all over his body, he allowed himself to examine her attire. She wore only what he would consider a corset. It wasn't a bodice, and she had no blouse on underneath it, so her arms were completely bare, and most of her shoulders. There was no gap between the laces and at least an inch, if not two, of her middle showing, which he found very appealing. Her snug fitting skirt went to her knees, but not over the knees, and her boots only went midway up her calf. So as he allowed his eyes to wander down her body, there was plenty to take in, and every curve was readily available to his eyes. When he finally went back to her face, her blush had increased tenfold.

"Stephen! …" but whatever else she was going to say died on her lips, as she stood there gaping, trying to find words.

Foster stood up slowly and pulled his tunic on with a groan, leaning towards her just a little bit. "Same place, seven o'clock, unless of course, you want to make me dinner." As her eyes widened, he laughed and headed for the door. He felt

150

something softly hitting him in the back. He turned around slowly and saw a roll of bandages lying on the floor. He looked up to see she was glaring at him. He carefully bent down and picked up the bandages and tossed it casually back at her. He turned and exited before she found something harder to hit him with.

Viktor waited until he was sure Stephen was gone before he said, "You like him."

Bloodrose turned and glared at him. "I do not. I find him a very annoying, persistent, arrogant man. He thinks I'm just going to show up."

"Bloodrose, you've worked here with me for nearly a year and I've seen you treat several men with concussions. I've never yet seen you manage to, forgive the expression, manhandle them as much as you just did him. In fact, I've never seen you deliberately stroke your hair over a man's shoulders as you just did him. My question to you is, were you trying to annoy him, or were you trying to arouse him? I will also state that if you do not have an interest in getting involved with him, you had better not show tonight. I've come to respect you very much over the past year and I never thought you were a tease as I just saw you doing. So if you are not truly interested in him and you show up tonight, after how you behaved in here, you will be a tease."

*****

Bloodstone lay with her chin on Eden's chest looking at him. "You know, I've wanted to say this for years, you sometimes have a most insatiable appetite."

He looked down at her. "Only where you're concerned, my love." With her chin still on his chest, she shook her head. Eden started laughing. "Don't do that, it tickles." She grinned at him mischievously, but before she could do anything else, they heard a slight murmur outside and then the tent flap opened. Eden cocked his head to the side. "Good afternoon, Sergeant Simon, how are you doing today?"

"Very good to see you, sir. I'm glad you made it back safely." Simon gave a slight bow to Eden, turned and walked out. A moment later they heard all the other guards burst into laughter. "You guys are a bunch of assholes. Y'all could have had the decency to inform me Eden was home," Sergeant Simon said angrily.

"But Simon, I thought you said you were used to things like this and it didn't embarrass you," Dex said smugly.

Simon continued to glare at him as he said, "It's different when I know I am going to walk in on them in the morning." The other men all continued to laugh at Simon's discomfort. "Shut up all of you … just shut up!"

Bloodstone slid out of bed, washed, and began dressing. Eden grumbled, "Killjoy," and followed suit.

Once they were both dressed Bloodstone called, "What did you need, Sergeant Simon?"

Sergeant Simon reentered the tent. "Sorry for the interruption earlier, Sir, but there are several wagon handlers here. They say they have your order and they're awaiting payment."

"Well, that was faster than I expected. Let's go see what they have for me."

As the three of them exited the tent, Dex fell in beside Eden. "At your earliest convenience, Your Majesty, I would like to have a word with you privately."

"As soon as we see what my woman is up to," Eden replied quickly.

When they arrived at the Eastern gate, to Eden's surprise, there were eight wagons full of saplings. Bloodstone examined their cargo and then paid the wagon handlers, tipping them generously. "Captain of the Watch," she called.

A young man Eden did not recognize approached and saluted. "Yes, General?"

"Would you and a handful of your men escort these wagons to the Western gate? Then have all of the men who were on punishment duty, bread and water, or any other penalty restrictions, called up. And then, going forward until I say otherwise, as long as the saplings hold out, their other punishments are suspended in lieu of planting saplings." She pulled out a stack of papers and handed them over to the Captain. "These are exact details on how I would like the saplings planted. Sergeant Simon will make arrangements for someone to replace you at the gate and for the rest of the day, I would like you to oversee this. I will assign someone to it tomorrow specifically. Any questions, Captain?"

The captain shook his head and looked amused. "No, Sir, but all the men on bread and water are going to be thanking you at least for the next day or two."

"And I've ordered a lot more, so hopefully before these run out, they will be here. I've decided I would rather have the men doing something productive, rather than sitting, pouting, and reflecting on their misbehavior."

As they turned and headed back to their quarters, Eden asked, "A lot more? Exactly what do you have in mind, Woman?"

"I think there's no reason we can't begin Seana's plan for rebuilding the forests now. We've done a lot of damage to the surrounding areas by building our walls. Why not do some replanting?

We've got plenty of men on punishment duty, why not put them to good use? We have nothing more urgent for them to do. They can be planting trees." After a moment she added, "You do not disapprove of how I'm spending your money, do you?"

"It's not my money. It's your money. Just because your peoples' laws say it now belongs to me, doesn't mean I agree with it. It's your money, they're your estates, they're your properties. Do with them as you see fit. You've done just fine running them this long, you do not need my help." He smiled at her and then added, "You two men stay with your queen, my commander here needs to report to me," he said, jerking his head in Dex's direction.

Eden turned and headed for the Mead Hall. Arriving, he entered and lit a lantern. He indicated a chair and they both seated themselves. "All right, Dex, what do you need to say? How badly has my woman misbehaved?"

"It's not that, Eden. It's just that I failed you in several regards, but beyond that there is a complication I did not foresee." Dex hesitated.

"Why don't we begin with you informing me of how you have failed me."

"First off, as I'm sure you're aware that your woman has some very horrible nightmares. In order to put a stop to them, or lessen them, I felt it

necessary to consult your grandfather and he recommended I consult her father. Her father decided it was a good idea, and I agreed with him, for her not to be alone in her quarters at night. Of course, the only appropriate person to sleep there with her was him, as he has done most nights. This, however, because of one of those differences between our two cultures, has created some unpleasant rumors. Apparently, Bretons feel that this Father/Daughter relationship is not a true Father/Daughter relationship because of the lack of blood. Bretons seem to think that there is something inappropriate going on at night, which of course there is not. And then, of course, I failed you utterly in the entire situation with their King." Dex hesitated a long moment organizing his thoughts, then he relayed the entire story from start to finish. "Fortunately, due to our absolute control of the area that night and with the help of Colonel Foster's men, no one has heard even a whisper of a rumor regarding the two of them. And now I must come to the reason - well the largest reason - of why I must resign. I have written a list of men I would recommend to replace me. Men who are older, wiser, and will not have the same problem that I have serving as your woman's protector. But for reasons I will explain, it is not appropriate for me to continue to protect your woman when I have such ..." The young man blushed. "...
inappropriate thoughts regarding your woman. Due to a nightmare, I entered your quarters and I saw your woman in a ..." He swallowed hard and looked uncomfortable. Eden had to bite his tongue

to contain his amusement. "... most alluring garment. It was also clinging to her in ways I should not even remember, but unfortunately, I cannot seem to get out of my mind. So you see, Sir, an older, wiser man who would not have such feelings would be a much better option."

Eden couldn't help it. He started laughing. "This is going to sound odd to you, Dex, but I often find it infuriating the number of men who can't see past the britches and the armor to see the beautiful woman underneath it all. So on those occasions I run across a man who actually finds my woman beautiful, as long as he can keep his hands to himself, I don't mind him admiring her. And since I do not feel I even need to ask the question of whether you can behave yourself, I see no reason for you to resign. As far as your perceived failures are concerned, I have learned in nearly a year of living with Bretons, they have filthy, perverted minds. If they think there is something inappropriate between Fletcher and his daughter, just ignore them. I do not doubt the content of their relationship; in fact, I hope it will continue to grow. Fletcher is a good man and will be a good influence on my woman. He is warm and loving, something she needs more of. And as far as the entire situation with their King is concerned; I will classify that as a Breton matter and handled by the Bretons. Hopefully, the next time you find yourself in that situation, you can, with my complete approval, stick a sword in his ribs." Eden hesitated a long moment, considering. "I also find myself compelled to tell you why I chose you for this job. When you were seventeen, you had a hard choice to make. You made the right one. You made the one I would've made if I'd been in your place, but it was not an easy choice for you to make. That has not made your life easy over the past six years, but you did it without complaint, and you did your duty, and you did it lovingly and gently. You may be young, but you were already well aware of how to handle a headstrong young woman, and since my woman and your sister are much of an age, I figured you would know how to handle her. Older, wiser men, as you put it, would be less willing to give on points where they should. I do not feel an older man would've handled the situation with the Breton King in the same manner in which you did. So unless you persist in your determination to submit your resignation, I would prefer for you to continue as my woman's protector."

Dex was staring at him surprised. "I did not know you knew about my sister."

"Do you think I would pick a man to protect my woman and my child and not know everything about him?" Eden gave Dex a pitying look. "Then that was not well thought out of you. I chose you because of your qualifications. You're also an excellent swordsman and are willing to go toe to toe with my woman. Not a lot of men are willing to do that. They know she's a superior swordsman, but I think you'd go up against her. You might not win, but you'd at least try."

"If you do not feel that the concerns that I have expressed will interfere in my duties as the protector of your woman and child, I would be honored to continue in the position. I do like your family, and I like her as a person. She's tough, but she's fair, and she and I have come to a tentative understanding."

Eden arose and the two men headed out of the room. "One more thing, Dex, there are occasions when I desire to make love to my woman without men listening, so you need to make sure that your men understand that when I order them to be gone, they will obey me."

Dex considered as they walked back to Eden's quarters. "With all due respect, Your Majesty, I would be remiss in my duties if I did not state that as her protectors, we should never be too far from her. Perhaps we could set a campfire about fifty or sixty feet from your quarters? Then we will be near, but not so near for occasions when you desire your privacy." Eden considered, then nodded.

*****

When Bloodstone returned home that evening, Eden was sitting at the table with a box in front of him. It was stained a cherry, and almost reminded her of a jewel box, but it was very large for a jewel box. "What is that?"

"This is what your father left you and, well, I haven't opened it. I figured it was none of my business." He slid it across the table. "Open it."

She crossed to the table and tentatively examined the outside of the box. The bottom of it had two drawers about two inches high each. From the top of the top drawer to the lid was at least eight inches, and the box itself must of been twelve by twelve square. She didn't know why, but the box gave her an uneasy feeling in the pit of her stomach. She decided it was better to open the bottom drawer first, rather than the lid. Tentatively pulling it out, she gave a little gasp. Eden stood up to move behind her. Looking down, he whistled. She closed the drawer with a snap and shook her head. Eden reached down and pulled the drawer open all the way. Inside was a bracelet at least an inch and a half wide of diamonds and sapphires. There was also a pair of earrings and a brooch, clearly part of the set. Eden closed the drawer, then nudged her. She opened the top drawer. It was the necklace to the set, with five hanging pendants, four of which were sapphires the size of grapes. The one in the center was a sapphire the size of a gold coin. At sight of the necklace, he'd felt his woman's entire body go rigid. He now knew why the Duke said he hoped Eden would make her use it. She would never wear it of her own accord. He closed the drawer gently and reached up with a single finger and flipped open the lid. Bloodstone began shaking her head. Inside was the diamond and sapphire tiara to match the entire set. Eden didn't even like to think what the cost of such a set would be. He whistled again. "You know, Woman, I think tomorrow you had better put a ward on this box if it's just going to be here in the encampment, where anybody can get ideas about it."

"Eden, you do realize I could never wear such a thing. That … that's not for me … that's for …"

"A Queen," he supplied.

She looked over her shoulder to glare at him. "I'm a soldier. Soldiers don't wear jewels."

He turned her around to face him and gripped her hips tightly and leaned down to put his forehead to hers. "But you've given me your word that when this war is over, you will not be a soldier anymore. Then you will be my Queen, and only my Queen. And my Queen will wear jewels."

XII

Foster had been standing at the bar for a quarter of an hour. He was just about to decide she wasn't going to show when she entered. "Do you want to stand at the bar, or would you prefer a table?" he asked as she approached.

"A table, we can talk more privately there." She went to find a table. He ordered her a light ale and got another glass of water for himself.

As he joined her at the table, he said, "I noticed last night you were drinking a light ale. I hope it's okay that I ordered you another one."

"What do you want?" she demanded abruptly.

"What do you mean, what do I want? I thought I was pretty upfront with it. I wanted some company tonight," he said, looking a little confused.

"So all you want is for me to just drink with you? Be one of your buddies?" she asked skeptically.

"Is there some reason you have a problem with being friends with a man?"

"I didn't think men ever wanted to be just friends with women."

"I've spent the past eight years being used to conversing with my daughter, so I find a woman's company very pleasing. Is that a problem? If you don't want to converse with me, you don't have to. I can leave."

She somehow found herself oddly disappointed. *Buddies, he just wants to be buddies.* "You mentioned your daughter several times, how old is she and where's your wife?"

"My daughter is twenty-two and I've never been married. Her mother died when she was about six and the man who actually fathered her, well, I gathered he wasn't a very nice man. I've only had her since she was fourteen." Despite himself, a little anger crept into his voice as it always did when he thought of Sidel when he first met her.

"You took a fourteen-year-old girl on to raise? Why?" she asked in surprise.

"Because if I didn't look after the girl, nobody else would've. I don't know much about the Barbarian lands, but around here for a runaway girl, there is really only one occupation available, and as long as I had any say in the matter, she wasn't going to be forced to survive by earning her income on the flat of her back," he said angrily.

Bloodrose blinked and looked momentarily confused. "On the flat of her back? You don't mean as a ... as a whore?"

"Yeah, that's really the only means of survival for girls who don't have a man to protect them, at least in my country." He picked up his glass of water and started to down it. And then, of course, realizing it was only water, he angrily slammed it back on the table. "I need a drink."

She reached over and picked up the water and handed it to him. "Have some more water." He tried to glare at her, but he couldn't seem to manage it, and he started laughing. A thrill shot through him as he was awarded with a dazzling smile. "You really love your daughter, don't you?"

He grinned back at her. "Like all kids, she can be a real pain in the ass, but yeah, I love her."

Bloodrose cocked her head to the side and looked at him, as a light slowly dawned. "Wait a minute, your daughter, you said she was a Soldier of Ares. Is she is the one who's married to that Wolf Tribesman, the one who got in so much trouble? Oh, what was his name ..." Her brow furrowed as she drummed her fingers on the table trying to remember. Finally she snapped her fingers. "Brynjolf, that was it."

His eyes narrowed. "Married?"

"Yes, it was a big to do. Probably not long before you arrived in the camp. He was in a lot of trouble with Wolf Tribe, but fortunately for him, Eden and Bloodstone both backed him. He's kind of on probation. If he gets in any more trouble, he's going to be cast out of the tribe." As she watched his face, she realized she'd really stuck her foot in it. "You didn't know that, did you?"

"Well, I guess I now know what my daughter was keeping from me. So she's married to a troublemaker? Just brilliant, somehow it doesn't surprise me."

"Sorry I'm the one to tell you. I wish you would've known, but in her defense, it was a Wolf Tribesman. There might have been unusual circumstances involved."

"What do you mean, unusual circumstances, and why is being a Wolf Tribesman different than anyone else?"

"Well, she might have just intended to go to bed with him, not realizing Wolf Tribesmen don't just go to bed with girls." He raised an eyebrow in question. "Wolf Tribe's men can't seduce innocent girls without consequences." To her great annoyance, she knew herself to be blushing. *You're a healer, you should not be blushing just because you're talking about, well, you know, with a man. It wasn't like you are, well, you know, with him. Oh by the gods, I'm sounding like an ignorant child again,* she thought.

Foster didn't know what was coming over him, but he found her blush and sudden discomfort appealing. He couldn't imagine what possessed him to say, "I'm sorry, I'm not following you."

Her blush increased. She mentally kicked herself. *Bloodrose, get a handle on yourself. You are a healer. You can discuss this dispassionately.* "All of the Barbarian tribes have different marriage laws. Some of us don't have marriage, for example, Amazons. We don't have marriage laws at all. Which is why one of our kings way back in the past, decided that there had to be some arrangement for when tribes intermarried. So it was decided whoever's tribal laws were the strictest where marriage was concerned, were the ones that would be adhered to. So if a Wolf Tribesman takes a woman to his bed who is a virgin, by law she is his woman. Wolf Tribesmen have no word for wife, for them to say 'woman,' means wife."

Foster found himself more attracted to this woman than he should be. He also found a deep rooted desire to yank her out of her chair, settle her on his lap, and kiss her. Deciding she would probably clobber him, he asked instead, "So Amazons don't ever marry?"

"Well, my sister, the Queen, did once, but that was long ago, and under interesting circumstances - and oddly enough, to a Wolf Tribesman. Amazons and Wolf Tribesman usually don't intermix, has to do with that whole male-dominated/female-dominated not getting along. Fortunately, Henry got himself killed by my ..." she cut herself off abruptly. "I think it's getting late. I think we should go for a walk. Yes, I definitely think you need to walk." *By the gods, he must think I'm a blithering idiot. I can't ever seem to put more than two words together coherently. What is wrong with me today?* she demanded of herself. He rose and gestured to the door. Fortunately, they walked in silence for some time, allowing her to regain her composure.

"So who killed your brother-in-law?" Foster hoped he managed to sound casual as he asked that question. She clearly didn't want to talk about it.

"My family relationships are complicated. I'm sure they would bore you."

"Since I have to stay up all night, I have plenty of time to hear a complicated story," he replied smoothly.

"It's complicated."

"You said that already, and I like complicated."

She stopped walking and turned to face him. "What do you want?" she demanded, with her hands on her hips.

"That's a very general question to which there are many answers, but I think what you mean is in the more immediate, to which the answer is 'Who killed your brother-in-law?' because clearly that had some impact on your feelings toward others. I want to know why you're so distrustful of men. I'm afraid it's because a man hurt you very badly, which is the only reason why I haven't kissed you yet. I don't want to frighten you."

She glared at him. *Boy, was he annoying and smug, thinking he knew everything.* She continued to glare at him. "What do you care anyways? You just want another buddy."

"You don't care about your friends?"

"You know what? Fine, I'll tell you. Then you'll leave me alone, because after I answer your questions, you are not going to want anything to do with me. Who killed my brother? My mother, because she wasn't going to have her heir married to a Wolf Tribesman. She was furious that he seduced my sister; which given my sister's age, I actually almost have to agree with my mother on this one. My sister left the tribe and came back ten years later and killed my mother." She waited for him to run or at least look horrified, but instead he merely looked surprised.

"It doesn't sound like you liked your mother very much."

"I hated her, and so did my sister. Our mother was completely insane, demented, and sick, emphasis on the sick."

He raised an eyebrow, but shrugged his shoulders, put his hand on the small of her back and gently propelled her forward. As he continued to walk with her he asked, "So why do you distrust men so much? Is that too because of your mother?"

"I told you my mother was very sick. Things other women would cry about, she boasted about, trying to teach her daughters they were good things. Fortunately, Xanhara and I are both too intelligent to buy into her sick and demented thought processes."

"For example?"

She let the question hang in the air a long time. She'd never discussed the matter with anyone, not even Xanhara. It was one of those few things in life that she and her sister just had a silent understanding not to talk about. They talked about everything else, but not this, not this one thing. When Xanhara came home and took her place, they'd even talked about Henry and what he was like in bed. Her sister had left nothing out, telling her everything she wanted to know. She and

Xanhara had a very special relationship that many sisters don't have. Growing up in an entire tribe full of women, she knew how sisters could be, and she knew how women could be. She had no illusions about the relationships women forged with each other. She glanced over at the man walking silently next to her. She liked him. She had to admit she really liked him. She reached up and put her hand on his shoulder. He turned to look at her. She stopped walking. She stretched up on her toes and slid her arm around his neck. It took no more convincing than that. He bent down and kissed her. After a moment, she pulled away and went back to walking.

"My mother believed that Amazons should only mate with the strongest of warriors," she said abruptly. Foster, realizing she was making up her mind on whether to tell him the rest, decided to just be quiet and continued to walk, but he already had a feeling he didn't like where this was going. After several more minutes she went on. "When my mother decided it was time for her to produce an heir, as was her duty, she knew that she was a superior swordswoman. So she started challenging men. And that if they could take it, they could have it, but she would bed no man who wasn't strong enough to take it." Foster sometimes really hated being right. "It was nearly two years before the first man defeated her in battle and took his prize. That man fathered my sister. After having an heir, she no longer felt the need to go out and pursue violent men. Occasionally, men who had heard of her challenge would show up and try to claim his prize. My understanding is over the next seven years, two men succeeded in claiming the prize. But it was nearly eight years after the birth of my sister, when my mother caught a man trespassing on our lands ..." her tone went cold. "Apparently, the fight was incredibly short. He defeated my mother in a few strokes of his blade and sent her crashing to her backside. She said she was just in the process of pushing herself up, when he put his sword to her chest and he told my mother, 'If you want to keep your life, you lay back down and pull up your skirt and spread your legs to me' ..." She choked on a little sob. Foster wondered what kind of demented psycho would tell their daughter of such a thing. "So you see how demented and sick my mother was. She actually boasted of the prowess of my father, that he defeated her so easily. Every man before him the battles have been hard won, but he did it without even breaking a sweat. My mother said it was remarkable, given his small stature. As you can guess, I followed nine months later. So now that you know what a crazy person my mother was, I'm sure you won't want to be my friend."

"Why would I desire not to be your friend? Just because your mother's insane? You do realize that you are not responsible for the sins of your mother, or the crimes of your father?"

"It really doesn't disgust you and make you want to have nothing to do with me?" she asked, looking dubious.

"I did not say that. It most definitely disgusts me; but not you. You were an innocent victim. In fact, you didn't even exist yet. I'm sure plenty of people will think what I'm about to say is strange, but I think it is a very good thing your sister put your mother to death. I know very well that we are not our parents. One of my very young soldier's father was an awful man. He raped more women than we even know about, beat them, abused them. Some of them he even held prisoner. He killed twenty before we caught him. We know he had dozens, if not hundreds more victims. The boy's mother was one of his father's many victims. Her father, being a true son of a bitch, cast her out when he found out she was pregnant. After being raped and beaten, not knowing what to do, she came to us. She's one of the cooks in our kitchen. She loves that boy though. He's a good man - well he's not quite a man yet, but close. He's going to be a good one, and he knows nothing of his father. We've all made very, very sure of that. He only knows that his grandfather was a son of a bitch."

Bloodrose turned to face him. "You have a thing for strays, don't you?" To her astonishment, he blushed.

His eyes went a little misty as he looked down at her. "I grew up on a farm. My parents never turned anybody away, no matter how rough that particular month had been. My parents always had food for everybody who needed a meal. We lived hand to mouth and it was glorious. I had two older brothers and two older sisters. I was the baby. My sisters both went on and married good men - one a soldier, one a farmer. It was the soldier, who was a Soldier of Ares, who I admired. It didn't take long before I decided I wanted to be just like him. My two brothers stayed on to take care of the farm, and here I am. But I do love going back to the farm and working with the animals, helping with the crops, but mostly my life is here now." She slid both of her arms around his neck and pulled him down and kissed him again. After several minutes of kissing, he pulled away. "I should take you back to your quarters. You need your rest, you're not stuck staying up all night." She opened her mouth to protest, but he put a finger over her lips. "I'll go stand an extra watch at one of the gates. I won't go to sleep, I promise." She nodded her consent.

After leaving her at her door, he went in search of the Wolf Tribesmen section of the camp. His daughter had a lot of explaining to do, and it didn't seem to matter to him that it was one in the morning. Asking directions, he found his way to Brynjolf's tent. He drew his dagger and slammed the butt of it into the post next to the tent flap. He instantly heard rustling and moving. He quickly sheathed his dagger. A moment later, the tent flap was cautiously pulled aside about six inches, and standing to Foster's left of the gap was a man holding a sword. He looked at Foster suspiciously. "What's amiss?" he demanded.

Foster was beginning to wonder if all Barbarian men were powerfully built. He hadn't yet seen one who was not. He also decided all Wolf Tribesmen must wear hunter green kilts, because again, this man was powerfully built with a few scars, and wearing only a hunter green kilt. "Is Sidel here? I want to speak to her now."

The man who Foster assumed was Brynjolf quickly pointed the blade at him. "Whatever you want with my woman, it can wait until a decent hour. Be gone."

"You mistakenly assumed that was a question," Foster snapped back at the man.

"No, I assume correctly. If you want to talk to my woman, you're going to have to go through me."

A voice interrupted them both. "Brynjolf, step aside and let the Colonel in. He would not be here if it was not important."

Brynjolf grumbled and turned back to the tent, holding the flap aside for Foster to enter. "Who gives the orders in this family, me or you, Woman?" he demanded angrily.

Sidel glanced at Brynjolf. "We'll have that argument later. In the meantime, this is my Colonel, Colonel Stephen Foster. This is my …" Sidel blushed. "husband, Brynjolf. Brynjolf, this is the man who raised me." To Foster's surprise, all irritation left the man. He nodded respectfully and extended his hand, and the two men shook.

"So, did you ever intend to tell me that you had married?"

"I was getting around to it, and who hit you?" she countered quickly.

"Eden. He gave me a concussion and broke some of my ribs."

Brynjolf and Sidel exchanged looks, but it was Brynjolf who spoke. "What did you do to piss him off?"

"Why does everybody automatically assume I'm the one who did something wrong?" Foster demanded, looking irritated.

"Because we all know Eden, and Eden wouldn't just deck you for no reason," Brynjolf replied.

"As it happens, it was a misunderstanding, and we're both now on excellent terms." Brynjolf shot a questioning glance at Sidel, who nodded.

"So what brings you to our quarters in the middle of the night, Colonel?" asked Sidel.

"Our quarters?" He groaned and rubbed his face. He was getting too old. "I just wanted to come and wish my daughter joy in her marriage, since you didn't even bother to tell me you were getting married. Any suggestions on a wedding present for you, daughter?" he said with irritation.

"Well, if you will have it, your first grandchild probably needs clothes and blankets. Helena is trying to teach me to knit, but I'm not any good at it."

Foster blinked and stared at his daughter. "What do you mean if I'll have it?" he demanded angrily.

"I didn't know how you'd feel about the fact that your grandchild's going to be half Barbarian." She looked concerned. He rolled his eyes and crossed over to her, gave her a hug, and kissed her on the forehead.

"The only thing I care about is that it's healthy and that you're happy." He glared over her shoulder at Brynjolf, who merely smiled. He extended his hand again to Brynjolf. "Congratulations to you as well, Brynjolf. I hope you realize if you hurt my daughter, I will make sure you regret it." Brynjolf shook his hand and nodded.

Sidel was watching the Colonel suspiciously. "What is wrong, you don't look happy."

"It's nothing for you to concern yourself with. Just be happy with your husband."

"Don't make me beat it out of you," she replied with a grin.

"Oh, I just met a beautiful woman. She's only six years older than you are, so needless to say it's not an appropriate relationship," he sighed.

"Colonel, you know I love you like a father. And in the eight years you've raised me, you've been a far better father than the man who raised me for the first fourteen years. But you actually aren't old enough to be my father. I think you're a few years shy of that. So what if she's only six years older than me, you like her. That's all that matters. Does she like you, and do I know her? What's her name?" she asked with excitement.

"Bloodrose."

Sidel turned to look at Brynjolf and shrugged her shoulders. "I haven't met that one. Do you know her?"

"I have not met her, but I do know of her. She is sister to the Queen of the Amazons and I believe she is now heir to the throne now that Amber, the Queen's daughter, is a Wolf Tribesman and married to Black Stone. But I am uncertain as to whether there any other sisters."

"You have the hots for an Amazon. Nice work, Colonel," she said, looking impressed.

"Sidel, that is not an appropriate way to be speaking," Foster snapped at her.

Sidel looked at him quizzically. "Colonel, have you been with a woman since you took me on?"

"Sidel," snapped the Colonel, looking horrified. "That is absolutely not an appropriate question for you to be asking any man, let alone your father!"

"Oh dear, this is worse than I thought. I knew in the four years I shared your quarters, if you'd been with any woman, you took discretion to a whole new level, but damn, that's even worse than I thought."

Brynjolf decided the Colonel needed rescuing. He gave his woman a pinch. She turned to glare at him and he gave her a silencing glance. "Woman, since I don't think any of us are going to get back to bed and the Colonel needs someone to stay up with him, why don't you make us all breakfast and stop bothering the poor man." She stuck her tongue out at him, but obeyed.

XIV

Six weeks later, Bloodstone was on her way to Black Stone's tent. He and Amber had arrived late last night - the last of the family to return, and Bloodstone had to admit she was so glad to finally have all of her family back together again. She was also glad that now that he was home, she could happily hand the reins of the encampment back over to him. She hoped he didn't think because he arrived late last night, she was going to give him a few days to acclimatize himself. After running the camp by herself for two months, she was more than willing to throw him to the lions.

Arriving at Black Stone's tent, Sergeant Henderson showed her in without announcing her. Black Stone was sitting at his desk looking a little lost. Bloodstone chuckled, crossed to the chair on this side of the desk and dropped into it. "What did you do to my desk, Woman?" he demanded, looking irritated.

"I organized it. Now you should actually be able to find everything easily. How you were able to work on that thing previously is beyond me." Snapping her fingers, she rose to her feet. "By the way, this is all of your personal correspondence. I didn't open any of it." She picked up a large crate and brought it back over and set it in front of him on the desk.

He groaned, as it was almost overflowing. "Why did you leave all of that for me?" he asked irritated.

She picked up one of the letters on top and turned it so he could see that written on it in a bold hand was 'personal confidential'. "Might have something to do with that," she said, tapping it with a finger.

Black Stone groaned again. "You could've opened them. I would not have minded," he replied with a laugh. Then he sighed again and began sorting his personal correspondence, as he listened to Bloodstone give a full and detailed report of the last two months. He was about midway through the crate when he discovered a large packet. Turning it over to see who it was from, he tossed it at Bloodstone. "There's that information you requested on that man Brown. Now, see, had you opened my personal correspondence, you would've gotten it sooner."

Bloodstone glared at him as she opened the packet and continued with her report. When she was finally finished, they sat in silence for a few minutes, Black Stone sorting mail, her reading the file. She turned back to the beginning and began reading the file again, asking as she did so, "Black Stone, how much would it cost for a Corporal to buy out honorably?"

"Depends on how many years he has left on his contract, and how long the contract was to begin with," he said, stopping what he was doing and leaning back in his chair. He surveyed her with curiosity.

"Two and a half years of a six-year contract," she replied, without even looking up.

"Has Brown asked you about buying out his contract?"

"No, I'm asking you how much to buy his contract. I want him."

"Two and a half years of a six-year … given my reluctance right now to give up any good fighting men, I would say a hundred gold. But what has he done to cause you to want to buy his contract?"

"I'll bring your money this afternoon. I want his contract, Black Stone, and my reasons are my own."

Black Stone pursed his lips together in disapproval, but nodded his head in agreement. "Very well, I will have the papers ready."

"I've also taken the liberty of calling a meeting of the officers here at two, since there's still the matter of that third party we have not yet had time to address."

Black Stone nodded. As he continued opening his mail, Bloodstone quietly excused herself. He waited until he was sure his sister was well away before he called for Sergeant Henderson.

"Yes, General? What can I do for you?"

"Go and find my brother-in-law. Tell Eden I need to see him at once, don't speak to him in front of my sister, and go yourself." The Sergeant nodded and excused himself.

A half an hour later, Eden entered. "You wish to see me urgently, Black Stone? Is something the matter?"

"My sister does not know we're meeting, does she?"

"No, why?"

"My sister just informed me she's buying out a man named Brown's contract. Are you familiar with him?"

"Not exactly, we dealt with him some immediately after we rescued the oracles, but to the best of my knowledge, no, neither one of us have had anything to do with him. Why would she buy out his contract, and what does that mean?"

"I'm not exactly sure what she intends. Once she owns his contract, ultimately he is her employee until the terms of the contract are met. It is not unusual for the State Knights to buy out the contract of a Lord's Knight because they want the man to work for them. It's not uncommon for the Church of Athena to buy out contracts of State Soldiers because they want their skills and experience, but she didn't say the church was buying it. She said she was buying it and I don't know, something just feels odd about it. I forgot to mention this. Right after the battle where we rescued the oracles, she asked me for his records. I sent for them. They arrived while I was gone; but she didn't open my personal correspondence, and they were marked 'personal'. It was while reading his file she demanded to buy his contract. I had no reason to deny her, but I don't like it. I thought you should be made aware of it."

"I appreciate that very much. I think perhaps I should go and have a conversation with this man Brown."

"I think you should too. Make sure to be back here by two. If you're late to the meeting, your woman will know something's up."

Eden nodded and excused himself. Remembering that Brown was part of Andrew's infantry, he went in search of the Twelfth. Once finding them, it didn't take long to find Brown. Everyone seemed to know him. To Eden's surprise, however, Brown was training a group of swordsmen. This surprised him since he never saw anyone but sergeants do training. As he watched, he saw the man was good. He was standing there with his arms crossed, observing, when he heard from behind him, "What brings you out here?" asked Andrew, with only mild curiosity.

"What do you know about that man Brown, and why is a Corporal training your troops?" Eden asked, without taking his eyes off the man.

"An enigma, that's what he is. I never can seem to figure him out. He's been in the Twelfth longer than I have, though not by much. He should be a Staff Sergeant by this time, if not a Master Sergeant, and yet he continues to be a Corporal. He'll be promoted, and then he promptly gets himself demoted. I myself have promoted him twice. That's the thing about him. He always does just enough to get himself demoted, not enough to suffer any great punishment. I just can't seem to figure him out. He's good, damn good, Eden. I wish I had a dozen more like him. He's smart, he thinks on his feet ..." Andrew cut himself off abruptly.

"But what, Andrew?"

"Some of the things he knows." Andrew made a face. "He shouldn't know them. They're not the kind of things a soldier knows. And the things he says one minute, he sounds like any other soldier, and the next minute, he's saying something no normal soldier ever says. It's like he wants to pretend not to be as well educated as he is. And

184

according to those who were here before him, he was fully trained when we got him. Showed up without a coin to his name, no weapons, no nothing, just wanted to enlist for four years. Then he turned around and enlisted for six more. He's a career soldier, be stupid for him to be anything else." Andrew turned to look at him. "Why the curiosity all of a sudden?"

"I'm not sure. Can I borrow him for half an hour?"

In response, Andrew bellowed, "Corporal Brown, I need to see you."

A moment later, Corporal Brown came walking up and saluted. "You wish to see me, Colonel?"

"Our Barbarian ally has asked to borrow you for a little while." Not waiting for a response, Andrew turned and went back to training his men. Brown slowly turned to face Eden. He knew the Big Barbarian's name. He had made it his business to learn everything he could about the General, though he, like so many of the Bretons, never thought of Eden as anything but the Big Barbarian. The two stood there staring at each other for a long moment. Finally, Eden jerked his head indicating Brown was to follow him. Seeing nothing else to do but to follow him, after all, his Colonel had ordered him to help him, he did as he was bid. Eden turned and headed in the direction of the Wolf Tribesmen's section of the encampment.

Eden went straight for the Mead Hall. Once inside, he turned to face Corporal Brown, crossed his arms over his chest, and asked, "How do you know my woman?"

Brown considered for a long time, then said, "I'm not sure I wish to have this conversation in here. Isn't this a place where you're supposed to meet and settle your differences nonviolently?" Eden nodded his head. "Then as I said, I think we should have this conversation elsewhere."

"Why do you say that this is going to end in violence?" Eden demanded.

"Because when I answer your questions, you're going to kill me ..." Eden raised an eyebrow. "but that's okay, I've had it coming for eight years so ..." he shrugged his shoulders, "might as well get it over with. Where do you want me to begin?"

"As General Black Stone is so fond of informing me, he always feels the best place to begin is at the beginning. So where would you say that was?"

"When I was eleven, my father was much lesser nobility and I am the third son, so needless to say, not very important to him. When it became time for me to begin training for the Knighthood, my father chose a man named Lord Wichcrest. Not a bad man, just weak. I spent the next seven years training hard for the Knighthood. I had only

186

been a Knight a few months when I was assigned the rather dubious honor of acting as guard for his son, the young Lord. Though I shouldn't say his young Lordship - he was older than I, nearly thirty. He was also a drunkard, a gambler, and opium addict, but despite these flaws, he was the son of my Lord. As a Knight sworn in service to his family, I had to do my duty whether I liked it or not. One morning early, I was informed that my charge wished to go for a long ride. It was a little before midday when we entered the mountains. I thought this strange, since I knew the Temple of the Mountain Pass was not far off, and that was an Athenian temple. My Lord and his son both had very strong objections to Athenians. I don't know if you've ever been that way, but there's a very large section of forest on the side of the mountain; it is actually rather pretty to ride through. His Lordship informed me that he wished some solitude on the mountain and told me to wait at the base and he would be back in less than an hour. I, of course, knew this was a lie. I assumed he was either going to get more opium, or perhaps to pay off one of his debts in private. This was not the first clandestine meeting I been forced to accompany him on and he always made me wait, but he was my Lord and I could not call him a liar, nor could I argue with his orders. After nearly two hours had passed and he had not come, I went in search of him. I found the boy first, just a kid, couldn't have been sixteen. His cold, sightless eyes still haunt my dreams. He'd been stuck to a tree with his sword. He clearly had been run through

187

the guts and left just to die there. It had to have been an excruciating way to go, and from the looks of his hands, I would say he tried to pull the sword free, but he had not the strength. I drew my sword fearing the worst, that I failed my Lord. I would find his son's body nearby. When I entered the little clearing, I found my Lord sitting slumped, breathing heavily, exhausted. He was covered in blood. It wasn't until I drew close that I saw the garments of the priestess. A little thing, by the gods, she was a bloody mess. I couldn't understand what had happened, and then I saw his knife. It was still sticking in her belly. His father'd given him that knife. It had an elaborate hilt, easily identified. I fear I must've stood there for a full minute like a fool. Though I did not like the man, I found it impossible to believe what I saw had actually happened, but clearly it had. From his own disrobed state and the girl's nakedness, he had clearly raped and beaten her. I grabbed him and yanked him to his feet and shook him. His face was bleeding badly. She'd clawed him viciously, fighting for her life. I honestly can't even remember what I said to him. I remember what he said though. He said, 'The little bitch deserved it. She clawed my face.' I looked back down on the corpse of the dead girl. He ordered me to take my hands off of him and to go and find his horse. I knew he had to pay for what he had done, but I couldn't take him to the temple of the Athenians. He was a noble, and not subject to their laws. I should have taken him to the Lord of that area, but I didn't. I failed her utterly. I thought my master

188

was a good man and he would deal with his son properly for his crimes. So, I went and retrieved the horses. When I came back, her body was gone. I don't know what he did with it, but clearly she was dead. Had I believed, or even thought for a second, she was still alive, no order he could have given me would have prevented me from taking him and her to the Athenians. But she was such a little thing and her eyes half open stared blankly. She was blue, so I truly believed she was dead. So I did what I thought was right. I took him home. I went straight to my Lord and informed him of everything. To my complete and utter shock, he ordered me never to repeat a word of what had happened. He promoted me and doubled my income, then sent me from the room. As I walked from it, it became clear to me that he intended to cover it up. He was my Lord and I must obey him and not repeat anything that had transpired, but I could no longer stomach being in his service. Later that night, I traded clothes with one of the stable boys who was about my size, traded boots with another, and disappeared, never to be seen or heard from again. I was working my way across country doing odd jobs when I heard the Twelfth was enlisting men. So I changed my name and enlisted. Here I am, I've been here ever since." As Brown's story came to an end, he was wondering why he had been permitted to finish it. He would've thought the Big Barbarian would long since have killed him, but instead he was just staring.

"I will never understand you Bretons. That man defiled, abused, and nearly murdered an innocent little child, a ten-year-old little girl, murdered a young boy, ruined your career and changed your life forever, and his life continues on unchecked." Eden stood there seething for a long time. "What is opium?" Eden demanded abruptly.

"You smoke it like tobacco, but it makes you very lethargic like you don't care. Why?"

"Did he use this a lot?"

"All the time, why?" Eden turned and walked out. Brown, seeing nothing else to do, did what he considered reasonable, he followed Eden.

Eden entered his brother's tent without announcing himself. Seeing Seva, he nodded to her and reached back and pulled the tent flap open, waiting for Brown to enter. Then he turned back to his sister. "You are an herbalist, are you familiar with something called opium?"

She slowly shook her head. "I might be, but not under that name. What does it do?" He quickly repeated what Brown had told him. She slowly nodded. "Yes, I believe I am familiar with it then, though we call it Scarlet. Well, Scarlet is how it would translate into the Breton tongue. Why?"

"Prolonged use of it, does it cause impotence?" She nodded her head and was beginning to look

190

worried. "If you used that and you were a drunkard, would that cause you to be irrational and maybe fly into unreasonable rages in addition to the impotence?"

"Yes. Eden, please explain what's going on. You're scaring me." Seeing how concerned his sister was, he crossed over to her and grabbed her by the shoulders. He bent down and kissed her on the forehead.

"I promise you, it is a very old matter and nothing for you to concern yourself with. I just wanted to make sure I understood things. Thank you for your assistance." Seeing she still looked worried, he hugged her tightly. "I promise."

Once they were several feet away from the woman's tent, Brown asked, "Are you going to explain to me what's going on and why you haven't killed me yet? I would've thought you would've killed me long ago."

"Why? You did nothing wrong. You're a soldier merely following orders. As a man who gives orders, I expect my men to follow them, and sometimes good men have to follow the orders of bad men. I cannot blame you for that, and now I know who I'm going to kill."

As they walked, Brown considered everything Eden had asked about. He asked abruptly, "Impotence, you asked about that twice. You also

asked about unreasonable rages, is that why he beat
her so badly? His own degenerate life coming
back to haunt him and he took it out on her? By
the gods, I knew I should've killed that man."

Eden turned and grabbed Brown by the tunic
with both hands. "Let's be very clear on this. He's
mine. I may not be able to kill him right now, but I
promise you I will make special time for it later."
Brown swallowed hard and stared up at the Big
Barbarian. Brown was not a man easily
intimidated. This man, however, managed to.
Brown gave a single nod. Eden released him and
continued walking. "By the way, I should warn
you, my woman has bought your contract from the
State Soldiers. I have no idea what she has in
mind."

XV

Eden arrived at Black Stone's tent with Brown. As the two of them entered the tent, Eden took a quick look around. He must be the last to arrive because Andrew, Murtaugh, Big Bear, Xanhara, Bloodrose, Victor, Autumn, Bloodstone, Daniel, Dex, Fletcher, and Foster were already present. A few eyebrows were raised in Brown's direction, but nobody questioned it. As Eden quickly surveyed the room, he noticed two large decanters and two trays of glasses sitting on the table in front of Black Stone.

Black Stone picked up one of the decanters and handed it to Eden. Then grabbing the other one, he began filling glasses. Eden, following his lead, also began filling glasses. When everyone had a glass, Black Stone said, "I hope you all join me in lifting a glass to the newest member of the Stone family - Lord Lewis Daniel Stone, second son to my brother Daniel, born eight days ago." They all drank to the health of the new infant, his mother and his father, then everyone took turns congratulating Daniel, who blushed slightly at the attention.

"Okay, I have a question," Eden said abruptly. All eyes turned to face him. "Who is the Stone Wall?"

Everyone looked confused for a long moment. Finally, Black Stone said, "Well, my understanding is the Stone Wall is what Murtaugh nicknamed my siblings and I," he hesitated a moment, "but I think I see what you mean. The Stone Wall isn't just Stones anymore, is it?"

"I don't know. That's what I'm asking. Who is the Stone Wall?"

"You know, I once heard Murtaugh call Father the head of the Stone Wall. I know there are plenty that would think that now makes me the head, but I don't think so, and I don't think I'm the right person to answer that question." He turned to stare at Murtaugh. "So who is the Stone Wall now?"

As all eyes turned to face him, Murtaugh looked horrified. "What, me? Why is everyone looking at me?"

"Because you created it. You started it. So you should say who it is," said Andrew.

Murtaugh considered a long moment, and then he realized without even thinking about it, he had expanded in his mind who he considered the Stone Wall. "The original Stones in the wall are the brothers and Bloodstone, and of course, His Grace, the late Duke of Stone Reach, but I don't think that's all the members anymore. But I also don't think it's for me to say who they are. I think like

194

any wall, it's built one stone at a time. So I think the Stones in the wall should decide who else is a part of it." Black Stone, Bloodstone, Andrew and Daniel all spoke simultaneously.

Black Stone, "Eden."

Bloodstone, "Murtaugh."

Daniel, "Now wait a minute, I would like to lodge a complaint."

Andrew, "Fletcher."

Black Stone said with a laugh, "Why am I not surprised. If somebody was going to complain about this arrangement, it was going to be you, Daniel. What is your complaint?"

"I think you have to have proven yourself an adult before you can be added into the ranks of the Stone Wall, which means in my opinion, Patrick and Edward aren't there yet." Everyone in the room nodded their head in agreement, even those not involved in the conversation. "Good, I'm glad we all agree on that. Now that that was said, I have no objection to the three new members. Does anyone else?" This time, only the members of the Stone Wall shook their heads. "Good, I would also like to add Big Bear."

Andrew said quickly, "I have no objections to Anthony." Big Bear sighed and shook his head.

"Anthony?" questioned Viktor.

"Yes, apparently Big Bear's mother didn't actually name him Big Bear, his name is Anthony," Andrew replied quickly.

As Big Bear blushed and looked uncomfortable at all the attention he was now receiving, Bloodstone decided to take pity on the big man and said, "Viktor, unless of course, you men feel that the only way to contribute to the Stone Wall is to be a warrior?"

Eden said, "I would like to add Xanhara, Amber, Tabitha, Helena, and Rebecca - two skilled warriors, one skilled healer, and two women I would not wish to be on their bad side." They all nodded in quick agreement. "I would also like to say that there's nothing wrong with looking at the younger ones as future members. I, myself, consider Innish a future member."

Black Stone laughed and nodded. "Then let's drink another toast to all future members, to good friends, and good allies." Everyone happily drank. Then Black Stone sighed. "It is unfortunate that I have to follow such good times with battle plans, but as most of you are aware, right before Bloody Fang showed up and everything went crazy around here, we had discovered the existence of a third player. A third player we have as of yet not investigated. The reason this meeting has been called is, we are going to decide who is going to investigate and who they're taking with them."

"Well, since I used to live on those mountains and have investigated some of the caves, I wish to lead the group," said Bloodstone.

"The difficult part about this is going to be deciding how many people are necessary to take. What's a safe number to take? On the off chance that these people are not hostile, we need to find the number that will be between enough to protect ourselves, and not so many that they'll feel they are being invaded," said Black Stone.

"Well, we all know if I'm going Eden's going. I don't know what other Barbarians he will feel it is necessary to drag along, but we will need to take a healer," Bloodstone added.

All eyes turned to face Eden. "Well, given the fact that a Bear Tribesman started all this, I think Big Bear should accompany us. And if I'm going, only one of my woman's guards need go, so we'll take Dex. I will also take Matthias, William, and Murtaugh. That is, of course, if Fletcher won't mind the responsibility of looking out for my son, Murtaugh's woman, and Big Bear's wife and child? They will, of course, have guards, but I would feel more comfortable with someone overseeing them," asked Eden politely.

"It would be my honor to look out for your ladies and children in your absence," Fletcher replied quickly.

"I would like to go, if you will have me, General," said Foster.

"I will go as healer." Everyone looked to see who spoke. To their astonishment, it was Bloodrose. Even Xanhara looked surprised.

"How many of your men will you wish to take with you, Colonel?" asked Bloodstone.

"I would prefer to know how many men you feel are necessary before I make such a request," replied Foster.

"Xanhara, how many warriors do you feel it necessary to send to protect your heir?" questioned Eden.

"With all of you going, I feel she will be in safe hands. But as my heir, she does need to take at least two warriors with her, and I would feel that that would be sufficient," replied Xanhara.

"Xanhara, please stop referring to me as your heir. We all know when you die, if I'm still alive, Autumn will wait maybe twenty-four hours out of decency before she pounds me into the ground and takes the throne. Fortunately, I don't feel she'll find it necessary to kill me to do it," Bloodrose replied peevishly.

198

"No, I'll beat you with my fists. Then you won't have to worry about any scars either," Autumn replied quickly.

"Please don't punch me in the face," Bloodrose said pleadingly.

Foster found he had to bite his tongue to keep out of the conversation between the Amazons. He did not like the idea of the large warrior attacking Bloodrose. The woman, Autumn, must be nearly twice Bloodrose's size.

"Well then, including Eden, that makes nine Barbarian warriors. So I will take eight additional Church Soldiers. Captain Daniel Stone - if you let me have him - and eight State Soldiers; which means in addition to you, Colonel, you may bring eight Soldiers of Ares. If that suits you, then nobody can say they're outnumbered - except of course, poor Bloodrose." At that, everyone turned to face the healer.

"That suits me just fine, General," replied Foster.

"Then I will meet you all at first light at the Eastern stables," said Bloodstone.

"Any further questions?" They all shook their heads. "Is there anything else anyone wishes to discuss at this time?" Again, they all shook their heads. "Then, dismissed," said Black Stone.

Foster was amongst the first to exit the tent, but he hung back waiting for Bloodrose to exit. She said a few parting words to her sister and then they separated. He waited a moment and then approached her. "You know, I don't think I thanked you properly for making me dinner last night."

"I do recall you saying thank you."

"Yes, but given how many times you have made me dinner over the past month, simply saying thank you again seems inadequate. I had this made for you. I hope you like it." He handed her a fabric wrapped parcel, only about two inches square. She took it and unwrapped it. Inside on a leather cord was a silver medallion, on one side was a tree, on the other side was a wolf curled up. She looked up at him in surprise. "I did a little investigating and it seems that this wild looking tree and a sleeping wolf are considered the two symbols of Seana."

She threw her arms around his neck and kissed him passionately. "I love it! It's beautiful!"

They walked in silence for some minutes before he said, "I've been thinking a lot about something the past few days. I feel I have to say what's on my mind, but before I do, I would like to ask you a favor. After I say what I'm going to say, please don't answer right away. Please do me the honor of considering what I have to say before you reply. I know it might not alter your decision, but it would make me feel better if you considered it before you answered." She nodded and looked at him with some concern. "I know that you've stated firmly that Amazons don't marry, ever. So I was wondering if you might be willing to meet me halfway. I'm very fond of you and I would like very much to spend the rest of my life with you, however long or short that time is - and let's be honest, I'm a Soldier of Ares. I could be killed in battle in a day. But I would like it very much if you would consent to live with me for the rest of my life."

Bloodrose turned to him and opened her mouth to speak; but then remembering, she changed what she was about to say. "I will consider your offer for a few days. We'll speak more on this matter later. For now, I think we both have much preparation to do for the coming journey." She took his face in both her hands and kissed him again.

XVI

When Bloodstone returned home, she sat down at her desk and began making a list of everything they would need to take with them. She determined that they were going to need two wagons and at least ten handlers to deal with the horses. She also decided that it was best to ask Sergeant Major Fletcher if his stables could deal with the horses for perhaps as much as two weeks; then the horses would only be a couple of hours from the cave, but would have sufficient shelter if by chance there was a freak summer storm. "Sergeant Simon, would you send for Sergeant Major Fletcher?"

Sergeant Simon peeked his head in. "Right away, General."

Sergeant Major Fletcher arrived an hour later. "You sent for me, General?"

"Yes, it appears as though our destination is not that far from your village. I was wondering if your stables might be able to accommodate forty horses."

"Yes, General. It will be a bit of a tight fit, but they'd only need to be in there if we're going to have a storm. Otherwise, the pasture would do very nicely. The only thing is that would be more horses than my family could handle."

"Then I see no problem. I was intending to take ten handlers and everything our horses will require. There would be nothing for your family to bother about, other than of course, allowing us the use of your stables."

"Of course, General. My stables are at your disposal. Is there anything else you require of me, General?"

"No, Fletcher, but thank you for keeping an eye on the baby while we are gone. I very much appreciate it."

"He is my grandson. It is my privilege to keep an eye on him. And I'll keep an eye on the older one too, if it happens that Lord Andrew and Lord Fitzwilliam have duty. I will make sure that the boy is not alone."

"Thank you, again, I appreciate it."

Bloodstone was at the stables at five checking the wagons' cargo, when the others started arriving. As soon as Brown arrived, he approached her. "Corporal Brown reporting as ordered, Sir."

She grabbed a large canvas bag and pulled him aside, tossing the bag down in front of him. She said, "You're in the wrong armor."

"I'm sorry, Sir, I don't follow you."

"Let's cut through the shit, Brown. You and I both know you're in the wrong armor. If you choose to continue to be called Brown, that's your decision, but I swore an oath to defend justice and you continuing to be a foot soldier is an injustice to you and an injustice to this army. A man named Brown may not be able to be a Knight in the State Knights, but he can be a Church Knight. So I say again, you're in the wrong armor. Get changed and mount up." With that, she turned and walked away. Brown knelt down and opened the bag. Inside was a suit of the leather armor the Church Knights always wore when they wanted to be stealthy. It was the exact same kind of armor General Bloodstone herself was wearing today. He quickly stripped out of his state soldier's armor and put on the leather. It felt strange to wear something so high quality, though it clearly had been fashioned for another man. She had obviously made alterations to it. He was impressed. Without ever having tried it on, it fit like a well-made glove. He wondered when she found the time. The woman seemed never to sleep.

As he approached the General, she glanced over her shoulder at him. "You know, Brown, I will find it very confusing having two Captain Browns under my command."

"Captain?"

"Yes, Captain Brown, unless you intend to give me another name." He slowly shook his head.

"Thought not." She gave him her full attention. "Looks good on you. When we return, you will not be returning with us. You're going to go to the village of Temple Hill. Our armorers here in camp are too busy to construct an entire suit of plate mail. I believe I can persuade the armorer there to make your suit a priority."

"General, with all due respect, this isn't right. The things that I've done should prevent me from holding such an honorable position. Besides, I could never afford a suit of plate mail, so perhaps I should go change into my old armor."

"Only if you want to end up in the stockade for being in the wrong armor, though I could charge you with being a spy. Fortunately for you, we're Church Knights, not State Knights. We don't expect our Knights to be able to afford to pay for their armor themselves. Now Captain Brown, if you don't mind, I'm busy and you need to go check on your men. You might find some of your other men interesting." She jerked her head in the direction of the Church Soldiers.

Brown, realizing he was never going to win this argument, went to check on his men and make sure that they were ready to go. To his amazement, five of them were very familiar faces. "What in Hades are the five of you doing in church armor?" he demanded, as he grabbed Tom's shoulder piece and shook him.

"General told us she was gonna buy out your contract and she was gonna to make you a Knight. Asked if we wanted to be under your command still, so she bought all of our contracts out, so you're stuck with us. You didn't get away from us," Tom replied with a grin.

Brown cuffed the boy upside the head affectionately, then remembering he was a Knight now, he sobered. "Well, unfortunately boys, I don't think we'll be allowed to socialize anymore."

Bloodstone, hearing that remark, tossed over her shoulder at them, "You keep forgetting, Brown, we're Church Soldiers, not State Soldiers. We're not quite so stuffy. You're allowed to socialize, you're allowed to drink with your subordinates, you're just not allowed have sex with them."

Brown looked embarrassed and turned to face her. "You don't have to worry about that, Sir, none of them are exactly my type."

Bloodstone laughed. "Again, Brown, you are forgetting that this is the church. A healer or rank one priestess are considered subordinates of yours. A rank two is considered your equal, a rank three is considered your superior." She turned and looked past him at the other soldiers. "Which means to you boys, all priestesses are off limits. The healers are fair game though." She nodded to her men. "Now if you men will excuse me, I have to go see what kind of humor Cedric is in this morning."

A quarter of an hour later had them on the road heading for the cave. Bloodstone moved alongside Big Bear. "Are you sure you can find the cave on this end?"

"Yes, most Bear Tribesmen explore the caves at some point in time. I know the cave Tobias was talking about, though I have never explored it much. There is cave that wanders from our side of the mountains to your side of the mountains. It would be safer to enter on your side of the mountains. Tobias drew me good map. I know how to find the path where he found the sword."

"You know, Big Bear, your speech is coming along very nicely. Brienna has done an excellent job improving it, however, you still drop your 'a'." He shot her a questioning glance. "Tobias drew me **a** good map. There is **a** cave that wanders."

"Damn, I will work on it."

Bloodstone reached over and squeezed him affectionately on the shoulder. "Don't let me discourage you, that was not my intention. You are doing wonderfully."

"Not discouraged, just frustrated. Why do you people have to use so many words? Why is less not better?" Everyone around started laughing.

"Because Tobias didn't use enough words, so consequently none of us could understand him," replied Murtaugh quickly. Big Bear sighed and nodded.

It was midday on their second day when Big Bear pointed. "There it is. I knew it could not be far."

Bloodstone looked up and up. "You could've mentioned that we were going to have to scale the side of one of the mountains to get to it," she remarked casually.

Big Bear looked up again. "Hmm, that could be problem." Bloodstone looked at him and nudged him with her elbow. Not following her, he continued to stare.

Eden cleared his throat and coughed out, "A."

"Dammit, that could be **a** problem."

They all dismounted and Bloodstone ordered the handlers to take all but six of the horses on to the village. She had brought along six extra men just to guard the gear. After all, they didn't know how many trips they'd have to make back and forth to retrieve more gear before they found what they were looking for. She tried not to think about the fact that they could spend months wandering around these caves and find nothing.

Bloodstone looked up at the cave. It was at least sixty or seventy feet off the ground with no easy path to it. It was going to have to be a careful climb. "So how many of you know how to climb a mountain?" She was not surprised that all of the Soldiers of Ares raised their hands. Nor was she surprised that only one State Soldier, Sergeant Halsted, a young man who had been promoted to the rank of Sergeant after the battle where they rescued the Oracles, raised his. Everybody else stood there and looked uncomfortable. Bloodstone sighed. "Well, Colonel, if you would do me the honor of accompanying me up the mountain, we'll throw ropes down to the others." She added under her breath, "Hopefully."

Bloodstone and the Soldiers of Ares, plus Sergeant Halsted, began climbing. They were a little over halfway up, when Bloodstone went to pull herself up with her left hand, reaching with her right. The rock beneath her hand gave way and she slid several feet down, struggling to grab a hand hold, when Colonel Foster reached out and grabbed her. She was amazed to find herself standing on a four inch ledge, pressed between the Colonel and the mountain. She swallowed hard and let out a soft sigh. Pressing her cheek against the cold stone, she glanced at the Colonel. "Thanks, that's another one I owe you."

"Anytime, General. Watch your handholds, boys, some of them are very deceptive." He looked back at the General. "The fun part is going to be getting ourselves off of this ledge. It isn't big enough for me to move to either side, nor is it big enough for you. I think you are going to have to up climb out, or I'm going to have to climb over you. Which would you prefer?" The two stood there looking around for their next handholds.

Finally, Bloodstone pointed at a large chunk of rock. "I think if I lower myself to my knees, you can put your foot on my shoulder and you should be able to then reach that handhold and then pull yourself up to that one."

"No, it's too risky. I could knock you off. I will get down to my knees."

"Colonel, you know that's not going to work, because I'm still between you and the wall. I'm the one up against the wall. I'm the one who has to get down on my knees. Just do as you're told". She carefully began squirming her way down between him and the wall. As Foster kept feeling her backside wiggling against him, he told himself, *This is not the time to become aroused, just because a woman is in close proximity.* He looked up studying his handholds, trying to concentrate on anything else. Finally, when Bloodstone knew she was as secure as she could be on her knees on the ledge of a mountain, she said, "All right Colonel, it's your turn. Carefully put your left foot on my shoulder and reach for that handhold - and Colonel, one more thing. Let's try not to die today."

The Colonel reluctantly put his booted foot on the General's shoulder, then carefully easing himself up, reached out and grabbed ahold of a chunk of rock. Bringing his other leg over, he found a foothold and then pulled himself free. A few minutes later, they were pulling the last of the Soldiers of Ares into the cave. It only took them a couple of minutes to find a large boulder they could tie ropes to, and throw them down to the others. Most of them were able to shimmy up the rope on their own, a few had to be carefully pulled. But finally, packs on their backs, torches in their hands, Big Bear led the way.

Bloodstone looked around, then said, "Now remember, we have to be careful to stay together and careful not to get lost. So we're going to have to mark the trail, which also means if somebody comes up behind us, they'll know we're here, but we can't afford to get lost."

After several hours, Bloodstone called a halt. "I think we could all use some food and some rest. I'm calling it for the night. We will begin again in the morning."

For the most part, everyone ate in silence then got out their bedrolls. Bloodstone established watches for the night. It was only as they were settling in Bloodstone heard Eden say, "You know, Woman, I'm already much older than you. Did you have to scare more years off my life with a stunt like that?"

"You know, Husband, you say that like I did it on purpose, because I promise you, falling to my death is not tops on my ways of dying."

Eden reached out and grabbed her and pulled her tightly against him. He kissed her passionately and then realized everybody was staring at them. He decided he better let her go before she throttled him.

Bloodrose was tossing and turning, trying to find a way to get comfortable on a hard, very cold stone floor. Though she was lying on one blanket and wrapped in another; she was still freezing. The cold didn't usually bother her this much. She didn't understand why, but it seemed to just be soaking right into her. After a few more minutes, her teeth were literally chattering. *If I try to spend the night like this, I'm going to end up dying from exposure wrapped in blanket.* She groaned, *Will you please stop being melodramatic, it's just cold.* She rolled over again.

"Bloodrose, are you okay over there? You sound like you're pretty cold. Do you need another blanket?" Bloodstone asked in a soft voice.

Bloodrose clenched her teeth together, determined not to chatter any longer. If she was going to die of exposure, she was at least going to do it quietly. "No, I'm warm enough, thank you." She hoped she managed to sound normal.

Bloodstone, lying on her back, rolled her eyes at that lie. She didn't even think her men were convinced by it, it was pretty pathetic. "Well, if you decide you want another blanket or you just need some extra body heat, you can always come and share my covers."

At that, there were several snickers and a few lewd remarks. "Be silent, all of you! She's not used to roughing it like the rest of us!" Bloodstone snapped with irritation.

"Well, if she just needs somebody to keep her warm, I would be more than willing to do that," replied a soldier Bloodstone didn't recognize.

Bloodrose tossed and turned a few more minutes before she decided it really was too cold for her to sleep like this. She picked up her blanket and went over to where she knew Foster had made his bed. He was lying on his back with his eyes closed. He didn't look at her. He didn't say anything. He just merely picked up the blanket she threw over him as she slid in with him. He slid his arm tightly around her and pulled her against him. "By the gods, Woman, you're half frozen!" He wrapped his other arm around her and began chafing her arms and back.

As she slid in with Foster, there were several more lewd remarks and disappointed noises. One soldier even said, "You should've chosen me, Love, the Colonel's not into petticoats."

213

Ignoring the men, she whispered softly, "I don't understand why I'm so cold. I wasn't cold before."

"It's the stone floor. Even though you have a blanket down, the cold is seeping through it and into your body."

A moment later, they heard someone groan. Bloodrose looked quickly to see someone, she thought it was Bloodstone, standing over a man who was holding his stomach and groaning. But before she could speak, and again, without even looking, Foster said, "General, did you just kick one of my men?"

"Yes, do you have a problem with that, Colonel?" she demanded angrily.

"As a matter of fact, I do. It doesn't sound like you kicked him hard enough." Bloodrose watched as Bloodstone kicked him again, this time much harder. He groaned, grunted, and banged the palm of his hand on the hard stone floor.

As he made choking and gagging noises, Bloodstone said, "If you can't speak with respect to your commanding officer, I'll break every bone in your body and that goes for the rest of you as well. And in addition, since clearly some of you are not aware of this, Bloodrose is my sister by marriage. You will not speak disrespectfully or lewdly about her again. Is that clear?"

All the men murmured, "Understood."

"I'm sorry, I didn't hear that!"

They quickly and clearly replied, "Understood, Sir!"

Foster chuckled softly to himself, then shifting her against him and pulling the covers up around her, he fell asleep.

Two days later, midmorning. To Bloodstone's surprise they had done no backtracking. They continued to wander further and further into the mountain, going down deeper as they did so. They had found no relics, no signs of habitation. Bloodstone was just starting to wonder if they were on a fool's errand, when she felt her entire body start tingling. She reached up quickly and grabbed Big Bear's arm. They halted. After a moment, she quietly moved forward and took the lead. About thirty feet down the corridor, they came to a crossroads. As they moved closer to the crossroads, the tingling increased. Taking a few steps to the right, the tingling subsided. Turning to the left and heading down the corridor, the tingling began to increase. She noticed Eden starting to twitch. She halted. Looking at him she asked, "What does it feel like?"

"Like my whole body fell asleep and is waking up, but there's no pain, it's just odd."

She nodded and turned back to the group. "Okay, if anybody feels one of the three things I'm

215

about to describe, you have to tell us. You don't want to keep that to yourself. If it feels like all the hair on your body is standing up, but there's something odd about it; or if your bones feel like they're quite literally vibrating; or if your entire body feels like it fell asleep and is now waking up. You have any of these feelings, come stand next to Eden." Big Bear moved to stand next to Eden, as did Bloodrose and Daniel. To her surprise, so did one of the young Soldiers of Ares. "No one else?" They all slowly shook their heads. "Okay, if that changes, come and stand with them and tell us."

They continued down the left corridor. It was only about fifty feet further when Bloodstone halted them again. "Dex, you still don't feel anything?"

"No, should I?"

"The rest of you wait here. Dex and I will go on ahead and then once we know where it is, we'll talk about it." They only had to go about another thirty feet before she found the runes, which were on either side of the corridor. She looked at Dex and asked, "Still nothing?" He nodded. "Good. Would you go ahead and tell us how long it is until you see another set of runes like this?"

He nodded and went down the corridor and came back. "About forty feet."

She beckoned the rest of them forward. "Still no one else feels odd?" Again they all shook their heads. "Okay, those of you who don't feel anything, it will have no effect on you. To those of you who do, your limbs will feel heavy. You will feel like you are moving through sludge, and then you will just slowly collapse to the ground and pass out. It is absolutely painless and will affect everybody a little differently. It is as though the more magic you have in your blood, the faster you pass out." She turned to face Foster. "I believe that you should carry Bloodrose to prevent her from injuring herself when she falls. Murtaugh and William, you are probably going to have to make two trips, as you probably are going to have to carry Eden and Big Bear. Matthias, I think you should be capable of carrying Captain Stone." She looked at the Soldiers of Ares. "I'm sure one or two of you can handle your brother when he passes out." They all nodded quickly. "And of course, it is up to you four whether you want to go as far as you can before you pass out, or just accept the inevitable and let your friends carry you. Dex, I'm afraid you're going to have to carry me the entire way. I can't guarantee how long we'll all be out - as I said, it affects everybody a little differently, though I can say with reasonable confidence, I will be out the longest." She turned to Brown. "Captain Brown, take eight men through to the other side. Go about ten feet past the other set of runes and wait for the rest of us to get through. Those of you who are not carrying something across will wait until the rest of us are through, then bring up the rear. Any questions?"

"Yes, you're actually going to accept the inevitable and just permit me to calmly carry you across?" asked Dex.

In reply, Bloodstone grinned at him, took two steps backwards, only one of which passed the runes. Before she had time to lift her foot a third time, she sank down and fell backwards unconscious. Everyone stared stunned for a moment. Eden went to grab her, but Murtaugh dropped his shoulders, and slipping one arm between Eden's legs, hoisted him over his shoulder. Eden had just enough time to utter a curse before Murtaugh walked between the runes. Two steps in, Eden went limp.

Dex walked forward and dropped to one knee, gently picking up his Queen and carrying her to the other side. He watched as Murtaugh unceremoniously dumped Eden on the ground with just enough care to make sure he didn't bash his head into the stone floor, but that was all. Then, he turned and headed back to the others. Once on the other side, Dex laid Bloodstone gently on the ground, using one of the packs as a pillow.

Foster moved towards Bloodrose, scooping her up in his arms. He kissed her. As he walked past the runes, her fingers slid into his hair and she kissed him back. Three steps and her hand slid from his hair. He paused only a moment to look down on her unconscious face, then continued walking through. Dex grabbed one of the bed rolls to be used as a pillow for the healer. Once the healer was settled comfortably, Foster and Dex turned back to watch Big Bear. Apparently, he had chosen to walk as far as he could. He made it nearly halfway before he dropped to his knees and fell to his side and was unconscious. William and Matthias picked him up and between the two of them, carried him the rest of the way. However, the young Soldier of Ares wasn't given the choice, as one of the bigger men grabbed him in the same manner Murtaugh had done to Eden and carried him to the other side. Though his backside was turned to them, they knew the minute he lost consciousness. He had remained conscious the longest, nearly three quarters of the way. Then they watched as Murtaugh repeated his maneuver on Daniel. Daniel barely had time to utter an oath before he lost consciousness. Once Murtaugh was on the other side, Foster let out a whistle and the others came to join them. It took the young Soldier of Ares a quarter of an hour to regain consciousness and Big Bear a half an hour. It had now been nearly three quarters of an hour and the other four had not yet regained consciousness, or even begun to stir.

Foster, Dex, Murtaugh, Big Bear, Matthias, and William all stood looking down on them. Finally, it was Dex who spoke. "Is anybody else starting to get worried?" To his surprise, the other men all nodded. They continued to stare for another minute, when Big Bear cocked his head to the side. A moment later, the two Amazon warriors moved to stand defensively over Bloodrose. All of the soldiers quickly began taking up defensive positions in front of their unconscious allies. They could hear several people moving around and occasional whispering, though whatever language they were speaking was not familiar to any of those present.

A male voice spoke in the same unfamiliar language from down the corridor. He was clearly directing his comments towards them. After a moment, Foster replied, "I'm afraid we don't speak your language, but we're not here to cause trouble. We would just like to talk."

After a moment and some more whispering, "You are People of Earth?"

"I'm not sure what that means, but if you mean we live above ground, the answer is yes." Foster looked at Murtaugh and made a face and shrugged. Murtaugh shrugged in reply.

"But are you People of Earth or People of Stone?" the man questioned.

This time, however, it was Murtaugh who replied. "I have never heard of the People of Earth. But in one of the old tales of my people, they called us the People of Stone. And they said there were two other people. And if Bretons are a different people, then perhaps they are your People of Earth."

"I think perhaps it is time we stopped talking around corners and come face to face. If you truly mean us no harm, my people and I will come to you."

"I told you, we're just here to talk. We don't want any trouble, especially right now," replied Foster.

A moment later, four glowing balls of light appeared down the corridor and ten lightly armored soldiers came forward. The man in front spoke. "How many men of yours are still unconscious?"

Foster found himself hesitant to admit it, but he also saw no reason to deny nor to lie about it. "Four."

"Do you know it has been more than a hundred years since one of your kind has broken through the barrier and crossed to our world?" He glanced past Foster to see the four unconscious people. "They have very strong magic. They will be unconscious for at least another hour, maybe two. They would rest more easily in our city. I am Lightfoot, Captain of the Watch. You've come this far, I figure you deserve a bed this night. Can you carry your friends, or do you need us to bring litters?"

"We have our friends and we thank you for your hospitality. I am Stephen Foster, Colonel of the Soldiers of Ares."

Lightfoot pounced quickly. "But you are not all Soldiers of Ares, and you do not introduce your friends. Do you not work together, Colonel? Or do you attempt to shield them from us? You also do not say you are in charge."

"We're a group of allies. We prefer to work together, though if push comes to shove, the woman is in command. She is the General of the Knights of Athena," replied Murtaugh with some heat.

Lightfoot nodded and turned, saying as he did so, "Follow me."

XVII

As Murtaugh and Foster turned back to their men, Murtaugh said softly, "Since you're currently in command, I think you should entrust Bloodrose to the Amazons. I know that that is not to your liking, but I think it would probably be advisable."

"I know. Already considered that myself. Are you going to be able to carry Eden that long?" Foster asked with some concern.

Murtaugh shrugged his shoulders and said, "I can carry him for some distance. If I become too wearied, I'm sure Big Bear can carry him. We might have to switch off." Big Bear nodded his agreement.

"I have the General," added Dex.

"You need have no concern about the Captain, we'll take care of him," supplied Sergeant Halsted.

Dex crossed to Bloodstone, dropped down to one knee, and carefully scooped her up in his arms. Rising to his feet, he shifted her in his arms so that her head was resting on his shoulder. The bigger of the two Amazons, Sorrow, bent down and carefully slung Bloodrose over her shoulder. The others did the same with their burdens. Once they were ready, Foster turned back to Lightfoot, who nodded and headed down the corridor. As they walked, Foster found himself fascinated by the glowing lights. They produced a truer light than the torches. It was almost as though the corridor was bathed in sunlight without the warmth. After a quarter of an hour, he was becoming concerned of how long his Allies could carry the other four when Lightfoot interrupted his thoughts. "You'll wish to watch your step on the stairs. There is no railing, and they can be a bit tricky if one is not paying attention." A moment later, they rounded a corner, and directly in front of them was a huge opening. Lightfoot stepped out and turned to the right and headed down the stairs. As Foster stepped through the opening, he stared in wonder. There was an entire city inside the mountain, bathed in a soft glow as though under a full moon - though a moment later he corrected himself. It was a little brighter than a full moon. He could see the entire city, and on the other side of the cavern was a waterfall that fell into a pool, and then the pool became a stream that ran through the entire city and back into the mountain somewhere. It was almost like something from a dream, not quite real.

Once they were all on the floor of the cavern, Lightfoot led the way into the city. He glanced at Foster and said, "I sent word ahead to make all ready for your visit. Rooms and beds are available for your friends." A few minutes later, they arrived at the largest structure in the center of the city. The stream actually ran right through the center of the structure. When Lightfoot opened the door and gestured for him to enter, Foster was amazed to see the inside was as bright as though the sun was shining. Lightfoot dismissed the soldiers and entered. Once everyone else had entered, Lightfoot removed his helmet and handed it to a servant. Running his fingers through his hair, he shook out what Foster could only call a mane. When he turned back to face Foster, Foster blinked in astonishment. Lightfoot was about his own age he guessed, nearly forty and was only about five foot four inches, which from the guards he had seen already, told him that was about average height for a man of his people. He had very pale skin that almost seemed to have a slight gray tinge to it, and his silky looking brown hair seemed almost unnatural to Foster. But his most astonishing trait was his amber cat's eyes. These astonished Foster so much, he glanced over quickly to see the servant. She too had cat's eyes, though she was not quite five feet tall. As the woman curtsied and walked away, he observed something sleek and feline about her. He swallowed hard as he remembered having the same thoughts about somebody else and those same odd amber eyes.

"If you will follow me, I will show you to your rooms for the night. It is still early here. We will give your companions some time to regain consciousness, then I will take you to meet our King. I can, if you wish, send for one of our magicians. They might be able to do something to shorten their time of unconsciousness - if you would trust our magic, of course."

"We greatly appreciate your offer, but I find myself reluctant to permit you to cast magic on our people," replied Foster.

"I do not blame you in the least. I would not wish to permit it either." A moment later, he opened a door. "These are the barracks of some of our officers. I feel your women will find these quarters more comfortable. The two barracks across the way should house all of your men." Dex stiffened. He was not comfortable with being in a separate room from his Queen while she was unconscious. But before he could utter a protest or say anything, he felt Murtaugh's hand squeeze his arm. He looked over his shoulder and saw an imperceptible nod of his head. Dex gave a slight nod in reply.

As he entered the quarters for the women, he saw a tiny woman in robes concentrating hard, looking at a bed that was glowing. She closed her hands around midair and started pulling them apart. As he watched, the bed in front of her grew longer. Hearing his entrance, she turned to face him. Her eyes widened at sight of him. For a moment, breaking her concentration, the bed stopped glowing. Looking back at the bed, then him, then back to the bed, she then mumbled to herself, "I think a little wider as well." Again the bed started to glow, and again her hands in midair were as though they were pulling and stretching the little bed. "Maybe a little thicker as well." She then turned her hands so that one was on the top

226

and one was on the bottom and pulled, and before his very eyes, the mattress became plumper. He was so startled, he almost dropped Bloodstone. She quickly did this to two of the other beds in the room. Curtsying, she excused herself and went to attend to the other beds. Dex, still stunned, laid Bloodstone on one of the beds.

"We will look after her, you need have no fear," said Sorrow, as she patted him on the shoulder. He nodded to her and excused himself.

Sorrow had been watching Bloodstone for the past two hours. She still had not so much as twitched. Sorrow was beginning to worry. She stood over the bed staring down at Bloodstone, crossed her arms over her chest and willed the woman to open her eyes. She was still standing there a quarter of an hour later.

Bloodstone stirred and stretched, she turned on her side and reached for Eden. A moment later, she sat up, looking around. She asked in a confused tone, "Where are we?"

"We're in a city inside the mountain with some very strange inhabitants, very strong magic, and they use it very … liberally." Sorrow had hesitated over the last word, as though she was searching for the right one.

"How long have I been out?"

"True to your word, you're the last to regain consciousness. Your brother and husband regained consciousness more than half an hour ago, though Bloodrose regained consciousness a little over an hour ago. No one else was out nearly as long as the rest of you, but I should go and inform Eden and the others that you have regained consciousness." She excused herself.

Bloodstone turned to Climber, concealing a smile as she always did when addressing the young Amazon. Her actual name was Lavender, but everybody just called her Climber. "Would you mind telling me everything that's transpired while I was unconscious?"

Climber quickly informed her of everything, being sure to include a detailed description of their hosts. When she had done this, she added, "They seem nice enough people."

She had barely concluded her tale before there was a tap on the door. "Enter," called Bloodstone.

Lightfoot entered and gave a little bow. "I'm glad to see you're awake, General. My King wishes to see you and your officers. If you would be so kind as to select who you wish to bring with you, I will take you to see him."

A few minutes later, they were following Lightfoot down the corridor. "We have not yet been introduced, General. I am Lightfoot, Captain of the Watch, Commander of the Army of the People of Mist."

"I am General Bloodstone 'the Dragon' Silvermane of the Battle Knights of Athena, and it is a pleasure to meet you."

"Likewise. It has been a long time since we have had visitors here. I must confess I find it most stimulating." At that moment, they arrived outside a set of double doors. Bloodstone had to conceal a smile as she realized that though the corridors were high enough the Barbarians were able to walk upright, however, to go through these doors, she, Daniel, and Foster would have to duck their heads, and the Barbarians would practically have to crawl. She had to bite the inside of her cheeks to keep from laughing at the thought of it.

The guards to either side of the door gave a respectful bow, then one of them opened the door and announced, "Lightfoot, the Captain of the Watch, is here at your request with the outsiders, Your Majesty."

He gestured for them to enter. Lightfoot entered and then announced her. "General Bloodstone 'the Dragon' Silvermane of the Battle Knights of Athena."

The King gave Lightfoot a withering glance. "I know it has been centuries since we have had guests, but have your manners fallen so far that you only announce her, when I see eleven others which you failed to introduce?"

Lightfoot bowed respectfully. "You will forgive my oversight, Your Majesty, but I had not yet had the pleasure to be introduced to the others, so I knew not how to properly introduce them. Again, forgive me, Your Majesty." The King waved his hand dismissively as though to say 'I will deal with you later.'

Bloodstone stepped forward a little and gave a bow. "If you will permit me, Your Majesty, it would be my great honor to introduce my Allies."

"Your Allies, not your subordinates?" questioned the King.

"I have but one subordinate present, Your Majesty, the rest are my Allies." He waved his hand as though to say go on with it. "This is Eden Silvermane, Commander of the Barbarian Army and King of the Barbarian lands …" Eden gave a nod of his head as he was introduced. "His right hand and second-in-command, Colonel Murtaugh Wolf …" Murtaugh gave a respectful bow and hoped none of the astonishment he was feeling showed on his face. "Big Bear, War Chieftain of Bear Tribe; Colonel William River; Captain Matthias Woodland …" All three men bowed respectfully. "Her Royal Highness, Princess Bloodrose, heir to the throne of the Amazons and the head of her guard, Sorrow of the Amazons …"

Both women nodded their heads. "Colonel Stephen Foster of the Soldiers of Ares, and Commander of the Fortress of Knee Deep ..." He concealed a smile as he bowed. The General was certainly making sure to pull out every title. "Colonel Dexter Wolf, Commander of the Queen of the Barbarian lands personal guard." Dex couldn't help it. As he bowed, he glanced at Eden. He had never heard any of these titles ever used. He could not understand what his Queen was up to, but as he stared at the face of his King, he saw nothing. This really didn't surprise him. Dex hoped his own confusion was not showing. "Lord Daniel Stone, Captain of the State Knights of Bretony, and Captain John Brown of the Battle Knights of Athena." Again, both men bowed respectfully.

"I am Silverleaf, King of the People of Mist, and this is my kingdom. What brings you outsiders here?"

"A boy from Bear Tribe found a broken weapon in one of the caves above. We felt it deserved investigation. We are currently at war and we wanted to know whose side you were on," replied Bloodstone.

"We left the surface and came down here because we no longer wished to involve ourselves in the quarrels between the People of Stone and the People of Earth. We tired of your excessive warring and thirst for blood."

"Why do you call our people the People of Earth?" questioned Foster.

"Is the story not known to you how our three peoples came to exist?" They all shook their heads. "More than fifteen hundred years ago, Lord Poseidon wagered Lord Hades and Zeus, King of the Gods, that he could create a more superior new being than the other two. This creature must be formed in their own image. Lord Poseidon created the People of Mist, Lord Hades created the People of Earth, and Zeus created the People of Stone. Each of our people has their own strengths and their own weaknesses. As you may or may not have realized, your people," he looked directly at Murtaugh, "have superior size, superior strength, your skin is denser, and you're more resistant to the elements, magic, and diseases. And because of your hardiness, you tend to live about twenty-five years longer than the People of Earth. However, your people have a very hard time using magic. Also, you're larger, and in many ways slower. This is because Zeus fashioned your people out of stone; that is why you are called People of Stone." He turned to look at Foster. "Your people were created by Lord Hades, and I apologize if I insult you when I inform you your people are really quite unremarkable. You are between us in strength and size. You can use more magic than the People of Stone, but less than we can. You're stouter and heartier than our people and survive more, however, your life span is greatly reduced compared to ours. Then again, so are the People of

Stone. The only true advantage Lord Hades gave you is that you are well balanced. This does give you several advantages over both the People of Stone and the People of Mist. And alas, I come to my people. We are quick and we're nimble, but our bodies are very frail. We live hundreds of years longer, but we are still a dying people. Our people lack the desire for physical companionship that your people have in excess. So consequently for every four, we produce but one child, and though we may live five to eight hundred years, our population is still dwindling. Despite our skill in magic and healing, accidents happen, lives are lost." He shrugged his shoulders dismissively.

"Your people live for hundreds of years?" questioned Dex.

"As I said."

Foster turned to look at Lightfoot. "How old are you?"

Lightfoot laughed. "Three hundred and twenty-eight."

Okay, not my age, Foster thought to himself.

"Did your people build the fortress in the pass between the mountains?" asked Bloodstone.

"Yes, nearly a thousand years ago. I only have vague memories of the structure. I was but a small child when we came underground, though I fear something's happened to the structure. More than a year ago, there was an awful earthquake and much damage was done to the caves and catacombs."

"For the most part, the structure is still there, though I do not know how much damage it sustained when I blocked the pass," replied Bloodstone.

"You blocked the pass? How interesting," replied the King.

"When you spoke of Breton, I mean the People of Earth, why did you address me and not the General?" asked Foster.

"Because you are merely of earth, she and her brother are not just of earth, as all of those of you who possess magic are not merely of your people. But each of them possess blood of another."

"I thought I lost consciousness because I'm a priestess of Seana," said Bloodrose.

"That had some to do with it, though it was not the entire cause. I presume it was your father who was of our people. Since you appear to share blood with the People of Stone and since our women cannot breed with their men, I assume it was your father. Is my assumption incorrect?" he asked with curiosity.

234

"I'm of your people, or half?" she asked with astonishment. He merely nodded in reply. "My father only stuck around long enough to father me, but my mother did say he was of a smaller stature than a Breton."

"How old are you?" asked Lightfoot.

"Twenty-seven, why?"

Lightfoot groaned. The King said, "Oh yes, I see."

"What's that supposed to mean?" Bloodrose demanded angrily.

"We merely have our suspicions on the man who fathered you. After all, we don't track every one of our people. It could be another, though the most logical conclusion would be the one who we cast out," replied the King, looking a little uncomfortable.

"Cast out. I know I shouldn't be surprised, but I am," she groaned.

"He was just an upstart and a trouble maker, nothing major. He was trying to convince our people that we should not live underground any longer." He hesitated a moment and then added, "But the hour grows late and you will return to your people in the morning. We will show you the fastest way out of the mountains, back to the lands of the People of Earth." He waved his hand dismissing them. This time Lightfoot did not escort them, but four young guards who were abuzz with questions about the surface. The Allies answered their questions and asked some of their own. When they arrived at their rooms for the night, they invited the men to continue the conversation. Bloodstone took Bloodrose by the arm and pulled her into their room.

"I hope you don't mind, but before the others return, I would like to have a private word with you. It's important," Bloodstone said.

"No, not at all."

"Well, first off, I would like to begin by telling you when he spoke of the man he believes fathered you, at the end he was lying through his teeth."

"I presumed that. Neither one of them seemed thrilled about it. Unfortunately, we'll probably never know more." She shrugged her shoulders. "What else would you like to discuss?"

"I don't know what's going on between you and Foster, but on the off chance it eventually comes out, I want to tell you something so you hear it from me, and not rumors. I want to make sure that you are fully aware of what had happened."

Bloodrose felt a hand squeeze her heart and a lump form in her throat. She didn't know how she managed to say calmly, "Oh really?"

236

Bloodstone said, "I know as my friend, you will not repeat anything I tell you in confidence. So I ask you not to repeat this, because it would make things very uncomfortable for Foster and Eden." Carefully, she relayed the entire situation involving the Breton King from start to finish, leaving nothing out.

As her tale drew to an end, Bloodrose looked furious. "How can Black Stone serve such a man? He is clearly a pig! Oh, how I wish Bretons were more like Amazons so that you could've challenged him on the spot for his throne! I am sure you would be a far better Queen than he is a King!"

"Do not judge my King too harshly because he has a fascination for ..." Bloodstone hesitated a long moment, "other men's wives. Despite this immoral streak, he's done many great things for our people. He has changed so many laws for the better, so many things he has done have made things better for my class, peasants. In his thirty-five year reign, he has improved the quality of life for peasants a hundredfold. His father was a good man too, and also did many things to lessen the gap between the two classes. When his grandfather was on the throne, a peasant woman like myself did not even have the right to tell a man like Black Stone no. He is a noble, and if he wanted something, he could have it. That's just the way it was, but his father changed that, and then the current King improved the housing situation. He made land owners improve all of the homes, and put rent restrictions on them so they couldn't charge exorbitant sums."

Bloodrose crossed her arms over her chest and looked annoyed. "He's still a pig!"

Bloodstone laughed. "Now that, I'll agree with you on." She hesitated a moment and then asked, "I hope this won't change how you feel about Foster or me?"

"Change how I feel about you, no. You're one of the few women I am truly proud to call my sister." She smiled. "Though it does change how I feel about him, but not in a bad way." She hesitated a moment. "If Eden would've asked you just to live with him, would you have done it?"

"You know it is not well known how Eden and I became married."

Bloodrose interrupted her. "Not well known, that is a major understatement. No one knows. That has to be the best guarded secret in the entire encampment."

"It's a long story, but I'll try to shorten it as much as possible, and again, I would ask you not to repeat this." Bloodrose nodded quickly. "I was sent by my general to do some spying in the Queen's training camp. I got caught and was going to be sold to the highest bidder ..." She gave an involuntary shudder at the thought. "But Eden was there spying, though he called himself something different, and he offered to buy me if I would live with him as ..." She turned a vivid shade of crimson. "Well, if I'd share his bed. We lived together like that for three months. Though of course, for Eden, I was now his wife. I did not know this and he did not inform me, the jackass. So when we were finally able to escape from the encampment, we each went our separate ways. And boy, did he give me a shock when he walked into Black Stone's tent. But had Eden not been a Wolf Tribesman and had he wanted me to just live with him in our encampment, no, I would not have been able to do it. I may have given in to him in a weak moment, but I would not have continued to behave so."

Bloodrose hugged her tightly. "Thank you for entrusting me with your secret. You know I will not repeat it to anyone, I swear, and thank you for your advice."

XVIII

The next morning, they were shown unceremoniously out the door. Fortunately, however, there was a secret exit which had them back to their horses and wagons in less than an hour.

Bloodstone said, "Captain Brown and I will go and inform the handlers to bring the rest of the horses around. Once they arrive, head back to camp. It will not take me long to catch up."

Eden said casually, "I know you don't think you're going without me, Woman, and from the look on Dex's face, I don't think you're going without him either."

Bloodstone stuck two fingers in her mouth and whistled loudly. A moment later, Cedric came through the woods. He charged right up to Bloodstone and bumped his head into her torso. "Was your journey profitable, General?" asked Cedric.

"Yes and no."

"Well, you can tell me all about it on the way home," Cedric said hopefully.

Bloodstone mounted up and looked at the others. "Well, are you coming or not?" The others quickly mounted their horses and followed her. A half an hour later, they were riding into the village of Temple Hill. "Eden, would you go and inform the horse handlers to go and retrieve the rest of our group. Brown and I need to have a word with Steel."

Eden nodded and then said, "Give Grandfather my regards." She nodded and turned her horse in the direction of the forge. Dex and Brown followed her.

As she dismounted, her younger brother Edward came out of the forge. "I'll take your horses."

She handed him her reins and patted him on the shoulder. "Thank you, Edward." He took the reins from Brown and headed for the stables.

Steel was drying his hands, leaning on a post watching her as she entered the forge. "What can I do for you, General?" he asked as his eyes were looking her up and down, appraising her armor. "That's a very nice suit of leather you have on. Did you make it?"

"Yes I did. I made his too, but I made it for someone else. I refitted it for him though, without him." He turned his expert eye on Brown and looked him up and down.

"Nice to see you didn't cut any corners. Well fitted for not having had him present when you did it, but leather is more forgiving in that manner than steel. What brings you to my forge?"

"He needs a suit of plate mail and I don't have the time to have it constructed in my camp. Do you think you might be a willing to make it a priority? I'll pay for the inconvenience."

"If I'm going to make it a priority, he'll have to stay. I'll need his body at my disposal, but if he's good at standing still and following directions, I see no reason I shouldn't be able to have him a suit in about two weeks. After all, I do have to deal with little emergencies like broken wagon wheels."

"Two weeks will be fine, and yes, I intended to leave Captain Brown with you."

As Brown watched the strictly business conversation, he wondered who her grandfather was. There was no one else working in the forge, and clearly she was not related to this man. His thoughts were interrupted when Bloodstone added, "Did you hear of the death of the Duke?"

"Yes, Fletcher did write us that your father was killed. My sincerest condolences to you and your family. He was a good soldier and a good man even if he was a …"

"Womanizer," supplied Bloodstone.

"Yes, but as it was pointed out to me, my daughter was not innocent in that affair. Have you spoken to your mother yet?"

"No, Grandfather, I came to see you first, and Eden sends his regards."

"Is my grandson here?" he asked hopefully.

"Yes, he's probably in the inn by now."

"Then I think I will be taking an early lunch." He headed out of the forge, slipping his arm around his granddaughter's waist, turning her to come with him. "You should come too, Brown, my daughter is a good cook."

As they entered the inn, they saw Rosie fussing over Eden. Bloodstone nodded to Rosie. "Mrs. Fletcher, I hope I will be able to rent a room from you for two weeks for my man Brown here," she said, jerking her head in Brown's direction. "And this is Dex. He's one of Eden's men." Catching sight of Eden's dirty look, Bloodstone rolled her eyes and sighed. "For Captain Brown, one of my soldiers." She looked past Rosie at Eden. "Better?" she demanded, irritated. He nodded. Only Dex didn't look confused.

"Of course," Rosie replied, looking a little disappointed.

"If you would please give me an estimate of the bill, I will pay you in advance for his room and

243

board. I will also settle up for what we owe you for the stables and the men who were responsible for taking care of our horses." A quick debate over money took place, but Bloodstone finally ended it by thrusting a coin pouch on Rosie. Turning back to Steel, she said, "I forgot to pay you for the armor." She produced a heavy pouch and handed it to him. "I think this should be sufficient, but if I end up owing you anything, hopefully you'll be kind enough to just send me a bill. But if you're reluctant to release the armor without full payment, send a note to the encampment and I will have a man bring out the rest of your money." Steel nodded, looking a little insulted.

"I hope you and Eden are going to stay the night?" asked Rosie.

"I'm afraid not this time, we actually need to be on our way." She extended her hand to Steel. "Good to see you as always. I look forward to a day when I have time to actually train at your forge under you."

"I will look forward to that day as well. Having my granddaughter around longer than a few hours would be a nice change." He shook her hand, then pulled her into his arms and gave her a warm embrace, kissing her on the cheek.

She turned to bid farewell to Rosie, but before she had a chance to speak, Rosie hugged her tightly. "Please come back soon and actually stay a while, maybe you can bring my grandson."

"We will make sure to do that soon," Eden replied. "And please give our apologies to our siblings. Tell them I promise the next time we come, it will not be a flying journey."

Bloodstone turned and headed for the stables, Dex only a few steps behind her. As soon as she was out of the inn, Eden sighed. He bent down and kissed Rosie on the cheek. "Give her time, she will warm up to you. She just takes her time. The past couple of months have been pretty hard on her."

"I know. Fletcher said she took the Duke's death very hard." Eden nodded, then he followed Bloodstone.

*****

Two days later, back in the encampment, Foster was lying on his bed with his hands behind his head. It was the one luxury he allowed himself. If he didn't have to sleep on the ground, he didn't. He heard the tent flap rustle and looked quickly. To his surprise, it was Bloodrose. He got to his feet. He opened his mouth to speak, but before he had a chance, she interrupted. "I hope you'll forgive the intrusion, but I've wanted to have a private word with you for a few days now, but unfortunately there just has not been an opportunity. Do you have some time now?"

He nodded and indicated a chair. "Yes, of course. Would you like to sit down?"

"No, thank you. I think I can say what I have to say better on my feet. You wanted me to consider your offer, and I have considered it. In fact, I have thought of little else since you made the offer. I wanted to reply at once, but you asked me to consider it, so I have. In truth, it was probably a good thing I did, though my answer has not changed. It will, however, be better thought out. I greatly appreciate the offer that you made me, but I'm not willing to have you on those terms …" Foster hoped he managed to conceal his disappointment at least somewhat. Though he was disappointed, he was not surprised. Eden had warned him. "If you and I were to live together, we would have to do so on your land around your people. And I have not lived in this encampment for more than a year and not learned how your people view such relationships and the offspring of them. And though I am not young, I do not feel that I am so old that I would not in time give you children. When I first came to this encampment, the Bretons would say terrible things about Bloodstone, and would still be saying them about her now, had Eden not bashed quite a few heads, as did Murtaugh. I do not think Bloodstone has even an inkling of how many fights those two got in over the first few months, silencing vicious, wagging tongues. Her brothers too asserted all of their influence to put an end to it, but I think nothing did as much as Eden's fist. I would not have my children suffer through that. If you are willing to allow me to have a garden shrine to Seana near your fortress and truly be stuck with me for the rest of your life …"

Realizing quickly what she was getting at, Foster put a finger to her lips. Slipping down to one knee, he took both her hands in his. "Please be my wife. You can take over the garden in the fortress. I don't think Lord Ares will care, though you will find it sadly neglected and overrun. It's all yours as long as you agree to be my wife."

She began nodding her head, and was surprised herself to find tears pricking her eyes. She tugged him to his feet, wrapped her arms around his neck, kissing him passionately. After a long moment, a horrible thought struck her and she asked, "You're not going to make me wait for a month like Black Stone did Amber are you?"

"Do you care who witnesses our marriage? Is there anyone you want present?" She shook her head. "Then as far as I'm concerned, we can go ensnare the first priest or priestess we find and two witnesses and be married at once."

"Then we should head in the direction of the infirmary. If nothing else, Viktor is there and two witnesses should not be far off."

XIX

Five days later, Bloodstone sat at her desk. She was nearly caught up with all of her paperwork after having been gone for a week. Sergeant Simon ducked his head in and said, "Forgive the interruption, General, but there's a girl here to see you and she claims she's your sister …"

Bloodstone heard an agitated voice outside say, "I do not claim to be her sister; I am her sister."

Unperturbed, Sergeant Simon continued, "… though she refuses to give her name. She arrived at the gates and the Captain of the Watch had her escorted here to see you, Sir."

Bloodstone groaned to herself as she recognized the voice. "Sergeant Simon, would you please be so kind as to show Jade in." He nodded and held the tent flap open, gesturing for the girl to enter. "I hope, Jade, you have a very, very good reason for why you are in this encampment, when you were supposed to be safely at home," Bloodstone demanded, her irritation evident. She looked the girl up and down. She looked tired, dirty, and frustrated. "When did you leave home?"

"Four days ago. I got a little lost. This place isn't as easy to find as one might suppose."

Bloodstone gestured to the chair in front of her desk. Crossing her arms over her chest, she continued to stare at the girl. "Are you going to inform me why you ran away from home?"

"I did not run away from home. I came to see my sister," Jade replied sweetly.

Bloodstone sighed. "Why did you come to see your sister?"

"Because I need your help. Mother and Father are being very unreasonable." Bloodstone raised an eyebrow in question as Jade hesitated. "Well, you see, I'm engaged. Father doesn't like him, and Father won't give his consent, and Philip is far too honorable to marry me without Father's consent, so I want you to help get his consent, please." She clasped her hands together and looked at her sister pleadingly.

"What makes you think that I would approve of him if Fletcher does not, and what gives you the idea that they would listen to me anyways?"

"Because you're my sister, you'll not look at him as Father does. You'll look at him as my sister and as the man I love."

Bloodstone was certain she could feel bile rising in the back of her throat. "I would not blindly assist you to marry some man I have not yet met."

To her surprise, Jade quickly clapped her hands together in excitement. "Oh, I knew you'd help me!" Bloodstone opened her mouth to protest, but Jade cut her off. "To try to prove himself to Father, Philip Evian enlisted. He is a private in the Twelfth. You can meet him immediately."

"I do not promise to assist you. I will meet him, but before I agree to meet him, Sister, you and I are going to have to have a conversation, because we will have to come to some kind of understanding about the price for my assistance in this matter," Bloodstone said firmly.

"You'll charge me for your assistance?"

"I do believe that in this particular instance, my assistance will not come for free. First off, I want you to explain to me exactly how far your relationship with Philip has gone."

Jade looked at her innocently. "Why, Sister, I can't understand what you mean."

Bloodstone narrowed her eyes at the girl. She was lying through her teeth. She clearly understood exactly what Bloodstone meant. Bloodstone hesitated only a moment, then deciding Jade had asked for it, she said in the calmest, most matter-of-fact tone she could manage, "I mean have you made the mistake of permitting him to lift your skirts and get between your legs? In another words, are you still a virgin?"

Jade turned red with a mixture of furor and embarrassment. "That is none of your business!"

"Very well. Sergeant Simon!" she yelled.

"Yes, General?" he said, re-entering.

"Would you be so kind as to go and inform Sergeant Major Fletcher that his runaway daughter is in my quarters and I wish him to take her away."

Jade jumped to her feet and looked at her pleadingly. "NO! Please don't do that!"

Without taking her eyes off Sergeant Simon Bloodstone demanded, "Are you going to cooperate with me?"

"Yes, I will do anything. Please don't send for Father!"

"You may return outside, Sergeant Simon, but if I tell you to go for him again, do not even bother to re-enter." Sergeant Simon nodded, concealing a smile as he exited the tent.

Jade glanced nervously at the tent flap and said in a very soft voice, "No I didn't," she blushed, "let him do that." Bloodstone continued to wait. Finally Jade added, "Yes, I'm a virgin. Why it is so important to you, I do not know."

"Because had he corrupted my younger sister, he would find out what my sword felt like in his gut; but since he has not dishonored my family, I will permit him to continue to live."

Jade gasped and put her hand to her mouth. "Oh, but you wouldn't," she barely breathed.

"Don't bet on it. Now I will make you a deal. I will meet your young man and if I feel that Fletcher is being an overprotective Father, I will assert all of my influence with him to persuade him to consent to your marriage …" Jade clasped her hands together and looked gratefully at her. "But, if I determine that he is indeed unsuitable, you will do whatever I determine is best in this situation."

"But that's not fair! How do I know you have not already determined that he is unsuitable?"

"I give you my word as a Knight of Athena that I have not prejudged him. I will judge him on himself and himself alone, not your opinion of him, nor others. I am not even going to consult Fletcher before I meet with him. He will stand or fall on his own merits, but this is the price I demand for my assistance. You will give your word that you will obey me absolutely in this matter, or I will not help you."

Jade glared at her and looked mutinous. "Very well, I give you my word." Bloodstone leaned back and looked up at her. Jade swallowed hard and looked annoyed, but then added, "To obey you absolutely in this matter. You have my word."

Bloodstone nodded then turned to the tent flap. "Sergeant Simon, Dex."

Both men entered. "Yes, General," they said simultaneously.

"Sergeant Simon, would you be so kind as to go and ask Katya if she would not mind a little company for a few hours?" He nodded and excused himself. "Dex, would you please place two guards on my little sister? I wouldn't want anything to happen to her." Dex - catching her meaning instantly and realizing that these guards were not only to protect her, but keep her out of trouble as well - nodded and excused himself.

Sergeant Simon re-entered a few minutes later. "Katya would greatly appreciate some company. If you follow me, Miss Fletcher, I will escort you to Katya."

"Sergeant, please return to me immediately." He nodded and offered his arm to Jade.

When Sergeant Simon re-entered her tent a few minutes later, she said without looking up, "Please go inform Colonel Stone I wish to speak to him and Private Evian immediately. When you return, keep Private Evian away from the tent until I call for him. I wish to speak to Colonel Stone privately first." Simon nodded and excused himself.

Three quarters of an hour later, Andrew entered. "You wish to see me, General?"

"Yes, Andrew, I wish to consult you on a personal matter. Please sit down." As he flung himself into the chair, something about it reminded her so much of Ares. She felt a small tug at her heart.

"So how can I assist you?"

"Tell me everything you know about Private Evian."

Andrew groaned. "He's not worthless as a soldier, he's just damn lazy. I should also inform you that Fletcher stuck me with him and told me he just wanted me to keep an eye on him and tell him what I thought of him."

"What do you think of him?"

"I think he's too pretty for his own good. I think he's lazy." Andrew shook his head to himself considering. "And though there is nothing I can say that that's why I don't like him, but I don't like him. He's not particularly popular with the men either, but lazy soldiers never are. He doesn't deserve to be in the Twelfth, that's for damn sure. Everybody knows he is there because Fletcher put him there. I think everyone figures it's either to shape him up or get rid of him, but he's only been with us for …" He considered for a moment. "He's only been with us about five months. He showed up in Spring and as you know, sometimes it takes a year to get a soldier properly trained; but

I still don't like him. Why are you so interested in him? I know it has nothing to do with his pretty face."

"Never ever clapped eyes on him. He's engaged to be married to Fletcher's eldest daughter."

Andrew raised an eyebrow conveying clearly, *oh I see*, but he said, "Don't you mean second eldest daughter?"

Bloodstone glared at him. "Don't you start that too." He shrugged and grinned. Turning to the tent flap, she yelled, "Show him in." Andrew immediately got to his feet and looked stern when Private Evian entered.

Bloodstone saw at once what Andrew had meant by his pretty face. He was indeed a beautiful man, not handsome, not good looking, beautiful. It was the only word that suited him. He was average height for a Breton, nicely built with wavy brown hair and green eyes. Bloodstone was certain many women would go weak at the knees just looking at him. Bloodstone, however, was not fooled for a minute. She sensed a darkness in him at once that she did not like. It hinted at a cruel, selfish nature. "Do you know who I am?"

"You're General Bloodstone, General of the Church Knights, second-in-command under General Black Stone," he replied quickly.

"Good, what do you know about me?"

"I know that you and the Stone brothers share the same father. I know that you're married to the Big Barbarian ..." he hesitated.

"Go on, what else do you know about me?"

"I know that you're having an affair with Sergeant Major Fletcher." The Private was unable to conceal his pleasure at Andrew's fury, though when he glanced back at the General, some of the pleasure left his face. She merely looked amused.

"I find it interesting that the camp gossip has not carried the rumors to your ears that Sergeant Major Fletcher is married to my mother, which means that Jade is my little sister." At that, the last of the amusement in his face died. "Oh, did that shock you? I'd like to say I'm not glad, but I'd be lying if I said that. So what are your intentions to my younger sister?"

"I hope that Sergeant Major Fletcher will permit me to take her for my wife," he said, bestowing a dazzling smile on her.

"Do you love my sister?" she asked out of mere curiosity.

He grinned at her again and said with almost a little gush, clearly well practiced, "With all my heart and soul." Again, Bloodstone felt bile rising in her throat, but concealed it. The urge to flatten the little liar was strong, but she refrained. Andrew, however, did not refrain from making gagging noises.

"Why don't you cut through the shit and tell me why you really want to marry my little sister, because we both know you were just now lying to me."

"With all due respect, General, it is not kind of you to trounce on my most tender feelings. I love and adore her and look forward to the time we are married."

"Well, at least part of that statement was true. Why do you look forward to being married to my sister?"

But to Bloodstone's surprise, it was Andrew who replied. "It's not Jade he wants, but her inheritance, and I would be quite surprised if she doesn't have a dowry. Fletcher's a careful man." Bloodstone laughed.

Evian looked indignant. "How dare you imply that I am pursuing her purely for her fortune!"

Bloodstone loved when people hung themselves with their own words. "You are only after my sister's fortune; you don't care anything for her. Get out and stay away from her. If you manage to persuade her to run off and marry you, I will make sure that Fletcher leaves her nothing as long as she resides under your control. You will never see so much as a copper of her money. Get out of my tent!" Her voice had risen as she became angrier.

Even she was startled when the tent flap opened and Dex walked in heading straight for Evian. Evian put up his hands quickly, looking at Dex. "I'm leaving! I'm leaving!" As he hurried out of the tent, Dex wordlessly turned and followed him.

Andrew remarked, "Have I mentioned recently how much I really like that guy?"

"Andrew, if you tell me you feel I need a bodyguard, I'm going to beat you within an inch of your life," she snapped angrily.

"Don't get pissy with me, Little Sister, and yes, I am well aware of the fact that you are an excellent swordsman. That doesn't change the fact that as your older brother, I like knowing somebody's around who is going to look after you, whether you like it or not. And I know it annoys you, but you're still a girl, and all my chivalrous male instincts prefer to know you have a man looking after you." Bloodstone continued to glare at him. "Is there anything else my General requires?" he asked, pretending as though he didn't notice she was glaring at him.

"No, Colonel, you are dismissed. Sergeant Simon, would you please go and inform Sergeant

Major Fletcher and Eden that I would like to see them both immediately."

"No need for you to go in search of them, Sergeant, I know where they are. I will send them to her immediately," Andrew said as he walked out.

"Sergeant Simon, Dex." As soon as the two men entered she said, "When my husband and Father arrive, I wish to speak to them privately, so I would like it if you and the guards would excuse yourselves. And Dex, before you protest, I will have two very strong warriors in the same room as me, so you need not hover over me, is that understood?" He grumbled, but agreed. Sergeant Simon merely nodded his head.

XX

Half an hour later, the two men entered laughing and talking. "Why did you require us, Woman?" asked Eden.

"I merely requested your presence, Eden, as a courtesy to you. It is actually Fletcher whose presence I required." Both men exchanged looks.

"How may I assist my General?" asked Fletcher, looking a little worried.

She gestured for him and Eden to sit down. As they did so, she said, "You may drop the general, Fletcher, this is not a military matter. It is a personal matter for you, a very personal matter. Your eldest daughter took it upon herself to run away from home, come here, and try to persuade me to persuade you to let Philip marry her." Fletcher groaned.

"Who's Philip?" asked Eden, in the tone of a man who is not sure he wants the answer.

"A worthless no good," replied Fletcher quickly. Eden shot a questioning look at Bloodstone, who merely nodded. "What in Hades am I going to do with that girl? I thought for sure a little time away from him would change her mind about him." Fletcher suddenly looked sharply at

Bloodstone. "Please tell me you're not on her side in this matter."

"What's the matter, Fletcher, afraid I am easily swayed by a pretty face?" she asked, looking irritated.

"No, I don't think you'd be easily swayed by good looks. A desire to make your sister happy, maybe, but not by his good looks."

Bloodstone said gently, "I don't think that man would be capable of making my sister happy even for a few months. I believe him to have a very cruel nature. I would not wish him on my enemy, let alone my little sister. My question to you, Fletcher, is what are you going to do about it? I hope you realize that she is clearly too headstrong and too much trouble for Rose to deal with on her own. If she were an only child, it might be possible; but with four younger children to worry about ... She does not need trouble from her eldest, but assistance, and I do not think that Jade will be in a very assisting mood."

"I don't know. I had considered sending her to school, but clearly that is no longer an option. She will just run away without someone's watchful eye over her. I'm sure she'll end up running straight back to that little idiot. She's too old to spank and too young to be reasoned with. I'm open to suggestions at this point."

"I do have a suggestion. I'm not sure either one of you will like it or approve of it, but given her age and the situation, I see no alternative." Fletcher nodded for her to continue. "I suggest that you make her someone else's problem - in other words, marry her off. I do not think that her fascination with this boy is purely on his looks. I think she feels that she is ready to be in love, so therefore, she is in love with him. I think she will stubbornly cling to her quote love for him unquote until she realizes the man she's married to is a far better class of man."

Fletcher was slowly shaking his head. "I agree with the idea, but I couldn't do that to her. You know what it would mean, she would in all likelihood end up hating him - justifiably so - and all of us for having a hand in it. I would rather her marry the idiot and then be there when it falls to pieces."

"That, Fletcher, is where we disagree. But then again, you are a Breton and you're thinking like a Breton." Fletcher stared at her for a long moment uncomprehending, then light slowly dawned.

"Do you think any of them would marry her on those terms? It would not be an easy way to come to your marriage," he asked, sounding hopeful.

"All right, clearly I'm not following some thread of this conversation that the two of you are.

Would one of you like to let me in on this?" asked Eden, looking annoyed.

"We cannot marry her off to a Breton. As much as I love my own people, there is a very large reason why one would not be suitable under these circumstances," Bloodstone replied, a little hesitantly.

"Why not?" Eden asked, still looking confused.

"Because a vast majority of Breton males would consider his wife's body his right, not a privilege, and would take what he was owed whether she likes it or not," Bloodstone stated matter-of-factly.

Eden face darkened. "You're telling me under the law a Breton woman does not have the right to tell her husband no?" They both nodded their heads. "That is repulsive!" They both nodded. "So Bloodstone's suggestion is to marry her off to a Wolf Tribesman?" Again they both nodded. "How old is she?"

"Two and a half months shy of her seventeenth birthday," replied Fletcher.

"Have any candidates in mind, Woman?" Eden asked wearily.

She smiled at him prettily. "I was going to ask you for suggestions, my love."

Eden sighed and leaned back in his chair considering. *In all reality, marrying the girl off to a Wolf Tribesman would not be a hard thing to do. Many men would seek an alliance with the royal family.* As he considered man after man, one name kept popping to his mind. He conjured an image of Jade up in his mind. *In body and beauty, they were very similar. Were she not his woman's younger sister and significantly younger than him, he himself would find her an appealing woman, which meant he knew she would appeal to ...* "Dex."

The room was silent a long moment before Fletcher finally said, "I like him a lot. I can't imagine any man not being proud to call him his son, but why?"

"My reasons are my own. You asked for my suggestion. I suggest him to you. If you do not wish to take my suggestion ..." He shrugged his shoulders dismissively.

"I like your suggestion just fine," replied Bloodstone quickly.

"It's a lot to ask of him," said Fletcher, looking a little concerned.

"In all reality, it's not our decision to make. If he is willing to have her on those terms, that is his decision and we should not make it for him. But when I speak to Dex on this matter, I prefer to do so alone. So if you two would not mind, I would appreciate it if you would leave," replied Bloodstone.

"What are you up to?" asked Fletcher.

"I told you, you would not approve of what I had in mind; so at this point you have agreed and I must ask you to trust my judgment. You asked for my advice, now trust my judgment."

Fletcher sighed and looked at Eden. "I sometimes wonder who's older, she or I?"

Eden started laughing. "Tell me about it. Come on, I'll buy you a drink."

As soon as they were gone, she crossed to the tent flap and called to Dex. Then returning to her desk, she seated herself. When he entered, she indicated a chair. "I wish to speak to you on a matter which is very personal, a family matter. How much regarding my sister did you overhear?"

"Enough to know that that man she wants to marry is no good."

"Would you find my sister an appealing mate?"

"I find her to be very attractive, but she's in love with someone else. She would not marry another man."

"I have managed to convince both Fletcher and Eden that the only proper solution to this situation is to marry my sister off, before she has a chance to do something stupid like marry that little fool. For reasons I would prefer not to get into at this time, I, nor Fletcher, are inclined to marry her off to a Breton …"

Dex interrupted her. "I've told you before I cannot help you if you conceal things from me."

Bloodstone sighed and wished Dex knew when to be a little less difficult. "My apologies, there are some differences between our two cultures that are painful to admit. One of the ways in which I find Wolf Tribesman superior to Bretons is their views on marriage. Not only do you feel that both parties should remain faithful, but you also believe that it should be a willing physical exchange, not something taken by force …" Dex's jaw tightened, but he remained silent. "And for this reason, I asked Eden for a suggestion of a Wolf Tribesman. Eden suggested you. My sister will not make it easy, nor be a good wife in the beginning. She will be difficult, to say the very least. I think in the end, she will come around and be a good wife, but of course, this cannot be guaranteed, which is why neither Fletcher nor Eden are aware of this next part of my plan. But before I go any further, is this something you are even interested in considering?"

"My King has suggested me for the task. My Queen asks it of me."

Bloodstone sighed and took a slow deep breath and let it out. "Dex, no one is ordering you, or even trying to persuade you into agreeing to this. If you do this, you must do it freely."

"I do not believe that I would find it unpleasant to take her as my woman. I agree, it does sound as though there would be difficulties, but I would rather endure those difficulties, than have her falling into hands such as his."

"As you know, the treaty accepts Wolf Tribe marriage laws, but as you are probably not aware, in some ways Breton marriage laws are very similar. Though we do always have a priest or priestess perform the marriage ceremony, the marriage is not binding if not consummated. This is the loophole - that if after a year, things are still unresolved between the two of you - we can use to have the marriage dissolved for both of you."

Dex looked appalled. "But it would not be right if we have lived together, to then cast her out. That would shame and embarrass her. No matter what the Council ruled, there would be talk."

"Yes, unfortunately there would be; however, since she would return to our lands and you would remain in your own lands, Wolf Tribe would consider you well rid of the troublemaker and no one in our lands need ever even know of it. And if at that point, she is not willing to see reason, then nothing any of us can ever do will prevent her from suffering."

"She is in love with him. She will not agree to marry me," he said with conviction.

"Actually, she already has. She just doesn't realize that's what she agreed to. But again, I must state, if this is not something you wish to do, you're not required to," Bloodstone stated firmly.

"I will marry her."

Bloodstone sent for Viktor, Eden, and Fletcher. Once they had all arrived and Viktor had been made fully aware of the situation, only then did she send for Jade. The smile died on her lips as she saw her father. "You agreed not to tell Father," she said angrily, glaring at Bloodstone.

"I never agreed not to tell him. I just didn't send for him then. And as per our agreement, I have met and spoken with both Philip and his commanding officer. I find him to be a repulsive little weasel and you are absolutely not marrying him. Your father has said so firmly and I agree with him, as does your brother-in-law …" Jade glared at all of them. "And as per our agreement, you will accept my judgment on this matter and do what I order you to do."

Jade stopped glaring and suddenly looked worried. "What do you mean?"

"This is the Commander of my personal bodyguard, and your husband, Dex." Bloodstone waited for protests.

"I didn't … agree … to … that," she stammered out.

"You gave your word to obey me absolutely in this matter. This is all part of the same matter," Bloodstone replied smugly.

"I hate you," Jade said firmly.

"Well, at least you're not lying to me, unlike Philip, who did nothing but lie to me. I would prefer honest hatred over lying devotion any day," Bloodstone replied coldly.

"I hate you with every fiber of my being. And I'll marry him, but that's only because you tricked me. I'm going to make his life miserable." Jade was watching the effect her words had on Dex, but to her surprise, he didn't even blink.

Viktor mumbled to himself, "I think the Conqueror's Wedding would be advisable." Eden choked on his laughter. As he tried to turn it into a cough, Dex grinned. "Dex, do you claim this woman as your mate, vowing to feed, protect, and be faithful to her?" asked Viktor.

"On my honor, I so swear" replied Dex without hesitation.

"Does any man here dispute his claim to this woman?"

"You didn't ask me if I agree!" Jade said angrily.

Viktor looked down on her. "Noticed that did you? Then on behalf of the Council of Wolf Tribe, in accordance with the treaty with the Bretons, I recognize your right to take her as your mate. From this day forward, she shall be your woman."

XXI

A half hour later, Dex showed Jade into their quarters. "It's not much, but it's home for now." Jade looked around. Not much was an understatement. There was a washbasin, cooking fire, a very large bed, a dining room table with two chairs, and one trunk. She stood in the center of the room and turned all the way around, nothing else. The two of them stood there staring at each other in awkward silence for a long moment. Finally, Dex said, "I think you and I had better come to an understanding of exactly what is expected out of this relationship ..."

He was interrupted before he had a chance to go on. "If you so much as think about touching me, I swear by the gods I will scream this tent down."

"Look, for now all I ask of you is to live here with me amiably. I will not touch you until you ask me to do so ..."

Again he was interrupted. "I will never ask you to do that, so you better get used to a long, lonely, cold marriage." To her great annoyance, he merely shrugged his shoulders.

"You know, Woman, if you keep interrupting me, this conversation is going to take all night ..."

"It's not like you're going to be doing anything else tonight," she said smugly.

Dex took a long, slow, deep breath, then he decided he needed to count to ten. He had forgotten how frustrating it was dealing with a young woman. When he was finished counting to ten in his head, he said in a calm tone that galled her to no end, "As I previously stated, I have no intention of touching you without your consent …"

"And I have no intention of ever, ever, giving you my consent! I will never share your bed!" she said, still angry.

"All I require of you is to do the chores that are expected of a wife. You will cook breakfast and dinner. I do not come home for the midday meal. You will also be responsible for keeping the tent clean and doing the laundry. Other than this, your time is your own. You may socialize with any of the wives you wish. You will not go near that man, or I will paddle your backside. And as far as sleeping arrangements are concerned, there is only one bed in this tent and it will be inhabited by both of us, and on this I am not negotiating. You will share that bed with me whether you like it or not …"

"I will not! You can sleep on the floor, and as previously stated you are not to touch me!" Dex noticed that though previously her anger had been genuine, her anger was now forced. She was more afraid than angry.

"You can stop worrying about me touching you. I don't want to touch you. I don't want a woman who doesn't want me back, and before I ever touch you, you're going to have to make it very clear to me that you want me badly. You are going to have to tell me in very clear, unveiled terms, exactly what you want out of me. And I'm not going to give you any more reassurances on this matter, so don't bother to bring it up again. I will return in a few hours. You had better not leave this tent in that time. One of my men kindly volunteered to go and bring you a basket of food. Be sure to thank him properly and don't be rude." He turned on his heel and walked out.

A quarter of an hour later, she heard someone clear their throat outside. She was a little nervous as she pulled the tent flap aside. One of the men she had seen standing outside of Bloodstone's tent was standing there carrying a large basket. At her appearance, he smiled. "It's a little heavy, would you like me to put it on the table for you?"

She smiled at him and pulled the tent flap aside. "Yes, thank you."

"Is there anything else you require?"

"If you would be so kind as to tell me where I could draw water, I would appreciate it," she asked with a smile.

"There's a well very near here. If you go out your tent and go to the left, it's a few rows down, but I'll bring you some water. Is one bucket enough, or do you require two?"

Looking around again, she asked, "Would four be too much to ask?" He smiled, shook his head, and excused himself. As soon as he returned with the water, she prepared dinner. As much as she didn't want to, she knew she had to at least eat. And she was sure if she didn't feed him, he'd starve her. Then she decided if she was going to live here, there needed to be some cleaning up around here. Not that it was particularly messy - actually, for a bachelor, she thought he was rather clean, but men just never cared as much about the little details as women did. She was just looking at herself in the mirror, trying to figure out how she was going to ever survive with only two dresses, when he reentered.

To her complete and utter astonishment, he looked around the tent and smiled at her. "It looks very nice, thank you." He sniffed the air. "Dinner smells good. I took the liberty of speaking to your Father about procuring any little things you might wish from home. He said he will send a letter out in the morning asking your mother to pack up all your things. A man will be along in a few days with a wagon to collect your possessions. I hope this meets with your approval."

She gave him a grudging smile. "Thank you, that was very kind of you. Your dinner's ready. Are you hungry?" He nodded, and she served him. They were just finishing dinner when they heard someone clear their throat outside.

Dex got up and opened the tent flap. To his surprise, Eden was standing there holding what looked to be a very large piece of wood. "My woman and I thought you might want this." Dex gestured for him to enter.

Eden entered and carried it straight over to where the washbasin was and began unfolding it. As Jade watched, Eden unfolded a large screen. She felt her heart lift. When he had it unfolded, he turned back to her. "If you tell me exactly how you want it positioned, I will arrange it so." A few moments later, it was carefully arranged how she wanted it.

"Thank you Eden, I really appreciate it."

"You should thank your sister. It was really her idea. I just agreed with it." She glared at him. "Right, I forgot, you hate her." He bowed and excused himself.

As soon as he was gone, she took her pack and went behind the screen, washing as thoroughly as one can do in a basin. She then brushed and braided her hair, and slid her nightie on. She felt a little shy about sleeping in it with a strange man, but there was no way she could sleep in her tight fitting, corseted dress. She'd suffocate in her sleep. As she exited from behind the screen, she kept her eyes down and crossed quickly to the bed, and slipped beneath the covers, pulling them all the way up to her neck. She was exhausted. All she wanted to do was close her eyes and go to sleep.

"Not that side. Move to the other side."

She sat up looking angry and said, "Why not? This side is perfectly comfortable and I'm already here. You can have the other side."

"Because the woman does not sleep on the side closest to the door. I would be surprised to learn that your father permits your mother to do so, and I can assure you Eden does not permit Bloodstone to do so." *Though in his absence she does,* he added to himself.

Jade scoffed and looked annoyed. He glared at her. "Oh, fine, it's not worth arguing over," she said, as she scooted to the other side of the bed and turned her back on him. As she snuggled her face into the pillow, she was surprised to find that it smelled nice and clean. She smelled the blanket. It smelled clean too, though she could smell him. She smiled to herself. It was a nice smell. He clearly liked things neat and tidy. She heard him rummaging around, but she didn't want to look.

She wasn't sure what he was doing. A moment later, she heard the lid of the trunk close. She decided to pretend to be asleep.

Dex went behind the screen, washed, and pulled on the britches he used to sleep in when he lived with his sister. He had them fashioned especially for that purpose. He couldn't stand sleeping in a tunic. Climbing into bed, he tried to go to sleep. It didn't take long before he decided it was going to be a very long night. Though the thought only crossed his mind once that she might stick a knife in his ribs while he was sleeping, he discarded it quickly. She didn't strike him as the murderous type.

Jade was sitting at the table with her arms crossed, trying to decide what she was supposed to do. Dex had left more than an hour ago, well fed, and in a reasonable mood. She admitted that if she was going to be married to a man, at least he wasn't bad to look at, even if he was a mean brute. She began drumming her fingers on the table. She knew she should get up and do the laundry, but who really wants to do laundry when you're mad at your husband. A woman's voice from outside interrupted her brooding.

"I'm sorry for intruding, but I thought I might come and check on you, see what you needed. May I come in?" Jade got up quickly and opened the tent flap. A lovely Breton woman was standing there with auburn hair and hazel eyes. She was also very, very pregnant. "I hope you'll forgive me for not waiting until we're properly introduced, but around here we kind of don't stand on ceremony unless we have to. I'm Helena, Murtaugh's wife."

"Please come in and have a seat. I'm afraid all I have to offer you is water, but would you like some?" she asked with a smile.

"No, thank you." Helena looked around. "Well, I've seen worse. Andrew's was actually much worse."

"I'm sorry, I'm not following you, and forgive me, but I didn't introduce myself. I'm Jade."

"I know who you are. You're Sergeant Major Fletcher's eldest daughter and sister to my husband's sister. What I meant was, it won't take quite as much to make you more comfortable here as it did to make Tabitha comfortable in Andrew's quarters. Apparently Andrew believed that less was more." Despite herself, Jade started laughing.

"Do you take it upon yourself to make all the new wives comfortable?"

"No, actually Amber and Bloodstone usually do that, but Murtaugh said you weren't exactly on good terms with your sister right now. So I figured you'd rebuff any assistance she would offer, and I don't know if Amber has learned of your marriage to Dex yet."

"Is anybody at home?" asked Amber.

Helena grinned. "I was just talking about you, Amber, come in."

Amber entered and looked around. "Well, Andrew's was worse." All three women started laughing. "I'm Amber. I'm married to the oldest of the brothers. Why don't you come with us and we'll show you around and see what things we can find to make this place a little less austere." Amber linked her arm through Jade's and then Helena's. "Though I should say if you want a competition for the most uncomfortable quarters, Bloodstone's quarters before she and Eden started living together would win. They are still pretty bad, but Eden has made some minor improvements."

Despite herself, Jade looked at Amber. "They looked pretty comfortable to me."

Amber started laughing. "Those are Eden's quarters. They still have separate quarters, though they primarily reside in Eden's." Jade didn't know why, but it upset her to think that her sister was so unhappy in her marriage that she would keep her own quarters.

XXII

Seven days later, Black Stone and Amber were sitting in their tent when Sergeant Henderson stuck his head in and announced, "Colonel Grayhawk is here to see you, Sir." Without waiting, he showed him in.

Grayhawk bowed to Amber when he entered. "I hope you'll forgive the intrusion, General, Duchess, but I'd like … Well, in truth, I would like a word with my brother and my General, kind of at the same time."

Amber rose, crossed to Grayhawk and gave him a kiss on the cheek. "Then permit me to excuse myself. You gentlemen play nice." She curtsied and left the tent.

"How may I be of service to you?" asked Black Stone, once Amber was gone.

"You may or may not recall my statement to Mother asking her to pick me a wife." Black Stone nodded grimly. "Mother has found several nice candidates, but I was thinking Lord Thomford's second youngest daughter, Sylvia would be a good choice. Mother has also recommended the Earl of Chamberlain's eldest daughter, Winifred. But I feel when you compare the two of them, due to the high station and wealth of her father, Winifred would not be happy in my small castle on my small estate with my meager title. Plus, she is the eldest daughter and I think he would want a little better for her than me; whereas Thomford's daughter is the second youngest of six. My estate is a little larger than his, though he is a little wealthier. I do not feel that she would overly tax my purse strings; whereas I am greatly concerned that Winifred would expect more than the estate could bear." He looked at his elder brother expectedly.

"I'm not sure exactly what you want me to say, Michael. Perhaps this conversation would go smoother if you tell me what to say and then I will say it."

"Eric, I don't want you to tell me what I want to hear. I want you to tell me what you think."

"If you truly want my honest opinion, then I would say don't do it. You do not know what either one of them is like, you do not even know if you would like either one of them. I understand you feel it is necessary to produce an heir, however, I feel it is a mistake for you to marry a woman that you are not at least fond of. If you cannot be at least friends with your wife, your life will be miserable. You do not have to love her, but you need to at least be able to socialize and be friendly with her. Since Mother picked these girls, I do not doubt that they are nice girls, but that doesn't mean you could tolerate them." Eric realized he'd spoken too harshly when he saw the wounded look on Michael's face.

"You forget, Eric, I am not the eldest son of a Duke, or even the son of a Duke at all. I am merely his stepson and stepbrother to the new Duke. My prospects are not as good as yours, they never have been. Unfortunately, I'm not even as good a soldier as you are, so I do not even have that to recommend me." Michael spoke without malice. He had accepted these things all of his life. He did not begrudge his brother them. In fact, if given a choice, he wouldn't change places with Eric for anything. He liked his quiet little estate with only a few tenants. When this war was over, he would live quite comfortably there. The only thing he did begrudge Eric was the truth, and Eric was right. But of course, that was the most annoying thing about Eric - he was almost always right. His quiet little existence on his estate would be marred by a woman he couldn't stand. But he needed to marry. He was not getting any younger, and if he died without producing an heir, his uncle would inherit the title. This, of course, would not bother him if he actually liked his uncle and respected him, but he did neither. He knew it would take his uncle less than a year to run through his money and ruin everything. Michael also knew good and damn well the only reason he had an estate to inherit at all was because the Duke took over the running of it until he reached the age of maturity. His uncle had fought the Duke hard, but with the support of the King, the Duke had won easily. He had had complete control of the Grayhawk estate since two months after the death of his father, before Michael was even born.

His thoughts were interrupted when Eric spoke. "Michael, I would rather you marry a nice, respectable, young woman of low birth and be happy, than marry the daughter of a nobleman and be miserable for the rest of your life. But I'm not our father, I'm merely your brother, so whatever you wish, whatever you do, I will support you. On my honor, you will never hear an 'I told you so' out of me. But I do ask that before you make any decisions, will you please consider what I have said?"

"I will take it under advisement, but I've already drawn up a formal request to marry this winter, and with your consent, to take two months off over the winter holidays to spend with my new bride. I know, of course, you and Amber and most of my brothers will be unable to attend the wedding due to the war, and that I do regret; but I do not feel I can wait any longer to marry."

He handed over the letter to his brother who opened it and read it. "As your commanding officer, I can see no reason to deny you your request. This is indeed a down time, and your presence will not be essential. You have my permission to marry under these terms, and I wish you all the happiness in the world." Eric hoped he managed not to sound grim. He didn't think he was succeeding.

Grayhawk nodded and rose. "Thank you for your time and consideration, General. I will not do anything until I return from patrol. I leave in the morning and I'll be back in two days. At that time if you would like, I will inform you of what my decision is."

Black Stone extended his hand and the two men shook. "I would appreciate that immensely. Gods speed and watch over you on your journey."

Eric watched until his brother had left, and then he said to his back, "I would trade places with you in a minute, Michael, if I could." He leaned back in his chair and considered how Amber was going to take it. When it happened, he knew she would stand by him no matter what, but he didn't think she was going to be happy about it. The King had asked to speak to him immediately after his father's funeral. Eric had invited him into his father's study, then he quickly corrected himself, my study. He closed his eyes and remembered back on the conversation.

*****

The King looked around. "You know, Black Stone - I hope you don't mind if I call you Black Stone. I always just called your father Grey Stone when we were alone. I would like our relationship to be similar."

"Of course, Your Majesty, you may call me anything you like," Black Stone replied, though he looked a little worried.

"Don't worry, Black Stone, I know you are not your father; but he was one of my dearest friends. And with his position and now your position, it will be necessary for us to work well together and get along. I would rather you view this more as a friendship, rather than being a Your Majesty/General formal, unbending relationship. I need my General to feel that he can speak to me without reservations when we we're in private." He paused and looked up at Black Stone, who nodded his head in understanding. "Good, we have an understanding, but I do not wish to speak to you as my General at this moment. I wish to speak to you as the Duke of Stone Reach, and the second most powerful man in all of Bretony. You do realize between your position as General and as the Duke of Stone Reach, you are now the second most powerful man in the country, which will put your life in peril on a regular basis. I don't know if you know how many attempts there have been to assassinate your father over the last ten years." To the King's surprise, Black Stone nodded.

"My father did not attempt to conceal such things from me. He knew I needed to know that there were going be dangers in inheriting his title. I have also informed my brother Andrew. Father was not thrilled about that, but he understood if something were to happen to us both suddenly, Andrew needed to be aware of the situation as well. The three of us, however, have done everything in our power to conceal it from the others, most especially the Dowager Duchess."

"Is it your intention to conceal it from your wife as well?" the King asked casually.

"My wife is currently in a delicate condition, but she is also not a fool, nor is my mother. Though we have made our attempts to conceal such things from Mother, I'm sure she is well aware of the danger - hopefully just not the extent of it. I know that my wife is well aware of the danger, unfortunately probably more aware of the extent than I would wish for her to be. But when you marry a warrior, you have to accept that they are not as naïve as other women in regards to military matters."

The King nodded his head. "Good, then hopefully your wife will understand that you don't tell her everything, because what I'm about to tell you must remain between the two of us. No exceptions, do I make myself clear?"

Black Stone looked insulted as he said, "You have my word, Sire, that nothing you tell me in confidence will ever be repeated."

"Good, because the only man who knew of this was your father; but now with his death, I must inform you of it. On my death, when my will is read, there's going to be quite an uproar. Because I have no son and no blood relatives at all, there is no one to inherit my title by blood; so it is within my right to bequeath the throne to whomever I see fit. During his life, that man was your father, now with his death, that mantle will pass to you. So at my death, you will be King. I do not want this known until after I am dead, because people will argue and people will fight and it will be unpleasant. Whereas when it becomes known after my death, there is nothing anyone can do about it. But make no mistake. They will try to rip you off the throne, and they might even succeed. You will have to fight to hold the throne, but I think you can keep it. I think you'll keep your life - after all, you have seven brothers to back you up. Your sister is in command of the Church Knights, and your brother-in-law, gods willing, will be the King of your neighbor within the next twelve months. All of these things will make it very hard to pull you off the throne, but not impossible. And your life, and the life of your wife and your children and your brothers, will all be at risk constantly until the civil unrest settles."

Black Stone stared. He didn't know what one was supposed to say to such a statement. The only thing that came to his mind was, *NO, not me, I refuse!* He swallowed hard and reminded himself that such comments were the thoughts of a coward and said instead, "I hope that I will not fail you and that I will prove myself to be worthy of the honor you bestow upon me, Your Majesty."

"If I did not think you were worthy, I would find someone else." The King gave him a curt nod, turned, and walked from the room.

*****

Black Stone's elbows hit his desk hard, his face in his hands. After a moment, he sat up and ran his hands through his hair. *Dammit! Dammit! Dammit! I don't want to be King!* A moment later, he started laughing as a thought struck him, as it always did when those thoughts ran through his mind. *Eden is going to enjoy gloating over me immensely. He could hear it now, 'What can I do for you, Sire? How may I serve you, Sir? Is there anything Your Majesty requires?'* He groaned and then laughed again.

XXIII

Two days later, late afternoon. Cora was
returning to her cave, her arms full of firewood,
when the sunlight glinting off something caught
her attention. She held her hand up to shield her
eyes, but all she could see was several large what
appeared to be rocks where she had never observed
rocks before. Something about it made her
stomach twist into knots with fear. She dropped
the handful of firewood and crept closer. She
could see no one moving around, so she crept
closer still. Hiding behind a large boulder, she
finally was able to see what it was. It was the
bodies of at least a dozen men. Slowly surveying
the area, she saw nothing moving. Only when she
was sure there were no Barbarians around she
hurried over. She caught her breath at the sight. It
had been a quick massacre, these men had never
stood a chance. They were Bretons, her own
people. Though she knew it was hopeless, she
began carefully checking each one of them. As she
did this, she was careful to disturb the ground
around the area as little as possible. She knew that
the Barbarians had left them here as a warning, a
clear message to the Breton army to 'back off'. She
was just about to decide it was hopeless when she
heard a soft moan. Moving towards where it came
from, she heard another. Finding the Knight who
was groaning, she put her hand to his lips, "Please
be silent." As she quickly looked him over, she

knew he needed more attention than she could give him right here. She had to get him back to her cave and out of sight quickly, but she could not do this until she checked the others. They were all dead. Returning to his side, she held her hands out in front of her creating an invisible board beneath him. She used it to lift him. He was so heavy that by the time she reached her cave, she was soaked in sweat from the exertion. Deciding she did not want to ruin her bedding, she grabbed a large piece of oiled canvas she used to cover the cave entrance when it stormed, and laid it over her bed. Then moving the board over her bed, she slowly lowered it and then released it, allowing herself a moment to catch her breath.

She then began stripping his armor, only pausing to bandage his wounds enough to stop the bleeding. Once out of his armor, she cut away his tunic so as to get at the two worst wounds. His side needed immediate attention. Fetching all of her healing supplies, bedding, and sewing box, she put on water to boil and then began cleaning his wounds. The pain was so great, he began to fight and struggle, but she had nothing to give him for it. For a moment she contemplated going in search of a healer, but quickly discarded that idea. They would be more likely to kill them both than help them. Though in truth, she didn't know why she was helping him. She had no love for the Bretons, even if they were her own people. She pushed all thoughts of that aside for another moment. "I hope you will forgive me, Sir Knight, but I am going to

290

have to tie you to the bed," she said to his unconscious body, realizing it was a little silly. Then finding whatever she could to tie him to the bed, she did so, and then went back to cleaning his wounds. Even with him tied down, she had to sit on his stomach. She finally had his side sewn up. She then moved to the wound on his thigh. It was not bleeding as badly, but definitely needed stitches. She knew she was being a coward leaving the arm to last, but she could see the bone and was not looking forward to the prospect of setting it. In fact, she didn't even like looking at it, she had covered it with a towel. Finally, all the other wounds treated, she had no choice but to turn her attention on the arm. Uncovering the wound, she almost gagged at the sight of the bones sticking out at least two inches. She decided she had better clean the wound first before she tried to put the bone back in. Once she was confident the wound was clean, she gently began tugging. Nothing happened. She gritted her teeth as she realized she was going to have to be much more forceful. Slowly and gently pulling with all her strength, the bone started to slide back in. Once inside, she concentrated hard, using her magic, trying to make sure the bone was perfectly aligned. When she felt it was as near as she was going to get, she cleaned the wound again and began sewing it up. Then she looked around for something to splint it with. Her eyes alighted on the back rods of her chair. They were nice flat pieces as long as his forearm. They would do very nicely. Using her magic like a pair of shears, she cut off four rods from her chair, then

bandaged and splinted his arm. She decided she
deserved a little break. She sat on the floor next to
him and laid her head on the edge of the bed. A
moment later she was asleep.

"Water," called an unfamiliar voice. Cora
couldn't understand why her dream was asking for
water, but a moment later she heard it again.
"Water." It sounded so pathetic and weak. Cora
sat up with a start. Looking down on the man, she
saw his eyes were barely open. "Water," he called
again.

"I'm sorry. I fell asleep. I will get you some."
Returning with a cup of cold water, she slid her
arm behind his head and allowed him to drink just
a little. "No more for the moment. I don't want
you to get sick. Just try to rest. I'm going to see
about making you more comfortable." She had no
idea how long she'd been asleep, but she didn't
think it could have been long. She concentrated on
carefully picking him from the bed. Using her
magic to hold him up, she cleaned all the blood off
of his body. Then she bandaged the wounds she
had not yet bandaged. When that was done, she
pulled off the oiled canvas, rolled it up, and
discarded it. She placed him gently in the bed.
She covered him up and then coaxed him to drink a
little more water. Then, so exhausted from her
extensive use of magic, she sat down next to him
and fell asleep again.

She awoke with a start. Sitting up, she looked at him. His teeth were chattering and his body was soaked with sweat. Putting her hand to his forehead, she could feel he was burning up with fever. She didn't understand why he was flushed with fever, but shaking as though he was cold. She hesitated a moment, looking at the fire that had died out. She didn't know if it was fear of the Barbarians or what, but she felt very strongly that the fire was not a good idea. Bemoaning, and not for the first time today, her complete lack of knowledge in the healing arts, she clasped her hands together and prayed to Freya for guidance, because she didn't know what to do. As she continued to pray for guidance, "The fire would be too hot. He needs the warmth of your body. The skin to skin warms and will regulate his temperature and help to stabilize his condition." Cora started as she heard the voice inside her head that was not her own. She always prayed to Freya for guidance, but did not actually expect a response. She considered what Freya had told her to do. *I'm not going to do that. He can just die if that's what it will take to save him,* she thought to herself. Then she looked down on him. He looked so vulnerable, very boyish, not at all like the men from her village. She gave a little shudder as she remembered. *Don't think about that now either,* she told herself angrily. Looking back down on him, she sighed. *If I go to all this trouble to save you, you damn well better not die.*

XXIV

Bloodstone was sitting at her desk when a guard was shown in. He saluted. "I hope you forgive the intrusion, General, but I bring bad news. The mountain patrol is an hour overdue." Bloodstone didn't even need to pull the patrol schedules to know that that was Grayhawk's patrol. She always paid particular attention when it was one of her brothers on patrol. She glanced at the hour candle, four.

Grayhawk was never late. She had a bad feeling about this. She looked at the guard. "Go and inform General Black Stone of the situation. Inform him that I am taking Colonel Stone and a dozen men, and I'm going in search of the missing patrol." The guard saluted and excused himself. "Sergeant Simon, send a man to the practice arena and have him inform Colonel Stone that I need him dressed in battle leather and at the Western stables in half an hour. Tell him he had damn well better not be late."

Sergeant Simon stuck his head outside and relayed the orders, then returning to his General he asked, "What else do you need me to do, Sir?"

"I need you to pull a dozen men from the watch and have them ready to go at the stables in light armor in half an hour." Sergeant Simon nodded and went to carry out his orders.

Dex, who had been listening quietly outside, turned to one of his men. "Go to my quarters now and inform my mate that I won't be back for a couple of days. Tell her you need the pack that sits next to my trunk. Bring it to me at once." The man nodded and turned on his heel. Dex turned to the other guard. "Go find Eden, inform him that our Queen intends to depart within the next half hour from the Western stables." The man nodded and left.

As soon as Sergeant Simon departed, Bloodstone quickly scribbled orders to Blacksmith. "Corporal." The Corporal entered and she handed him the orders. "Have this delivered to Colonel Blacksmith at once." The Corporal saluted and left the tent. Bloodstone quickly changed into her battle leather, then grabbed her pack and Eden's, smiling to herself as she did so. She knew she had no need to inform Eden, Dex would've already taken care of that for her. Grabbing the small trunk of herbs and a pack full of nothing but bandages, she exited her tent. Three packs slung over one shoulder and the box tucked under one arm, she didn't even look at Dex. She turned and headed for the stables, saying as she did so, "Come on if you're coming." Arriving at the stables, she wasn't surprised to see Sergeant Simon saddling his horse.

Andrew and Eden arrived a few minutes later. She quickly informed them of the situation. Both men looked worried. "What's the plan?" asked Andrew.

"We're going to set out on their return journey. Hopefully, we'll find them just a few hours away, something having delayed them." Both men nodded in quick agreement.

Once on the road, Bloodstone decided to take their minds off of the situation for a moment and asked, "So, Dex, how is married life treating you?" Dex looked uncomfortable and did not answer. After a long moment, Bloodstone added, "I know my sister's being a pain in the ass, but other than that, how are things going?"

"Despite her promise, she's not making my life miserable if that's what you mean, General," he replied hesitantly.

Eden said, "That's good to hear. I was a little worried."

"Is she giving you the silent treatment?" asked Andrew.

Dex shrugged his shoulders. "I'm not sure how talkative she normally is, but she doesn't not talk to me. She just doesn't go out of her way to talk to me."

Eden considered for a moment. "I seem to recall from the inn, she is a little bit of a quiet girl, or at least I should say she didn't seem to chatter endlessly."

Andrew considered for a moment and then added, "She also didn't flirt with the soldiers."

Bloodstone reached out and punched her brother in the shoulder. "Not helping, Andrew."

They rode as late into the evening as they dared before stopping to make camp. They had as of yet seen no sign of their men, which told them something bad had indeed happened. Bloodstone heard one of the men speaking unguardedly that they would only find corpses if anything at all, and as much as it pained her to admit it, he was probably right.

They were up and ready to go before sunrise. As soon as the first fingers of dawn lit the sky, they were on their horses. Less than an hour later, they saw them. Bloodstone brought them to a halt more than fifty feet away from the bodies of their friends. "Who here besides Eden and I are good at tracking?" asked Bloodstone. One Church Soldier, one State Soldier, and Dex raised their hands. "Let's circle them before we go in. There's no need to hurry, they clearly have been here all night." The men all nodded grimly as they dismounted and handed the reins to their friends. They each slowly worked their way to the center.

"General, I have some strange tracks over here," the State Soldier said. Bloodstone and Eden both went to investigate.

Eden knelt down near one of the better tracks, examining it carefully. He then slowly rose to his feet and followed it. Once he got close to the center of the battle, he lost it, only occasionally finding it. "She arrived after the battle. From the amount of blood she tread in, I'd say at least an hour, if not more."

Andrew had dismounted and had slowly been working his way closer and closer. He asked, "Scavenger?"

"I don't think so, nothing appears to have be taken," replied the Church soldier.

"Don't speak too hastily, Corporal. One of our men is missing. I counted twice, there's only twenty …" Bloodstone hesitated a long moment. "I'm pretty sure it's Grayhawk. I haven't checked all the faces yet, but I don't see any emerald green. There are only two Knights, one in blue, one in yellow, which means either the Barbarians took him or she did. But I saw no signs of drag marks. I don't know how something so small carried him away. Eden, for the length of her stride, how tall would you say she was?"

"Five four, five six, no more, maybe a hundred and twenty pounds," he replied quickly.

"She didn't take him away, General. I found her tracks leaving, headed in that direction," replied Dex. A moment later he said, "Eden,

General, would you mind coming and joining me over here?"

Bloodstone and Eden both turned and quickly joined him. He spoke in a soft voice. "These are her tracks here, but I keep finding drops of blood about a foot or two away from her, heading in the same direction. But unless she was holding out her arm that was dripping blood, I don't know how there's blood drops over here," he said, looking confused.

"You know it occurs to me, we keep assuming she's a woman, but it could be a child," said Andrew from behind them. They all turned to look at him. He shrugged his shoulders.

Bloodstone hesitated a moment, then called for the men to follow them as they began searching the side of the mountain. Bloodstone watched her men carefully for any sign that they found something. When she saw a Corporal gesturing to her, she joined him and the Sergeant. The Sergeant was just inside a cave. The Corporal was holding aside a curtain made out of what appeared to be vines and moss. She looked inside past the Sergeant. She saw a woman sitting in a bed holding a sheet up against her naked body, turned in an awkward position. It took Bloodstone only a moment to realize that she was trying to hide something, or more importantly, someone behind her. "Wait outside," she ordered. As she entered, the soldier retreated. Bloodstone watched as the woman twisted her body more, trying in vain to conceal what was in bed with her. What surprised Bloodstone more than anything was that the woman was Breton. "Do you speak Breton?"

The woman looked at her as though she was an idiot. "This is my home. Get out, whoever you are. Get out, you have no business here."

Bloodstone moved further into the cave, looking around. It was a rather nice little home she had made for herself. Then her heart lifted as she saw the tattered remains of Grayhawk's surcoat. "If the man you are trying to conceal behind you is my brother, or one of my men, it is my business." Hearing movement behind her, Bloodstone cursed under her breath at Dex.

The woman quickly looked from Bloodstone to Dex and back to Bloodstone. "I don't want to hurt either one of you. Get out of my home. I don't know who you are, but Bretons and Barbarians working together can't be good. You're both probably traitors - now get out!"

"I'm not leaving here without my brother. I know that's my brother. That's his surcoat over there. How badly hurt is he?" Bloodstone said firmly.

"Just because he's your brother doesn't mean you two are friends. He is a Breton and all those men out there who were slaughtered were Bretons.

How do I know you're not mixed up in it? How do I know you're not a part of it?" she demanded angrily.

"I hate to admit it, General, but she does make a good point. But I don't know how we're supposed to convince her that we're on the same side," Andrew said from the entrance.

The woman looked more frightened. Now Bloodstone looked over her shoulder. Eden, Andrew, and Sergeant Simon had joined Dex in the entrance. "This is your final warning, if all of you don't get out of here I'm going to hurt you!"

Bloodstone had been standing to one side of the entrance, she now moved to the center and took a few steps further forward trying to shield the others as much as possible. She heard someone start to move behind her and said quickly, "Dex, I swear to the gods if you try to interfere I'll kill you." Bloodstone took another step forward. "Listen, I don't know what I'm supposed to say or what I'm supposed to do to convince you that we mean you no harm. We also mean him no harm, he's brother to four of us."

"He can't be brother to four of you. Two of you are Barbarians and you don't look like him," she said angrily, as she held her hand up, palm out.

Bloodstone quickly held up both hands, palm out. "Please wait just a minute. Hear me out."

The woman lowered her hand. Bloodstone pulled off her helmet, Andrew did the same. "He and I share no blood. Andrew has the same mother as Grayhawk. Grayhawk favors his father as does Andrew. Andrew and I, we share the same father. Dex here, his wife is my sister. We share the same mother and Eden is my husband. That's why he's brother to four of us. Our family relationship gets a lot more convoluted than that I promise you …"

Before Bloodstone had a chance to go on, the woman interrupted her. "You're a woman?"

"Yes, why don't I send the men away and you let me look at my brother. If I do anything you don't like, you can torch me or whatever you were intending to do to me if that would make you happy. But let me look at my brother, please, I'm begging you." Bloodstone lowered herself to her knees. "Please?"

"If you give the men all your weapons, I will let you stay, but they have to go away." Bloodstone quickly stripped out of all of her weapons, handing them over to the men. Dex stood there as though he was going to refuse, when Eden grabbed him by the back of the tunic and pulled him out.

Once the men were gone, the woman slipped quickly from the bed and grabbed her dress. As she pulled it on, Bloodstone saw a scar on her shoulder, as though someone had carved a symbol into her flesh. Bloodstone gave an involuntary shudder as she felt her temper rise. No wonder the woman hated Bretons. She waited until the woman was dressed and then she crossed to Michael and knelt down next to him. He had a fever, but this was expected. She examined the broken arm through the splint, then his side, and then his thigh. The wounds all looked angry, but not infected. After satisfying herself that none of them were life-threatening, she began unsplinting the arm carefully.

"What do you think you're doing?" demanded the woman angrily.

"I'm Bloodstone, and you are?"

"Cora, and I asked you a question. What do you think you're doing?"

"I want to look at the broken bone." She carefully examined the stitches and the broken bone. As she gently felt it, Michael moaned and groaned in pain. "I'm sorry, Michael, I will give you something for the pain in a minute. You did an expert job setting the broken bone, couldn't have been easy on your own. I thank you for the care and attention you gave my brother." She turned to look at the woman. "Why are you out here, Cora? This is no place for you."

"My reasons are my own."

"Is it because they believe you are a witch?" Cora began stepping backwards, looking terrified.

"Cora, we mean you no harm, but you shouldn't be out here. It's too dangerous. The Barbarians are increasing their patrols. It's only a matter of time before they find your cave."

"I can take care of myself, and what do you care anyways? You don't know me." she said angrily.

"No, you're right, I don't know you. I only owe you for the life of my brother, and that is not a debt I intend to take lightly."

"You don't owe me anything and I'll be fine out here by myself. Don't worry," she said, with more confidence than she felt.

Bloodstone sighed and grimaced. She always hated it when she had to be harsh and nearly cruel, but clearly kindness was not going to convince Cora to come with them. "Cora, I promise you they will find you. We found you easily enough. And when they find you, if you are lucky, they will take turns raping you and they will kill you. If you're not so lucky, they will take you with them and they will sell you, trade you, and will torture you for as long as they can."

Cora's eyes widened in terror, then she said, "Not if I kill them first."

"I don't know a lot about magic, but I know it takes a lot out of you to use it. Do you have enough to kill twenty grown Barbarian males who are resistant to magic? Because I promise you, if they see you use magic, you will become breeding stock. Barbarians believe magic runs in the blood. I know you think I'm saying these things to frighten you, and in a way I am, but only to frighten you to come with us. My men and I will protect you. My men and I will not use you. We will not abuse you. Yes, I know you're a witch. I saw the brand on your back. I'm not afraid of you and I promise you my men won't be either. I owe you a debt, let me protect you."

"I'm not your prisoner? I can come and go as I please?"

"You can live in the encampment. I can send you somewhere else where you will be safe. It is your choice, but you will be no one's prisoner." Cora nodded her head. "Thank you. You and Grayhawk will stay here for now. With your permission, I will have one of my men bring my herbs and I'll make Grayhawk something for the pain." Again, she nodded.

Bloodstone sent for her box and bandages. Andrew brought them in to her, then he went and sat next to his brother. Bloodstone began mixing a potion.

"I see why you're not afraid of me, you have magic too."

Andrew turned to look at her sharply. "What do you mean?"

Cora's eyes widened and she looked nervous. Bloodstone gave a little laugh. "Don't worry, Cora. You only startled him. But yes, I have magic, but in a very limited capacity. Just enough to infuse potions. My husband's brother, Viktor, he's very good at infusing potions. He has a lot more magic than one would expect from a shaman of Freya, but in addition to his potions, he's the High Shaman of Freya. That's why I'm not afraid of you. I grew up in a temple around magic all the time. Magic doesn't frighten me. Sometimes surprises or startles me, because I didn't expect it to come from that quarter, but it never frightens me. I think sometimes people don't realize how much magic is really in the world. Here Andrew, give this to your brother." Andrew took the potion and roused Grayhawk just enough to coerce him into swallowing it. Bloodstone reached over and squeezed his shoulder tightly. "Don't worry, he'll live. He's just gonna be uncomfortable for a while, but you should remember what that's like." Andrew shot her a dirty look, but smiled nevertheless. "Why don't you stay here, I'll go help bury the bodies."

"No General, you should stay here. I'll go," Andrew replied, rising.

"Neither one of you need stay if you have other things that need your attention, I can attend to him," Cora said softly.

"If you're sure Grayhawk won't give you any trouble?" Andrew asked with a grin.

"Why you do call him Grayhawk and Michael?" Cora asked, looking puzzled.

"Most of the time I just call him Grayhawk, but occasionally when I'm feeling more brotherly, I call him Michael. Knights are often referred to by their last name. Technically, if you want to address him properly, it should be Lord Michael Eric Grayhawk, Colonel of the State Knights of the King." With that, he bowed and excused himself.

As he and Bloodstone were heading out to the bodies, he slammed his shoulder into hers playfully. "Fifty gold says they're married within a month."

Bloodstone immediately began shaking her head. "No bet." Bloodstone laughed. "You'll have to find another sucker for that one; I saw the way she was looking at him."

XXV

Cora awoke with a start. Sitting up, she could hear her guest shivering. Turning to look at him, she was surprised to see his eyes open. "You're awake."

He nodded, teeth chattering. "Where are my men? Where am I?"

She got up and crossed to him, picking up the cup Bloodstone had left for him. "Your sister said if you awoke I could give you this. She said it would help with the fever and any pain." She slid her arm behind him and helped him to sit up.

"My sister?" He looked around. "Where is she?" She put the cup to his lips and would not answer until it was empty.

Finally, she put the cup on the ground and turned to him. "Your family's outside, or some of it. I gather your sister would have stayed in here with you, but apparently she is not permitted to go anywhere without one of the Barbarians. And the other one, her husband, he, of course, would not want to be far from her either. One of your brothers would have stayed in here, but I was not comfortable with that." She blushed slightly. "Your sister would've had you moved outside, but I insisted you were more comfortable and would rest better here in my bed."

Grayhawk couldn't understand why he was freezing. Try as he might, he couldn't seem to stop his teeth from chattering. It made it hard to focus on the woman's words. "My men, you didn't tell me about my men," he demanded. She suddenly looked very sad. He sighed and said, "All of them?" She nodded sadly, refusing to meet his eye. He leaned back on the pillow and cursed silently. Lifting his head and banging it against the pillow, he cursed himself again. *WHY! Why did you spare me and not my men?* he demanded of the gods. They didn't answer. They never did, but it made him feel better to ask.

As Cora sat on the edge of the bed watching him brood, her concern was growing. Despite the potion, he was still shaking like a leaf. She touched her hand to his forehead. He felt cold. This surprised her. She had to warm him back up. She stripped out of her dress and slid into bed next to him. He stared at her. "And what in Hades do you think you're doing?" he asked in shock.

"Freya says that you're too sick for fire, but you need to be warm. She says body warmth is the best thing." Lying down on his left side, she pressed her body against his, rubbing his chest with her hand trying to warm him. He felt cold everywhere she touched.

Grayhawk groaned to himself. He knew this was a very bad idea and he should put a stop to it immediately, but he was freezing and couldn't seem to get warm. Her warm body felt so nice next to his. He decided he better ask a mundane question before he focused too much on the very lovely body pressed up against him. "How does a Breton come to live in the mountains of the Barbarian lands?"

She stiffened and hesitated. "I ran away." She hesitated a moment, then added, "I like it here, no people here."

Grayhawk shifted uncomfortably. She was squishing his arm. "Forgive me, but you're lying on my arm."

"Oh, my apologies." She lifted herself off his arm.

He instinctively wrapped his arm around her and pulled her back against him. His teeth had stopped chattering and he was finally starting to feel warm. He was reluctant to give up her heat, but nevertheless he forced himself to say, "I think I'm warming. I should move to the floor and let you have your bed back."

She lifted her head off the pillow and looked down at him. He forced himself to maintain eye contact, which was very hard given what was directly in front of his face. "Don't be ridiculous, you'll catch your death on that stone floor. Besides, you're still shivering." As she settled back in next to him, this time she placed her head on his

310

shoulder. He curled his arm around her again and pressed his hand into her back. Her skin felt nice and soft. He slid his hand up her back to squeeze her left shoulder. When his hand felt a patch of rough skin, he stiffened. As he ran his hand across it, she pulled away quickly and started to turn her back to him, but then turned on her knees to face him. Covering her breasts, she would've backed away, but he grabbed her arm quickly.

"Turn around," he said calmly as he sat up.

She tried to pull her arm free, but despite his weakened condition, he had a grip like a vice. "Please, just let me go. I don't want to hurt anyone," she pleaded softly.

"And I don't want to force you to turn around, but I will," he said calmly.

"If you try to make me, it'll pop all your stitches," she cautioned.

"You say that as though I care. Turn around." He took advantage of her momentary indecision and jerked her around. Pulling her hair aside, he stared at the mark on her shoulder. He felt his blood begin to boil. Someone, most likely a man, had carved the symbol for witch on her left shoulder. It was a warning to anyone who saw it that this person was dangerous. He stared at the crude carving of an upside down bird. He placed his hand over the scar, mentally cursing any human being who would disfigure another. He felt her stiffen, then she hugged herself tightly and started to sniffle. He gently slid his arm around her waist and pulled her onto his lap. Forgetting for a moment the throbbing pain in his right arm, he wrapped his other arm around her and squeezed her tightly, gritting his teeth when he remembered. "I am so sorry." He placed his cheek against the back of her neck. Still holding her tightly against him, he asked, "Who did that to you?"

She sniffled again and wiped at her eyes. "It doesn't matter, it was a long time ago."

Grayhawk clenched his teeth tighter. A long time ago did not make him feel better - if anything, it made him feel worse. That meant whoever had done this, had done it to a child. He cursed the man again. "Is that why you came to live here? Is that why you don't like people?" He felt her nod. "Tell me about it. How did you end up here? This is no place for a woman by herself."

"You shouldn't be questioning me, you should be sleeping."

"Very well." He leaned back, pulling her down with him. Shifting her in his arms, putting her head back on his shoulder and wrapping his good arm tightly around her, he said, "You can tell me a bedtime story."

She scoffed at him. "Only if you want nightmares."

"I'll take my chances. Tell me. Anyways, you should learn I may not be a Stone, but I was raised by one, and I am as stubborn as they are."

She sighed and shrugged her shoulders. She'd never told anyone. Granted, there never been anyone to tell. She'd lived alone a very long time, having as little to do with others as possible. "Why aren't you afraid of me? I'm a witch!" she demanded suddenly.

"Are you dangerous?" She nodded her head solemnly. He couldn't help it, he started laughing. "I don't believe it. I don't believe you'd ever hurt a fly."

"I killed a man once," she said in a hollow voice, then she squirmed and wiggled against him.

Grayhawk groaned to himself. Then he cleared his throat and said in the calmest voice he could manage, "If you're going to keep wiggling against me like that, I won't be held responsible for what I might end up doing to you, Woman." He looked at her sharply. "You know, it just occurred to me, I don't know your name. My name is Michael Grayhawk, but most everybody just calls me Grayhawk."

"Cora, just Cora." She pushed herself up so her chin was resting on his chest and looked down at him. "Why is it I said I killed a man and you don't even look worried?"

"I figure you'll tell me in a minute how you killed him, but I get the sinking suspicion he deserved it. But of course, if you want me to try you for murder, I could do that, but I'd rather you just tell me what happened. After all, I am a Knight, and you just admitted to me that you killed somebody, so now you have to tell me the whole story." He grinned at her. She looked frightened as she remembered that Knights had the authority to act as judge, jury, and executioner, and their authority was absolute. She trembled in his arms. "Just tell me what happened from the beginning," he said gently.

"As you gathered from the mark on my back, I'm a witch. I was born this way. There are some things with magic that come as easy to me as breathing does to you. Of course, there are things that take much more effort, but moving small objects around ..." A moment later, the empty glass was floating over his head. "Like things like that, I can move them around all day. I can make them dance and swirl and do any number of things. Unfortunately, I often do these things without even thinking. I think I want them and they come to me; so consequently, my parents were terrified of me. I guess I was about eight or so when the children in the village started learning that I wasn't normal. Mostly they just threw mud pies at me, but they threw a lot of rocks too. The meanest of them was the magistrate's son. One day he hit me in the head with a rock, then knocked me into a mud puddle. He jumped on top of me and started hitting me. I didn't even think, I just put out my hands and pushed him away. He flew back about twenty feet and slammed into a building, falling unconscious. The other children all scattered. I ran home. The magistrate wasn't far behind me. He dragged me from my home and as we entered his office, he slammed my head into a bar. I guess I lost consciousness. When I woke up," she reached for her shoulder, "my shoulder was throbbing. The next day he took me from my village. He took me to a ... well, I didn't know what it was then, but I would later learn it was a ... a whorehouse." Grayhawk stiffened with disgust, but he forced his face to remain neutral. "He haggled with the proprietor, and finally they agreed on twenty gold. I guess I should've told you, at this time I was about ten maybe. The proprietor was actually very nice. He treated me better than my parents had ever treated me. I was one of six women he employed to serve as a drudge. You know the kind, invisible, who scrubs floors, do laundry, things like that. It was hard work, but nobody bothered me. I guess I worked there about two years before the proprietor called me to one of the rooms one night. It didn't happen often, but it did happen occasionally that they would need a room cleaned during ..." she hesitated over her choice of words, "business hours. As soon as I entered though, I knew something was wrong. The proprietor and a man was in there. Usually it was just the proprietor and he would tell me what I needed to do, and then he would leave. But as I entered, the other man, he looked me up and down in a way I was very familiar with. I had seen men look at the whores that way." She swallowed hard and shuddered. Grayhawk instinctively tightened his grasp on her, trying to lend comfort. "He was a hideous looking man. Someone had mauled his face. He told the proprietor that I'd do fine, exactly what he was looking for. The proprietor excused himself and left us alone. He … he grabbed me and started … kissing me and … touching me. I screamed and I didn't even think …" She began shaking and sobbing uncontrollably. "I just brought up my hands to push him away … I didn't want to hurt him … but he flew back, slamming into a large mirror. It shattered. I just ran. I ran to my room and I grabbed my things and I ran away and then I just kept running and I ended up here. You see, he was dead. I know he was dead. There was so much blood." She pressed her face into his shoulder and cried.

Grayhawk wished he could believe the man was dead, but he doubted it seriously. "Unfortunately, I believe you probably didn't kill him. What a shame. But even had you killed him, he got what he deserved, and so did the magistrate's son." She pressed her cheek on his chest and hugged him tightly. "Cora, I warned you, stop that."

She slid her body up on his just a little more so that her chin was resting on his chest again. She said, managing to look quite innocent, but he knew she was anything but innocent at this moment. "Stop what?"

"If you don't stop rubbing your body against mine like that, I'm going to roll you on your back and show you exactly what you're doing to me."

She giggled. "You're too badly wounded to do that. You'd hurt yourself before you even managed it," she giggled again.

To her surprise, she was on her back in a moment, with him half on top of her. She looked up at him, startled as his mouth came down on hers. She hesitated for only a moment before her arms wrapped around him and her hand slid up his back. After several more minutes of passionate kissing, he wrenched his mouth free. "If you think a scratch on my leg and a scratch on my side is going to prevent me from making love to you, you are under an extreme misapprehension. The only large hindrance is my damn arm, which I fear will prevent me from giving a brilliant performance, but nevertheless, I think I can get the job done." As he stared down at her, he allowed his eyes to rake over every inch of her exposed flesh; then breathing hard, he forced himself to say, "Fortunately, however, I am not in the habit of seducing and ruining innocent girls." He started to pull away when one of her arms wrapped tightly around him. Fingers pressing into his back, her other hand slid up into his hair and grabbed a handful of his hair, forcing him back down to her mouth. Grayhawk needed no other encouragement.

Grayhawk awoke when he felt her shift in his arms. He had slept badly. His arm was throbbing like crazy and his thigh was alternating between cramping and throbbing. He told himself the pain was his punishment for what he had done last night. It had been wrong of him to take advantage of her and steal her innocence. He was staring down at the fiery red curls draped over his chest when he heard a rustle. He looked up to see Eden entering the cave. The smile on his lips died instantly. And the disapproving look Eden gave Grayhawk was more painful than any harsh words he could've said. Eden narrowed his eyes and gave an almost imperceptible shake of the head. Grayhawk felt Cora stiffen in his arms. A moment later, Eden turned and walked out.

"Dammit, one these days that man is going to explain to me how he always knows everything," Grayhawk said angrily.

She lifted her head to look at him. "What do you mean?"

"Nothing, you probably think me ridiculous, but I would swear that that man knows that I stole your innocence last night."

"It's his wolf's blood, and what do you mean you stole it? I thought I gave it to you," she asked, looking annoyed.

"Just because someone gives you something," he caressed her cheek, "doesn't mean you have the right to take it. And though I'm honored by what you gave me last night, it was wrong, and I should not have allowed it to happen. I behaved as a cad."

She looked annoyed and climbed out of bed, washed, and dressed. She had just begun brushing her hair when he asked, "What do you mean wolf's blood? You mean because he is a Wolf Tribesman?"

Cora, realizing she was about to out someone else's secrets - because clearly Grayhawk did not know - was trying to think of a plausible lie when she was saved by one of the Breton males entering. Grayhawk sat up, but before he could speak, the other man spoke. "Here we all were worried about you, though apparently you are doing just fine."

"What in Hades is that supposed to mean, Andrew?" demanded Grayhawk, looking furious.

Andrew shrugged his shoulders as though he couldn't understand. "I just mean Eden says you're doing well - though he does, however, seem to be incapable of speaking to you right now. So he had me bring in your clothes, though since he was already in here, I wonder why he couldn't leave them?"

"Listen to me, Little Brother. You had better watch that mouth of yours before somebody bashes it in. I'd hate for Tabitha to suddenly find you revolting to look at."

"Anytime you're ready, Big Brother, bring it on. I will take you on any day," Andrew replied with heat. The two brothers glared at each other for a long moment. Finally, Andrew just threw the clothes at him and turned and walked out.

Grayhawk grunted and began pulling on his clothes. "Did my boots survive?" he snapped.

She retrieved them and handed them over to him. "Your boots and most of your armor, though your sister removed your armor last night."

"Thank you. Please don't mind Andrew. He can be a bit of an ass sometimes, but he's a good guy. Definitely the kind of man you want on your side." He stood up slowly and examined his arm, then the tunic. He had to split the sleeve for his arm to fit through, but other than that, he didn't look so bad. "You do realize you're not staying here, right?"

"Yes, your sister won't let me stay either. She says it's too dangerous." Remembering what the woman had said, she gave a little shudder. "Yes, she made it very clear exactly how dangerous it is."

320

A quarter of an hour later, Grayhawk and Cora were approaching the group. Eden turned and headed their direction, putting his left hand on Grayhawk's right shoulder, he looked down on him. "How are you feeling?" he asked, his concern evident.

"My arm is killing me, but other than that, I'm fine." Grayhawk pressed his lips tightly together. He didn't have long to wait. Eden squeezed his shoulder and then delivered a hard right into his stomach.

Grayhawk doubled over and would've slumped to the ground, but Eden held him. "Thanks for not punching me in the ribs," Grayhawk choked out.

Cora screeched, "How dare you! He's wounded, why would you do such a thing? I thought you were friends?"

Grayhawk straightened himself, still holding his stomach with his good arm. "We are friends, that's why he punched me in the stomach. If Eden didn't like me, he would've just broken all my ribs."

"But why?" she demanded angrily.

"He knows why," Eden replied calmly.

Bloodstone said, "All right Eden, you've expressed your displeasure, now leave poor Grayhawk alone." Turning to Cora she asked, "Is there anything myself or my men can help you with?"

"No, I've packed up everything I want to take with me. It's not much." Bloodstone ordered two of her men to go and retrieve Cora's possessions.

"Searched the area last night, our men found a few of the horses, none of which, unfortunately, was your horse. So I suggest, given your injuries, you ride Cedric. He'll give you less trouble than the others might." Glancing at Cora she asked, "Do you know how to ride a horse?"

Cora fiercely shook her head and looked nervous. Grayhawk said, "Cora can ride with me."

"Very well, since you are injured, we'll let you set the pace," replied Bloodstone. "Get mounted, men."

Once they were all mounted and on their way, Cora looked at Grayhawk. "Why did Eden hit you?"

"Because Wolf Tribesman do not approve of the way we Bretons whore and Eden is one of the most vocal about it. But of course, what Eden doesn't realize, especially since he's not speaking to me ..." Grayhawk shouted to no one in particular.

"I am not not speaking to you, I'm just mad at you. I knew the brothers enjoyed their women. I just thought you had the decency not to take advantage of innocent girls and ruin them."

"See what I mean, high-minded ideals, but as I was going to say before he interrupted me, he can stop fretting because I'm going to marry you," he squeezed her waist tightly, "if you'll have me?"

She said softly so that only he could hear, "I don't think this is the right time to be having this conversation."

He looked grim. "In other words, the answer is no."

Though he had spoken in a normal voice, she still spoke softly when she replied, "You're only asking me because of last night, not because you want me. I won't have everybody saying I tricked you into it."

He laughed. "No one will say you tricked me. They will all say I was bewitched by your beauty and your fiery red hair, so I married you before you had a chance to be swept off your feet by someone else." He kissed her passionately. "And they'd be right, but I'm the man in possession and I don't intend to give it up," he added, pulling her even tighter against him and kissing her again. After a moment, he let go of the reins and ran his hand up and down her back.

She pulled away quickly. "The reins, the horse, won't he bolt?" she asked, looking frightened and clutching at him.

He laughed again. "Do you think I would have let go of the reins if I thought he would? Had it been any other horse then Cedric, I wouldn't have; but I don't think I've pissed him off enough that he will throw me, and I certainly don't think he'd do anything to hurt you."

Cedric said, "You know General, I so like Lord Greyhawk. He's such a nice man, very intelligent too."

As Cedric snorted, whinnied, and tossed his head, Cora's eyes widened. She looked down at the horse for the first time. "Oh, my apologies Sir Knight, I didn't realize you were a person. I was too afraid of being put on a horse. Do forgive me?"

Everyone turned to look at her, but it was Eden who spoke. "You mean you can understand Cedric too?"

"No, unfortunately, I can't understand what he's saying, but I can see him. I can see the spirit of the Knight in him."

"How disappointing, and here I thought I might get a real conversation," Cedric said mournfully.

"Ha ha very funny, Cedric," Bloodstone replied without looking amused.

"Well, it's not like you ever talk to me."

"I'm talking to you right now aren't I?"

"Only because you are forced to," he said sadly.

Bloodstone groaned. "I'm sorry Athena stuck you with me."

After several minutes of silence, Cora asked Grayhawk softly, "Do you want to be married to me?"

"I think I would find your company very enjoyable." He leaned in and whispered in her ear. "You already know I enjoy making love to you."

A soft blush colored her cheeks. "If you're really sure, I'll marry you."

"Very sure, but I can't actually ask you yet." She looked at him curiously.

"Sure you can, just ask Bloodstone first. She is our General, just not the General. I'm sure if she gives permission, Black Stone won't punish you," suggested Andrew.

"That's not a bad idea, Andrew." Grayhawk turned to face Bloodstone. "General, may I have your permission to marry this woman?"

"Yes, you may have my permission. I'll deal with Eric."

"Eric?" Cora asked.

"The eldest brother and our General," replied Grayhawk.

"Hold up, I'm the eldest. Murtaugh is the second oldest, followed by Eric, then you, Andrew and the rest of the brothers," replied Eden, looking annoyed.

Bloodstone hesitated a moment, then asked in a curious tone, "I thought the eldest was Viktor, followed by Foster, Xanhara, then you and everyone else … or were you men only talking about men - but in that case Viktor's still older," she added, with just the faintest hint of satisfaction.

Eden turned and glared at her, grabbed her, yanked her off her horse and settled her in front of him. "If you're going to be difficult and run on at the mouth, Woman, I will stop your mouth," he said, kissing her roughly.

XXVI

Ten days later, Black Stone, Eden, Murtaugh, Bloodstone, Xanhara, Andrew, Fletcher, Foster, Big Bear, Dex, Daniel, Grayhawk, and Sergeant Simon were all in the practice arena sparring. There were currently six combatants in the ring, with the rest surrounding them in a circle.

Xanhara was currently fighting Fletcher, and Dex was going up against Sergeant Simon. Black Stone was facing off against Big Bear. Everyone else was taking turns shouting words of encouragement, offering advice, or heckling the combatants. This was a game they had been playing for over a year. The number of participants may alter depending on the day, but the rules were always the same: no mercy, no quarter. They stopped only short of serious injury. Bruises, cuts, and scrapes were all part of the fun.

Xanhara sidestepped Fletcher, bringing the back half of her spear up into his ribs. Fletcher quickly countered with an elbow to her back. Taking advantage of her close proximity, he brought his knee up into her stomach. She staggered and Fletcher brought his arm back, quickly placing his blade at the side of her neck. "Shouldn't have tried to get cute, Xanhara. Had you brought your point across my stomach, I'd be the one dead and you'd still be in this fight."

"Yeah, you're right, I shouldn't have tried it, but that's okay, hopefully," she looked up and called out the name of the first person her eyes alighted on, "Bloodstone will trounce your ass." Fletcher groaned as Bloodstone came in sword swinging.

Simon was breathing hard. He hadn't realized how out of shape he was until he had been initiated into the Stone Wall and they started asking him to join them in sparring. This particular group of soldiers took their fighting ability very seriously. They were not your run-of-the-mill officers who felt a few hours of practice a week was enough, a few hours a day maybe. And he hadn't practiced more than a few hours a week in months now. Two hours straight, three days in a row, he could barely lift his arms, but he wasn't going to tell them that, even if he was pretty sure they knew it. And Dex was showing no mercy. He'd been hammering him from the start and hadn't let up. Simon was amazed he hadn't been killed and eliminated yet. But as he had learned, they played till all but one was dead. They had just begun their second round of the day. Eden had killed him quickly the first round, and now he wasn't sure whether Dex was toying with him or tired himself, but it was all Simon could do to block blow after blow. He barely had been able to strike one of his own. Dex brought his sword down hard over Simon's head. Sparks flew from their blades as they ran along each other.

Big Bear put another large dent in Black Stone's shield. "Bloodstone, I think my shield is going to need to be replaced after this fight. Big Bear's hammering it to pieces."

"Good for Big Bear. It's a piece of shit anyways," Bloodstone replied, as she dodged a blow from Fletcher.

"You only say that because you didn't make it," Black Stone countered, as he went on the attack against Big Bear, landing three hard blows in rapid succession on his axe. Big Bear pulled back quickly, then thrust the top of his axe into the center of Black Stone's chest. Black Stone rolled with the blow to the right, saying as he did so, "You know, Big Bear, that's the second time I've seen you do that move today. If you are going to keep doing that, you should have Bloodstone put a spike on that thing." Then stepping in, he brought the flat of his blade across Big Bear's stomach. "But since you're dead, I think you should pick my opponent."

"Dammit, I thought for sure I had you this time, but maybe Murtaugh will have better luck against you." Murtaugh stepped into the ring, tossing his sword from hand to hand, spinning the heavy blade lightly.

Black Stone rolled his eyes as he watched him show off. "Are you going to stand there and look pretty, or are we going to fight?" taunted Black

Stone. Murtaugh moved so quickly, catching Black Stone off guard, he nearly killed him in the first blow.

Murtaugh laughed. "Tisk, tisk, shouldn't allow yourself to be distracted," teased Murtaugh.

Bloodstone and Fletcher exchanged a flurry of blows, neither one giving ground. "Simon, switch with me, I want to teach Dex a lesson," Bloodstone called out suddenly. As Simon quickly attacked the Sergeant Major, then he mentally corrected himself, Fletcher. That was the only real rule when they were sparring. There were no ranks, no titles, just skill against skill.

Bloodstone and Dex exchanged a quick flurry of blows. "What's the matter, Bloodstone, Fletcher too much for you? Thought I'd take it easy on you?" Dex taunted.

"No, I just figured you were getting sloppy and needed the practice. After all, the way you've been swinging that blade, Blackwolf could take you with one hand tied behind his back." Dex couldn't help it. He busted out laughing, though he did regret it a moment later when she kicked him in the chest and he hit the ground hard. Sliding across it, he rolled quickly, barely managing to miss the blow that was intended for his head.

Getting quickly to his feet he added, "Really, are you that tired that you have to resort to taunts and tricks?" he teased.

There was another rapid exchange of blows, the final one of which had Bloodstone holding her sword with both hands. She strained with all of her might to keep Dex's blade out of her shoulder. "Really, I'm not the one who was just on my back," she taunted.

A moment later she regretted that, as Dex kicked both her legs out from underneath her and sent her crashing to her back. He fell on top of her, sword to her throat. "You're good. I'm stronger and I'm better, don't try to win a fight against me with strength. You'll lose every time. You have to use your speed to beat me," he said, all joking aside. He stood up and offered her his hand. She took it and he pulled her to her feet.

She turned and was just about to pick his new opponent, when she saw a guard on horseback charge up and dismount quickly. He saluted. "Forgive the intrusion, Generals." He turned and nodded to the rest of the officers. "Sirs, ma'am, the Captain of the Eastern Gate sent me to inform you there's about a hundred and fifty people approaching. They don't look like an army, but there are some soldiers, and they're not Bretons."

"Eastern Gate … but that's the Breton border," Xanhara said incredulously.

Black Stone shot a questioning look at Foster. "More Soldiers of Ares?" he said hopefully.

"No, but I can take a guess," said Foster.

Eden looked at Foster sharply. "Boy, do I hope you're right, that would be a tremendous advantage. Why don't we go find out who our new visitors are."

As they walked in the direction of the Eastern Gate, Bloodstone felt her ego was a little bruised. She knew that that fight wouldn't be over had she been willing to hurt him. She only would've had to bring her knee up and he would've been the one on the ground, but that was something she would never do in a fight with her friends, even if occasionally she might wish to. But he was right, she should never have tried to overpower him. Perhaps that was the thing that stung the most, her own ill judgment. She mentally kicked herself for her stupidity and vowed not to make that mistake again.

Arriving at the gates, they saw at a glance that they were indeed people from the underground city. They all walked out to meet them. Two of the men who stepped forward to speak with them, they recognized at once as two of the four guards who were so curious about the surface. Eden stepped forward and offered his hand, greeting them by name. "Quicksilver, Shadowrock, it's good to see you. I never thought we would again. Permit me to introduce our friends."

Introductions having been performed, Black Stone asked, "Would you and your officers like to join me in my tent? I'm sure you could all use some refreshment after your journey. I can have my men see to your ..." he hesitated a moment over his words, then added, "soldiers."

"Yes, we would like to have a few words with you if you do not mind, General, and my people are tired," replied Shadowrock.

Black Stone gave orders for their guests to be attended to and showed the few officers to the War Room. Once everyone had been made comfortable, Shadowrock said, "I would first like to say that it has been decided amongst my people that I would lead us here. Please allow me to introduce the others with us, this is Lydia ..." She gave a little curtsy and Dex recognized her as the woman who had made the beds larger. "And this is Rivermoss ..." the young man bowed. "And this is Ivy."

"Your names, Rivermoss, Shadowrock, are those warrior names?" asked Big Bear.

"No, when our people are born, they're taken before the Council of Elders and then they are examined. It is determined what they will be when they grow up. Once this is determined, parents often give their children names that have to do with what their abilities will be. Rivermoss has a natural affinity for water, creatures of the water, and basically anything that grows, lives, or has to do with water. I have a natural affinity for stone and shadows." He looked around. "There is no dark corner in this tent or I could demonstrate."

Black Stone nodded, then said, "My apologies, but it was my understanding that your people showed us the door and didn't want anything to do with us. So what changed your mind?"

Shadowrock said angrily, "That was our King, not our people as a whole. We were not given a choice in the matter. After talking with your people that night - we kept them up most of the night - but they were very kind about it. They answered all of our questions and only asked a few of their own in return. The four of us, we started talking amongst ourselves. And then four of us turned into twenty, and by the time we were all done talking, we were the hundred and sixty one of us you saw. The old may be content to hide in the mountains and read their books and practice their magic, dedicate themselves to their arts, but the younger ones like myself, we're not so content. There were those of us who knew nothing but the inside of the mountain and did not wish to venture out into the world, but there are also those of us who felt a restlessness these many years and longed to see the sunshine. Our people were not born into darkness, but thrust into it. And though our people would try to blame yours and yours," he nodded to Eden and Black Stone, "it was their decision and no one else's. We do not wish to dwell in darkness any longer. We would like to join you, and perhaps when the war is over, we could carve out a little holding of our own. Do not misunderstand me - I do not want to be a king. I don't want to control a country. I just mean a small section in one of your countries, maybe where we could live as a community under your rule."

"Would you require the section to be exclusively yours, or would you share it with others?" asked Bloodstone.

"We would not wish to drive people from their homes, if that is what you mean. I can see no reason why we could not live in peaceful harmony with others," replied Quicksilver.

Black Stone said, "Then I'm sure between our two countries we could find some place for you."

"That is all that we ask, just to live in the sunshine again, a place to raise our children. I should also warn you that most of the people I have brought with me are not warriors. They are either archers or sorcerers. In truth, I don't think any of us could survive open combat with the People of Stone," cautioned Shadowrock.

"We have no shortage of soldiers. What we do, however, lack is sorcerers," replied Foster.

335

Shadowrock looked a little nervous as he said, "You also may or may not have noticed some of us who left the darkness had children and we brought them with us, others who are in expectation of the arrival of their first ..." he shifted and started to turn his head, but then stopped himself at the last moment.

Before he had a chance to go on, Lydia stepped forward and slipped her left hand into his and wrapped her right arm around his left. "What my husband is reluctant to tell you is that we are expecting. He fears you will not want us if you know that we have not brought as many warriors as you might wish."

Bloodstone looked at the woman with surprise. She hesitated a moment and then decided that was a lie she was not willing to overlook. "I think you'd better explain why you're lying to us, Lydia."

Lydia clutched at Shadowrock's arm tighter, but it was he who replied. "She meant no harm by her lie. I was unaware that any of you have magic, or I would've corrected the lie immediately." He looked uncomfortable and shifted. "Amongst our people, all marriages are arranged by the Council of Elders, based on ability and birth." They all watched as the young man struggled to find words. He was clearly uncomfortable discussing whatever this was.

Quicksilver stepped into the gap. "They are not married because Shadowrock is considered beneath her in birth and ability, and his relationship with her is considered a crime. Had the King discovered it, he would've had him put to death or banished, probably the former. I heard the King tell you that we were a dying people and that our people are more passionate about their abilities than they are physical relationships. The reason our people are dying is because no one is ever happy with who the Council chooses to be their breeding partner. Though there are those who can find it in themselves to do their duty and produce a child, there are many who cannot." He glanced apologetically at Ivy. "Ivy only came with us because in ten days time she was to be married to a man she hates, because the Council feels his water abilities and her plant abilities could create an interesting power combination." Everyone glanced at Rivermoss, who immediately held up his hands and began shaking his head. "No, it was not Rivermoss. It was actually an older man, much older. She did not want to leave her home, but she would not marry him. So she joined us instead."

"Having once had the misfortune of being in an arranged marriage for ten very long years, I can't blame any of you, and I don't think Eden will blame you either. His first marriage was arranged as well. But since most everyone in the room is married and at least half of them already have a child or a child on the way, I don't think we'll hold it against you for adding a few more to the mix.

Since I'm assuming that Lydia's condition has been kept secret, I hope you will permit me to be amongst the first to congratulate you. I would wish you both joy," Black Stone added with a grin. "In fact there's quite a few bets on when the others will produce offspring."

"And don't forget about the bet on when Bloodstone and Eden will have a second one," added Xanhara.

Bloodstone added, "Hey, I still have twenty gold on when Brienna and Big Bear will have their second."

To everyone's surprise, Big Bear blushed and looked uncomfortable. All eyes slowly turned to stare at him. After a long moment, he cleared his throat. "About that, we expect a new arrival very late winter or very early spring." Everyone quickly congratulated him, even their new allies.

"Well, I think this calls for another celebration. I think we should toast our new alliance and all of our future arrivals," Black Stone said, as he went into his private quarters and came back with three bottles of wine.

XXVII

Bloodstone had just finished preparing the midday meal when Sergeant Simon stuck his head in. "Forgive the intrusion, General, but a Wolf Tribesman just stopped by with a message from Helena. She's going stir crazy cooped up in her tent and wondered if you might have a few minutes to spare her." Bloodstone laughed and nodded. Grabbing her cloak, she headed in the direction of Murtaugh and Helena's tent. She felt bad for Helena; Murtaugh didn't like her straying far now that she was so near her time. She entered the tent without announcing herself first.

A moment later, she was shaking her head at Helena. "If I might have a minute to spare? Please tell me you sent for Viktor."

"No, I didn't, and I don't want you to either. There's no reason for the entire camp to get into an uproar just because I'm having a baby. What good would it do anyways? All you'd do is upset poor Murtaugh. And what good would that do? There's nothing he can do. Allow him to continue to spar with the rest of the men and be happily ignorant …" She was cut off abruptly by a contraction. Bloodstone discarded her cloak and crossed to the other woman. Sitting down on the edge of the bed, she gripped her hand tightly.

When the contraction was over, Bloodstone looked down at her sternly. "You should've sent for me sooner, that was a very strong contraction. How close together are they?"

"Only a few minutes," she said sheepishly.

Bloodstone sighed and shook her head again and began rolling up her sleeves. Looking around, she saw that Helena had already made all the preparations. "You know Amber might just kill you if you don't send for her?"

"I definitely don't want Amber here. She's nearly as far along as I am. She doesn't need to be involved. She'll forgive me when I let her hold the baby," Helena said, with more confidence than she felt.

Bloodstone sighed again and crossed to the tent flap. Opening it, she glared at Dex. "Helena does not want her husband to know right now. So you better not send for him - do I make myself clear?" He grumbled but nodded. "Good, and if you see Murtaugh heading this way, you better give me warning." Again, he grumbled but nodded.

Looking back at Helena, she said, "You do realize that your husband will be coming home for the midday meal in just about two hours, so he will probably find out before your child actually makes it here?"

"That'll be two less hours he has to worry, and anyways I don't think this baby can wait that long. I went into labor right after Murtaugh left, maybe even a little before," Helena said, looking apologetic.

Bloodstone sighed and rolled her eyes again. "And Eden says I'm a stubborn pain in the ass."

Nearly an hour and a half later, Bloodstone was looking down on mother and child, both clean and resting. "Now may I send for your husband?"

Helena was staring down at her son. "You think Murtaugh's going to mind that he's so small?" she asked with genuine concern.

"I don't think Murtaugh will even notice. He will be too happy and too relieved that the two of you are both safe and healthy." Helena nodded, still looking worried. "Helena, he's just going to be happy he's here safely. May I please send for your husband?"

"Yes, but will you do me a favor?" Helena asked with a smile.

"Delivering your son this morning by myself wasn't enough of a favor? You have another one to ask?" Bloodstone said laughing.

"Yes, when Murtaugh arrives would you go and tell him that his son, Logen, is healthy - though a little small. Maybe if he hears it first, he will take it better when he sees him," she asked sweetly.

Bloodstone stared at her. "Helena, I will, of course, go out and tell him that you are both fine, but he's not going to care, and I don't know why you're suddenly so worried."

"I expected him to be smaller than a Barbarian baby, but he's the size of a normal Breton baby. Blackwolf was much larger and he was earlier."

Bloodstone rolled her eyes again, but before she could say anything, Dex announced from outside, "Murtaugh and Eden are headed this direction."

She pointed a finger at Helena and said, "You owe me big." Turning, she exited the tent and went straight for the two men. "Well, I don't know about you two, but I had a busy morning. How are you doing today, Murtaugh?"

"Very well. Is Helena still mad at me for asking her not to leave our tent any more than necessary?"

"No, I think she's too tired to be mad, but she also seems to have this unreasonable fear that you are not going to want your son because he's too small. I keep trying to tell her that you just care he's here safely and she's fine."

Murtaugh blinked at her and stared. "I have a son?"

"Yes, Murtaugh, you have a very fine healthy son, a little on the small size by Barbarian standards, but he's a healthy size baby for a Breton. He has all of his appropriate body parts and has already settled in for his first meal, so I would say all in all, Logen is a very healthy, happy baby ..."

She was interrupted by both men saying simultaneously, "Logen?"

"That's what she called him. I assumed you had a hand in picking it," Bloodstone replied.

"No, I had no hand in it. We hadn't even discussed names yet. My father will be thrilled and honored. Why is she afraid I will not want him because he is small?"

"I think Blackwolf's reception probably has a lot to do with it. She's afraid that they'll look down on him because he's small, or maybe even say he's not yours because he's so small, though he does have the skin tone of a Barbarian."

Murtaugh looked furious. "Any man says he's not my son, I'll kill him, Barbarian or Breton, it doesn't matter." After a moment he grinned. "You don't think she'll be mad if I call him Runt?"

Eden shoved Murtaugh. Murtaugh started laughing. "All right, will one of you please explain what the joke is about Runt?" she demanded.

"When we were kids, I was a full head taller than Eden. Everybody called him Runt. He was so much smaller than all the other kids. It wasn't until about twelve, or maybe thirteen, he started growing two to three inches for every inch I grew - well, and you know how that story ended. Now he's a full head taller than me, but seeing as how one of my best friends growing up was a Runt, I kind of have a fondness for them. Can I see them now?"

"Absolutely, she's waiting for you." Murtaugh moved away swiftly. Bloodstone looked up at Eden. "Runt?"

"Don't you start, Woman," he said, feigning annoyance. He pulled her into his arms and kissed her. "Do you think we should go away and come back, or just give them a few minutes?" he asked, pulling away.

"I think Helena will be furious if you don't come in and see your nephew. I also think we should send messengers to notify everyone, before everyone kills Helena."

Eden nodded and laughed and they both sent messengers to notify the rest of the family. "Dex, you should go and inform your mate. She and

344

Helena have become friends over the past couple of months. She'll be hurt if she's not informed," Eden ordered. Dex nodded and excused himself. They waited until someone else arrived before they disturbed Helena and Murtaugh. When they entered, Murtaugh was laying on the bed on his side propped up on his elbows, staring down at his woman and his child, looking incredibly happy and proud. When Andrew and Black Stone arrived, they carried with them a case of glasses and two bottles of wine. They waited for everyone to arrive and then they toasted the new arrival. After the toast had been drunk, they each congratulated the couple, then started excusing themselves.

As Eden left, he stopped by Dex, put his hand on his shoulder, and leaned in and whispered in his ear, "Take your woman home and stay with her. I would like to spend some time alone with mine." Dex nodded.

Dex decided he was going to wait until Jade had a chance to hold the baby before informing her that they should leave them alone. But to his surprise, as soon as she held the baby, she handed him back, congratulated them, and took her leave. He followed her out, then moved to walk alongside her. "Don't you have to go back on duty?" she asked.

"No, apparently Eden intends to spend the rest of the day at home, so he said I should do the same."

She nodded and asked, "Have you eaten? Would you like me to prepare you something?"

"Thank you for the kind offer, but I do not find myself hungry at this time." They walked inside their quarters. Upon entering, he sat down and picked up a book he had borrowed from Bloodstone to practice his Breton reading. He had been reading for several minutes when he was startled by his woman's hand on his shoulder.

"Are you sure you want to read? Is there something else maybe you'd like to do?" she asked. Pressing her chest against his back as she leaned over his shoulder to read the book, tossing her head slightly so that her hair brushed against his cheek and neck, she shifted a little to the side and said in a soft, sweet voice, "You didn't answer me."

Dex turned his head to discover her breasts were only a few inches away from his nose. He allowed his eyes to explore every inch of exposed curve, and with her leaning over, he could see right down her cleavage. It was quite pleasant to admire. After a long moment, he slowly lifted his eyes to her face and said quite calmly, "I am content to read. If there's anything else you wish to occupy yourself with, you need not trouble yourself over my entertainment." He concealed a smile as he saw her eyes widen with irritation.

He went back to reading his book. He continued to read his book until she announced that dinner was ready. He put his book down, washed, and returned to the table. As had become their custom, they conversed amiably over dinner. The past two evenings, however, she had gone out of her way to be much more cordial to him, and had taken any opportunity she found to press her body against his. Last night, she had even gone so far as to cuddle up against him in bed murmuring that she was cold.

Dex found himself enjoying the new attention. However, he was uncertain as to whether she was playing some kind of game, or genuinely interested in his affections. But if she thought these little affections were going to sway him, she had another thing coming. He had made it very clear to her what he expected from her before he would fully share his bed with her, and she did not even come close to fulfilling such requirements. Though, by Wolf Tribe standards, she was starting to push the bounds of what would've been permitted of a courting couple, she had not yet shown a true desire for him. After dinner, he decided to torment her and go back to reading.

"Well, I'm very tired. I think I'm going to turn in," she announced with a fictitious yawn. She arose and went behind the screen. When she emerged, Dex almost dropped his book. She was wearing some pink, filmy looking nightie that was practically see-through, with thin little shoulder straps so that her arms and shoulders were bare. It was cut so that it curved across the top of her breasts, and plunged between her breasts at least two inches so that the hollow was fully exposed. As if this garment wasn't scandalous enough, it was cut so it was nearly snug across her body. As his eyes raked down her body, he swallowed hard as his eyes came to rest on her bare feet and ankles, for the garment stopped at least six, if not eight, inches shy of the ground. As Jade watched the look on her husband's face, she found it quite rewarding. The nightie had been a gift from her mother, though it had been billowy until she took it in just a little and cut it off just a little. She walked calmly around to her side of the bed, then tossing the covers aside, she dropped onto the bed pulling the nightie past one of her knees as she settled in. She could feel Dex's eyes on her. *Ignore me last night, will you? I will make sure you pay for that,* she thought to herself with a smile. After a minute or two, she shifted and twisted in the bed again, then grabbed the covers and threw them over herself, mumbling as she did so, "Boy, is it getting cold outside."

Dex read for another half hour before turning in. He hadn't been in bed a quarter of an hour when she snuggled against him, wrapping her arm around his waist. She murmured, "It's too cold." Dex thought for sure he was going to have to count to a thousand tonight before he'd fall asleep.

XXVIII

Five days later, Dex stood on guard outside the General's tent. He was glad she hadn't gone anywhere today, it gave him time to think about what his woman was up to. She had continued with her attempts at ... he hesitated before using the word seduction. It didn't quite feel like the right word, because if she was trying to seduce him, she would be a lot more aggressive in her physical contact, however, her physical efforts had been much more restrained. He was still pondering this when Viktor, Matthias, and Murtaugh approached. The look on Viktor's face put him on his guard at once. Viktor walked straight up to him and said softly, "I think you should go home. I ran across your woman on my way here. She seemed very agitated, and when I spoke to her, she almost shrank and avoided looking at me."

Dex hesitated a moment. Before he had a chance to reply, Murtaugh said, "I will stay with our Queen. Go and see to your woman."

At that, any hesitation Dex might have felt left him. He merely nodded his head and headed straight for his quarters, his pace increasing with his worry. As he entered his quarters, his woman gave a little start, then quickly turned her back to him, but not before he saw her busted lip. "Please leave," she sobbed out.

He felt his temper rise and his guts twist and knot. He carefully removed all emotion from his face before he walked up to her and gently gripped her by the arm. She winced with pain. He gently slid his hand around her waist and turned her to face him. She resisted him, but only for a moment, and then she burst into tears, pressing her body against him. He wrapped his arms tightly around her and held her to him. "Jade, you're going to have to tell me what happened," he said gently. She shook her head against his chest. He gently gripped her shoulders and pushed her away from him. Her head and shoulders slumped, trying to avoid his gaze. He caught his breath and gritted his teeth as he saw scratches on her left shoulder going down to the top curve of her breasts where her dress was torn away. He only had a brief glimpse before she covered herself again. She struggled to be free of him, but he pulled her tightly against him.

Again she sobbed out, "Please, just go. I want to be left alone."

Still holding her by the arm, he gently guided her to the table and sat her down. Going to the washbasin, he retrieved a bowl of water and a rag. Returning to the table, he knelt down and gently began cleaning the blood from her face. She tried to push his hand away, but he ignored her. "I think I need to send for a healer," he said after a long moment.

She clasped his hand tightly and looked at him pleadingly. "Please don't send for anyone. Don't tell anyone. I'll go away and I'll be quiet and nobody ever has to know. Please, if you send for a healer, everyone will know."

Dex maintained a tight control on his emotions. After a moment, he said gently, "Jade, you need more attention than I can give you. Let me send for a healer. I can send for Tabitha, Bloodrose, or Viktor, but you're going to have to tell me what happened." She shook her head fiercely. He gripped her hand gently. "You're going to have to tell me everything that happened."

"I'll tell you anything you want to know, just please, don't send for anyone. Don't tell anyone," she said in a hollow voice.

"Why are you so afraid for anyone to know? It's not your fault ..." He gently caressed her cheek. "Someone attacked you."

She started crying hysterically. "It is my fault, and everybody will say so. They will say it's what I deserved for ever getting involved with him in the first place, and they'll be right. I should have seen him for what he was. Father knew. Mother knew."

Dex cut her off abruptly. "It is never a woman's fault when an animal attacks her ..." He gently caressed her cheek again. "But you have to tell me everything he did to you. You can't hold anything back no matter how … painful it is to admit."

"You promise you won't send for a healer. You won't tell anyone?"

Dex took a deep breath and said a quick, silent prayer to Freya, *Please, please let Viktor or Bloodstone come of their own accord.* "I give you my word I will not tell anyone or send for anyone, but only if you tell me everything."

She nodded her head slowly. As she began speaking, he went back to gently cleaning the blood off her face, and then applying the cool, damp cloth to the scratches on her chest. "I had just finished the wash. I was bringing it back. I lost the basket somewhere, I don't remember where it was, wherever he grabbed me. He pulled me into an alley. I can't believe I was so stupid … for a moment to actually be happy to see him. But then he kissed me, and he tasted of ale. He was clearly drunk. I pulled away and told him that we shouldn't do that. He grabbed me around the waist and slammed me into one of the pillars and went back to kissing me roughly. I pulled away and told him to stop it. I told him I was a married woman and that it wasn't right. He replied that I didn't love my husband, I loved him and he had a plan. We were going to run away, find somewhere to hide until …" She started crying again, but continued to speak through her tears, "Till he had had a chance to get me pregnant, and then we'd come back and you'd cast me off and he could marry me. He was sure once I gave Father a grandchild, Father would forgive any bad behavior. I don't think he knows my father as well as he thinks he does. I told him he was speaking foolishly. What was done was done and could not be undone. Like it or not, I belonged to Dex. He actually laughed and said you were an idiot. And you had mush for brains. That all the Barbarians were stupid oafs. I don't know why, but that made me mad and I slapped him." She tentatively touched her busted lip. "That's when he backhanded me. Then he went back to kissing me, but when he slammed me against the pillar again this time, he started trying to hoist up my skirt. I pushed him away, but then he punched me and grabbed my dress." This time it was several minutes before she could speak again. "He tore it away from my breast and I tried to pull away. I slipped out, but he grabbed my arm and wrenched it so hard it still hurts. He went back to trying to pull up my skirt. When he grabbed my bare thigh, I remembered once a man attacked Mother. Before Father even had a chance to do anything … she'd … she'd … " She whispered so softly he barely heard it. "Brought her knee up between his legs. The man had crumpled to the ground before Father had even reached her side. I didn't even stop to think. I just did what Mother had done and he doubled over in the alleyway and I ran away." She put her face in her hands and began sobbing hysterically.

Dex was so relieved that all she had had to endure was a few vulgar kisses he almost slumped with relief. "Will you let me help you get cleaned up and out of this dress?"

"I just want to be left alone."

"Well, I'm not leaving you alone, and since you won't let me send for anyone else, I guess you're stuck with me. Do you want me to have a bath brought in?"

Before she had a chance to respond, they heard Eden clear his throat outside. She grabbed his arm quickly. "Please, you promised. I don't want anyone else to know of my shame," she whispered.

"You have nothing to be ashamed of. But if I don't go out and talk to him, he will come in." She nodded her head. He rose and pulled aside the tent flap. He was not at all surprised to see Eden, Murtaugh, Bloodstone, and Viktor. As he exited his tent, he was trying desperately to figure out a way not to break his promise, but to convey to them that there was a problem.

"Why is there blood on your tunic?" demanded Eden. Dex, surprised by the question, looked down. To his surprise, there was indeed blood on his tunic. He opened his mouth and gaped for a minute, genuinely unable to come up with a response. Bloodstone and Viktor didn't even hesitate, they headed into the tent. Eden waited a long moment before he said angrily, "You haven't answered the question."

"Because there is no answer I can give. I was just about to order a bath for my woman. I'll be right back," he said, looking dazed.

Eden and Murtaugh exchanged worried looks and waited impatiently for someone to tell them what in Hades was going on. Eden hesitated. Though he didn't know what was going on, he knew something bad had happened. He decided he should send for Fletcher. Turning around and grabbing the first Wolf Tribesman his eyes alighted on, he ordered him to go in search of Sergeant Major Fletcher. The man nodded and did as he was bid.

Dex returned only a few moments later. As the bath started being brought in, Viktor exited. Stopping the first guard he saw, he asked, "Would you please go get the priestess Tabitha. She's in Colonel Stone's quarters." The guard nodded and went to carry out his orders. Tabitha and Andrew arrived a quarter of an hour later. Viktor and Tabitha had a quick, quiet conversation, and she entered the tent.

Fletcher arrived only a few minutes later. His eyes went from Eden, Murtaugh, Viktor, and Andrew's worried faces, to Dex's back. Dex's head was erect, his arms were crossed, and his back was as stiff as a board. Fletcher turned to Eden. "What in Hades is going on?"

"I've no idea. No one as of yet has condescended to inform me. All I can tell you is there's blood on Dex's tunic. Viktor's not talking either, but he sent for Tabitha. And Tabitha and Bloodstone have been in your daughter's tent with your daughter for more than half an hour now."

Fletcher's jaw tightened as his stomach heaved. He turned to Viktor. "Tell me what you know," he demanded.

"I would rather not misinform you," Viktor replied cautiously.

Fletcher snapped back, "Dammit Viktor, you're a father! Tell me what you know!"

Viktor sighed. "Someone has struck her at least twice, bloodied her lip, given her a bruised cheek, scratched her breast, and tore her dress away. I don't know anything more than that. She wouldn't talk if I was in the room."

"When I get my hands on that little weasel, I'm going to tear his head off," Fletcher said angrily.

To his astonishment, Murtaugh, Andrew, and Eden replied simultaneously, "He belongs to Dex." Fletcher hesitated a moment, groaned, and then gave a curt nod in agreement.

After that, the men stood outside for a full hour in absolute silence. The only time they moved was when they heard a scream and then crying coming from inside. Murtaugh and Eden had both moved to restrain Dex from entering, and Viktor put his hand on Fletcher's shoulder. When Tabitha finally exited, she approached Dex and spoke as though he was the only one there. "She's resting comfortably. Fortunately, he was unable to accomplish his goal. She's a little bruised, but she'll be all right. The worst of the injuries is her shoulder. He nearly wrenched it out of its socket. It was misaligned, so we had to put it back into place. It was worse than if he had completely dislocated it, but she's strong and healthy. There's nothing that time will not heal. Bloodstone and I assume you men would like us to stay with her for a little while. We assume you have urgent business to attend to?" she said, her disapproval evident.

Dex nodded slowly. It took him a minute to find his voice. "Thank you, Priestess, I am eternally grateful to you, and I would indeed like you to stay with her for just a little while. Tell her I will return as soon as my business is concluded. If she doesn't understand, don't explain it to her." With that, he turned on his heel and walked away. The other men followed in silence.

"You do realize, Andrew, I'm about to kill him," Dex said in a voice that shook with rage.

"If you don't, I will," Andrew replied quickly.

357

"Are you sure you want to come along for this, Viktor?" asked Eden.

"And if you're going to moralize, Viktor, and tell me it's wrong to murder him, save your breath. Nothing you could say would stop me from beating him to death," Dex said angrily.

"I don't believe it's murder when you kill somebody who was asking for it as clearly as this man was asking for it," Viktor replied grimly.

"I would appreciate it, Viktor, if you would not refer to him as a man. He's not a man. He's an animal and like any rabid dog, he needs to be put down," commented Murtaugh.

As they arrived in the section of camp where the Twelfth was billeted, Andrew said, "He's in the privates' quarters, second to last tent."

To Dex's pleasure, he was sitting outside around the fire, laughing with the other soldiers. When he looked up and saw them there, all pleasure died. He rose quickly to his feet and saluted, as did the others, though he was the only one stupid enough to speak. "Colonel, is there something we can do for you?"

"Yes, you can stand right there. The rest of you – back off and stay out of this," Andrew said angrily.

The other soldiers did as they were ordered without hesitation, but they only drew far enough away to give them room to work. They stuck around to see what was going to happen. "Am I in some kind of trouble, Colonel?" he asked casually.

"You punched my woman and then you have the audacity to ask if you're in some kind of trouble?" Dex demanded angrily.

"Hey, that was just an accident. We got a little too enthusiastic and things got a little out of hand," he replied with a little laugh.

Dex didn't even hesitate. He just started walking forward. Phillip turned to flee, but found a wall of the Twelfth in his way. He turned to go the other direction, but saw it was no use. Other men had come out of their tents to see what the commotion was, and no one was going to give him the opportunity to run. "Which do you think gives you a fighting chance against me, a sword, or your fists? After all, I'm just a slow Barbarian with mush for brains," Dex said without heat.

"You can't kill me just because I got fresh with your wife and got a little rough with her. Anyway, she likes it. She was begging for it. You can't murder me just because you're jealous because she likes me better than she likes you," he spat out angrily.

"I heard him say fists; didn't everybody else hear him say that?" To Philip's dismay, everyone in the area either was nodding their head, or murmuring in assent. Dex gave him another moment before he went for him. To his surprise, Philip was putting up more of a fight than he had expected. He was not particularly strong, but he was quick, and he knew to get inside Dex's reach. He was landing four blows to every blow Dex landed. After several more exchanges, it was becoming obvious Philip was becoming winded. Dex waited for his moment, waited for Philip to overextend himself, as he knew he was going to. His inexperience was obvious. When it finally happened, Dex sidestepped him and wrapped his arm around his neck pulling Phillip against him.

Philip cried out, "You can't murder me just because I bedded your woman!" He was clawing desperately at Dex's arm.

Dex said in his ear, only loud enough for him to hear, "I'm killing you because you beat and tried to rape my woman, and I'm not going to let you live to do it to another woman." Philip's eyes widened for just a moment before Dex snapped his neck like a twig. He released him, allowing the body to fall to the ground. After a moment, he turned to face Andrew and asked calmly, "What do you want me to do with the body?"

To his surprise, it was the Sergeant who stepped forward and said, "With the Colonel's permission, we'll deal with the garbage."

"I would appreciate it," replied Andrew, then he offered his hand to Dex. "Welcome to the Stone Wall."

Dex looked at him with surprise. "Me, a member of the Stone Wall?" Eden nodded in agreement.

"Come on Dex, we'll buy you a drink. You look like you need it," added Murtaugh.

"No, thank you. I appreciate the offer, but if my Queen is done with me for the day, I would like to stay with my woman." The other men all nodded and escorted him back to his quarters.

Once they were out of hearing of the soldiers, Eden reached up and squeezed Dex's shoulder saying gently, "Take as much time off as you and Jade feel you need to. And if you ever feel you need to talk, my door is always open. No one knows better than I the strain such incidents put on a man."

Dex nodded and said, "Thank you. I appreciate the offer."

When they arrived, they saw that someone had placed a basket of clothes just outside the door. He nodded to the men, bent down and picked it up, and entered his tent. He was surprised to find his woman alone and sitting at the table. She was wearing her gray linen nightgown with a high collar, long sleeves, and it went all the way to the ground. He didn't know why, but it pained him to see her in it. "You shouldn't be out of bed. Let me put you back to bed," he said, as he dropped the basket at the foot of the bed.

"No, thank you. I think we should talk first, and anyways, I can walk back to bed myself," she said sadly.

He crossed to his trunk, opened it, and pulled out a bottle and grabbed two glasses. Pouring just a little in one, he set it in front of her, saying as he did so, "Burns like the dickens, but it will make you feel better." Then he poured himself at least two inches, then put the open bottle on the table. Seating himself, he asked, "What would you like to talk about?" He took a large pull of his drink and waited for her.

"When are you going to send me away? Were you going to get rid of me first, and then send me away?" She sounded weary.

He reached out with the hand that was holding the glass, and gently nudged her glass closer to her. "Drink." He waited until she picked it up and tentatively took a sip. "All of it." She wrinkled her nose and downed it. After a moment, she coughed and held her throat. "That's the second time you've mentioned me sending you away. Why in Hades would I do such a thing?" He took another long drink.

"Because of what happened," she said, refusing to meet his eye.

He downed his drink and poured himself another one. "You want some more?" She quickly shook her head. He gave a laugh. "Probably for the best, I don't think you'd like being drunk. Look, I'm not going to send you away. You're my woman, and even had he succeeded in raping …" She shrank before him. "… you, I wouldn't send you away. I wouldn't blame you for what he did." He downed the rest of his drink, set the glass down, and picked her up in his arms. "But you're hurt and you need your rest, so you're going back to bed. If you need me, I'll be on the floor tonight."

As he carried her to bed, she wrapped her arms tightly around his neck. "Why are you sleeping on the floor if you're not mad at me?"

He shrugged his shoulders. "I thought you would prefer for me not to be near you … for a while."

"Please don't sleep on the floor." He nodded his head and tucked her gently into bed, kissing her on the forehead. He washed and joined her in bed. He'd scarcely settled in before she cuddled tightly against him and asked softly, "Will you hold me?" He wrapped his arm tightly around her, pulling her snugly to him. Resting his hand on her waist, he forced himself to close his eyes and go to sleep.

Two days later, Eden cleared his throat outside Dex's tent. A moment later, Jade pulled aside the tent flap. Eden saw at once she wasn't glad to see him. "I was wondering if you might spare me a few minutes time?" he asked.

She held the tent flap aside. He entered and she gestured to the table. "Would you like some coffee?"

"Thank you, that would be nice." As she went to pour him coffee, he said, "Forgive me if I speak out of turn, but you are my sister and Dex is one of my men. And because he's married to you, by our customs that makes him my brother. I respect him a lot because of what he stepped up and did. He's done a lot of things he shouldn't have had to do and he's never complained about them, not once, and he has not complained about you either."

She interrupted him. "What do you mean, what has he had to do? What makes him any different than any other man in this encampment?"

"He didn't tell you about his family?" She shook her head. "Dex doesn't come from my village, in fact, very few people are left from his village. A large group of men - and boys who were about to become men - went on a hunting party. When they returned, nearly everyone in the village had been slaughtered. Many of the women were taken and have never been seen again. His mother and older sister were amongst the lucky ones, they were killed ..." Jade put her hand to her mouth as tears started to slide down her cheeks. "... his younger sister, she was twelve, and a few of the other children about that age had gone on a picnic and weren't in the village at that time. His father, mother, two brothers, and a sister were all slaughtered. He and the younger sister were the only ones who survived. Though he was only seventeen, he asked the council to permit him to take and raise his little sister. He's put his life on hold to raise her. She only recently married, but that's not what I'm here to talk to you about." He hesitated a moment.

"Why are you here? Clearly you have something on your mind, and I think you're dancing around it. Why don't you get to the point."

"Look, you're my sister, and I don't want to insult you, and I also don't want to think ill of you, but given your infatuation with Philip, I find myself anxious for my friend. Before Philip's death, he said some uncomplimentary things about you. That doesn't mean they're true and I don't want to believe them, but you promised to make Dex's life miserable. I can think of a very easy way you could accomplish that. I can even see you regretting it afterwards. I can even see Philip wanting more and you refusing and then things going badly. I don't doubt for a minute that he was slime and deserved to die. I don't doubt for a minute that he hurt you, but what I want to know is: did you make a foolish mistake with him after being married to my friend?"

For a moment Jade was angry, then she realized he had every right to be worried. She had vowed to make Dex's life miserable, and though she had meant it at the time, she regretted it later. Eden was right. That would've been a very easy way to make Dex's life miserable. Were she less of a woman, then she could've even seen herself doing it, though in truth, the thought never entered her head. She was married to Dex. She quietly poured Eden a cup of coffee, then sat down. "You know, I do want to be very angry with you, but I can't seem to find it in me to be angry with you for what you just said. I guess I kind of deserve it. I haven't made Dex's life very easy, especially not the past couple of weeks. In fact, I've probably made his life very uncomfortable, but I have too much respect for him, and too much respect for myself to have ever degraded myself in such an immoral manner. Whatever Philip told you, whatever he told all of you, they were lies. I swear." She hesitated a moment, then started drawing circles on the table with her finger. "Do you like being married to my sister? Does she like being married to you? Have you always enjoyed it?"

"Our marriage is complicated." He hesitated a moment. "Not that yours isn't complicated, but let's just say mine is a lot more complicated."

"What do you mean, you're not happy?"

"I am happy, and I believe she is as well."

"Of course she'd be happy. She's married the man she loved."

Eden couldn't help it, he started laughing. "I know you judge your sister harshly for forcing you to marry Dex, but she knew what kind of man Philip was and she wanted to protect you from him. Clearly you have made some assumptions about your sister, and I'd like to set you straight. The first of these is we may be happy now, but it wasn't always so. What I'm about to tell you is known by virtually no one. When your sister and I were first married, we'd known each other all of five minutes. In those five minutes, our conversation consisted of me promising not to beat her or take her against her will, and I would protect her from the others who would rape her. The price I demanded for these promises was for her to share my bed and to keep my house. It used to pain me that she wears my mark, but as our relationship has grown, that pain has lessened and finally faded away altogether. I know I'm going to sound like an old man here, and compared to you, I am an old man. It's easy to love, and you can love many people, but love alone would not make a happy marriage. There has to be respect, trust, understanding, and faithfulness. I truly believe if you have those four things in a marriage, love will come rather easily. But if you don't have those four things, love will fade very quickly."

"Dex doesn't want me." She gave a little shrug of her shoulders as though it didn't matter, but Eden could tell it did.

"Why do you believe he doesn't want you?" he asked, taking a sip of his coffee.

She blushed. "I may have said some very mean things on our wedding night and he may have laid down some firm rules, rules I apparently can't get around."

"You may have said?"

"All right, I did say some," she said with a huff.

Eden laughed. "Why don't you tell me what he said and I'll see if I can help you," he said, taking another sip of his coffee. To her surprise, she did. She repeated the whole conversation and she didn't even feel too embarrassed about it. "Let me guess. I've been married to a Breton long enough. The problem is Bretons don't exactly talk as openly about the intimacies between a man and a woman as we Barbarians do?" She blushed and nodded. "I think the solution to your problem is actually quite simple. Do your best to explain that to him, and then do your best to express what you want."

He arose, downed his coffee, set the cup on the table, nodded to her, and left without another word.

Three days later, Dex was walking back to his quarters, pondering the alteration in his woman's behavior. She didn't seem afraid of him, or even reluctant for him to be near her. In fact, every night she cuddled up against him and asked for him to hold her. All of her little flirtatious tricks had come to an end. He wasn't sure how he felt about this. In one way that seemed a sign of progress, but they'd also hinted at a game she was playing. A game that he was unaware of the rules. As he entered his tent, he swallowed hard at sight of his woman. She was standing in the middle of the room, as though she'd been waiting for him to come home. She was again wearing that very alluring pink nightie. She gave him a dazzling smile as he entered. "I was wondering how long it was going to be before you got home."

He hesitated a moment before he asked, "Is there something you require of me?"

She gave a shy little nod. "I know you were immune to my toying with you the past couple of weeks. And the past few days I've thought a lot about what you said you wanted me ..." She swallowed hard as he crossed his arms over his chest. "I don't want to tease you or play games with you anymore. It was wrong of me to do that, or even attempt it. Though I may have grown up in a bar, I did not fully understand what it meant to tease a man, and if you tease the wrong one, what can happen. I've also realized it's wrong to tease the right one. It is not fair to him. As I said, I've thought a lot about the things you wanted me to say to you or tell you or whatever. And I can't quite bring myself to say the things I think you want me to say; not because I don't want them, but because I just ... I just ... well, Breton girls are taught not to say things like that to a man. In fact we're taught quite the opposite, so I hope you will understand me and accept what I'm about to say ..." She hesitated and blushed. "I would very much like to be your wife, not as we have been ... but properly. I would very much like to belong to you ... I would like for you to give me a child." Her cheeks blazed an even deeper shade of red. She faltered and was no longer meeting his eye and she looked down at the ground.

He crossed over to her and tilted her chin up with his knuckle. Staring down at her, he asked in a deep, husky voice, "Are you sure that's what you want, because if I do this, I will never give you up." She nodded her head. He shook his head. "A nod is not sufficient. I want you to tell me you want me."

She tried to look at down at the ground, but he forced her to continue to stare into his eyes. "I want you," she said softly. He slid his arms around her and pulled her tightly to him, kissing her passionately. He started inching up her nightie. Once he had it high enough he could slide his

370

hands underneath it, he cupped her bottom with both hands. She pressed tighter against him and her hand slid up his back and into his hair. After a moment, he slid his hands higher and pulled the nightie off over her head. Then picking her up in his arms, he carried her to the bed and dropped her on it, covering her body quickly with his. After several more minutes of passionate kissing, she began tugging at his tunic. He moved his arms so she could pull it off over his head, then her hands were on his bare chest. After another minute, he pulled away and stood up, discarding his boots, belt, and kilt. While he did this, she pulled back the covers and slipped between the sheets. He froze for a moment as he stared down at her, then he slipped quickly beneath the sheets and covered her body with his. He allowed his hands free reign over her body as he kissed her mouth, her neck, her throat. When his mouth found her breasts, she stiffened and started to squirm away from him.

He pushed himself off of her and looked down at her. "If you're lying to me, you'd better tell me now. It is not too late to draw back," he said, gritting his teeth, trying to get control over his desire which was rapidly burning out of control.

She ran her hands along his hips and his back and said in a shy voice, "I'm sorry. It startled me. But I do want you. I mean it truly; I want you so badly it actually hurts." She blushed at her boldness. He needed no more reassurances. His mouth was again on hers. She continued to rub her body against him. He felt his desire burning beyond control. He gently pulled apart her thighs. As he moved between her legs, he hesitated, kissing her gently. She looked at him puzzled. "Why do you look so worried? I'm the one about to be hurt here," she asked with a little laugh, as she caressed his cheek.

He swallowed hard and stared down at her. "Because I know I'm about to hurt you, and I'm concerned I won't be able to be gentle. I'm afraid in my inexperience, I won't be able to please you."

"Your inexperience?"

He leaned down and nibbled on her earlobe, then pulling away he touched his forehead to hers. "This might surprise you, but this is my first time too." He hesitated, clearly having something more to say, but reluctant to say it. She gave him an encouraging smile. "I'm afraid if I hurt you too badly, you won't ever want me again."

She gave a little laugh. "I know it's going to hurt, but I also know it's going to be very, very enjoyable."

XXIX

Two hours before dawn the following morning, Black Stone and Andrew arrived outside Foster's tent. Black Stone drew his knife and gently tapped on the beam next to the tent flap of Foster's quarters. They heard nothing. Black Stone waited another moment and was just about to tap louder when they heard from behind them, "What in Hades are the two of you doing here this early?" They both turned around quickly to see Foster standing there, sword in hand.

"Do we have the wrong tent?" asked Andrew.

"No, those are my quarters. I just came out the side," Foster replied casually, as he examined the two brothers. He had now been in this encampment for nearly four months, and though he had seen Andrew and Bloodstone in all manner of armor, he had never seen Black Stone in anything but full plate. However, this morning he was in battle leather. "What do the two of you require of me this early in the morning?"

"A family matter that I have put off long enough requires my attention. I'm going to be gone hopefully no more than three days, if the weather turns bad, it might be four. As the second oldest, Andrew insists upon joining me; however, he is the Colonel in charge of the watch for the next five days. You're the only Colonel whose duties would not interfere with covering for Andrew for the next five days. Would you do us this favor?" asked Black Stone.

"Is General Bloodstone aware of your absence?" questioned Foster.

Black Stone shifted uncomfortably and looked sheepish. "I did not wish my sister to ask a lot of questions, so my sergeant will deliver a message to her in a few hours informing her of our unexpected departure."

"You can attend to your family business. I will gladly cover Andrew's duties."

Andrew handed him a stack of papers. "These are the watch schedules, the patrols' disciplinary requirements, everything you need to know for the next five days. Of course there will be alterations, but General Bloodstone will inform you of those as they occur."

Foster took them and nodded. "If I have any questions, I will ask the General. Good luck gentlemen, and gods speed." He nodded his head and stepped past the two men to enter his quarters.

The following morning, Foster awoke with a start, reaching for his sword. As he did so, he was acutely aware of the fact he was not alone. As he reached for his sword, he heard a voice say, "Why is it every time someone finds me in their quarters, they automatically reach for their sword? It's almost offensive."

Foster got to his feet and stared in open mouthed astonishment as Lord Ares turned to face him. "Lord Ares, how may I serve you?"

Ares laughed. "Funny you should ask. I have a difficult task for you ... actually several. The most difficult of these tasks is going to be dealing with my daughter. I have recently acquired a new fortress, and this fact is going to displease my daughter immensely. Since I do not wish to go to war with the Athenians, I would like this transition to be as painless as possible for both parties; so I wish you to work hand-in-hand with my daughter to coordinate the final evacuation of the Athenian Temple of the Mountain Pass by the Athenians, and our occupation of it."

Foster rubbed his forehead. "You want me to inform the General of the Battle Knights of Athena that she has to relinquish control of the Temple of the Mountain Pass to the Soldiers of Ares?"

"Yes, and though I do wish you to go ahead and negotiate terms, I do not wish for the change of guard to the fortress to take place until after the war is over. After all, the fortress' new commanding officer is going to be a little busy for a while. It's going to take a considerable amount of his skill, tact, influence, power, and authority to control and command the entire Army of Ares."

"The Soldiers of Ares have not functioned as a single army in more than a hundred years!"

Ares cocked his head to the side. "Was that supposed to be a statement or question?"

Foster hesitated a moment. "Both."

Ares laughed. "Well then, I guess my new General has his work cut out for him." Ares grinned broadly. Foster suddenly found himself grateful he only had to negotiate terms for new ownership. He found himself feeling very sorry for the new General of the Soldiers of Ares. Ares laughed again. "I didn't think self-pity was a trade of a Soldier of Ares. I guess even generals feel sorry for themselves once in a while, just don't let it become a habit."

Foster's eyes slowly widened as the full ramifications of what Ares had just said struck him. "Me!?"

"Unless, of course, you don't want the job, General Foster." Foster hesitated for a moment, wondering if all generals felt as unworthy as he felt in this moment. "I think anyone who doesn't feel overwhelmed at the task before them isn't worthy of the position; and remember - courage doesn't mean you're not afraid. It merely means you do not permit fear to stop you," remarked Ares.

"What else do you require of your General?"

"Right now, all I require of you is to lead my army and make arrangements to control my new fortress after the war is over; which of course, as my General, since it will be the largest of all my fortresses, you will command." Ares turned to leave, then stopped and tossed over his shoulder, "And as far as I'm concerned, your wife can have the garden. I don't do gardens. Just make sure Seana knows it's my fortress." Then he exited the tent.

Foster sighed, washed, dressed, and donned his armor. As he headed in the direction of Bloodstone's quarters, he contemplated the correct way to announce himself. "Sergeant Simon, would you please inform General Bloodstone that the General of the Soldiers of Ares would like a few minutes of her time?"

The Sergeant nodded, opened the tent flap and announced him. "The General will see you now, Sir." Sergeant Simon held the tent flap aside.

Bloodstone was leaning back in her chair, staring at him as he entered. "General?"

"Yes, Lord Ares awoke me this morning with tasks for me to attend to for him," he replied, a little hesitantly.

"Had you known he was our father before that, or was it a surprise?"

"I knew you were of his bloodline, I did not know how close the connection was. The oldest of our fortresses does have some murals, paintings, tapestries, things like that devoted to him; though most of our fortresses do not. He's not exactly into statuary or tapestries. He leaves those things to his sisters."

Bloodstone nodded in understanding. "I guess in that we are alike; though I would ask that you not inform my brothers of this as of yet. I'm awaiting my father to get off his butt and do it himself," she said, her irritation evident.

"Your brothers as of yet are unaware?"

"I was not aware until after his death, and for some reason, he's dragging his ass on telling my brothers; though in truth, I've not spoken to him since five days after the Duke's death. So what is it my father requires of you that has you in my quarters?" she said, clearly intending to change the subject.

"Lord Ares requires his new General to negotiate the transfer of ownership of the Temple of the Mountain Pass from the Soldiers of Athena to the Soldiers of Ares."

She closed her eyes and took a deep breath and pinched the bridge of her nose, then let it out slowly. "Ares, did you win the Temple of the

Mountain Pass in your damn bet?" she demanded angrily.

A moment later, a ball of fire appeared and coiled around something. When the fire disappeared, Ares was sitting in Eden's chair - which was now sitting in front of Bloodstone's desk - lounging in it casually. "Why are you so angry with me? She's the one who bet one of her temples. It's not my fault she did not specify which temple. And as you and I are both aware, it is the only one of her temples which suits the needs of the Soldiers of Ares."

Bloodstone took a deep breath and angrily ran her hands through her hair. "When are you going to inform your sons so I can stop worrying about accidentally informing them? After all, Andrew, I believe, is growing suspicious."

"I'm waiting for Black Stone to finish something. When he finishes it, I will inform them, but not before then," he stated firmly.

"It will take at least a month to clear the library alone," she said with irritation.

Ares waved his hand in a dismissive gesture. "As though I care about the library. You can take forever for all I care. It's the forge I want possession of - and the fortress."

Bloodstone was quick to pounce. "Well then, if you don't require the library, than I see no reason for us to vacate it at all. The library does have its own entrance. Why can we not just maintain possession of the library and our scholars may come and go at their will. They can, of course, camp outside the fortress when they need to use the library and we can build a little cottage downhill for the caretakers." Foster was wondering why he was even present as he was watching the interchange.

Ares stroked his chin as he considered. *All in all, it isn't a bad idea, and in fact, if I allow my sister to maintain control of the library, I could, of course, require her to pay some of the repairs, therefore lessening the strain on my coffers. This is not a bad idea.* "I will allow the Athenians to maintain control of the library and to permit four of the priests or priestesses, preferably priestesses, to be housed in the fortress, if the Athenians are willing to pay one third of the repairs. After all, they did break it."

Bloodstone considered for a moment. "Twelve servants of Athena and a quarter of the repair costs and you have a deal, Lord Ares."

Ares couldn't help it, he grinned broadly. Every time he had dealings with his daughter, she impressed him more. Not many people would sit calmly across from the God of War and negotiate terms and haggle prices; even if he was their father. In fact, he seemed to recall a few of his sons cowering before him. "Done."

"Now wait a minute, that's not fair! Why does Athena get the library and Seana get the garden?" demanded Freya angrily.

"Who invited you?" demanded Ares, without looking at her.

Bloodstone casually glanced at Foster. "Bloodrose lay claim to the garden, did she?"

Foster gave a slight shrug of his shoulders and nodded. "One could say it was a condition of our marriage; though I correctly assumed Lord Ares doesn't care about gardens."

"Now wait a minute, if Athena gets the library because you don't care about libraries, and Seana gets the garden because you don't care about gardens, why can't I have the infirmary? You don't care about them either!" Freya demanded.

Ares ran his hands through his hair angrily and bemoaned his father's lust for goddesses. If he only would have stuck to seducing mortals, Ares would not now be stuck having this conversation. *Wait a minute, if Athena is willing to pay a quarter of the costs to control the library, if Freya is willing to pay a quarter she can have the damn infirmary, then I only have to pay half the repair costs. This is not a bad idea.* He turned to his little sister. "I'll make you the same deal I made Athena. You can have control of the infirmary and twelve servants of Freya can be housed in the fortress if you're willing to pay a quarter of the repair costs; but don't bother to negotiate because I won't be budged. If I lessen it for you, I have to lessen it for Athena and that's just not going to happen. A quarter, or no deal," Ares said sternly.

She crossed her arms over her chest and pouted. After a long minute, seeing Ares wasn't budging, she sighed. "Done."

XXX

Andrew looked around; it was nearly dusk. Finally catching sight of the castle, he and Black Stone rode straight for the gates. They slowed their pace about two hundred feet out. When they got within fifty feet, a voice called out, "That's far enough. State your business."

"His Grace, the Duke of Stone Reach, General Eric 'Black' Stone, Commander of the Army of the King, and Lord Andrew Stone, Colonel of the State Knights, seek an audience with Lord Woodridge and shelter for the night," Andrew replied.

Less than a quarter of an hour later, the gates were opened and they were shown in. Two men from the stables came out to take their horses. As they approached the main entrance of the castle, they were not at all surprised to see Bulldog coming out. "All right, last time you told me your general was here, it wasn't Black Stone. This time it is. So what in Hades brings him out of his encampment?" demanded Bulldog.

Black Stone extended his hand, laughing. "You do realize, Bulldog, I'm standing right here."

Lucas started laughing and took his hand and shook it warmly. "You know, Black Stone, I just can't get used to the idea of calling you 'Your Grace'," he replied a little sadly.

"Neither can I," Andrew agreed.

"My condolences to you both and my apologies. I did not learn of the Duke's death until it was too late to attend his funeral."

"No apologies necessary, wouldn't have expected you to make the journey anyways, not for a funeral. A wedding, maybe," replied Andrew.

"Well, you didn't give anybody the chance to attend your wedding. You just ran off and married the girl," Eric scolded.

Lucas held up his hands. "Now wait a minute, are you telling me that he actually got married? You're teasing me, right? But where are my manners? Let us take this conversation inside. Have you two eaten?"

"No," said Black Stone.

"We are starved," Andrew added quickly.

"Well then, why don't we take this conversation into the dining hall, and I will have my cook prepare something for you. We can start with a bottle of my best port." Lucas showed them into the dining hall and gave the orders. Quickly seating himself at the table, he said, "There now, do go on, when did Andrew actually decide to get married? Tell me, is she as beautiful as one would imagine for her to catch Andrew's eye?"

Eric replied quickly, "She's not bad to look at, I guess." Andrew shot him a dirty look. "My apologies Andrew, but I think Amber's prettier."

Andrew considered for a moment, then shrugged his shoulders. "I guess when you ask any man who truly loves his wife, he would say she is prettier. Eden would probably say the same thing about Bloodstone; but yes, Tabitha is very beautiful. But I'm not the only one who's recently taken on a wife. I'm sure you already gathered Amber is Eric's wife and they're literally about to have their first. Grayhawk married not even two weeks ago. She's a pretty little thing with fiery red hair, and since you're familiar with Fletcher; his eldest daughter Jade also recently married …"

Lucas narrowed his eyes and looked displeased. "If you tell me that idiot girl married that no good drifter, what was his name, Evian? I'm going to lose a lot of respect for Sergeant Major Fletcher."

"Of course, what I'm about to tell you will remain just between us," Andrew said. Lucas looked insulted. "I know, I know, but it had to be said, and you can put your mind at ease. Evian is dead. He died at the hands of Jade's husband after he attacked her. Fortunately, no harm was really done, just a few bruises."

Lucas was shaking his head with disgust. "Didn't like that man from the moment he showed up outside my gates looking for work. My steward gave him a meal and sent him on his way. I'm glad to hear Jade wasn't hurt, she's a good kid - or woman, I guess. Hopefully, her husband will treat her well."

Eric said, "Not to worry, she married a Wolf Tribesman. He'll treat her well."

"So, do you take an interest in all of your village girls, or did Jade just catch your eye?" Andrew asked, as he took a sip of his drink.

"As I said, I view her as nothing but a nice kid; but I like Fletcher and I like Steel. They're both good men. Because of his work, Steel travels a lot, and Fletcher's gone a lot now because of the war. I kind of took it upon myself to keep an eye out for Fletcher's family. Got a problem with that, Lord Stone?" Lucas said, looking offended.

Andrew replied apologetically, "No, I don't. In fact I appreciate it, especially now that Fletcher's family is my family too."

"You know, you two still have not answered my question. What brings you here?" Lucas asked, taking another sip from his drink.

"It's a private family matter I don't wish to get into. A night's hospitality is all we ask of you. We'll be out of your hair early in the morning and on our way back to the encampment by afternoon," replied Black Stone.

"You know, that's one trick of being a soldier I never managed to master. Being able to go from friend to soldier in an instant. I always found it interesting how you and Andrew could do that. One minute I'd be talking to Andrew, and the next I'd be talking to Sir Stone. You just did it to me, too." After that, they fell into the easy pattern of swapping stories and remembering past transgressions.

They took their leave early the next morning, and arrived in Temple Hill midmorning. Arriving at the Forge, they dismounted and tied up their horses. Black Stone pulled a large, wrapped parcel off his horse and entered the forge. Steel stopped working and rose, turning to face the brothers. He took a deep breath and let it out. As he looked from brother to brother, so like their father, it startled him. Though this was not the first time encountering Andrew, the family resemblance between the three siblings still startled him; it truly was remarkable. "What brings two of the Stone brothers to my forge?"

"I hope you will forgive the intrusion, Master Blacksmith, but I'm Eric Stone, the new Duke of Stone Reach, and I came here to ask you about this." He offered the parcel to Steel. Steel took it, but didn't unwrap it. After a very long moment Eric added, "I would appreciate anything you can tell me about it."

Steel gave a curt nod. Still not unwrapping it, he asked, "Before I look at it, what do you know of it, and specifically, what do you want to know about it?"

But it was Andrew who replied. "I know that it's my father's sword. And he's used it as long as I can remember. I remember no other. Eric says he has vague memories of one before it."

Steel turned his cold gaze on Eric. He lifted an eyebrow in question. "It was a long time ago. I wish to test my memory. I have but a child's memory of that time. Things that would've been important for adults were not important to me. Now, as I look back on them ..." He gave a slight shrug of his shoulders. "My adult mind wars with my child's memories. Some things that were unclear to me then are clear to me now." He shrugged again. "Others, not so much. I think this sword is very important and I want to know what you can tell me of it. I think it might hold the answer to many questions."

Steel sighed and unwrapped the parcel. It had been a long time since he'd seen this blade. He knew what it was before he even unwrapped it. It was, without a doubt, one of the finest pieces he had ever crafted. Over the course of his career, he had on many occasions been asked to craft the finest weapons he could; but his craftsmanship was always limited by their money or the time in which they were willing to give him to complete the project. The Duke merely had asked him when it would be ready. He told him six to eight months. The Duke didn't even raise an eyebrow, he pulled out a coin purse and handed it over and informed Steel he would pay the balance upon delivery. But when you are the most powerful Duke in all of Bretony, how could one really be surprised? He carefully unwrapped it. As he turned to his workbench, laying the uncovered blade on the bench, he gazed down at it lovingly. This weapon had not been crafted for beauty, though it was pretty to look at. It had been crafted for functionality. It was a Longsword; overlong for most Bretons, but given the height difference between Grey Stone and the average Breton, nearly a foot. There was no gold, only a little silver in the handle. There was a large ruby to either side of the hilt, and the pommel stone was a large onyx stone. The Duke had brought the two gems with him. Steel had added the onyx of his own accord. It was the only time in his life he'd ever been asked to craft a weapon of exceptional quality without being asked the cost. He picked it up and examined it carefully. The Duke had clearly taken good care of it. It was well maintained, and in good order. "Again I say, tell me exactly what you want to know. There are many things about this blade I could tell you, but I believe it is a specific question you seek the answer to. So rather than answering a hundred questions that you do not wish the answer to, why do you not just tell me what you do wish the answer to."

"Did you craft that blade for our father a little over nineteen years ago?" Black Stone said abruptly.

"Yes, he told me he needed a new sword. He said he had broken his last one. It was not his habit to carry anything but the finest. The man who'd crafted his last, had died of old age. He asked around and was told that I was, for lack of a better word, his replacement in skill. We argued over what he wanted. He gave me exact specifications for the blade. I told him he would regret it if I made it that way. He ended the conversation with him informing me that he was the man paying for it, and I should just make it the way he wanted and make him happy, which of course I did not do. I made this instead." He smiled to himself, remembering the conversation with his granddaughter. "He was furious when he saw it, but I convinced him to try a few swings. The first time he held it in his hand he, knew it was a better blade then the one he'd ordered. He paid for it without question."

"Did it not occur to you then to tell my father that your daughter was about to have his child?" Andrew demanded angrily.

"As a man, the thought had crossed my mind once or twice; but I'm a peasant blacksmith and your father was the Duke. There was no way that that conversation was going to end well for me or mine. If I was lucky, he'd do nothing about it and have no interest. He could've convinced my daughter that she was better off being his mistress for the rest of her life, and taken her away and put her in a house and used her for his own pleasure until he tired of her. Or he could've just taken my grandchild. So I held my tongue and kept my peace. Besides, though I suspected that your father was the father of my grandchild, I did not know. My daughter never told anyone. Everyone suspected, but no one knew. And what if I was wrong?" He hesitated a long moment, staring at Eric as he did so. "You know, it occurs to me, the way you spoke earlier, like there was a lot more involved than what passed between my daughter and your father."

Black Stone ignored the question. "Thank you very much for your time, Master Blacksmith. My brother and I will be going now." Black Stone picked up the sword and carefully rewrapped it.

As Steel watched the younger man, he said, "I'd completed the blade and was delivering it when your sister was born." He found himself concerned. There was clearly a lot weighing on his mind and something troubling him deeply; but whatever it was, he clearly was not willing to share or to discuss it. Steel looked back at his brother, and from the concerned look on his face, Eric apparently was not willing to share it with anyone.

Black Stone finished with his task, turned, and headed for his horse. Securing the blade, he mounted up and rode off without so much as a word to his brother. Andrew sighed deeply as his worry increased.

"Whatever he's struggling with, he'll share it with you eventually. I think his mind is just at war with itself."

Andrew nodded, turned, and said, "Thank you for your time. I know you're never happy to see any of us, but I do appreciate your courtesy."

"I no more blame you or your brothers for the actions of your father, than I do my granddaughter for the actions of her parents. As you have stated, you were all innocent bystanders in this unfortunate event." The two men shook hands. Andrew excused himself. Mounting up, he followed his brother.

XXXI

Black Stone rode hard, arriving back in the encampment late at night. He entered the War Room quietly, so as not to disturb his wife. He set his father's sword down on the table, then grabbed two glasses and a bottle off the side table. He poured himself a drink and sat down in front of his father's sword. He then sat up all night trying to make order of his disorderly thoughts. Finally, shortly before dawn, he sent for Grayhawk.

"You wish to see me early this morning, or did you just to delight in the idea of dragging me out of bed with my wife?" he asked as he entered. Then all mirth died on his face the moment he set eyes on his brother. Seeing his unshaven, still dirty face, a half-empty bottle, and a glass sitting in front of him, he changed his tone instantly. "What troubles you?"

"What do you remember of the six months before we went to be trained as Knights?" he asked, taking another sip.

"Are you drunk?" Eric slowly shook his head. Michael pulled out a chair and sat down across from his brother. "Not much. Mother and Father went back and forth between not speaking and screaming at each other. It's the only time in my life I ever remember them not sharing a room. Why? Why is it so important to you now?"

"You remember what happened to Father's first sword?"

Michael shifted uncomfortably in his chair. "Father shattered it, slamming it into the stone pillar on the side of the Castle. It was after that last fight with Mother, before he left home. He stayed in the barracks for two months before he was reassigned." Michael reached forward and grabbed the bottle, pouring himself a healthy dollop. Taking a long swig, he asked, "You think any of our younger brothers remember those horrible months?"

Eric took another sip and slowly shook his head. "At least I hope they don't. Andrew doesn't seem to. If anyone would, it would be him. He's only a little over two years younger than we are; that would've made him not quite eight at the time I guess, or about that. But it was nearly twenty years ago."

"What did Steel tell you about Father's sword? Were you right?" Eric nodded his head and relayed the whole story, not that there was that much to tell. Michael nodded his head in understanding. "Do you still blame yourself for those months?"

"I was the one who started it all. Pleading with Father, begging him, insisting that I wanted to be a Knight. Insisted I was old enough, big enough, strong enough. I'd no idea Mother was going to take it so badly, but I don't think two years time would've made her take it any better."

Michael shook his head. "No, I think two years wouldn't have made it any better. If anything, it might've just made it worse, but it wasn't your fault."

"I wish I could agree with you, but it doesn't matter. It was twenty years ago. I can't go back and change it. I just have to live with it." Changing the subject suddenly, Eric said, "I think Amber and I will have the family over for dinner tonight. After dinner we can deal with it."

Michael nodded. "Sounds good, it will be the first time that Cora socializes with the family as a whole. All right, maybe not as a whole, sixty percent of them." Eric nodded grimly. Michael sighed, downed his drink, and excused himself.

Amber thought it had been a lovely evening dinner. She very much enjoyed having all of the brothers here with their wives: Andrew, Michael, Daniel, though unfortunately, Bridget, of course, was not present, Fitzwilliam, Terrance, Patrick, and of course Eden. Growing up an only child, she was surprised at how much she enjoyed having such a large family. She was sorry that Murtaugh and Helena had been unable to attend due to the new baby; but they were so selfishly keeping him to themselves. She smiled and patted her belly. She would do the same and she knew it. As her eyes alighted on her husband, she remembered the only thing marring the atmosphere was the dark expression on his face. She had tried all day to find out what was wrong with him, but he refused to discuss the matter in any way. She was almost relieved when he stood up and excused himself. To her surprise, he returned almost immediately, carrying a sword she had never seen before. "I hope you all forgive the interruption to your conversations, but I had an ulterior motive when I invited you all here for dinner tonight. Though of course, all of the brothers, with the exception of Eden, are aware of it as I've spoken to each one of you in turn on this matter. As soon as I learned that Bloodstone's grandfather was a master blacksmith, it occurred to me he was probably the man who crafted Father's sword. So as you all know, I took a trip the past few days and went to Steel. He verified that he did indeed craft Father's sword. I feel, and my brothers all agree with me, given the fact that the sword was crafted by Bloodstone's grandfather for our father, the sword rightfully belongs to her." He moved to stand beside her. She rose to her feet and looked at him as he offered her the sword.

But she was already shaking her head. "Black Stone, you're the oldest and the new Duke. Father's sword belongs to you."

"If I were to take Father's sword, it would be a crime as good as theft. If you ask me, the sword was forged by your blood for your blood. Any

396

way you look at it, it belongs to you." All of the brothers murmured in agreement.

"If you do not want it, perhaps Michael or Andrew would like it?" she asked quickly.

"Stop arguing. We've all discussed it. We all agree. No one disagrees; Father's sword belongs to you," Andrew said firmly.

"But I truly believe Father would wish you to have it, Eric," she said, clasping his arm.

"I find it interesting how often people say they know what I would want," said a voice from the head of the table. They all turned quickly, drawing their swords as they did so, only to see a twenty-five-year-old version of the Eighth Duke of Stone Reach, General Grey Stone, lounging in Black Stone's chair. That is, all but Bloodstone, who merely sighed and dropped back into her chair.

Everyone else stared in shock, but it was Daniel who recovered the quickest. "Who in Hades are you and what in Hades do you think you're doing?"

"See, here we go again. Why does Hades get brought into it and swords get drawn on me? I'm really starting to feel unloved," he said sarcastically.

"If you want love, perhaps you should switch from war to gardening," suggested Bloodstone.

"Now daughter, you're just being cruel. You know I hate gardens."

"Yes, but you also hate libraries and infirmaries, but you know how to read and you have healers, so perhaps you could learn gardening," she replied with equal sarcasm.

"Daughter?" demanded Andrew.

Ares turned to look at Andrew. "Yes, Son, Daughter," he gestured to the other boys, "Sons, Father, it's how a family works. I thought you would know this. I did raise you this way, did I not?" Ares snapped with irritation.

Cora said with understanding, "Well, that explains it. I'd been trying to figure out why all of you had magic except you, Greyhawk. It was no kind of magic I'd ever seen."

"What do you mean, we all have magic?" demanded Black Stone.

"You're all half gods. You are all sons of Ares," replied Ares.

"You're telling me, the reason I was unconscious for hours after walking into that magic booby-trap is because I'm a son of Ares, as in Ares, God of War?" Daniel demanded with irritation.

"Don't forget Battle and Bloodshed. If you're going to use my title, at least use all of it; though as

I informed your sister, I prefer you all to call me Father."

Again, with the exception of Bloodstone, who merely picked up her glass and took a drink, they all stared in stunned silence for a long moment. Finally, Black Stone slowly turned to face Bloodstone and asked incredulously, "This is an elaborate joke, right?"

"I wish it were. I'm not any happier about this than you. It's rather an uncomfortable spot to find yourself in. A devout servant of Athena being the daughter of Ares, and that's before you take into account all of the unfortunate side effects that have popped up lately," she said, glaring at Ares.

"Don't look daggers at me, Girl. You'll learn to control it in time. You're nearly there now," Ares replied nonchalantly.

"Why did Ares, God of War, take the, what, sixty? eighty? year sabbatical from his duties to slum it as the Duke of Stone Reach?" Eric demanded angrily. Then he added, "Does Mother know?"

"You forgot Battle and Bloodshed," supplied Daniel. Eric glared at him.

Ares grinned. "I informed your mother as soon as all of you boys were on your way back here. So yes, she knows, and I'll say she took it a lot better than any of you are taking it."

399

Eric felt his temper rising. He began turning and pacing back and forth, only a few steps at a time as he ran his hands through his hair angrily. Two steps, turn, two steps, turn, as all the thoughts of the past few months rushed through his mind; all of his anger and guilt over the past twenty years. To those who were watching, it happened in an instant. Eric turned his back on Ares, who was still lounging in the chair, took two steps, and as Eric turned around, he was nose to nose with Ares. "If you have questions, Eric, ask them, don't brood."

"Could you have prevented it?" he asked, his voice shaking with emotion.

"If I could have, I would have. But even as a god, by the time I heard her scream and stepped into the hallway, she was at the foot of the stairs and there was nothing I could do. I'm the God of War, healing is not in my realm. My healers have no magic healing abilities to speak of. Their abilities are entirely skill and training, and those few that do actually have magical healing abilities, they get them from Freya, not from me. If you think I did not feel the loss acutely, you're wrong Eric; but it wasn't your fault. Your mother and I had been fighting for weeks, and yes, we were fighting over you and Michael; but that doesn't make it your fault. She and I had very different ideas about what the two of you needed to become men. She believed that there was no need for you both to enter training as Knights until you were fourteen. As we both know, I did not agree with that. When I informed her that come spring you were both entering training for Knighthood, that Lord Sanford had agreed to take you both on so you could stay together, she was furious. You know what happened after that." Eden swallowed hard as he watched Ares' face cloud over with darkness - though to anyone watching, they knew it was not the look of rage and fury, but tremendous grief. Eric stood there stiff and unbending for a long moment, then his lip quivered slightly, his shoulders slumped, and his forehead fell forward on to his Father's shoulder. Ares wrapped his arms tightly around his son and he said firmly, "If anyone is to blame, it was me."

Andrew turned to look at Michael. "What happened, Michael? I don't remember," he said with confusion.

"Father made his announcement that we were to begin training early to mid winter, and over the next few months, Mother turned Stone Reach into a living Tartarus for Father. She challenged him at every turn. She argued with him. How Father managed not to strike her sometimes, I don't know - she certainly pushed him hard enough. If there was a mean, hateful thing to be said, Mother found a way to say it. It became so bad, Father requested a transfer anywhere and he was given one. The King arranged it so that he would be able to take us and deliver us for our training, and then go on to his new post. The day he came home to inform Mother that we would all be leaving as soon as the roads were passable, they were in Mother's sitting room at the top of the stairs. It's not her sitting room anymore, she changed it. She has a sitting room downstairs now. We could hear her screaming and yelling at Father and things breaking. I heard the door open and Mother threw one more hateful comment over her shoulder as she turned to head down the stairs. I guess she must've tripped on the hem of her skirt. As she screamed, I looked up, but I didn't even have a chance to move. We were both in the hallway. She tumbled down the stairs. Father was out as quick as he could be, though he must've been on the other side of the room. He carried her up to her room and sent for healers. Still in his armor, I remember that he paced up and down the hallway for hours until the healer finally came out and told him that Mother would live, but she'd lost the baby. Father's face went as dark as night. He went down the stairs and out the front doorway. He banged the door open so hard, it chipped some of the stone of the sidewall. You can still see it. I saw him pull out his sword. He made an almost inhuman noise as he slammed it into the stone pillar. The blade shattered. Mother refused to have him in the room. She didn't see him again until … I don't know when. We were gone by then. We didn't come home for Solstice that first year; only came home the following year. Everything was normal, and I think Patrick was on the way."

Greyhawk didn't care if his brothers were watching. He reached over and grabbed Cora around the waist and pulled her onto his lap, pressing his forehead into her neck. She instantly wrapped her arms around him.

Eden turned in his chair and slid one arm around his woman's back, placing his other hand over both of hers and squeezing them tightly. His own heart ached with the knowledge of his own loss. He couldn't imagine how more acute that pain would be had he been in any way responsible for that loss. Though in truth, as much as it pained him to admit it, much of her suffering the Duchess had brought on herself. Dowager Duchess, he corrected himself with a mental kick.

The room sat silent for several more minutes before Ares grabbed Black Stone's head and pulled him away. Looking deep into his son's eyes, he said firmly, "You have nothing to reproach yourself for. Stop raking yourself over the coals." Eric nodded grimly.

"I hope everyone won't think me heartless for what I'm about to say, but I think that there are two very large reasons why this is all bothering Eric so much. One is the death of his father," Tabitha said, looking at Ares and shrugging, "combined with the imminent birth of his own child. Perhaps more than anything, what is bothering him is he knows in ten years he will make the same decision and he fears how Amber will take it." All the men turned to look at Amber and all the women turned to look at Eric.

Amber spoke slowly. "I'm a warrior. I understand the need for a child to be trained and if it is the custom that Knights leave their home to do this, then it will be difficult, but I will not protest."

Andrew reached over and placed his hand on Tabitha's belly, gently. "We were all ten when Father sent us away to be trained. How will you take it in ten years?"

Tabitha slowly blushed as all eyes turned back to her. "First off, it's going to be more like eleven - and that's assuming your first is a boy."

Andrew laughed and pulled her onto his lap and kissed her. "True my love, very, very true."

Amber scoffed and looked annoyed. "And were the two of you planning on getting around to telling us anytime soon?"

"Technically, she still hasn't told me," Andrew replied, still laughing. He sobered at once though and said, "That didn't answer my question."

"Well, I left home to begin my training as a priestess of Anna when I was twelve, so can we split the difference and do eleven?" she asked a little hesitantly.

"Done." He kissed her again.

Everyone laughed. The mood in the room immediately lightened. Ares reached down and picked up Grey Stone's sword from where Eric had dropped it. Turning, he offered it to Eric. "Don't you want it back?" asked Eric.

"Ares, God of War, has his own sword. This sword belonged to Grey Stone, and the only reason I didn't come and tell all of you boys sooner was because I was waiting for you to give it to your sister. I knew that that was what you intended, and I did not wish to interfere. It meant more you giving it to her when you didn't know who I was."

"You forgot Battle and Bloodshed," supplied Daniel, with a grin.

Father and son turned identical glares on him. Daniel only laughed. Eric took it and met the eyes of his Father. "So who is our father, Grey Stone or Ares?"

"That is a very interesting question. Ares was born Grey Stone, or Michael Stone, I guess you should say. I think somehow the two got mixed up and I don't think there will ever be any separating them. Should be interesting to see how the next few decades go, but at least for the moment, they are one and the same."

Eric turned and grabbed his sister by the arm and pulled her to her feet. "Take it. It's yours, it belongs to you and everyone in this room agrees except you." She nodded as she took it and unwrapped the belt, strapped it on, then she looked back up at her oldest brother, then hugged him tightly.

XXXII

Five weeks later, Bloodstone was awoken from a sound sleep by a huge clap of thunder. She listened for a moment. She could hear the rain pouring down. A moment later, there was another loud crack of thunder, followed by another and another. She smiled to herself as she could hear between claps of thunder, Blackwolf's uninterrupted snoring. As she lay there listening to the storm, she wondered how Eden could sleep through it. The storm seemed to be getting worse and worse, unusual for a fall storm. She rolled over and tried to go back to sleep, and then something caught her attention, a noise outside. As she sat up and slid out of bed, Eden sat up and reached for his sword. A moment later, she was pulling aside the tent flap. To her surprise, Brynjolf, looking like a drowned rat, was just stepping under the canopy. Seeing her, he turned to speak to her instead of her guards. He said in a quick rush, "I'm sorry for disturbing you, but Sidel has gone into labor and with Viktor's tent so far away, I didn't like to leave her alone that long."

"No, of course not, but let me send my guards for Viktor, Foster, and Bloodrose. Eden, why don't you quickly dress and take Brynjolf for a drink at the main bar. I will have the guard inform Foster to join you there. At least you'll be dry, and as soon as we have word I will bring it to you there."

She turned to Reef. "Would you please go and inform Katya that a friend of ours has gone into labor and ask her if she would be willing to come and spend the rest of the night here with Blackwolf?" He nodded, pulled his cloak over his head, and left. She quickly dispatched the other two guards on their errands, then beckoned to Brynjolf to enter. As she walked past him beginning to pull up her nightie, he quickly turned his back.

"You do realize, Woman, I'm not going to put up with your immodest behavior once you're just my Queen, right?" Eden asked, with only the faintest trace of amusement.

"When the day comes I cease to be a soldier, I'll practice modesty. Until then, forget it," she said as she quickly dressed, grabbed her cloak, and headed out the door. Tossing over her shoulder as she did so, "You boys can wait for Katya."

*****

Viktor was lying in bed staring up at roof of the tent, listening to the storm. He had been doing so for at least a quarter of an hour. He knew it was pointless to go back to sleep. He always got dragged from his bed on nights like this. Inevitably, some baby always decided they couldn't wait any longer. He was just wondering who it was going to be. If he was a betting man, he would say it was going to be Sidel. She seemed

408

the more impatient, but it has nothing to do with the woman and everything to do with the baby. Another loud clap of thunder decided it for him. He swung his feet out of bed and began to dress. His woman sat up and looked at him. "Should I dress?"

"Only if you wish to aid me in my endeavors. If you wish not to get out on a night like this, I truly understand." He moved to the bedside and bent down to kiss her on the cheek. She got up and quickly dressed.

He was just pulling on his boots when he heard someone knocking at the tent flap. He pulled it open and gestured the man inside quickly. The guard entered without hesitation. "Forgive the intrusion, sir, but General Black Stone sends me to inform you your niece has gone into labor and the General would greatly appreciate your immediate presence."

Viktor laughed to himself as he picked up his bag. He gestured the guard out. Seva and Viktor pulled on their cloaks as they followed him out. As they walked, Viktor turned to the guard. "Has anyone informed Colonel Stone or Colonel Grayhawk?"

"No, sir, I was the only one sent and I was sent for you."

Viktor hesitated only a moment. "Go and inform Eden and General Bloodstone, then move on to Colonel Stone and Colonel Grayhawk, and best not leave off Captain Stone."

The guard turned to him in question. "Which one?"

"Yes."

As Viktor entered his niece's quarters, he found Black Stone sitting calmly on the side of the bed, holding her hand. "All right, Black Stone, you can go now."

Black Stone bent down and kissed her on the forehead. "I'll just be in the other room if you need me."

"Oh no, you will not be; go to the bar. I'll send word for you when your child is born. Until then, give me room to work," Viktor said, practically shoving him out the door. Once they were alone, Viktor performed a brief examination. "Well, Niece, you appear to be doing just fine. Things are progressing well, but don't expect it to be anytime soon. I say you still have several more hours to go. Have you sent for your mother yet?"

"I didn't want her fussing over me."

Viktor looked over his shoulder at his woman, who merely nodded and exited the tent. A moment later, she returned. "I sent a guard for her."

An hour later, as Viktor stood back and watched all the women fuss over his niece, he quickly took stock of who was present. There was his woman of course, Xanhara, Autumn, Carmen, Sorrow, Tabitha, Jade, and Cora. Where on earth was Bloodstone and Bloodrose? The only other woman missing was Helena, but that was to be expected. He exited the private quarters and entered the War Room. Opening the flap, he looked at the two guards. Seeing the one who fetched him, he demanded, "Where is my sister Bloodstone?"

The guard looked at him in confusion. "When I arrived at her quarters, the guards informed me that she'd been summoned to the bedside of a friend who was having a baby. I thought she was here already." *Sidel.* He nodded to himself, and went back to Amber. He gave the other women another hour before he threw half of them out.

*****

Eden and Brynjolf had not been in the bar a quarter of an hour when Black Stone entered looking irritated. Seeing them, he headed straight for them. "Sidel too?" Both men nodded. "Well, at least we don't have to wait alone."

Foster was the next to arrive. Seeing them, he gave them a nod and went to the bar. "A dozen mugs of ale." The bartender gave him a tray. Picking it up, he crossed to the table where the other men were sitting. Setting the tray down, he pulled two other tables over. Quickly counting, he grabbed another table and pulled it over too. "Anyone want to play cards?" A half an hour later found Eden, Black Stone, Brynjolf, Foster, Andrew, Grayhawk, Dex, Daniel, Fitzwilliam, Terrance, Patrick, and Innish all sitting and nursing their drinks, playing cards. When Murtaugh and Big Bear joined them at the table, they were dealt in.

The men continued nursing their drinks, playing cards, until the Amazons entered nearly two hours later. Black Stone got to his feet looking at them anxiously. They waved him back in his chair. "Viktor kicked us out. He said that there were too many people in there. So the three of us thought we'd come and drink with you boys," Sorrow said, pulling out a chair.

Foster yelled out to the barkeep, "Another round plus three for our new friends."

The bartender grumbled to himself as he poured three ales and refilled two pitchers. "If it was anybody other than you officers, I'd worry about being stiffed." He headed over to the table carrying the three mugs in one hand, and the two pitchers in the other. He sat the three fresh mugs down in front of the Amazons and started topping off the men's mugs.

As he got near the young Barbarian, Captain Stone put his hand over the boy's mug. "No more for him, switch him to water." The barkeep nodded but grumbled.

As he circled around to the youngest Stone, the Big Barbarian put his hand over the mug saying as he did so, "Him too."

"Now wait a minute, I'm sixteen, nearly seventeen! I understand you cutting off Innish, he's only twelve. Why do I have to switch to water? I've only had two," demanded Patrick.

"Thirteen!" Innish snapped.

Eden replied without hesitation, "Because I said so, and I'm older."

Six hours later - not only had they all switched to coffee, but even their bartender had changed - they were all startled by Viktor's entrance. They all shot to their feet. He grinned. "Boy, if all of you aren't the sorriest looking bunch of uncles I've ever seen; however, the aunts all look lovely." He crossed to Black Stone, extended his hand. "Permit me to be the first to congratulate you on your fine, healthy son."

The two men shook hands warmly. "May I see them now?"

"Yes, the women were nearly ready when I left. She should be ready to be seen now. We'll give you a half hour." Black Stone didn't wait to hear the last words, he was already out the door. Viktor turned to look at Brynjolf. "Are you here to lend comfort, or to receive it?"

"If that is your backwards way of asking if Sidel is in labor too, the answer is yes."

"Well then, if you'll excuse me, I guess I have another patient to go attend to." Viktor nodded and excused himself. The brothers gave Black Stone and Amber three quarters of an hour before they started taking turns going to see their new nephew, though each one returned afterwards to await the arrival of Brynjolf's child.

Another two and a half hours passed before Bloodstone entered the bar. Again, they all shot to their feet. She gave them all a warm smile. They all relaxed. She crossed to Brynjolf and patted him on the arm. "You have a beautiful baby girl, and mother and daughter are doing very well and await the arrival of Father and Grandfather."

Brynjolf gripped her tightly by the shoulders, bent down, and kissed her on the cheek. "Thank you. I can't thank you enough."

As Brynjolf and Foster headed for the door, Andrew said, "We'll give you some time alone, then we'll all come and oooh and ahhh appropriately over your new baby." Brynjolf either didn't hear him, or merely didn't respond.

"Well, I'm going to go and visit Amber and Black Stone." Bloodstone turned and headed out the door. As she quietly entered their quarters, she saw Amber looking down on her son and something about it struck her as familiar, though she could not immediately place it. She smiled as she looked up at her brother standing there, arms crossed, just gazing down on his wife and son. She crossed over to him and wrapped her arm around his waist. "You did good. He's beautiful. Have you named him yet? And please tell me at least the two of you named your child together. No one else around here seems to."

Black Stone laughed and nodded. "Xavier Nathan Stone."

"Tell me, what did Sidel and Brynjolf have, and do you know what they're going to call it?" asked Amber.

"They had a beautiful baby girl, and apparently Sidel is determined to call her Jasmine."

"Jasmine, that's a pretty name. I can't wait to meet her," Amber replied with a little yawn.

Bloodstone smiled down on her nephew, then reached over and caressed his forehead. As she did so, it struck her right between the eyes. The look on Amber's face, the look on Seana's face when she looked down on Big Bear. It was a maternal look; the way a mother looks at her child. But Big Bear remembered his mother. He talked about her. Then she remembered Big Bear had said his father was given to his grandparents by an Amazon, and Seana very much looked like an Amazon. She put her hand to her mouth reeling under the weight of that discovery.

Amber looked at her concerned. "Bloodstone, are you all right?"

"Yes, of course I am. You needn't worry about me. Something I've just been trying to figure out for about six months suddenly struck me. But now that I've met my beautiful nephew, I should excuse myself so you three can be alone." She ignored their protests and left the tent heading for her own quarters.

Rounding one of the tents, she saw a Barbarian girl about seven or eight years old with pale blonde hair and very blue eyes. The little girl moved to walk alongside Bloodstone and said, "You know, I was wondering if you were ever going to figure that out."

Bloodstone stopped walking and looked at the girl. The girl smiled at her. "I'm sorry, little girl, I'm not following you. Figure out what?" She continued on her way.

The little girl giggled. "Figure out that Big Bear was my grandson. You know, almost any other woman would've figured it out on the spot.

That maternal look of mine gives me away. I do so love that boy, though I must say, he's not as wild as I would like anymore. You fixed that. I did like him much better more unkempt; but I guess if he was going to find a mate, he needed to be tamed."

Bloodstone stopped walking and stared at the girl. "Seana?"

"Who else, silly?" Bloodstone blinked as she stared down at the delicate little girl in front of her. Only the pale blonde hair and very blue eyes reminded her of the large Amazon warrior she had seen before. "You won't tell him will you? I'd hate to damage our relationship." Bloodstone continued to stare down at the little girl in disbelief. "Will you please stop looking at me like that? It's almost as though you don't believe I am who I say I am," the little girl said, bouncing from foot to foot, giving off the appearance to anyone watching her that she was your typical eight-year-old little girl.

"My apologies, I'm just … surprised, that's all."

"Yes, I guess people do find me somewhat startling. I've never understood that," the little girl said twirling. "But you didn't answer me. You're not going to tell him, are you? He might not like me anymore if he knows that I'm his grandmother," the little girl said with a pout.

"If you do not wish me to, then of course I would not. But I don't believe he'll ever ask the question, so I see no reason I cannot say with reasonable certainty I will not tell."

The little girl jumped up and down clapping her hands. "Oh thank you, thank you. I knew we would be just such fabulous friends." The girl threw her arms around Bloodstone's waist and hugged her tightly, rubbing her face against Bloodstone's belly. She said, "That under thing you wear is very uncomfortable. How does your mate stand it? I would not like it if you were in bed with me."

Bloodstone reflected momentarily on the absurd conversations she sometimes found herself in before she replied, "I don't wear it to bed."

"Oh, that would make a difference. That would make your pillows much more comfortable. I like soft pillows." With that, the little girl beamed and disappeared, leaving behind only a soft amber glow.

*****

Seana - Goddess of the Wilderness. Like the wilderness, she is wild and untamed. She is often considered quite mad. Unlike most of the gods, who have the capability, but lack the inclination to assume other forms; she often appears as a woman, a man, or a girl child. She is a fierce defender of

418

the forest and shows no mercy to those who would destroy the natural resources of the earth. Seana has rugged features, bronze skin, and is pretty. She has white hair and ice blue eyes. She is six feet three inches tall and muscular. Her animal is the wolf. Her preferred weapon is the spear. Goddess of the Barbarians.

XXXIII

Five days later, Bloodstone was watching the Soldiers of Athena drill when a guard on horseback rode up, dismounted, saluted, and began speaking before she even acknowledged him. "Captain of the Watch sent me to inform you that the patrol that left this morning just returned. They have wounded. They were taken to the infirmary."

Bloodstone felt a cold hand squeeze her heart. Eden had been on that patrol. She forced herself not to think of it and to reply as she would any other time she received such news. "My compliments to the Captain and thank him for his quick response."

Dex watched as General Bloodstone calmly walked over and exchanged a few brief words with Hawthorne. He wondered if anybody other than himself would've found her movements to be deliberately calm; but he had watched her face go from concerned, interested, to blank in an instant at the mention of the wounded patrol.

Bloodstone patted Hawthorne on the shoulder and turned and headed in the direction of the infirmary. As they neared the infirmary, they heard a loud commotion. As they came in sight of the disturbance, they saw about twenty soldiers trying to keep the group back. Over the heads of everyone else they could see Eden, his face half covered in blood, his back was pressed up against the side wall of the infirmary, his sword out for some reason. The soldiers were trying to keep everybody back from him. There was something so incredibly wild about his appearance. As Bloodstone quickly scanned the area, she saw several wounded men lying about, though from their body positions, they clearly had been placed there, not fallen.

Bloodstone started pushing her way through the crowd. As she broke through the crowd, she grabbed one of the soldiers. "What in Hades is going on?" she demanded angrily.

"I don't know, General. The patrol came in and they had a lot of wounded. We brought them straight here. He was unconscious and all I know is, one minute he was unconscious, the next he just started swinging."

Bloodstone started forward when a hand grabbed her by the shoulder. She looked over her shoulder to see Dex standing there. He spoke before she could. "I know you don't think you're about to go toe to toe with your mate."

Bloodstone glared at him. "I don't have time to argue with you. Remember what I told you previously about interfering with me as a General." She jerked her shoulder free and turned, saying to the soldiers as she did so, "If he tries to follow me, you have my permission to treat him just like any other member of the crowd."

"Yes, General," replied the soldiers quickly.

"Push the crowd back another twenty feet," she added, as she slowly started moving forward towards Eden. Now that she was in front of him, she could see that more like three quarters of his face was covered in blood. And though the left side of his head was entirely covered in braids, even the braids seemed soaked with blood, it ran down his neck, soaking into his tunic halfway down his chest and arm. He had other wounds, but none of them seemed to be life-threatening. As she observed him, she realized his eyes were darting from left to right and he was breathing hard. He was gripping his sword with both hands so tight his knuckles were white. She hesitated only a moment, and then she decided to speak in Barbarian. "Eden, you look like shit. Why don't you let me clean you up?" His eyes and his sword darted back and forth a few inches as though he was searching for something. It took her a full minute before she realized the eyes that were staring at her were sightless.

Bloodstone quickly searched her mind for something to say that wouldn't be a lie. "Soldiers, I've got the situation under control. One of you get those healers back to work on the wounded. Eden's calming down; he's just a little disoriented from the head injury. Get the rest of the bystanders

out of here. The healers need room to work." She
heard her men giving orders. She took a few steps
closer, just outside of his blade range. She said
very softly, "Eden, you recognize my voice?"

He lowered his blade just a little. "I don't want
to hurt anybody. Just go away and leave me
alone."

"Eden, you didn't answer me. Do you
recognize my voice?"

"You look and sound like my woman, but my
eyes have been deceived before; I'm sure my ears
could be just as easily deceived," he lied.

She took two more steps forward. Now she
was inside of his blade reach. "If I'm not your
woman, how do I know you are lying to me right
now?" She pitched her voice a little lower and
took another step forward. "What about your
smell, your hands, can those things be deceived?"
She tentatively reached forward and put her left
hand over his on his sword. His hands jerked and
she pulled up her shoulder and jerked her head
away just in time for his blade to bite into her
forearm.

His blade slid from his hands as he murmured,
"Oh, by the gods, what have I done?" He started to
shake uncontrollably. Bloodstone stepped in
quickly and wrapped her arms tightly around him,
pulling his face into her neck. She pressed her

cheek against his and barely breathed in his ear, "They ought to recognize me, to know me, smell me."

"You know I can't see, don't you?"

"Yes, do you recognize me?"

As Eden inhaled deeply several times, he felt himself begin to calm. That oh so familiar smell of lavender and vanilla, and though he could smell that she had washed this morning after he had left, he could still smell him all over her. He pressed his hand tightly into her back. "Yes, I can smell that I made love to you last night."

"You have a few wounds that I need to stop the bleeding on, and then I'll take you back to our tent. Will you give me just a minute? I'm going to push you up against the wall, just stand there. Don't move, okay?"

Bloodstone crossed to the nearest healer and grabbed a couple of rolls of bandages, quickly and sloppily tying off her own bleeding arm. She returned to him, bandaging his arm and stomach, saying as she did so, "As soon as I'm done, I want you to slump down like your strength is fading."

He nodded his head, then groaned with pain. "I shouldn't have done that," he said with a weak laugh.

"There, all done. You're going to need a lot of stitches, but we can do that back in our home." A moment later he slumped and would've fallen to his knees; but she caught him, pulling his left arm over her shoulders and wrapping her right arm around his waist so that her wounded left forearm was on the other side from him. She hoped he wouldn't notice the wound until his eyesight returned. Her nagging healer's voice said, *If his eyesight returns.* She ignored the cynical part of her brain and said, "Dex, would you come help me get Eden back to our quarters. I don't think he'll make it without us."

Dex moved quickly, grabbing Eden by the other side. Once he was sure he had him, he said, "I've got him, you can grab Eden's sword. He wouldn't like to leave it."

She hesitated a moment, then Eden said, "I'm fine with Dex."

She grabbed his sword and told one of the guards, "If Viktor is not in the infirmary, would you send for him and ask him to join us in our quarters?" The guard nodded.

Dex waited until they were in their quarters before he said, "He's blind, isn't he?"

"I'm afraid so." Bloodstone seated Eden in one of the wooden chairs next to the table. Getting rags and water, she began cleaning him up. It took forever digging through the mass of his hair before she found the wound.

"I'm going to have to un-braid a couple of your braids and probably shave a small section of the side of your head to stitch this up."

"Which ones?" asked Eden and Dex simultaneously.

"Do they have names?" she asked with surprise.

Again they both replied simultaneously, "No."

Eden elaborated. "They don't have names, but you get some of them for specific tasks. For example, it probably completely escaped your notice that after Dex married Jade, he got a second braid above his ear. The braid at his temple - that one was given to him when he went hunting for the first time. The first one above his ear was for his first kill. The one directly behind that was when he became a man. These are standard. We all get them, or I should say we all have to get them, or we're not considered a man. But the second one directly above the ears, not all men get that one. You only get it when you marry. It shows that you're a married man. Have you noticed that these are the only four braids Viktor has? You also may have noticed these are four of the five I gave you. I also gave you one directly behind the ear,

426

distinction in battle, though I know you should have at least a half dozen more."

"How do you know I distinguished myself in battle?" she asked, merely to take his mind off of his eyes. When he was speaking about the braids, it was the only time he seemed relaxed.

"You were in command of the men that took over the prison, for nothing else, you deserve it for that, though I'm sure you distinguished yourself in the battle of the Temple of the Mountain Pass."

"Well, it looks as though you're going to lose two braids, and only part of them. And it should grow back anyways, but you won't lose any of the four you mentioned."

He wrapped his left arm tightly around her waist. "I don't mind the loss of any but one." She was just finishing stitching up his head when Viktor and Black Stone entered.

"Damn, Eden, you look like shit," Black Stone said helpfully.

"Well, it looks as though your woman has everything well in hand. Why did I get sent for?" Viktor asked, unconcerned.

Bloodstone turned to him, hesitating, trying to find words that wouldn't upset Eden anymore; but before she could think of them, Eden spoke. "I think my woman's afraid she's going to frighten or upset me if she tells you I'm blind. So I'll just say it, I'm completely blind. I can't see a damn thing."

Viktor swallowed hard and looked at Black Stone, who suddenly looked contrite for his flippant remarks. "Well then, let's get all your braids un-braided and your hair washed so we can take a better look at your head."

Three quarters of an hour later, Eden sat stripped to the waist, hair thoroughly washed, while Viktor was gently running his fingers through Eden's hair, examining every inch of his scalp carefully. As if this wasn't obnoxious enough, Bloodstone was busy stitching up his arm. She had already attended to the wound on his stomach. It made him very uncomfortable having so many people so close and he couldn't see them. It made him want to scream. Viktor moved behind him and began carefully examining the back of his head. After a few more minutes of this, he moved back around to his front and tilted his chin up. Eden could feel him very close, but his inability to see him was making him very uncomfortable. Finally Viktor said, "I'm going to examine your eyes themselves now, so don't move." After what seemed to Eden an eternity of pulling up his eyelids and examining them, tilting his chin this way and that way, holding a candle so close he could feel the warmth, but not see any of the light, Viktor finally said, "I can find no apparent reason for the blindness, which leads me to believe that this head injury here on the side has caused your

428

brain to swell and it's pinching something. That happens on occasion. When the swelling goes down, your eyesight will return. Unfortunately, sometimes the swelling can take months to fully recede and vision to be restored."

"But I will get my sight back?"

Viktor looked at Bloodstone. She gave a single nod of her head. "Yes, but it could take a few months, and there is nothing I or any other healer can do to speed this process. It is essential that you take it very easy; the angrier or the more frustrated you get, the harder it will be for the swelling to recede. You also probably are going to have a lot of headaches. Unfortunately, the more headaches you have, again, the longer it takes for the swelling to recede. As long as you're having headaches, the swelling won't recede, so if you have headaches for the next month, it could take three months for your vision to restore."

Eden nodded grimly. He sat considering for a moment. "We have to keep this amongst ourselves, as the usurper cannot learn that I'm blind. I'm sure she would find a way to sway supporters in her direction."

"I agree with that, but there are those who are going to have to know, for example, Simon. And I'm sure some of the other brothers are going to be here to check on you as soon as they learn you were injured."

429

Eden sat silently brooding for a quarter of an hour, when Andrew, Daniel, and Innish were announced. "Wow, that has to be a first," Andrew said as he entered, looking at Eden.

"What?" Eden demanded with irritation.

"I don't think I've ever seen you without all those braids in your hair. You look kind of funny this way," Andrew replied quickly.

"You know, come to think of it, I don't think I ever have either," added Daniel. Black Stone nodded in agreement.

"That's because he is a man of Wolf Tribe, and once they're awarded braids, they're never seen without them. They're status symbols, kind of like your rank and your surcoats," Innish added helpfully.

Eden shifted uncomfortably and looked moody. Bloodstone bent down and kissed him on the cheek. He flinched and pulled away. "Don't do that."

"Don't worry, Eden, I will put your braids back as soon as I have a chance to cut your hair. It's a little shaggy," she said with a laugh.

"I like it shaggy, and I don't need your help."

"Who pissed in his porridge this morning?" demanded Daniel.

430

"Why don't we all talk about it outside," Bloodstone said, seeing Eden's discomfort increase.

"You don't have to go outside to talk about me behind my back. You can just talk about me like I'm not here," Eden snapped.

"Eden's feeling a little temperamental right now because his head injury has caused him to lose his sight temporarily," Viktor said gently.

"But I thought you were a healer. Why can't you just heal it?" Innish asked with surprise.

"There are some things as a healer of Freya we're not allowed to do. If it is considered fate, then we are not allowed to do it. Freya does not want to go up against the Fates. No one wants to end up on their bad side. Things like the loss of a limb or your eyesight are considered fate, and therefore under the domain of the Fates," Viktor said gently.

Innish's confusion had increased. "So an Athenian can do something healing wise that a servant of Freya can't?"

"No, servants of Athena are permitted to do even less healing than we are," Viktor replied, looking confused himself.

Innish was shaking his head in confusion. "But I don't understand."

431

"Innish, I think we should save this conversation for another time," Bloodstone said firmly.

"What if an Athenian did something that they should not have, healing wise?" Innish asked quickly.

"Athena has very definite ideas about it. They could suffer a very large punishment," Viktor replied. Then he caught Bloodstone's eye. She was glaring at him. Viktor blinked as he stared at Bloodstone for a long moment, then his head snapped back to Innish's eye and then back to Bloodstone. Her glare increased tenfold. "You fixed his eye," Viktor said in awe.

"But you said she'd be punished for doing such a thing!" Innish turned a heartbroken gaze on her. "Were you punished for fixing my eye?"

Bloodstone continued to glare at Viktor, who swallowed hard and looked apologetic. "That's between me and Athena; nothing for you to concern yourself with," she said in a voice that left no room for argument.

Black Stone, deciding he had better change the subject, said quickly, "Well, since winter's upon us and we're going to have the first snowfall any day now, I see no reason for you all to remain in camp. Eden needs to convalesce. He needs to be somewhere where he can be more comfortable than he can be here. So I'm making a command decision as General of this encampment that you both have to go somewhere for the winter. Where you go is up to you, but you will not remain in this encampment. Eden needs to rest and be comfortable - and you could use a break too."

Bloodstone opened her mouth to protest, but Eden's voice came out. "Temple Hill, we'll be in Temple Hill if you need us for the winter. I'm sure Jade misses her family and she would like to introduce her new husband, and I promised our younger siblings I would make you return and spend more time with them. This is as good an opportunity as any."

Bloodstone pursed her lips together and didn't look happy, but she nodded. "Very well, I will begin making arrangements for us to leave day after tomorrow. Good enough for you, General?"

"Good enough."

"Well, if I'm going to get us ready to travel by the day after tomorrow, I'll have to make some arrangements. Daniel or Andrew, would you mind staying with Eden for a little bit?"

"Not all," replied Andrew.

"Of course not," replied Daniel.

"I don't need a babysitter, and where are you going?" Eden demanded moodily.

"As I said, if we're going to leave the day after tomorrow, I have to make some arrangements. I need to inform Katya. I'm sure Jade would like some warning, plus I actually have to make the arrangements for travel, speak to my second-in-command, and any number of other things," she snapped back. Eden grumbled, but nodded.

Bloodstone turned and exited the tent with Black Stone and Viktor. Once they were a safe distance, Black Stone asked, "Were you telling the truth back there, Viktor?"

"Yes and no. I do believe that his vision is only a temporary loss; however, I did lie when I said it could take a couple of months. In reality it should be back in a few days, a week or two at the absolute most; but I was afraid if I told Eden that it should be back in a few days and it took longer, he would despair. This way, hopefully his vision will be back before he starts to panic about it." Viktor turned to Bloodstone. "How bad is that arm?"

"It's fine. It just needs a few stitches. I'll deal with it later." She looked at Black Stone. "Black Stone, if you can spare Fletcher over the winter, I think you should give him most of it off. After all, he worked almost all of last winter while we were on break."

Black Stone nodded his head in agreement. "Also, I'm more comfortable knowing he's along with you."

434

Bloodstone informed Jade and Katya first that Eden had been injured and needed to convalesce, so they were going to Temple Hill. Then she went in search of Sergeant Major Fletcher. Arriving outside his tent, she pounded her fist on one of the side posts. A moment later, he pulled aside the tent flap. Whatever he was going to say, he changed it. "General, is there something I can do for you?"

"May we speak privately?"

"Of course." He stepped aside, gesturing her in.

She motioned for Dex to follow her. Once inside, she turned to face Fletcher. "I'm assuming you heard that the patrol was attacked and returned early?"

"Yes, I was informed that about an hour ago, though I was told none of the injuries were life-threatening. Was I misinformed?"

"No. However, one of the wounded was Eden."

Fletcher immediately looked concerned. "Nothing serious, I hope."

She shifted and looked uncomfortable as she struggled to find words. Her instincts were to speak positively, but positive was not always truthful. And though Viktor had managed to lie convincingly to Eden and Black Stone, he of course could not fool her, and he had serious doubts. Though in truth, she had to admit Viktor was quite a doubter. What was it Eden had called him once? A worrywart. Her thoughts were interrupted by Fletcher. "You're really starting to worry me. Perhaps you should just come out and say it. What happened?"

"Eden is blind. Viktor believes it's only temporary."

Dex added quickly, "He says we'll know more in a few months, but for now Eden needs to just relax and not strain or stress himself." Bloodstone looked at him gratefully.

"And for these reasons, General Black Stone has ordered us out of the encampment by the day after tomorrow. He wants Eden somewhere where he can rest more comfortably, and Eden has chosen Temple Hill. Black Stone has also given permission for you to take the winter off, and he says I am to take you with me. But of course, all of this doesn't matter if you and Rose aren't willing to have some long-term tenants at your inn."

"As far as I'm concerned, the inn can be closed to visitors for the whole winter. We'll just keep the bar open." Bloodstone nodded grimly. "Though of course, if we're taking the winter off, we will have to come to a new understanding on the family relationship."

"Exactly what is that supposed to mean, Sergeant Major?" she demanded, crossing her arms over her chest.

"That means, Daughter, that you will remember you are my daughter, not my general, and there's certain things I expect of my daughters in my home," he replied smugly.

Bloodstone narrowed her eyes at him. "For example?"

"For example, I expect my daughter to be appropriately attired for her sex most of the time and I also expect her to remember she is a young woman and behave as such." Bloodstone silently cursed Eden for picking that place to spend the winter. But even her willful nature would not defy a man in his own home.

"Very well, Sergeant Major, but don't expect me to be happy about it."

XXXIV

Three days later, late afternoon, they rode into Temple Hill. As they turned their horses and headed for the inn, Bloodstone looked at Eden astride Cedric. He looked moody. Granted, he'd looked moody the past two days and had scarcely spoken to anyone. He also seemed to have no appetite. As they halted outside the inn, Bloodstone dismounted and tied off her horse and moved to stand beside Cedric. "Do you need a hand, Eden?" she asked. He awkwardly slid from the saddle in response.

"My goodness, I didn't expect to see all of you," Rose said from the doorway.

"I hope we've plenty of rooms available, my love. We have somewhat of a large entourage," Fletcher said, walking up to his wife and kissing her.

"I don't need a room, just a hole in the ground," Eden supplied bitterly.

Rose and Jade both looked horrified. After a moment, Rose recovered and said, "As it happens, we've been kind of slow lately, so we have plenty of room."

"Eden, here, take my arm," offered Bloodstone.

"I don't need any help. I'm not a child."

"Very well, about three paces forward and four steps up," she replied with a sigh. Rose shot a questioning look at Fletcher, who merely put his finger to his lips. She nodded and squeezed his hand.

"I'm sure you're all starving. Shall we have an early dinner?" Rose asked hopefully.

"That sounds wonderful, Mother. Mother, permit me to introduce my husband, Dex of Wolf Tribe. He is one of Eden's men, and this lovely woman is Katya. She's Blackwolf's nurse." Jade smiled as she took Blackwolf from Katya and bestowed several kisses on his cheek. She said, "And this adorable little creature is your grandson, Blackwolf." She offered him to her mother, who took him and cuddled him close. "This is Sergeant Simon. I don't believe you'd met him before. He's Bloodstone's personal aide. He's sweet on Katya, but we all pretend we don't notice. These other three men are also members of Wolf Tribe. They're all part of Bloodstone's personal bodyguard, of which Dex is in command. They're Reef, Broderick, and Grim."

Rose looked a little worried. "My daughter needs a personal guard?"

"After the death of the Duke of Stone Reach, our King decided he no longer wished his mate to be unprotected," supplied Dex.

*****

Two weeks later, Jade and Bloodstone were setting the table for dinner. Jade had been trying for the past quarter of an hour to figure out a way to start a conversation with her sister. She hadn't heard her speak in at least five days. Eden hadn't left his room in three. She had made several attempts already, but as of yet, Bloodstone had said nothing. Her thoughts were interrupted by Annabelle bringing in a large dish of cooked greens and setting them on the table. As Jade caught a whiff of them, she felt her stomach churn as a wave of nausea swept over her. She closed her eyes and gripped the table with one hand, as she put her other hand to her stomach. For a brief, horrifying moment, she thought for sure she was going to be sick. To her surprise, she heard Bloodstone give a little laugh. "That is the pits, but hopefully it will pass quickly. Have you told Dex yet?"

Jade blushed deeply. "I haven't figured out how one broaches such a subject. I mean, do you just blurt it out, or do you lead up to it?" she asked with genuine curiosity.

"How late are you?"

"Nearly a month," she replied shyly.

"You do realize, you are a married woman and these things are supposed to happen. To answer your question, I've always wondered how men don't know, or at least suspect; but I guess some are more obtuse than others. What I mean is, I understand Eden not realizing it; I wasn't late when the Duchess informed him. But being a month late, I will be surprised if Dex doesn't at least suspect. But whether he suspects it or whether he doesn't, he does expect it to happen eventually. So I would just tell him. He's not going to be angry."

As though he'd been summoned by the repeated use of his name, Dex entered. "Is there anything I can do to help?" he asked with a grin as he surveyed the table. Grabbing a roll, he stuffed it in his mouth.

Bloodstone caught Jade's eye and nodded encouragingly. Jade picked up the stack of plates and went back to putting them out. Looking at her husband shyly, she asked, "How many children do you think we should have?"

He moved behind her, wrapped his arms tightly around her, and bent down and kissed her on the neck before he said, "How many will you let me give you?"

"You know it's not fair to answer a question with a question," she replied. Then she got a mischievous grin on her face as she wiggled her backside against him. As he groaned, she looked over her shoulder at him innocently. "Something the matter?"

"Yes, I thought I married a young innocent girl and instead I married a little minx." He grabbed her jaw tightly and bent down and kissed her roughly. She turned in his arms and wrapped her arms tightly around his neck.

She slid her hand up into his hair and grabbed a handful of his hair. Pulling his mouth away from her, she said, "I'm pregnant." He grinned broadly and went back to kissing her.

A moment later they heard the door open and then they heard gagging noises. They both turned just in time to see Edward making gagging noises, his eyes focused on them and not where he was going. His arm caught on the back of a chair and he stumbled, sending a full tureen of gravy splattering all over the floor and Bloodstone's lower half.

"Oh my goodness, Bloodstone, are you all right? You didn't get burned, did you?" Jade asked, moving quickly to her side.

"No, fortunately I'm fine. It's just my skirt."

Dex walked around the table and cuffed Edward upside the head. "You're damn lucky!

You could've hurt her! Go get a mop and bucket and clean this up."

Edward turned and glared at Dex. "Who do you think you are? You're not the boss of me. You can't tell me what to do."

"I think I'm your older brother. I also think I'm older, wiser, and a bigger man than you are. You can go and get a mop and bucket and you can clean it up, or I can make you lick it up. It's your choice, which do you prefer?"

"If I were you, Edward, I would go and get a mop and bucket before Dex uses your face to clean it up. I will remind you in the future, he is your older brother and you will treat him with respect, or I'll put you over my knee and spank your backside, and don't think because you're twelve I can't do it," Fletcher said entering the room. Edward grumbled, but did as he was told to do. "You sure you're unharmed?" he asked, looking at his eldest daughter.

"I'm fine. I'm more concerned about how much of dinner is on the floor," she replied quickly.

"Fortunately, it was only the gravy. We'll just have to enjoy our potatoes and beef without gravy this evening," Rose said, entering the room looking at the mess.

Bloodstone bent down and carefully picked up her skirts so as not drip all over the floor. Seeing that it soaked through some of her petticoat and her shoes were covered in it, she walked to the edge of the mess, slipped out of her shoes, and stepped onto clean floor. Picking her shoes up, she wrapped them up in her skirt. "I hope you'll forgive my immodest display of leg, Fletcher," she said sarcastically, as she gathered up her skirts to her knees. She turned and headed through the kitchen adding, "Don't worry, I'll take the back stairs so as not to appall your other guests."

Rose turned to her husband laughing, but all amusement died at sight of his face. She put her hand on his shoulder. "Oh, Edward, don't look so severe. I think she's been pretty good about adhering to your wishes. I only ever see her in britches in the morning when she goes out and trains with the Wolf Tribesmen, or is working in the forge with Father. She was only trying not to track gravy through the whole house."

Fletcher slowly shook his head. "It's not that at all. Dex, would you join me on a quick walk while Edward cleans up this mess. We'll be back in just a few minutes." Once outside, Fletcher turned on Dex. "That mark on my daughter's calf, that's a slave brand, isn't it?"

Dex stood there in silence as he contemplated the answer to that question. He didn't like the idea of lying to his father, but he also felt he shouldn't answer. Maybe answering wouldn't be so bad. *Fletcher's probably never seen the mark on Eden's arm.* Then he mentally kicked himself for his stupidity. He didn't need to see Eden's arm. It hung on a damn banner in front of his damn tent.

"So that's how the two of them came to be married. Eden bought her," Fletcher said wearily.

"We don't know that, she might've just decided to get the mark and put it there."

"Do you really believe that?"

Dex slowly shook his head. "No, I don't; but I'm also incapable of believing that Eden did anything wrong. Circumstances may have made him buy her. Circumstances may have even made him brand her. But he would never have forced anything on her." Fletcher considered a long moment and nodded in agreement.

As Bloodstone entered her room, she immediately began stripping out of her dress. She glanced at her husband sitting in the corner. She wondered if he'd even moved today. She washed and redressed. She turned to face her husband. "Dinner is almost ready. Would you like to come downstairs?" In response, he merely looked the other way. She sighed and left the room. As she moved down the hallway, she decided she'd give him a few more days to mope before she beat some sense into him, one way or another.

*****

Seven days later, Bloodstone was returning to their quarters after weapons training with the Wolf Tribesmen. She found every day as she reached for the door handle, she had to take a deep breath to steel herself. As she gripped the door handle, she told herself she should be grateful. He may not be leaving his room or talking, but at least he still got up, washed and dressed, and changed his clothes. The only thing he wasn't doing was shaving, but he had a beard when she met him and she didn't find it so terrible, though she preferred his clean-shaven face. She entered, saying as she did so, "After I wash, you want to come down for breakfast?"

"No, but I do have a request to make of you."

She was so startled when he spoke, she jumped and turned to face him. "Of course, what do you wish me to do?" *Please say shave me,* she hoped desperately. She didn't know why, but she felt strongly that that alone would show progress.

"If I don't have my sight back in another week, I want you to take me to Appleshire and leave me there. Return to the encampment and get on with your life without me. Tell everyone I'm dead," he said bitterly.

She absentmindedly rubbed her left shoulder feeling the stitches. That, coupled with his remarks, propelled her into action. "That's it! I've had it! I've allowed this to go on long enough!

You need to take your head out of your backside, get off your butt and get over it!" she said angrily.

He got to his feet. "Get over what, my insufficiencies as a man? I'm just supposed to forget that I'm completely incapable of protecting my woman or my child? I can't even walk down the damn stairs by myself! I'm completely useless!"

Bloodstone stormed over and slapped him across the face. "Don't ever say that again!"

Eden clenched his teeth and took a deep breath. Letting it out slowly, he said, "I can't help it if I feel that it would've been better for you and my son had I died." She slapped him again.

"Dammit, Woman, stop hitting me!" She went to slap him again, but this time he blocked it. She hesitated a moment and then went to slap him again; this time he caught her wrist.

"I thought you said you were incapable of protecting me. You just stopped me from hitting you. Clearly, you can learn, or are you too busy feeling sorry for yourself and being lazy?"

"Oh, yes, I can try. I can try to get myself killed. It's one thing to stop my woman who I know well from hitting me, it's an entirely different thing to stop a stranger."

447

Bloodstone growled in frustration. "You may think it would have been better had you died, but you don't even give a thought for what that would've done to me. To lose you would've killed me …"

He cut her off rudely. "You will come to wish I'd died. Better that than being a stone hanging around your neck that you can't shake off."

She went to slap him again, and again he caught her hand. "Are you so stupid that you think your only value to me or to your people is your ability to kill? You're a better man than that, Eden Silvermane. Your value to your people is about your ability to lead them. Your inner strength, your kind and generous heart has nothing to do with your ability to kill."

"My value to my people is my ability to protect them, and I do not kill men just to kill them. You make it sound as though I'm a murderer."

"Your people have plenty of skilled swords who are willing to stand up and fight for you and for them. I can name at least a half a dozen of your best warriors who would be willing to be your sword. And though your stubborn, arrogant, male pride might prevent you from asking them for their help, they would give it in an instant. Though this might pain you, but you know what you might actually have to do, is ask me to be your sword and your eyes. I know I gave you my word that I

448

would step down and cease to be the General of the Knights of Athena, and I will, but that might not be the best way for me to serve you. If you need me to serve you as your General and to be your eyes and your sword, then that is what I will do. If you need me to serve under Murtaugh, or even Dex, or even to be a common soldier, that is what I will do. You might have to swallow that male ego of yours and ask for help."

"No, I don't need anyone else to fight for me. I sure as Hades don't need my woman to fight for me …"

It was her turn to cut him off rudely. "Really! I'm your woman? You could have fooled me. You haven't so much as touched me in a month."

Eden sank back into his chair, saying as he did so, "Cripples don't have the right to bed beautiful women."

"If that is what you want to think of yourself, as a cripple; then that is what you are going to be. But just remember - no one else thinks that about you. Only you do, and if you ever decide to stop feeling sorry for yourself, let me know, because I'll be waiting." With that, she turned and stormed out of the room, slamming the door behind her. She charged down the stairs, grabbing her cloak off the peg, and heading for the stables. Entering the stables, she grabbed her bow, quiver, and a parcel of extra arrows she had left there. Saddling Cedric quickly, she left the stables before Dex even knew she was gone. She rode hard across the frozen field headed for Marcus' family's farm.

XXXV

Eden sat in his room considering what his woman had just said. She was, of course, quite right. He had been pouting like a petulant child, but it was hard to feel worthy of your woman when you couldn't even see her.

He must've fallen asleep, because he awoke with a start. He was lying in bed looking around. He sat up and swung his feet out of the bed knowing he must still be dreaming. He looked around, marveling at his imagination. He was in a beautiful garden in the clouds. He was sitting on a large, four poster bed. He stood up and turned slowly in a circle. When he came full circle, he was startled to see Freya standing there. "What do you think of my home?" she asked in Barbarian. He had forgotten how musical her voice was.

"It's very nice. Is this a dream, or am I actually here?" he asked in awe.

"You're actually here. This is Olympus, and on Olympus all mortals have no defects, that's why you can see." She gestured. He turned to see a large mirror that hadn't been there before. It was part of the dressing table, and to either side of the dressing table were two large lemon trees, heavy with fruit. As Eden stared, he was surprised to see his younger self. He couldn't be more than twenty-one or twenty-two. As he turned his head, it also surprised him to see the scar on his neck was gone. Freya smiled. "As I said, you have no defects."

He nodded and then asked, "Why did you summon me here?"

She moved to stand before him, looking up at him. "You offered to serve me. You said if I ever had need of you, I had but to ask. So I brought you here to ask."

"What is it you wish to ask of me, Lady?" Eden didn't know why, but he was slowly becoming uncomfortable.

She placed her hand on his chest and slid her hand up his chest to wrap her arm around his neck, then pulled him down and kissed him. Eden was so startled, her lips actually touched his before he reacted. He pulled away quickly. "You said you had something to ask of me, ask it."

"But that is what I demand of you. I demand you in my bed," she said, stepping forward and wrapping her arms around his neck again. This time he gripped her arms and pulled her away before she had a chance to kiss him.

"That is not within my power to do."

"Nonsense, you are a very young, healthy, strong male. It is absolutely within your power, and as I said, it is what I demand, so stop trying to resist me and just enjoy it," she said, trying to kiss him again.

"You are correct, the physical action is within my power; but it is not something I can give you, because I'm a married man and I would never be unfaithful to my mate. I'm not a fool. I do not make blind promises to gods. I told you I owed you one, and if it was within my power to do, I would do it. I did not say I owed you anything, nor did I promise to do whatever you required of me," he said firmly.

She smiled and shook her head. "I think we both know that wasn't exactly true. And besides, your woman has no need to ever know of it. This is Olympus. It's not like she could walk in on us. You may have your pleasure without fear of being caught," she said with a coy smile, as she twitched her shoulders ever so slightly causing the shoulder of her dress to slide down, almost exposing her left breast. She then gave him a look so full of heat, he felt desire welling up inside of him.

He swallowed hard and forced himself to say, "I would know."

She crossed to the bed and lounged on it seductively, managing to bare one leg almost to the hip. "You know, there are other benefits to being the lover of a goddess. For example, I could fix your eyes," she said, as she moved both of her hands over her head and wiggled more seductively into the pillows.

"I will not trade my soul, my self-respect, or the love of my woman, for one night's pleasure in your bed," he snapped angrily.

"I do not think it is the love of your woman you are worried about so much as the allies you would lose. And who said it would only be one night? I'm sure your woman would rather you share my bed than remain blind for the rest of your life. I'm sure if you were to broach the subject with her, she would tell you to share my bed. My offer's not good forever, but perhaps a little more time in darkness might change your mind." She lifted one hand from the pillow and waved it in his direction.

He found himself thrust abruptly back into darkness. Fortunately, he was seated in a chair, wherever he was. He inhaled deeply several times, recognizing all the scents of the room. He was back in his room, the room he'd been sharing with his woman. As he sat there considering, he thought, *This has to be the worst part about being blind. No way to tell time.* As he sat there, he suddenly found the room stifling. He got up, found the window, and threw it open, inhaling the fresh cool air. He felt a little better. He hesitated a moment, and carefully started feeling his way around the room. Finding the other window, he opened it too. He stood there leaning against the window, thinking for a very, very long time.

*****

When Bloodstone returned late that evening, she found Dex waiting in the stables. "What in Hades do you think you're doing going off on your own?"

"Getting some room to breathe, something I haven't had much of lately. If you have a problem with that, take it up with your King. I'm sure his comments on the matter would be enlightening."

Dex looked at her with surprise, but changed his tone as he said, "Dinner's nearly ready. You better get cleaned up and changed."

She nodded and headed for the room where they had been hanging the wash to dry. Finding all the appropriate garments, she pulled them down and then went to the little washing room. She had no desire to come face-to-face with her husband right now. She also had no desire for dinner. She washed and redressed, then entered the bar room. She was surprised to see they were a little busier than they'd been the past few weeks. She started clearing tables and helping serve drinks. After a quarter of an hour, Rose came up and wrapped her arm around her waist. "I'll watch the bar. You should go have your dinner."

Bloodstone smiled at her. "I appreciate it, Rose, but I'm not hungry. Why don't you go dine with your family and I'll watch the bar."

Bloodstone stayed working in the bar till Fletcher closed it. Taking a deep breath, she sighed and reluctantly mounted the stairs to her room. As she approached the door, she was startled by a noise coming from inside. She caught her breath as she felt her heart lift. She knew that sound very well. She just hadn't heard it in more than a month. Eden pacing. She was afraid if she just opened the door, he'd walk into it, so she tapped on the door and waited until the pacing stopped. She opened the door carefully.

Eden turned in the general direction of the door, saying as he did so, "Bloodstone?"

"Yes?" She entered and closed the door behind her.

"You know, I was thinking, when we met, I had a beard didn't I?"

"Yes."

"Do you prefer me with a beard, or without?" he asked casually, as though it was a normal thing for him to say. In fact, his entire demeanor seemed normal.

"Without, most definitely without."

"Me too, would you help me shave it off?"

Bloodstone had to bite her lip to keep from bursting into tears. She blinked away tears as she

456

took a steadying breath and said in what she hoped sounded a calm voice, "Of course." A quarter of an hour later, she was wiping away the last remnants of soap, looking down on her clean-shaven husband.

He stuck his arm out, wrapping it around her thighs, just beneath her bottom. As he pulled her tightly against him, he rubbed his cheek against the bottom curve of her breasts. He pulled his head away and kind of looked at her funny. He started rubbing his free hand from side to side across her belly, slowly working his way up, saying as he did so, "What are you wearing?"

"A dress, why? Do you not like it?"

He pulled back. Finding her hips easily with both hands, he then pulled her between his thighs. Then, eyes closed, concentrating hard, he slid his hands up and down her body. She found it interesting. It didn't feel sexual, it was as though he was feeling the dress and the fabric. He felt her arms and her shoulders as though he was visualizing it all in his mind. After a long time, he asked, "What color is it?"

"The skirt and bodice are blue, the under dress is white, and so are my petticoats."

To her surprise, he suddenly grinned very broadly and stood. He found her hips again with both hands and then thrust her arm's reach away from him. Again to her surprise, he started pulling her in the direction of the bed. When they were halfway there he said, "Do you know how many times I fantasized about hoisting up your skirt and taking you on the table?"

"Eden!" she gasped in shock and smacked him on the arm. As they got near the bed, he reached out, touching and feeling the bed, then he picked her up and plopped her backside on the bed. Then his fumbling fingers found the ties to her bodice and started unlacing it.

"Not that I'm complaining, but why all of a sudden are you wearing a dress?"

"If you'd care to pay attention, you would've learned that I've been wearing dresses the whole time we've been here. Fletcher wouldn't permit us to stay otherwise. He said he wasn't going to have his daughter dressed unbecoming of her sex in his home." For a man who couldn't see, he had her bodice unlaced very quickly, though he did not pull it off. He just pulled it back and down her arms. Gripping her belly tightly, he groaned. "What's the matter?" she asked with concern.

Finding her mouth, he didn't answer right away. He just kissed her for a long time, allowing his hands to continue to see her body for his eyes. Finally, he pulled his mouth free. "Nothing's the matter, you're not wearing a corset. I hate that damn garment. When I'm King, I'm going to outlaw it." Bloodstone couldn't help it. She let out an unladylike giggle, which turned into a gasp as Eden stuck his hands under her skirt and found her bare thighs.

"Eden, I'm sure this isn't appropriate. I'm sure married couples do not behave like this."

She gasped again as he started nibbling her ear, then he deliberately breathed up and down her neck, finally whispering in her ear, "Prude." She couldn't help it. She started giggling again.

As the first fingers of dawn started to shine through their bedroom windows, she cuddled closer to her husband and wondered what on earth had come over him. It'd been a very long time since he'd made love to her all night, and even now he was still awake, caressing her thighs. "Eden, it's not that I didn't thoroughly enjoy our very wonderful night together, but what changed?"

"My woman slapped me repeatedly, told me what I needed to hear even if I didn't want to hear it, reminded me how much I love her, reminded me that I can't live without her, and I would suffer anything as long as I can keep her, even the loss of my eyes."

Bloodstone didn't know why, but that sounded funny in her ears. She pushed herself up to look down on him. "What aren't you telling me?"

"Well, in accordance with our agreement not to keep secrets from each other anymore, I have to tell you something and I'm very much afraid of the answer … I was made an offer yesterday; an offer to restore my vision, but at a price. What would you say if I could restore my vision … by spending one night in another woman's bed?"

Bloodstone was truly glad Eden did not see the look on her face. She felt as though her heart had just been ripped out. *Is that the only reason he made love to me last night? He wanted to butter me up for this?* she asked herself. *Now, now Bloodstone, look at this rationally. Are you being selfish?* She considered that for a long moment. Her mind went over and over all kinds of answers, all kinds of thoughts, and finally she said, "Hear me out before you interrupt me. If your eyesight is that important to you, and if you're willing to meet her terms, then I'll try to forgive you, but I won't like it. And you certainly don't have my permission."

He moved so quickly, she didn't even have a chance to respond before she was on her back and he was on top of her kissing her. "I love you! I love you! I love you so much! You have no idea how terrified I was you were going to tell me I should do it, that my eyesight was more important." After making love to her again, Eden passed out with his head on her chest.

When she awoke sometime later, she wasn't sure what time it was. The windows in their room faced neither East nor West. As she tried to slide quietly from the bed, Eden sat up and stretched. "What time is it?" he asked with a yawn.

"I have no idea, because apparently we completely neglected the hour candle yesterday, and from the direction of the windows, I've no idea. Whatever time it is, I'm starving."

"Me too. Why don't you wash, dress, and go downstairs first and scare us up something to eat and I'll come downstairs. If you hear a loud noise, can you come pick me up from the bottom of the stairs?" he said with a big grin.

"Are you sure you can make it down the stairs by yourself?"

"Sure, I just can't guarantee I'll do it on my feet." They both laughed.

*****

"So, sister of mine, how much longer are you going to torture my son with blindness before you restore his sight?" Ares asked casually.

"What makes you think it's not permanent?" Freya asked, turning around.

"Even the God of War knows his sight should have been returned weeks ago. Why did you keep him blind so long?"

"I didn't like his tendency to feel sorry for himself. It was unlike him."

"And what would you have done had he taken you to your bed last night?" Ares asked with curiosity.

"Never - not in ten million years would Eden have ever done that. Not even had Bloodstone told him to do it, he wouldn't have. He would've been so heartbroken, he would never have spoken to her again; but I also know my niece well enough to know she would never have agreed to it."

XXXVI

Four weeks later, Bloodstone and Steel finished securing the load. "You know, Granddaughter, I'm going to miss you immensely. It's been nice having an apprentice around I didn't have to hold their hand every minute."

Bloodstone looked up at him sharply. "Apprentice! You say that like I'm some wet behind the ears greenhorn! Though I've enjoyed training in your forge, I taught you a few tricks too, and don't forget it, old man."

Steel laughed. "That you did. I guess I'm living proof, you can teach an old dog a new trick."

Rose came out of the inn carrying Blackwolf. "Are you sure you can't stay another couple of weeks? I know the roads have thawed some and there might be another storm and you want to get back before that, but if the storm hits while you're out, you'll be stuck between us and them. Then what will you do?" she asked, looking worried.

"Mother, stop fretting. We'll be fine," Bloodstone replied with exasperation. It still surprised Rose when Bloodstone called her Mother. It had only happened once or twice, but she treasured every one.

As Eden, Fletcher, and Dex exited the inn, Rose turned to them and looked at them pleadingly. "Can't one of you manage to talk some sense into her and convince her to stay a little longer?"

Eden bent down and kissed her on the forehead and shook his head. "Afraid not, especially since I am as anxious to be home as she is."

"I'm afraid none of us are on your side on this one, Mother," Jade said from the doorway.

"Is there anything I can help you with, my love?" asked Eden.

"No, everything is packed and ready to go. The horses are saddled, all that's left to do is to say our goodbyes." Bloodstone looked up at Eden who was staring down at her. "Something the matter?"

He reached out and caressed her cheek. "Nope, I just never get tired of looking at you." Bloodstone couldn't help it, she blushed.

Katya came out and said her goodbyes and then took Blackwolf. Bloodstone hugged her four youngest siblings goodbye, then she gave her mother a tight hug. "Mother, you can stop worrying. I'll take care of them. I'll make sure all your men make it back to the encampment safely, I promise." Rose laughed through her tears. As Bloodstone pulled away, she said, "Last chance,

464

Fletcher, you don't have to come back with us.
You can stay another couple of weeks."

"As much as I'd love to stay with my family,
I'm concerned about the condition of my men.
After all, I left them to those Knights to keep in
line. The gods only know what condition they'll be
in when I get back."

Bloodstone laughed and shook her head. "I
will be sure to mention to General Black Stone you
were concerned about his ability to train and
maintain your soldiers' abilities. Well then,
enough procrastinating, men. Let's get mounted
and get on the road." With that, Bloodstone turned
and made sure the other women were comfortable,
then mounted her horse.

Midafternoon the next day, Bloodstone had just
finished making sure Katya and Blackwolf were
comfortable in her quarters. Now she needed to go
and check in with her general. Arriving outside
Black Stone's tent, she smiled at Sergeant
Henderson, who pulled aside the tent flap and
waved her in. Black Stone looked up, surprised to
see her. He leaned back in his chair. "I seem to
recall ordering you to rest for the winter. I think
winter still has a few weeks to run, don't you?"

"Eden and I were tired of resting," Bloodstone
said as she took a seat.

"I can't even express how relieved I was when I received your letter that Eden had his sight back. Granted, I know I wasn't nearly as relieved as he was."

"So what have all of you been up to this winter in my absence?" she asked.

"Well, our brothers and myself decided we were going to see if you were the only one who's good at playing with fire." Bloodstone raised an eyebrow in question. "And we've all learned we're actually quite good at it. Surprisingly enough, Patrick's actually not as good at it as the rest of us. Fitzwilliam either can't put it out, or just has not learned. The rest of us can put it out, but Fitzwilliam can definitely make it."

"Did any of you have trouble controlling it once you started playing with it?"

Black Stone started laughing. "If you mean did all of us have a few problems with setting random things on fire; the answer's yes, and some of us worse than others. But enough about family fun and games, let's get down to business. I had a lot of time to think these two months. I'm sick and tired of playing this game with that woman. I've asked around. She only has two major fortresses. I say we take them both in succession. We have to take one to get to the other. I say that we stop playing with her and just go for it."

Bloodstone sat up in her chair and leaned forward, eyes wide with excitement. "What's the plan, General? You know I'm in."

"First off, I'm going to order a council of war tomorrow morning. I'm going to tell everybody to clear their day. Then you and I are going to spend the rest of today going over our troops and discussing the best way to use them." The two of them spent the rest of the day in quiet conference. As Bloodstone left Black Stone's tent that night, she went in search of Big Bear and William.

The following morning, as Bloodstone and Eden walked to Black Stone's tent, Eden asked, "Are you going to tell me what's in the box?"

"Nope."

As they arrived at Black Stone's quarters, Sergeant Henderson showed them right in. Bloodstone saw that Black Stone had had another table brought in, making it one large square. He also had a piece of paper on each side of the table. They said Church, Barbarian warriors, Sorcerers, and State. She crossed to the side of the table that said Church and sat the box down. Opening it, she pulled out a Corinthian helmet. She artfully arranged the helmet at the place to her right, then discarded the box to a side table and seated herself. Black Stone and Eden both stared at her. Eden shrugged his shoulders and seated himself on the

Barbarians' side of the table. The Council started arriving and slowly began taking their places.

When Foster arrived, Black Stone said, "Now that you are the General of Ares, would you please take your place at the right of General Bloodstone. That way, the two Generals are to center."

Foster moved towards the other end of the table. Seeing a Corinthian helmet sitting directly to the right of Bloodstone, he reached for the chair next to it. As he started to pull out the chair, Bloodstone said, "I believe you were told to sit at my right."

He indicated the helmet. "I thought someone was already seated there."

"Does it look like anybody else is seated there?"

"Someone's helmet is there," he replied, looking confused.

"Yes. I'm starting to think he must not like it since he won't sit in front of it," she said with irritation.

"But that helmet looks like the one Lord Ares wears."

"Not quite, I tweaked the design a little. After all, I figured his General shouldn't wear the same helmet as the rest of his men." She indicated the helmet. "What do you think?"

He reached down and picked it up, examining it carefully. It was truly incredible craftsmanship. He'd never seen its equal. His conscience smote him a bit as he thought to himself, *It's even prettier than the one Lord Ares wears.* Like Lord Ares', this one was made of shiny steel with crimson horsehair. The red horsehair began at the forehead and went straight down the back. It stood about eight inches high until it got all the way down the back, then it had a long tail which must've hung at least eighteen inches. However, the design on this one was not on the cheek protectors, but on the forehead to either side of the horsehair. It was an exquisitely etched head of a war dog, with its snout pointing towards the center of the forehead, as though it was staring at the horsehair ridge. As Foster turned it over in his hand examining it, his thoughts were interrupted.

"Are you just going to stand there admiring it all day, or are you actually going to try it on?" Andrew asked with a grin.

With all eyes on him, Foster pulled the helmet on. Foster was surprised at how well it fit; it didn't seem to need any adjustment at all. "How's it feel?" asked Bloodstone.

"It seems to fit perfectly, and of course I won't know for certain until I practice with it on, but it's the best fitting helmet I ever had."

Bloodstone stood up and pointed to the bridge of her nose. "Look right here." Foster did as he was told. Bloodstone quickly looked from side to side, occasionally touching or handling it, pulling it one direction or another. "Looks like a good fit. Shouldn't need any adjustment, unless, of course, you decide to get hit in the head."

"Well, if the two of you are done playing dress-up, the rest of us would like to do some real work," Black Stone said with a grin. They both looked duly chastised and sat down. Black Stone took a mental roll call: Eden, Xanhara, Viktor, Murtaugh, William, Matthias, Brynjolf, Dex, Bloodrose, Big Bear, Shadowrock, Quicksilver, Lydia, Ivy, Rivermoss, Cora, Tabitha, Bloodstone, Blacksmith, Foster, Fletcher, Andrew, Daniel, and Grayhawk. "Good, now that everybody who was requested to be here is here, let's get started. I don't know about the rest of you, but I'm tired of playing this woman's games. I'm tired of being on the defensive. I think it's time we go on the offensive. I've been asking a lot of questions. I've been drawing a lot of maps and it has come to my attention that the castle she is hiding in only has one fortress between where we stand and where she stands. I say we give the snow a little bit more time to melt, and I say we march on it, and I say we go straight from that fortress right to her door.

We've gathered our allies, we've whittled down their forces, time stop playing with her." The warriors all murmured in agreement. Black Stone turned to face the sorcerers. "This isn't exactly your fight, how do you feel about this?"

"It was not our fight before we came to join you, but you have given us sanctuary and you have offered us freedom in your land. This is our home now, and these are our people. It is not our intention to stand back and watch. It is our intention to fight and to help. As I said, I do not feel we can go toe to toe with one of the People of Stone, but we will use whatever magic we can to aid you in your fight," said Shadowrock.

"You know, if we are going to be doing a battle strategy, it might not be a bad idea for us to ask the sorcerers what exactly they could do to help us. I don't know anything about magic," suggested Eden. All eyes turned to the sorcerers.

"I don't know anything about fighting a war. I'm not sure what talents would be useful," stated Shadowrock.

"When I entered the barracks, Lydia was making beds bigger. I know that this might sound silly, but could she possibly do that with catapults?" Dex asked a little nervously. As all eyes turned to stare at him, he felt he must've asked a really stupid question.

After a long moment, Lydia said, "Absolutely brilliant! I would have never have thought of doing that."

Dex blinked and stared at her. "You mean I didn't just ask a really stupid question?"

"No! Aren't catapults large and slow-moving? Wouldn't it be a really good thing to make them small enough that we could fit several in a wagon, like maybe cat size? Then all I have to do is make them bigger."

"Are you forgetting the fact that you're pregnant?" asked Viktor.

Lydia waved her hand dismissively. "I won't actually be in the fight and you know, Ivy, you can bring plants back to life; would it be possible to bring their bows back to life?"

Ivy shot her a dazzling smile. "I've never tried it before, but I bet I could. If the army doesn't mind sacrificing a few bows, I can practice."

"Not at all, the Barbarians are willing to sacrifice as many as you need to practice," Eden said, turning to look at Matthias. "Matthias, you're an archer. Can you see to it, help her do whatever she needs?" Matthias looked stricken as he gaped stupidly trying to find words.

Ivy apparently had no problems finding words. "No, absolutely not, anybody but Matthias," she snapped.

Eden, still looking at Matthias, asked, "Did you do something to make Ivy mad?"

Matthias continued to open and close his mouth, completely incapable of finding words. "So now you can't find words? You seemed to have no shortage of them the other night," Ivy shouted.

"Forgive me for butting into your personal affairs, Matthias, but are you two sleeping together?" asked Andrew casually.

What happened next, happened simultaneously. Ivy burst out laughing, Black Stone elbowed Andrew hard, Eden glared at Matthias, and Bloodstone said, "Andrew, really?" Matthias looked even more uncomfortable than he did before.

After a moment, Dex said, a little confused, "But I thought the King of the People of Mist said that their women could not mate with our men?"

Ivy stopped laughing and glared at Dex. "So that's where you got that idiotic notion …" She turned her glare on Matthias. "You can't believe anything that man says; half the things he told you were probably lies."

Matthias replied hesitantly, "I'm sure that there is a better place for us to have this discussion than right here and now, Ivy."

"Well, since I tried to have this conversation the other night, and all you kept telling me is 'it wasn't a good idea', maybe now is the best place to have this discussion. Maybe now you will actually tell me what the problem is," she said, crossing her arms over her chest.

Matthias looked pleadingly at Black Stone who merely shook his head. He turned hopefully to look at Eden. "No, not with my woman at the other end of the table. I'm not getting involved in this," Eden said firmly.

"There, see, you're not getting out of it. We're going to have to have this discussion right here and right now," Ivy said smugly.

"Fine, you want to have this argument in public? I am not willing to lose another wife. Your King says your women can't breed with our men. I can't be with you and not ..." Matthias kept putting his hand to his chest as he struggled for words. Finally, he blurted out, "Love you. I don't want to lose you. I would rather just be your friend."

"You know, my King said that the People of Stone had rocks for brains. I thought he was just being prejudiced, but apparently he must be right, at least some of you do have rocks for brains."

Matthias opened his mouth to retort, but someone else spoke. "I was wrong."

Everyone began looking around to see who spoke, except Eden, who said, "Viktor, did you say something?"

"Yes, I said I was wrong. I know to some of you that doesn't make sense," he gave an apologetic smile to Bloodstone, "but I know to some of you it does. I was not as vocal about it, but I was not thrilled with the concept of People of Stone marrying People of Earth. I felt it was too dangerous. But in the nearly two years I've been in this encampment, the women of this encampment have proven me wrong time and time again. Most of you are probably completely unaware of the fact that in two years, the healers have delivered more than a hundred children. Of that hundred children, nearly half of them were half-bloods. Both Breton and Barbarian women alike having half-bloods, and the only child that was lost came far too soon - and it was a Barbarian woman having a Barbarian baby. I did lose one of the Amazons in childbirth - her child survived, she did not. Her son was half Breton. I can't feel that that had any impact on her loss. She started bleeding and I just couldn't stop it. So I state again - I was wrong, and from where I stand, the only risk I see from a woman of Mist and a man of Stone choosing to make a life together is, she will remain relatively young while he ages and dies."

The room sat silent for a long moment, then Bloodstone stood up, pushing her chair out all the way. The Barbarians shot to their feet. She took the two steps required to her right so that she slipped between Foster and Viktor. She hugged Viktor tightly. After a moment, she pulled away and looked up at him. "Thank you, Viktor, that really means a lot."

Matthias had been unable to take his eyes off Viktor. He slowly turned his head toward Ivy. He didn't know why, but he was surprised to see tears in her eyes. He stared for another moment, then he walked around to the other side of the table, gripped her by the arm and pulled her out of her chair, then tilted her chin up with his knuckle. He bent down and said, "I'm sorry."

She punched him in the arm. "You should be." Then she hugged him.

Black Stone cleared his throat and said firmly, "Well, now that that's settled, and hopefully going forward everybody will be able to work together, because we can't be squabbling amongst ourselves. Bloodstone and I spent all of yesterday devising the battle strategy. I asked you all here to fine tune the details, to make sure that every branch of our army, every culture present, every skill set is used and utilized to its very best advantage so that we can work as one cohesive army. We need to put aside our differences, stop bickering, and remember we're all friends. And if the twenty-five of us in this room can't get along and work together, the thirty thousand of them out there sure as Hades won't, because they follow where we lead."

XXXVII

Three weeks later, Black Stone, Bloodstone, Eden, Foster, Dex, and Shadowrock stood on the hilltop looking down across the valley. On the other side was a very, very large fortress. "Tell me again why they call it the Prison of the Lost?" asked Foster.

"Because once you go in, you never come out," Eden replied grimly.

"Well, as I see it, they already know we're coming. Their scouts had to have carried word to them by now. The building looks like it's made up of three parts: that over there ..." Black Stone said, pointing to the structure on the right, "it looks like a common barracks; the center structure itself looks like the old castle, it appears to be the oldest of the three structures; the one to the left, that's probably the prison and dungeon. Which means once we get into the fortress we'll have to break ourselves up into four groups. One group will remain outside with the bulk of our force. We will need three smaller groups to go in and clean out those three structures. As the highest-ranking general, it is my duty to stay behind and command the bulk of the forces. Until we have primary control, I will remain at the head of my army; which leaves the other three tasks to you. Who

wants what and who are you taking with you?"
They all replied simultaneously.

"My men and I will take on the barracks,"
stated Foster.

Bloodstone said, "Prison."

Eden said, "I want the castle."

Black Stone laughed. "Good, none of you want
the same thing. That makes our lives much easier.
Who are you taking with you?" he asked, looking
at Eden.

"I'll push through with a group of four hundred
men and I'll make it easy; I will just take a hundred
of each - unless any of you have a problem with
that." They all shook their heads.

"Do you require any of my sorcerers?" asked
Shadowrock.

Eden considered for a moment and then shook
his head. "I can't think of any reason I need a
sorcerer unless you can suggest one. I think I'm
good with swords and as far as individuals are
concerned, I'll take Murtaugh, Big Bear, and
Daniel with me." They all considered for a
moment, then nodded their heads.

Black Stone turned to Foster. "Your turn."

"There shouldn't be very many soldiers in the barracks. The hardest part about this is going to be getting through the army to get to the barracks; so unless General Black Stone objects, I'm going to take five hundred of my own men with me. Which means the rest will remain under your command, General. And like Eden, I see no particular need for sorcerers. They'll probably be of better use working with the bulk of the army."

Black Stone shook his head and looked at Bloodstone. "You're up."

"I don't have need of a large force. I will take two hundred men, and so as to not diminish the bulk of Black Stone's army, with Foster's permission, I'll take two hundred Soldiers of Ares. That will leave Black Stone with two thousand Knights, one thousand archers, seventeen hundred Soldiers of Ares, one hundred Amazons, nine hundred Barbarians, and thirty-three hundred Breton foot soldiers; which leaves him with a fighting force of … just a shade over nine thousand. Would be nine thousand even if wasn't for the eighty sorcerers. Which by the way, Shadowrock, do you have any people who can disintegrate metal, melt metal without hurting somebody? I'm thinking chains that we can't get off."

Shadowrock considered for a moment. "No one instantly springs to mind, but metal shatters under extreme cold if hit, right? I have an ice sorceress - could she be of use?"

"Yes, that will work perfectly. I'll just make sure to take a chisel and hammer with me." Bloodstone sighed deeply and decided it was now or never. "One more thing, Eden. Dex and all of my personal guard go with you."

Both Dex and Eden opened their mouths to protest, but Black Stone forestalled them both. "I'm on Bloodstone's side on this one. It would be impossible for them to look after themselves and her at the same time, and if they are near her, they're going to feel obligated to look after her. They need to be separated from her. They need to be focused only on the job at hand and not on the job they're used to doing."

Eden nodded his head and said, "Very well. Dex, you and your men report to me."

The following morning, Black Stone watched in amazement as Lydia made the second catapult bigger. He continued to watch her as all six catapults grew before his very eyes. As soon as she was finished, he gave orders for them to start being loaded. He checked the position of his armies. Everyone was where they were supposed to be. He now rode alongside Eden. "All right, Eden, I think it's time you gave your people a chance to surrender."

"Do you honestly think that's going to work?" Eden demanded.

"No, but I think we need to give them the option anyways."

Eden rolled his eyes, sighed, and moved to the head of the army. Eden and four randomly selected men rode within shouting distance of the walls. "I am Eden Silvermane, only surviving warrior son of Henry Silvermane, rightful King of all the Barbarian lands. I swore an oath to unseat the usurper. You stand between me and my goal. This is the only time I will ask you to surrender." Eden got the reply he expected, just not the one he hoped for, as a half a dozen arrows were stopped five feet from him. It was as though they'd hit a stone wall. They shattered and fell to the ground. Eden shouted back, "You should have surrendered!" He turned his horse and rode back to the army. Approaching Black Stone, he turned and glared at him. "I told you it was a waste of breath."

Black Stone shrugged his shoulders, drew his sword, and swung it over his shoulder in a downward arc, saying as he did so, "Fire!"

Three hours later, Black Stone watched as another ballista caught fire in the enemy fortress. He idly wondered whether one of his brothers had done it, or a sorcerer. He looked back to where they had been hammering the walls nonstop. The wall was starting to weaken. He slowly turned his attention to the battering ram. Unfortunately, they had as of yet been unable to do any major damage to the gates. On the plus side however, the sorcerers had managed to completely stop all attacks on their men. As he watched, the battering ram prepared to strike the gates again. Just as the battering ram struck the gate, the enemies lifted and poured a large cauldron of what he assumed was pitch over the wall. Halfway to his men, the pitch turned solid. When the pitch struck the log, it shattered and a few of his men were knocked to the ground; but were apparently unharmed, as they got quickly to their feet and went back to their work. A few of his men on the battering ram stopped what they were doing and began clearing away the large chunks of what he could only guess was now frozen pitch.

"I'm sorry for interrupting you, General, but we have an idea," Shadowrock said.

Black Stone turned to face him and saw that Ivy was standing next to him. "Go on, I'm listening."

"I'd like to begin by saying I don't know if it would work. I've never tried anything that large before and I don't know how thick the stone is. But what if I could make the stone to one side of the gate soft or maybe even intangible, and if Ivy were to make the wood brittle at the same time? If we managed to coordinate all of this right before the gates are struck by the battering ram ..." asked Shadowrock.

"You can make stone intangible?" Black Stone said in awe.

"Where do you think I get my name? I can meld with stone and I can make shadows longer." At Black Stone's confused look, he laughed. "It's hard to explain."

"I think it sounds like a great idea. And even if all you can do is make stone a little weaker on one side; that should be enough for the battering ram to do its work. The problem is that damn thing seems to be set in there but good. But what about the two of you? I know Shadowrock is a soldier, but you'll both be right in the thick of it."

"Don't worry about me, General. I, unlike Shadowrock, don't need to touch it; I just need to see it," Ivy said with confidence.

"If I get into any trouble, I can just become one with the stone and sit out the rest of the fight. I can stand in stone all day; though of course I'd just walk through it and go find a nice, quiet place." At the stunned look on Black Stone's face, he just laughed. "We are going to take a lot of getting used to for you aren't we?" Black Stone nodded dumbly.

"Well, General, why don't you make whatever preparations you need to make for when the gates come down and then we'll bring it down," Ivy said with a grin.

Three quarters of an hour later, Black Stone was watching as Shadowrock took his place at the front of the battering ram. He jumped out right before the battering ram hit the gate and pressed himself against the gate. The battering ram pulled back. Black Stone watched as he moved along the gate towards the stone wall. As Black Stone continued to watch, he would've sworn that the stone blurred and the wood changed color. A moment later, the battering ram started moving forward. As it struck, there was a horrible sound of wrenching metal as the gates were torn away from the left side. The castle wall and part of the walkway above collapsed, wood splintering. Black Stone swung his sword again and yelled, "First wave attack!" A soldier to his left lifted the emerald green banner signaling Eden to attack. He heard his commands being echoed through his men. He watched as enemy soldiers came pouring out of the castle trying to prevent them from entering. He scanned the walls. They seem to be less occupied on the right. "Second wave!" he bellowed. Another soldier standing to his left lifted the crimson banner signaling the Soldiers of Ares to attack. A few minutes later, he watched as Foster and his men went up the ladders and over the walls. As he watched, he decided the opposition from the enemy forces was too great coming out of the gate. He turned to a messenger on horseback. "Report to Colonel Stone; inform him our central position needs reinforcement." The soldier did not even salute, he spurred his horse and headed for Andrew.

Black Stone watched as the Twelfth moved in to reinforce Eden's group. He watched a little longer and then he ordered, "Third wave!" A sky blue banner shot up. He turned to one of his messengers. "Go inform Colonel Weatherford as soon as General Bloodstone and the Soldiers of Ares are over the wall, I want him to follow them as reinforcement." The messenger nodded and rode off. Black Stone turned back to watch as Bloodstone and the two hundred Soldiers of Ares went up and over the walls. He turned his attention back to the main entrance. Eden and Andrew had forced their opponents back inside. Black Stone decided it was time for him to get personally involved. He pulled his face mask down and ordered the Third infantry to storm the castle and the rest of the army to close the distance and take up the defensive position outside the walls. He dismounted before reaching the walls and appraised the situation. There was little to no fighting going on in the courtyard. Andrew approached him and immediately saluted. "Report, Colonel."

"The courtyard is yours, General Black Stone. Eden, General Foster, and General Bloodstone have each moved on to their primary objective. I await your orders."

"Order the Ninth and the Twelfth to clear the grounds. As soon as we have control of the castle, order the healers to take over whatever section they want and start getting the wounded treated. Once we have control of the prison, we'll house any prisoners there."

"Yes, General." Andrew saluted and went to carry out his orders.

An hour and a half later, Black Stone stood in the Great Hall, which Viktor had turned into a temporary infirmary.

Eden approached him. "I put all of the household staff into a couple of the rooms and have them under guard. I don't think they'll give us any trouble and I've had my men sweep the castle twice. There are no lurkers."

"Good, and Foster just reported he has control of the barracks. I'm currently holding all prisoners in the courtyard." Black Stone cut himself off as William approached. "Colonel Stone sends his respects, Sir. We searched the grounds twice and any small outlying buildings. We met with no resistance. Everybody surrendered without a fight. They were mostly stable boys and household staff."

"Good, that means everybody's reported in except the prison, but that doesn't surprise me. It would be the hardest to clear," replied Black Stone.

William suddenly looked concerned. "The prison hasn't reported in? Who is in command?"

"General Bloodstone," replied Black Stone.

William's eyes widened in horror. "You let her take the prison?" he demanded angrily.

"Why not, and don't take that tone with me!" Black Stone snapped back.

"Because this is the same prison where Bloody Fang held and tortured her for two months," he said incredulously. "How did you two numbskulls not know that?"

Eden grabbed William by the arm and jerked him. "Show me where!"

XXXVIII

Bloodstone's attention was divided between her General and the battle. She watched calmly as Foster and his men went up and over the walls. Then she watched as Andrew came in to reinforce Eden. Then she saw it - the blue flag went up. She turned and swung her sword, yelling as she did so, "Attack!" She and her men started forward. A moment later, she heard Black Stone's order of 'Third wave' echo through the army.

As the ladder in front of her went up, one of the Soldiers of Ares turned to her and said flippantly, "After you, my lady."

Bloodstone didn't even hesitate. She headed up the ladder, saying as she passed the Soldier of Ares, "Nothing to be afraid of, boys, I'll clear the way for you." When she was nearly to the top of the ladder, a Barbarian moved to push the ladder away from the wall. Bloodstone swung her sword, cutting across both forearms. The man cried out in pain and fell backwards. She hustled up the last few rungs, swung her leg, and climbed over the wall. Just as both feet were hitting the stone, the man started to get up. She brought her foot back and kicked him hard in the head. He fell back unconscious. The Soldiers of Ares started swarming over the wall. As she cut down the man in front of her, she looked for the stairs. Finding them, she turned and headed in that direction, shouting as she did so, "This way men, follow me!"

As they fought their way across the courtyard, Bloodstone cut down two more men. When they reached the doors to the prison, Bloodstone was not at all surprised to find them barred. "Frostbite, where are you?"

The Soldiers of Ares moved aside for Frostbite to make her way to the front. "Yes, General?"

Bloodstone gestured to the doors. "Would you do the honors?"

The young sorceress grinned as she slowly ran her hand along the right of the door and then the left. They all watched as the edges of the door iced over. "The hinges should be frozen solid. Are you sure this is going to work, General?"

"Positive." Bloodstone pointed to three Soldiers of Ares. "You three give me a hand. Put your shoulders to the door." It only took the four of them three tries before the doors, still intact, fell over, their hinges shattered. Bloodstone looked and saw about a dozen guards standing about ten feet down the corridor. She pointed her sword and said in a firm voice, "Surrender now!" The guards hesitated for a moment, then a commotion behind them caught their attention. They looked over their shoulders. Two dozen reinforcements arrived on the scene.

Bloodstone sighed and said, "Fine, we'll do it your way." As she stepped forward to meet the first of the defenders, he brought his sword up in a narrow arc, clearly well trained at fighting in close quarters. She deflected his blow and brought her sword down. He sidestepped, bringing his sword back across her chest plate. *That was a narrow miss. Let's not do that again, okay?* she told herself, as she sidestepped and thrust her blade into the man's thigh. She pulled her blade out and brought it up his belly to his shoulder. He fell to the ground. Her next opponent she took down in a single swipe. Looking from left to right, the corridor was empty. "Captain Thomas, have a half dozen men stack these bodies to the side. We'll need to keep the corridors open. Put twenty men on guarding the door, the rest of your men follow me." As they moved down the corridor clearing rooms she said, "Don't attack anyone who doesn't attack you first. There are a few prisoners they allow to roam around in chains. You don't want to kill an innocent person."

Captain Thomas looked at her sharply. "How do you know so much about this place, General?" he asked.

Bloodstone could tell from the tone of his voice he had just gone on his guard against her. "I lived here for three months, give or take, as a prisoner," she said emotionless. Without breaking stride, she pointed her sword. "Two dozen men check this corridor; these are barracks, so be on your guard."

Three quarters of an hour later, Bloodstone stood in front of the door leading to the cellblocks. She had removed the keys from an obliging guard. She took a deep breath and looked over her shoulder. "Have any of you ever been in a prison before?" They all shook their heads. "It's dark, damp, and it smells. If you think you're going to be sick, just leave. The last thing you want to do is contribute to the stench. Is that understood?" They all nodded. "There shouldn't be more than a half dozen guards down here and most likely they'll all surrender." She turned back to the door and unlocked it. She took a deep breath, steeling herself for what was to come. Reminding herself that she was in command here and she had a job to do, she pushed the door open. As the first whiff caught her nose, she realized the smell was even worse than she remembered. She wrinkled her nose, but did not allow herself to show any sign of discomfort. She headed down the narrow stairwell.

A guard stepped out, sword in hand. Her eyes had not yet adjusted to the darker room. All she could see was his outline, but his evil, cruel soul told her all she needed to know. She didn't bother to give him a warning, she merely cut him down where he stood. "There are four cellblocks, twenty cells in each. They run East/West. Captain, you take twenty men and clear the East. I'll take twenty and clear the West. Remember what I said about prisoners."

"Yes, General," all the Soldiers of Ares replied.

Bloodstone turned down her first cellblock. Halfway down, there were two guards. At sight of her and twenty Soldiers of Ares, they threw down their blades. Bloodstone sensed the cells, she went to the first empty one she felt and turned the key. Throwing open the door, she turned back to the two prison guards and said, "Remove your armor and any weapons. Just leave it there on the ground. Gesturing to the Soldiers of Ares, she said, "Search them and make sure they're not hiding anything. When you're done, lock them in." Bloodstone started opening the cells with innocent men in them, asking them as she did so to please be patient and stay in their cells. The cellblocks weren't completely clear yet and she didn't want anything to happen to them. They would get them out of here as soon as they could and get them cleaned up and fed. She had half the cells on this block opened when she heard someone calling her from the other side. Looking down the cellblocks directly across as she exited, she could see that only a few soldiers remained. They pointed to the other cellblock. She moved towards the second cellblock on the eastern side when she saw the Captain.

"You'll forgive me for calling you, General, but we don't speak Barbarian and though he doesn't look afraid, I don't want to frighten him."

Bloodstone moved past him to look down the cellblock. Standing at the other end staring at them was Broch. She pulled off her helmet and handed it to one of the soldiers. As she moved closer, Broch slowly grinned. "You shouldn't be here, girl. This is no place for you."

"I told you I'd come back and rescue you. It just took longer than I thought. I want you to come out of here and go sit in one of the chairs while my men and I finish our work, and then I'll talk with you." Broch nodded and did as he was asked. As Captain Thomas watched the old man walk past him, he stared in surprise. The man had to be at least seventy if he was a day. From his gaunt body, his stooped shoulders, his long hair and long beard, he guessed the man must have been a prisoner for a very long time.

Once all four cellblocks were cleared, Bloodstone opened all the doors of the men who should be released. She was actually surprised to find that there were two men in cells who actually belonged there. She would have to question them later to find out what they had done. For now, she had to attend to Broch and send word to General Black Stone that the prison was clear. With her help, Broch managed to make it up the stairs and into a chair. "Sergeant, would you please go and inform General Black Stone that we have control of the prison and ask for further orders. Does anyone know where Frostbite got off to?"

"I'm right here, General," replied the young woman, moving forward. "What do you need me to do now?"

Bloodstone opened her mouth to speak, but a commotion caught her attention. Hearing Eden, she didn't even bother to look. "These chains have no key. I'm going to put some fabric between the metal and his leg. Can you freeze it so I can break them?" The girl nodded, and as Eden approached, Bloodstone was breaking the first of the four chains.

"We need to talk now, Woman!" Eden said angrily.

"You're going to have to wait; I'm busy." Eden glared at her, but seeing the old man; he bit his tongue and stepped back.

As soon as the last of the chains was broken, Eden grabbed his woman and turned her to face him. "You gave me your word you wouldn't keep any more secrets and you did!"

"Actually, as I recall the conversation, I said you would not accept my word; so how was I to prove it to you? You said you would accept my word, but that I could not give my word until I ceased to keep secrets from you. So my word was actually never given. And even had I given my word; I would've broken it because I swore an oath to him long before I swore an oath to you. I swore to him I would do anything and everything in my power to get him out of here. Because I could not get his chains off, he is the only prisoner I did not free that day. He's the only one who was stuck behind. If I would've told you that this is where I was in prison, you would never have allowed me to have anything to do with this battle. So all I can do is ask you to forgive me and swear to you on my honor as a Knight to keep no more secrets from you. And this is a vow I will not break."

Eden wanted to swear. *Why were women so damn frustrating?* He wanted to wrap his hands around her throat and choke the life out of her, but he knew she was right. He hated admitting that she was right, but as he recalled the conversation, she was correct. She had kept no other secrets from him. She even told him about several of her awful nightmares. "Woman, as the gods are my witness, I swear if I ever catch you keeping another secret from me; I will blister your backside."

Bloodstone grinned up at her husband. "You won't do that."

"I've done it before, what makes you think I wouldn't do it again?" Eden snapped.

Bloodstone beckoned him to her with a single finger. Eden, looking suspicious, bent forward.

Bloodstone stretched up on her tippy-toes and whispered in his ear, "Because if you do that, I swear I will make sure that every dress I own requires a corset."

Eden pulled back and glared at her. Grabbing her braid tightly and jerking her head back, he said angrily, "That, Woman, is not playing fair," then he kissed her roughly. Movement to his right caught Eden's attention. The old man was staring at him thunderstruck. "Something the matter, old man?"

The old man chuckled. "Not at all, boy, not at all. I just know who your father is." The old man laughed again. "By the gods, it's really remarkable! You're the spitting image of your grandfather! How is my old friend, Hafgrim?"

Eden, who had only been listening to the old man ramble with half an ear, now gave him his undivided attention. "You know my grandfather?"

"Oh, yes, and I know your mother and your father. In fact, the last conversation I ever had with your grandfather was about our two daughters. It's strange, it seems like I've spent a lifetime in this prison; but I dwell on all those conversations with my friends. Sometimes I think they're the only thing that kept me sane in here."

Eden didn't know what made him ask, maybe it was just the fact that no one ever talked about his mother, even his grandfather. "What did you two talk about?"

The old man chuckled. "How things never turn out how we expected. You'll forgive me for what I'm about to say about your mother; but I've known her since she was born, so I think that gives me the liberty, does it not?" Eden nodded. "Your mother was always the wildest little creature, even as a babe. She was so beautiful, that kind of beauty that makes all men, young and old, turn to watch her just walk down the street. We all knew for sure she was going to marry some wild young man. Then there was my daughter, the kind of quiet beauty that grows on you as you get to know her better and see her true sweetness. We all knew for certain she was going to marry a nice respectable young man, but of course that didn't happen. She married an awful man, an evil ogre, and your mother, of all people, married to the stern Viktor. I would never of guessed it. Surprised me when he asked."

Eden's jaw dropped. "My mother married Viktor Silvermane?"

The old man looked confused. "Is not Viktor Silvermane your father? They were betrothed when I was thrown in prison."

Eden was shaking his head as though he couldn't understand what he was hearing. He said again, "Viktor Silvermane, second oldest son to

King Henry, betrothed to Desiree Wolf, Hafgrim Wolf's only daughter?"

"Yes, they were to be married in three months when I was thrown into prison." Eden turned and took two steps, then he quickened his pace and was practically running out of the prison.

Bloodstone turned and followed him, shouting over her shoulder as she did so, "William, you're in command."

XXXIX

Eden entered the Great Hall and scanned the room. Seeing Viktor near an open door, he went for him, grabbing him by the tunic with both hands and walking him backwards, quickly shoving him through the door. Once they were in the room, he flung him against the wall. Eden neither knew nor cared that two of his brothers had followed him in.

"Eden, what in Hades is going on?" demanded Black Stone.

Andrew shouted with concern, "Eden, stop this! You're going to hurt him!"

Eden grabbed Viktor again and pulled him away from the wall and slammed him into it again. Eden demanded in a voice that shook with rage, "Who fathered me, Viktor?"

Bloodstone, entering the room, slammed the door behind her and shouted, "Eden, let your brother go! Let's talk about this calmly."

Viktor stared at him in confusion. "Eden, I don't know what you're on about. What do you mean?"

"The old man … there's an old man in the cells, he says you were betrothed to marry my mother." Viktor's eyes widened in horror. Eden snarled at him as he slammed him into the wall again. "Who, Viktor?"

"Eden, it's not what you think."

"Then tell me what it is!"

Bloodstone put her hand on Eden's shoulder. "Eden, let him go so he can talk. I'm sure there's a logical explanation for this."

Eden growled, but released him, then took several steps back. "This better be good, Viktor."

"As an older brother, there are some things you never want to admit to your younger brother - and we are brothers, Eden, I swear. We share the same father ..." Viktor swallowed hard as he remembered back over those painful days he'd buried long ago. "Desiree and I were only a few months apart. She was beautiful and I couldn't see past her beauty. I guess we were about seventeen when I asked Hafgrim for permission to marry her. He gave his permission readily; but he thought we were both too young, so he agreed to a year's betrothal. I deliberately allowed you to believe that Father's and my quarrel had everything to do with me becoming a shaman; that's not exactly true. He was not happy about it, but the part about Father really having no use for me was true even before I became a shaman. When I informed Father of my betrothal, he was very pleased. Hafgrim was well respected and his daughter marrying into the Royal family made Father look better. Looking back on it, I guess Father had never met Desiree until the night of our engagement party, which was held in the palace. Father insisted everything was going to be elaborate. I was the first one of his children to marry. Everything was going to be a huge celebration. He even insisted we have a wedding like Bretons do. As you know, all of Father's wives had weddings because he was the King and he thought it looked better. Our engagement party was in early spring, not long after the equinox. Desiree disappeared for two hours, and I didn't realize Father had disappeared too. When she returned, I could tell there was something different about her. She seemed excited and nervous all at the same time. Henry asked her to dance. When he was done, someone else asked her to dance. Henry came over and stood next to me. He asked if I was okay. Even at the time, I thought that was strange; Henry never seemed concerned about me. I guess with Henry's animal senses he could smell it. The next morning, Desiree broke our betrothal and insisted she be taken home. I said, of course I would take her, but she refused to go with me, insisted someone else had to do it. I was so heartbroken and confused I hid in my room for two days, which is why I didn't realize that Father escorted her home personally. I returned to my village. I did already live with Wolf Tribe; I hadn't lived in the palace since I was fifteen. It was about ten days later, or ten days after the engagement party, however you look at it; people stopped

502

talking when I walked by. I didn't understand why. I thought it was just because Desiree had proven to be as flighty as she had always been; but it was because Father already had permission to marry her. Desiree avoided me for the next few days. I accidentally ran into her coming out of the Mercantile store. You know, I heard Bloodstone once say it sucks always knowing when someone's lying. That is the only time in my life I ever regretted being a shaman of Freya; because I knew the second I saw her she was already two weeks gone with you. And this is why I told my father I would never speak to him again, and you know the truly shitty part? He married her on the day that was supposed to be my wedding day. All the plans he had made for my wedding, he just used for his." Viktor pursed his lips together as he watched his younger brother struggle with that.

Eden started shaking his head again. "But what about you and Seva? She's said the two of you have been together since you were children. It just took you forever to get around asking her?"

Viktor sighed. "Well, if I've told you this much of the story, might as will tell you the whole story. But I should warn you; if any of you ever let on to Seva that you know this, she might just kill us all. Our village was about five days from the palace, so I guess you were probably about six days old when I learned of your birth. Not that I wasn't glad that you were here safely, but ..."

Eden cut him off. "You weren't thrilled about my arrival, I can understand."

"No, I wasn't. Not when I was still angry and foolish enough to of thought that you should've been mine. I went to the tavern to get drunk. I didn't even have time to finish my first ale before the toast to the new prince started making me nauseous. So I decided to buy a bottle and go back home and get drunk there, better company. I just had no idea what company was waiting for me …" He grinned as he remembered back. "I walked in, set the bottle on the table, went to get a glass, and as I turned, I saw a woman in my bed. I knew this woman; I just didn't understand why she was in my bed. As I stared at my bed, I saw the trunk at the foot of my bed had her clothes laying on it. I looked back; she was clearly naked under the covers. Finally, I found my voice and I asked Seva what in Hades was she doing in my bed." He laughed as he remembered. "That little minx sat up in bed holding the blanket so that it barely covered her breasts and asked in such an innocent voice, 'Would you like me to go?'" He coughed and cleared his throat. "She went on to say she was tired of seeing me mope around and she knew she wasn't as pretty as Desiree; but she'd be very happy to console me if I thought I could find comfort in her arms." He laughed and shook his head. "I think my eyes must've bugged out of my sockets. Seva was nothing like Desiree; she was calm and quiet and steady." He laughed again. "I'm not telling you anything you don't already know; you all know her very well. She hasn't changed in thirty years; she's still that same person I remember. As I stood there staring at her, she clutched the covers tighter and said, 'I'm not a whore. I've never been with a man. I'm offering to console you for the rest of your life if you'll have me. I don't mind living in her shadow as long as I have you' …" Viktor blushed. "Let's just say I didn't spend the night alone, nor did I sleep that night. In the morning, I went to speak to her father. I told him that I had married his daughter last night, but I told him I didn't think it was a good idea for everybody to know it was that day. Everybody would get the wrong idea that I only married her because I was a drunken idiot. I promised him I wasn't drunk that night. He agreed. We kept our marriage quiet for about three months. Fortunately, Justin, our oldest, had the decency to wait a little more than two years before he decided to come along." He turned to look at the three Stones. "You're probably not aware of it, since you've never met him; but he's three years younger than Eden. You've also never met our oldest daughter, Hope. You only know the younger two."

They all stared in astonishment. Bloodstone was the one who finally broke the silence. "I always knew Seva was just like Helena, that quiet shyness is really just an act. They're both just as wild and stubborn as I am; they're just not as loud about it."

Viktor grinned and nodded. He turned to his younger brother. "You still want to kill me?"

Eden slowly shook his head. "My mind is reeling. I am sorry for any pain I may have caused you by …"

Viktor cut him off. "You better be about to say by shoving me against the wall, because if you say for being born, I will hit you. I know it won't hurt you, but I'll try anyways. Neither one of us is responsible for what our father did, and though I was mad at Father, and I was mad at Desiree, the best thing that woman ever did for me was not marrying me. I would never have been as happy with her as I am with Seva. I love that woman as much as you love Bloodstone. I know this is going to sound cruel and heartless, Brother, but the best thing that woman ever did for you was die having you. You would not be half the man you are now had she lived; because you would not have been raised by Murtaugh's family. Murtaugh's father and mother were better parents to you than yours would have ever been."

Eden stared at Viktor. He'd never in his life heard him say it was good someone had died. "I know you're right. Murtaugh's father turned me into the man I am. I don't know where I'd be if it weren't for Logen." Eden hugged his brother tightly.

XL

Three days later, Eden yawned loudly at the breakfast table. "I shudder to think what you and my sister are doing all night that has you this tired in the morning," Andrew said with a laugh.

"Sorry, she hasn't been sleeping well at night, and if she doesn't sleep well, I don't sleep well," Eden said with another yawn.

Black Stone said sadly, "Yeah, I heard she has nightmares, but I thought she didn't have them if you were around."

"She doesn't usually. It's been this awful place. I can't wait to get her out of here. I'm sure once we're gone, they will stop."

Grayhawk sighed and shook his head. "I know what you mean. Cora occasionally has nightmares about the man who attacked her. She says she sees his ugly, mauled face in her dreams."

Eden slowly turned to face Grayhawk. "When was this?"

"I'm not really sure. She said she was about twelve and I guess she's about twenty, so I guess that was about eight or nine years ago. Why?"

"Because when I hear mauled; I think clawed. When I think clawed, I think there can't be that many Bretons in the world with a clawed face, can there?" Eden asked.

"I can't imagine so. I've certainly never seen any," added Andrew.

"Do you know where this was?" Eden asked.

"Eden, what about this has you so curious?" asked Black Stone.

Eden hesitated a long moment, then he leaned back in his chair and looked around. The only people who were at the breakfast table were Black Stone, Andrew, Grayhawk, Murtaugh, Dex, and himself. "Ever since I heard the story of the man who attacked Bloodstone when she was a child, I've been trying to find the man responsible. A few months ago, I got his name. I don't know if he's the son, or if he is now the Lord. It was nine years ago, but the family name is Wichcrest, and when he attacked her, she clawed his face very badly. One could say mauled. That was about nine years ago. It would've looked worse when it was still fresh and raw," he added hopefully, "and infected."

Grayhawk leaned forward and put his elbow on the table. "She said that. She said it was fresh, raw. By the gods, are you telling me the same man who attacked my wife is the same animal who

508

attacked my sister? It's in his holdings, the village she said she came from. It is the same man!"

"Lord Wichcrest has a son. He's older than us, probably about forty, maybe forty-five. When I was stationed at one of the garrisons near his land, I heard rumors that his son was a sick son of a bitch. I even heard rumors he liked little girls; but try as I may, I could not substantiate it. I kept my ear to the ground and I put out feelers; but all that kept coming back to me were rumors. Nothing I could act on; though something did happen to his face. He said he was attacked by a dog. I've seen it, and I never saw a dog do that. It definitely looked like a woman did it." Black Stone shook his head with disgust. "I knew I should have killed that bastard; but I never had anything to go on. I say after the war, boys, we go pay him a visit." All the men at the table nodded.

When they had all finished their breakfast, they rose and went to the new War Room. As they entered, they were surprised to find everyone else already there. Bloodstone and Viktor were talking to someone. As Eden moved to see who they were talking to, he was surprised to see it was the old man. He was clean, shaved, and looked quite respectable; but what surprised Eden more than anything was he now wore the braids of a Wolf Tribesman. Then he reminded himself that the man had said he and his grandfather were old friends. That definitely implied he too was a Wolf Tribesman. "Eden, I don't think you were ever properly introduced. This is an old friend of mine, Brochan," Viktor said as he approached. "I can't tell you how surprised I was he was still alive."

Eden extended his hand and shook the older man's. "I'm sure any friend of Viktor's is a friend of mine." He hesitated a moment. "Yes, I remember you said you were thrown in prison before I was … born. You have really been a prisoner for thirty years?"

Brochan tried to rise but Bloodstone put her hand on his shoulder. "Please remain seated."

"I am not so old or so infirm I cannot stand on my feet before my King. And yes, I was thrown in prison before your father married your mother."

Eden took a deep breath and looked at the ceiling. He let it out slowly. He didn't think he'd ever get used to being called King. "I've not yet seated myself on my father's throne, so I do not like being called King. So please remain seated, and anyways …" he wrapped his arms around Bloodstone's waist, "you would not wish to disobey your Queen, would you?" Bloodstone squirmed uncomfortably and tried to push Eden's arms away. Eden squeezed her tighter and looked over his shoulder at Black Stone. "Why do Bretons have such a thing against showing affection publicly?"

Black Stone shrugged his shoulders. "I don't know. I've never understood that either. My parents certainly didn't have a problem with it, and neither do I. I will take any chance I get to kiss Amber, and I don't care who's watching. Fortunately, neither does she." Andrew and Daniel nodded in agreement.

Andrew said with surprise, "I was under the impression people didn't survive being a prisoner in there much over a year?"

Brochan said, "Occasionally a prisoner would be brought in who either the Queen, or someone else, wanted to remain alive and reasonably unharmed. Those prisoners would remain alive as long as they remained useful."

"What did you do that kept you useful for thirty years? I think I would've found a way to become not useful," Andrew said.

"Oh, I tried that on many occasions, but all it ever got me was a sound beating. Because Colonel Fang, as he was then, wanted to make me suffer for daring to oppose him, challenge his right to claim my daughter as his woman." The old man looked down at the ground as though he'd become overwhelmed with emotion.

Viktor sighed and squeezed the older man's shoulder. "Libby was a quiet, proud, young girl, a little younger than I was at the time. I guess she

511

was not quite seventeen when she didn't come home one night. When she did return the following afternoon; it was with Fang, and he announced their marriage. Broch was furious. He accused Colonel Fang of corrupting his daughter. He said he would take his charges to the King. I wasn't present; I only heard about it later, and everybody seemed to tell the story differently. I don't think I heard two alike versions. The only thing everybody agreed on was the two men fought and Colonel Fang arrested Broch and put him in prison. He was never seen again."

"That's not true, Viktor. Fang saw me at least once a year. He liked to come by and tell me whatever new horror he'd inflicted on my daughter. And after she died trying to give him another child; he delighted in gloating over the atrocities that his oldest son was doing." The old man reached out and squeezed Bloodstone's hand tightly. "This is not an appropriate conversation to be having in front of our Queen."

Daniel said with surprise, "You're Innish's great-grandfather."

"Innish?" Broch asked, in confusion.

"Do you remember the young boy who ended up in here?" The old man nodded. "Bloody Fang fathered him. I took him away with me. He's my son now …"

512

Eden cut her off. "Our son, our oldest, he's a good boy, kind of boy any man would be proud to call his great-grandson," Eden said firmly. Then he turned to Black Stone. "Well, General Black Stone, now that we're all here, why don't you tell us what we're doing from here?" said Eden.

Black Stone shook his head. "Oh, I'm not in charge here anymore. I merely command the army. I am not the King." All eyes turned to stare at Eden. "Though, if his Majesty will grant me a moment, I would like to say something."

Eden felt a deep rooted desire to wipe that grin off Eric's face, but he tapped down the urge and turned and said instead, "Of course, General."

Black Stone turned to William and extended his hand. The two men shook as he said, "Welcome to the Stone Wall." Then he turned to Matthias and offered his hand.

Everyone nodded in agreement. Bloodstone crossed to Foster and offered her hand. "We would be honored to have you join us in the Stone Wall."

Eden said, "Well, General Black Stone, now that that's handled; I would like your permission to leave the Ninth under the command of its Colonel. You'll forgive me, I don't remember his name."

Black Stone interrupted. "Colonel Weatherford was amongst the casualties. He succumbed to his wounds yesterday."

Viktor added, "And Major Franklin's leg was broken in the engagement. He was on a ladder when it was pushed away from the wall. His femur was shattered. I doubt he'll ever fight again. I've done everything I can to repair the bone, but I think he'll have a very pronounced limp."

Black Stone nodded and continued. "Which is why I've drawn up the battlefield promotion of Captain Daniel Stone to Acting Colonel of the Ninth, provided the King has no problems with it. As soon as I have an opportunity to communicate with His Majesty, the position will be made permanent. He is the senior captain in command of the Ninth." Everyone congratulated Daniel on his promotion. Daniel still looked a little stunned.

Eden nodded and said, "Good, then I will ask that the Colonel of the Ninth reinforce the two hundred Barbarians I am leaving to control this fortress under the command of Colonel William and Major Matthias, unless of course, they don't want the job."

"I think I can speak for Matthias as well as myself when I say that we are honored by your faith in us," William said quickly.

"Good, then I don't have to worry about losing this fortress and having to retake it. Well, now that that's settled, I would like to be on the move in the morning. Let's go pull that woman off my father's throne."

Viktor said a little hesitantly, "Eden?"

Eden turned to face him. "Viktor?"

"You know I've never involved myself in your battles before, but I wonder what you remember of the palace?"

Eden closed his eyes, trying to remember as much as he could. He still had a lot of memories of the palace, though he sometimes wondered how much were true, and how much were his own imaginings. After a long moment he said, "I remember once Father showed me something, but I don't … I don't remember if it was a childish imagining, or if it really happened."

"Father showed you the emergency escape, the secret passage?"

"I didn't imagine it?"

"No, and I doubt anyone else knows about it. Father didn't show just anyone, only his children. I don't recall him ever showing any of the wives before. Father didn't really care about his wives; he could just get another one. It might be the way to get in. You couldn't get a lot of troops in, probably not more than a hundred. It was designed for the Royal family to escape. It's hundreds of years old. I mean, it hasn't been maintained, and I don't even know if it could be used, but it is there."

Eden closed his eyes remembering wandering and wandering through a long, dark tunnel with his father. Though the tunnel did wind, he could recall no offshoots. His eyes flew open. "The river, the opening is in a cave near the river, practically in the river, and the other end is the armory. Is it the armory?"

"It was the armory then, I don't know, she might have changed things around a bit; but it could get you a hundred men into the center of the palace. But of course, all of this is betting she doesn't know about it." Viktor hesitated, struggling with what he knew of his father. Finally, he shook his head fiercely. "Father may have been easily led around by his cock, but he was no fool. He'd never trusted one of his wives before; he wouldn't have told her. The only way she knows is if one of our brothers told her. Father swore us all to secrecy, and I think at that time, the brothers would have been more afraid of him than of her. And she killed them all outright, she didn't torture or question any of them." Viktor spoke firmly and then nodded his head for emphasis. "She doesn't know."

"Then that is how I will get in and that is how I will find her and I will kill her. That means you're in charge of the outside force, Black Stone. You keep her busy and I will kill her."

"I'm going with you," Bloodstone said.

516

Eden shook his head firmly. "No, if I fail or get trapped in there, I will not give her the King and Queen in one fell swoop. She has to fight to get us both. You will stay outside. The reason I let you take the prison is because I didn't want you with me in the Castle. We can't be together in battle - if things go wrong, then we're both dead. I would rather you stay here, but I know you won't. I know I can't ask it of you, but you will not come with me and if you try to argue or fight or sneak your way in with me, I will tie you up and leave you somewhere safe with … with a hundred guards. Is that clear, Woman?"

"I give you my word I will stay with the bulk of our forces. I will not come in until we move in as an army, but if you think you're not taking Murtaugh, Dex, and Big Bear with you, then you're insane."

He turned to face her and leaned forward, putting his forehead to hers. "I love you."

She smiled at him. "I love you too - and you haven't agreed."

"As though the three of them would give me any choice," he said with a laugh.

XLI

Four days later, Eden crawled along the riverbank, Shadowrock and Ivy in front of him. They crawled for another quarter of an hour before Shadowrock said softly, "I see the cave now, there, another fifty paces, a little to our left." They continued crawling.

As soon as Eden was in the cave, he stood up and stretched his aching back. He was too big to crawl. "I just hope this cave is as big as I remember it being."

"No worries about that; it goes on forever. I can see it's a huge cave."

Once the hundred Wolf Tribesmen were inside, Shadowrock turned to Ivy and said, "You think you can close the door?"

"Not a problem, there's plenty of green life around. I'll grow an ivy curtain," she said with a little laugh. As Eden stood there, a few minutes later he could hear rustling. "Now let's shed a little light on the situation." A moment later, a half-dozen little balls of light appeared around Ivy. "Don't. No! Don't do that!" she said with irritation to the little balls as she gestured them down. Eden stared as he thought they were protesting. They blinked and fizzled; some even crackled, others changed color slightly. Ivy stamped her foot.

"Don't get an attitude with me. We need you to light the corridor, not my head."

Shadowrock laughed. "I am so glad I don't get light from a spirit," he said as he held up his hand and a large ball of light appeared.

"Well at least I don't have to hold mine."

"True." Shadowrock gestured for Eden to lead the way. "Do you remember how far down it is?"

Eden shook his head. "I only have vague memories, but I seem to recall in the cave a large stone that looks like it can't be moved, but Father moved it." As they moved through the cave, Eden had been watching the ground. "I've seen no signs of anyone being in this cave anytime recent, not for years."

They came to an offshoot. As Eden examined the ground, Shadowrock put his hands to the wall. "This way, the secret entrance is this way," he said, turning down the offshoot.

Eden looked at Ivy who smiled. "He can talk to the stone. It's kind of odd, but then again, most people think me talking to plants is kind of odd; so to each their own, I guess."

As soon as Eden saw the cave-in, it all came back to him. He walked up to one of the stones in the middle, grabbed it, and pulled it. The large stone to the side moved and revealed an entrance.

Eden gently laid the stone down. Once all of his men were through, he entered the passageway, grabbed a stick attached to a heavy rope, and pulled it down. The stone moved back in place. He pointed to another stick. "Pull down hard on that one and it will open the door again." Shadowrock and Ivy both nodded. Eden moved past his men to the front of the line, then continued down the long passageway. He seemed to recall it took several hours for them to walk through it; but as he had expected, that was merely a child's exaggeration. It only took about half an hour.

Eden stared at the large stone blocking their path. He walked up to it and put his ear to it. He could hear nothing. He stepped back and gestured to Shadowrock who put both of his hands to the stone; then he slowly moved forward, his body sinking into the stone till they could no longer see him. After several minutes, he came back. "Everyone's in a tizzy. Apparently our army has begun the attack."

*****

Black Stone sat on his horse, watching the palace, considering. He looked up at the sky, another hour till dawn. He didn't know why he had this itch on the back of his neck; something told him not to wait till dawn to start the fight. "Catapults launch!" The six catapults fired in rapid succession. "Reload!" He fired four more volleys before the enemy decided to retaliate. He laughed as they wasted arrows; his men were safely out of range. He fired two more volleys before the sun started to rise. As he watched the enemy start to load two heavy ballista, he turned to one of his messengers. "Go ask General Bloodstone to put a stop to those ballista before they get started." The messenger rode off quickly. A few minutes later he watched as both ballista burst into flames. "Catapults launch!" Black Stone chuckled to himself as he watched the small boulders that they had loaded it with strike several of the guards, knocking them off the walls.

A quarter of an hour later, a man on the wall was waving his hands. Then he threw something at them. A few minutes later, a messenger from the Twelfth delivered it to him. Black Stone took it and read it and looked back at the messenger. "Did Colonel Stone see this?"

"Yes, General, the Colonel would like to be the one to meet with them. He says he doesn't trust them. He thinks it's too dangerous for you or General Bloodstone to do it."

"Take this message to Xanhara, Queen of the Amazons. Tell her I agree that Colonel Stone should do it, but I think that there should be a Barbarian representative."

A few minutes later, Andrew, Xanhara, and two members of the Twelfth crossed half the distance between the gates and their army. They were made to wait a quarter of an hour before the gates opened and three men on horseback rode out to meet them. The man in the center rode up to Andrew. "I am General Fang. Who is in charge here?" he demanded harshly.

"I am Colonel Andrew Stone, Commander of the Twelfth Infantry of the King. This is Xanhara, Queen of the Amazons." Andrew resisted the urge to say 'and I burnt your son's body', but he thought that wouldn't be a good way to start this conversation.

"I thought you had two generals who commanded your army. Are they too afraid to speak to me?" he taunted.

"My General is not afraid of you. He merely feels you are not worth his time, unless of course, you and the usurper intend to surrender. Then he would gladly come down here and speak with you; but only when the usurper is sitting next to you. But since I'm fairly confident you have no intention of surrender; I'm assuming you're going to tell us, the Breton Army, to leave again, for the third time. Probably offer us another deal that you'll let us control our lands when we already control half of your lands; so explain to me how that is a beneficial arrangement for us?"

"You are meddling in affairs you cannot even begin to imagine. You have no concept of the evil of the Silvermane bloodline, or did your ally not tell you that his family is cursed. They will all give way to the madness and end as prisoners in their own dungeon, as all of his forbearers have done. All of his descendants will be consumed by the same bloodlust and madness." Xanhara watched Andrew, but his face was completely blank. "Answer me this, did your brother tell you of the beast's blood that runs through his veins? Your sister's son already carries that same tainted blood." General Fang laughed. "That blank expression you wear might fool others, boy, but I know you knew nothing of this. I speak the truth. Ask her, ask any of the Barbarians, and they will tell you that the Silvermane line is cursed."

"Is there a point to these ramblings, or are you just trying to scare me, which is not working. Eden is as sane as I and I would trust him with my life and the life of my woman and the life of my child. You will not frighten me and you will not convince me that he is a threat to me or mine, to my country, or to his own people. The only people that man is a threat to is all who willingly serve that backstabbing bitch of a usurper. Her reign ends today when we rip that hag off his throne and kneel before my brother as King." The General swallowed hard as he saw flames leap into the man's eyes.

"My Queen and I will crush you and your army and then we'll conquer your people and kill your King." Despite his harsh words, his voice shook a little as he spoke.

"That will never happen, and this conversation is done." Andrew took the reins of his horse and headed back to the Twelfth. Xanhara, right beside him, heard him say, "Father, I hope you're listening. Please tell me that I did not just make a foolish mistake." Turning his horse and taking his position at the head of his men, he looked past Xanhara who had followed him, to a messenger. "Go and inform General Black Stone that it was nothing but inane drivel and not worth our time to repeat." He turned his head to face forward, still ignoring Xanhara's presence.

As a bright blue light appeared in front of him, he stared in awe as a white warhorse, fully armored, appeared in front of him with a woman seated sidesaddle in flowing robes wearing a shiny, steel chest plate, her pale blonde hair pulled back and dressed in a severe manner. "You know, Nephew, you spoke with such confidence a moment ago, you almost fooled even me. That's not an easy thing to do. You need have no fear of Eden; you never did. What he said was lies. The Silvermanes were cursed, but only a few of them have ever given over to the madness in the past three hundred years. Many of them have borne the scars, but no more. Your nephew will not be haunted by it. Though Eden will carry it for the rest of his life, he is now in control. His love, adoration, and respect for Bloodstone as a warrior broke the curse. When he first recognized her in his own heart as an equal, the curse shattered." Andrew blinked and turned to look at Xanhara, who was staring just as dumbfounded as he knew himself to be. He glanced at his men. His eyes widened as he realized they could not have seen her. They looked as bored and impatient as they had looked before her arrival, ready for a fight. He heard a soft musical laugh. He looked back to the woman and saw she was laughing. "Xanhara sees me because I permit her to see me. Your brothers and your sister see me because I permit them to see me, but I don't feel the need to proclaim my presence to all." She laughed again at his confusion and then glowed a bright blue and disappeared.

"Nephew?" questioned Xanhara.

"Yeah, you don't know about that do you?" She shook her head. "It's a long story and I'll explain later, but the shortened version is Ares is our father. I'm pretty sure that was Athena because she definitely didn't look like how I would imagine Freya looking, so process of elimination, Athena." Xanhara nodded, still looking confused.

Black Stone listened to the messenger from Andrew. He watched the woman on horseback who was speaking with Andrew. He hesitated a long moment. He didn't like standing back and spitting at his opponent. It just wasn't in his nature. "First and second waves!" The red banner for the Soldiers of Ares and the blue banner for the Soldiers of Athena both shot up. He turned to a messenger. "Go inform Colonel Stone when

Shadowrock succeeds in bringing down the gates, I want the Tenth and Twelfth through those gates before they have a chance to get them back up."

*****

"Is it still the armory?" Shadowrock nodded. "Is there anyone in there right now?" He shook his head. "Good." Eden pulled the lever that released the secret door. The heavy stones slid backwards and then to the right. They stepped out into the large armory.

"Where do you think you will find your prey?" asked Big Bear.

"I think I will find her in my father's Throne Room." He turned to Shadowrock. "Are you sure you don't want to take any men with you?"

"No, I'm going to move through the castle stones as much as possible. I'll be fine on my own, just keep Ivy out of trouble." Ivy glared at him.

Eden turned and headed for the door, gesturing with his sword for his men to follow him. He said a quick prayer to Athena that Viktor had remembered the layout correctly. He had drawn them a map and they had gone over it at least a million times till Eden could give the directions with his eyes shut. As he moved through the corridors, Eden found himself glad that his woman only felt the need to make him a chest plate. She had tried to persuade him to wear a helmet. He had said he was sure he couldn't think with it on. As he glanced over his shoulder at Murtaugh, Dex, and Big Bear, he idly wondered if he looked as uncomfortable as they did. They were just approaching another corridor when a guard, sword in hand, stepped out in front of them. He was so surprised at the sight of them, he froze before he even brought his sword up defensively. "I don't want to kill you, boy. Surrender and save me the trouble."

The boy lowered his sword. "I don't want to die for her."

"Good call, boy," Murtaugh said, as he stepped forward and took the boy's sword and knife.

"Tie him up and gag him. Bring him with us. If we leave him, they might kill him for failing," Eden said quickly.

Murtaugh tied the boy's hands, but as he went to gag him, the boy said, "You're heading the wrong way. She's in the Throne Room."

Eden turned to the boy. "I thought the Throne Room was in this direction."

The boy shook his head. "No, the Great Hall is that way. The Throne Room is the other way."

Eden closed his eyes, concentrating hard on the map in his mind. He was certain that Viktor said the Throne Room was this way; but the castle was laid out in a square with four towers. The right and left of the castle were two identical rectangles with the armory on the right side and the kitchens on the left on the ground floor. The Throne Room was in the center of the first floor. Viktor could have gotten it confused, after all, he wouldn't have had much to do with either the armory or the kitchens. "If you're lying to me, boy …"

"I'm not, I swear! The stairwell to get up is a little further back the way you came in. The Throne Room is in the center, though …" the boy hesitated for a moment, "if you want to run into less guards you won't take that stairwell. Take the one further to the back, the one that leads to the bedrooms. All the family rooms are completely deserted. Nobody lives in them. The only rooms that are occupied are the King's chambers and those are occupied by the Queen."

Murtaugh grabbed the boy by the throat and squeezed. "The usurper, do not ever refer to that woman as the Queen again." The boy nodded frantically.

"Lead the way," said Eden, then gestured with his sword.

The boy led them back the way they came. He indicated a stairwell, then he led them past it down a long corridor to another stairwell and then up it. As Eden had followed the boy, he'd been looking around. He may have only had vague memories of this castle, but he never remembered it being this dark, dirty, or smelly. It clearly had been neglected; but that's what happens when you have a mistress who doesn't care and servants who are frightened for their lives. He smiled to himself as he imagined Bloodstone on her hands and knees scrubbing floors. No amount of argument would stop her, though he did not like the thought of her on her hands and knees scrubbing. He did like the image of her wiggling backside. He shook his head to clear that out of his mind; now was not the time. As they reached the top of the staircase, he put his hand on the boy's shoulder and pulled him back behind him. Eden carefully peeked around the corner. The boy hadn't been lying. No one was around, and from the state of the floor, he would say virtually no one ever came up here. After a moment, he gestured for the boy to continue to lead the way.

When the boy reached a set of double doors, he looked at Eden. "You want the long way or the short way? The short way's going to have several men between you and the usurper, the long way, not so many."

"We'll take the long way," Eden replied quickly. He didn't want to kill any more men than he had to. He knew plenty of these men would side with him if given the choice, and he wanted to give them that choice. The boy put his hands on the door handle and pushed down, then leaned heavily against the door. It didn't budge.

Murtaugh gestured the boy away and gripping the door handle, he put his shoulder to the door. It took twice more before the long unused door opened. Murtaugh made a face. A moment later, Eden knew why, when his nose caught the first stench of the long unused corridor. He could smell mold and dirt and air that had not stirred for years. He was starting to wonder if this castle could ever be inhabitable again. As they moved down the corridor, they passed by numerous doors. Finally, they reached another set of large doors. The boy gestured with his hands, then kneeling down, he wrote on the dirty floor, 'War Room. Door on other side opens into Throne Room.' Eden nodded and gestured the boy back. He put his ear to the door; he could hear a few men in there talking. He indicated using sign language to two of his men that they were to push the door handles down and put their shoulders to the door simultaneously. Then he indicated that he, Murtaugh, Dex, and Big Bear would go through as soon as the doors were open. The rest of the men were to follow. They all nodded.

*****

Black Stone sat on his horse watching as Bloodstone and Foster led their men across to the walls. The first ladders were just going up when the portcullis went up. Black Stone turned his full attention on the gates. A moment later they opened just a little, but it was enough. "Third wave!" he shouted, but a moment later he knew

Andrew had already given the order to charge. The Twelfth started moving, followed quickly by the Tenth. "Close the distance! Prepare to reinforce our men!" he ordered. Pulling his face mask down, he spurred his horse. He decided he was not going to be the last one in this fight. He wanted to have some fun this time and he thought that General Fang's armor was just distinctive enough he could find him on the battlefield. A few minutes later, in thick of it, he wasn't disappointed. He caught sight of General Fang's helmet. He cut down the man in front of him and changed directions, heading for Fang. A large Barbarian wielding a club stepped in front of him. As he swung for Black Stone's head, Black Stone blocked the blow with his shield and brought his sword across the man's belly. The man fell to the ground clutching his stomach. Black Stone kicked him in the head as he stepped over him. Another man wielding an axe tried to remove Black Stone's head. He shouted to no one in particular, "Didn't they teach you all anything but head shots? It's kind of monotonous." The man stared at him in blank confusion. Black Stone hit him in the side of his head with the flat of his blade. The man fell to the ground unconscious, or so Black Stone hoped. Like Eden, he had a reluctance to kill any of these men.

Two more men fell before him in his quest for Fang, but now they were face-to-face. They exchanged a quick flurry of blows. Despite the fact that Fang was using a Two-handed Bastard

Sword, he was good and he was quick; but Black Stone had the advantage with his shield and Longsword. They exchanged a few more blows, just testing the waters. As Black Stone sidestepped a blow aimed at his head, he got a good look at the hilt of Fang's sword. There was a large emerald on the rain guard, the pommel was the head of a wolf. Black Stone didn't know why, but he knew instantly that that sword belonged to Eden's father. He blocked another blow and asked as he did so, "Did you take that sword off the King's dead body, or just claim it after he was dead?"

Fang laughed as he pressed the advantage and forced Black Stone on the defensive. "I took it off the mantle, walked over, and severed his unconscious head," he laughed again.

Black Stone moved as though he was going to bring his sword across Fang's belly; but at the last moment he shifted, sidestepped and dropped his blade, bringing it down into the outside of Fang's left thigh. Fang brought his sword down hard, aimed at Black Stone's chest, but he deflected it with his shield. Thanks to his new shield with a reinforced back Bloodstone had put on all of the Stone siblings' shields, he was able to easily deflect the blow. He also countered quickly, bringing his sword right into the side of Fang. Fang faltered and staggered backwards. Black Stone didn't even hesitate, he removed Fang's head from his shoulders. As General Fang's headless corpse slowly sunk to the ground, the fighting immediately around them stopped. Several men murmured that he had just killed the General. Fighting in the entire area was dying down. Almost everyone stood in stunned silence. Then someone cheered. As Black Stone looked up to see the face of the cheering man, he was astonished to see he was wearing Queen's men's armor. More men started cheering. He looked around. There was still a few scrimmagers, though they were easily defeated. He pulled out a cloth and wiped the blood off of his sword, sheathed it, then he bent down and picked up the other. Examining it carefully as he cleaned the blood from it; it was a beautiful sword. It had a silver hilt and there was a large emerald to either side of the rain guard. The pommel was the head of a Wolf with the snout pointing down so it gave the illusion of having a point.

*****

As the doors opened, the six men in the room turned to face the intruders. Eden said quickly, "Is she worth dying for?" The six then drew their swords and attacked. The first four men went down before they even brought their swords to bear. Eden and Murtaugh dispatched the other two in a few quick blows. The doors to the Throne Room were thrown open. At a glance, Eden knew the room had at least fifty guards in it. Eden went through the open doorway; he cut down the first man who challenged him without hesitation. He looked for the usurper. Seeing her, he turned and headed in her direction. Murtaugh, Dex, and Big Bear were keeping the area around him clear. As one of her guards got in front of him, Eden snarled and brought his sword down on the man's as hard as he could, shattering the blade. The man dropped the hilt and fled. "Call off your dogs! This fight is between you and me."

Eden started as the woman standing in front of him disappeared. A moment later, a flock of birds came out of the walls and attacked them. Eden cut one of the birds in half and it disappeared.

Ivy yelled from the doorway, "They're not real, men. They're just an illusion. They cannot hurt you." The men stopped attacking the birds and though they kept clawing at them, they were doing them no harm. "Eden, she's an illusionist. Don't believe anything you see. Trust your other senses."

My other senses? That's just stupid! I can't fight without my eyes. I can't fight what I cannot see, he told himself angrily. As he was looking from side to side, he suddenly felt something hitting him in the back. A moment later, something hit him in his stomach. He looked down to see a scratch on his armor and a little dot like the point of a blade would have left. He smelled the air. Though still dirty, this room was much cleaner than the others had been. He caught a faint smell of several flowers he didn't recognize. As he turned from side to side trying to follow the scent, one of the corpses of the fallen queen's men rose with his sword. He moved to challenge Eden.

"That's not an illusion! That's a puppet! He's real and he can hurt you! Watch out! He doesn't feel pain; only severe dismemberment will stop him!" Ivy shouted. Eden was starting to find it useful having a sorceress on his side. He didn't think he would, but he guessed he was wrong. As he moved to attack the puppet, it brought up the sword to block his blow. As Eden attacked it several more times, he understood why she called it a puppet. It did indeed look as though it was a puppet with the master pulling the strings. It moved in the same jerky manner. After two more tentative attacks, he learned that whoever was pulling the strings did not themselves know how to use a sword. Once he realized that, removing the puppet's arms and legs was quite easy. The puppet fell to the ground useless. Eden quickly sniffed the air, catching a whiff of her flowered perfume. He charged in her direction. She was nearer than he thought and he slammed into her. Wrapping his arms around her, he struggled to hold the invisible woman. She tried to knee him in the bollocks, but he realized she was going to try this and twisted just in time that she kneed him in the inner thigh instead. He flung her hard against the wall.

Still invisible, Alyshia quickly moved away from him. *My god, I have served you faithfully these many years; do not abandon me now. Give me the strength to defeat these invaders.*

"If you do not wish to have all the gods against you, Bastion, you will not interfere," Athena cautioned.

"You, your brother, and your sister have done nothing but interfere, and now you warn me?" Bastion snarled back.

"If you will look back over these battles, you will see that my siblings and I did not in any way interfere. All my brother has done is father some remarkable children; but he is not responsible for the actions of his offspring, as the gods declared many, many centuries ago. And yes, I did appear on the battlefield earlier, but that was merely to have a conversation with my nephew. I did not in any way interfere with the battle; and if you interfere now, you will interfere in the course of these two countries. That will be a grievous violation of the agreement of the gods," Athena stated firmly.

Anna spoke with the gentle grace that she was known for. "I hope the two of you will forgive my interference in this charming argument of yours, but Athena is speaking the truth. I've been watching this war since it has begun, and neither Athena, Ares, nor Freya, have ever directly interfered in the war itself. They have on occasion advised, which is permissible. And they have permitted their followers to act, but they themselves have never interfered. She is right; myself and the other gods will not stand for direct interference, especially at this moment. So if I were you, Bastion, I would only give counsel to your follower, no more."

Bastion roared and snarled, "And what will you do if I do not heed you? What do you think you can do to me, Goddess of the Hearth? You're pathetic and weak; you do not have the power to stop me."

Atropos cackled, "You may be able to take her on by yourself, but you cannot take us all on. Do you want another war of the gods? It's been a long time since I've snipped the thread of a god. I would not mind at all if the next one was yours. Do not be a fool; she is but one follower. You can build another army. You can start another revolution; but you cannot grow another thread."

*****

Alyshia tried to catch her breath, then it slowly dawned on her that her god had indeed abandoned her. She drew her two poisoned daggers. She knew any attempt to poison Eden was foolish; his Werewolf's blood was immune to poison. Turning the blades in her hand, she aimed them at her belly, then plunged both knives in. Eden's jaw dropped as the woman became visible. She slowly sank to the ground, still gripping her blades. Eden watched as her body convulsed. "I will not give

537

you the pleasure of avenging your father." A
moment later, her sightless eyes stared at him.

A noise to his right caught his attention. He
looked sharply to see Black Stone, Andrew,
Bloodstone, Foster, Greyhawk, Fletcher, and
Viktor entering the Throne Room. Black Stone
walked up to him, turning the blade he held over in
his hand; he offered it on its side to Eden. "I could
be wrong, but I think this belongs to you." As
Eden took his father's sword, he stared at Black
Stone. "We have primary control of the castle,
Eden. We'll need to sweep it several times and
have Bloodstone analyze your soldiers, but other
than that, the Castle is yours."

Eden turned and touched Bloodstone on the
arm, gesturing for her to follow him. He mounted
the two steps of the wooden platform. It only had
a single chair. Turning and dropping into the chair,
he plunged the point of his father's sword into the
platform. Bloodstone moved to stand at his right
and placed her hand on the back of his chair. Eden
kept his eyes forward as he looked at his men.

"Now, you may call me King."

66779230R00297

Made in the USA
Charleston, SC
30 January 2017